alethea
P.P.

DEBORAH'S LEGACY

BY
STEPHEN MARLOWE

PUBLISHED IN HARDCOVER AS *1956*

ZEBRA BOOKS
KENSINGTON PUBLISHING CORP.

With Ann More Than Ever

ZEBRA BOOKS

are published by

KENSINGTON PUBLISHING CORP.
475 Park Avenue South
New York, N.Y. 10016

Copyright © 1981 by Stephen Marlowe
Reprinted by arrangement with Arbor House Publishing
Company. All rights reserved.

All rights reserved. No part of this book may be reproduced
in any form or by any means without the prior written
consent of the Publisher, excepting brief quotes used in
reviews.

Printed in the United States of America.

Prologue

1

On the last afternoon of his life, Gideon Parr lunched at the Café Hungaria at the corner of Lenin Boulevard and Dohány Street in downtown Budapest.

He ate roast goose, its skin golden and crackling, with red cabbage and chestnut purée. The wine, a hearty red *bikavér*, suited the food and would ward off the chill of the late winter day outside. An icy wind off the Danube had lashed the streets with rain on Gideon Parr's walk from the bus terminal.

His face ruddy, his graying hair clipped short, Parr looked more German than American. The passport he carried said he was an Austrian named Fritz Neumayr born in Innsbruck and now residing in Vienna's Fourteenth District. Herr Neumayr's date of birth was 27 April 1906, which, this March Sunday in 1956, would have made him a few weeks short of fifty years old. Gideon Parr was, in fact, forty-seven.

At half-past three precisely, the maître d', wearing tailcoat, high stiff collar and white tie, appeared at Parr's elbow. From Parr's small table in the rear of the Hungaria, the two men could see the mirrored walls, the twisted majolica columns, the crystal chandeliers that seemed so out of place in the drab capital of the People's Republic of Hungary. Most of the tables had been cleared and reset for dinner.

"The Herr has enjoyed his lunch?" the maître d' asked in German.

Gideon Parr bit off the tip of a cigar and with proper Germanic disdain spat it on the carpet. The maître d' at once produced a lighter, gold, as had been specified.

Parr drew on the cigar and leaned back expansively, watching the smoke rise to dissipate beneath the high gilded ceiling.

"Phone for a taxi," he said. "The West Station."

"The express to Vienna?"

"Yes, that's right," Parr said. The cigar had made his face more ruddy and he began to cough. His heart was beating too hard. He wasn't supposed to smoke, but it was part of the ritual of identification. He let the cigar go out.

The maître d' clicked his heels. *"Sofort, mein Herr!"*

"Oh, and have this ready for me, will you?" Parr told him, producing his coatcheck.

Ten minutes later, in dark-green loden cloak and loden hat, carrying a bulging briefcase, Parr entered the waiting taxi for the two-minute drive to the West Station. The rain was just then turning to snow.

Parr felt for the envelope in the inner pocket of his cloak.

At the rail junction of Györ, Hungary, almost exactly half the 166-mile distance from Budapest to Vienna, the afternoon express had a scheduled eight-minute stop. Parr stood in the corridor outside his compartment, watching the activity on the station platform. Dusk had fallen. Snow swirled golden past the platform lights, a few passengers got off, a few boarded, a fat woman trudged by pushing a cart heaped with sandwiches and bottled drinks from the station buffet.

The wind increased, moaning in unseen high-tension wires. Parr wished he could stay aboard in comfort for the ride to Vienna, but the risk, while slight, was there. Frontier police would come aboard at the next town down the line. This would not be the first time an agent had been hooked and caught by the lure of information as important as the contents of the envelope in Parr's pocket. Not that he was an agent anymore, but then an agent could not have accomplished what he had, not so quickly.

A train pulled in across the platform. It was empty, its windows dark. When it stopped, the lights went on and an old man wearing a visored cap placed a card in the slot near the door of the carriage directly across from where Parr stood. The card said: Line 8, Györ-Csorna-Sopron. Parr watched a few passengers emerge from the stairwell and cross the platform to the Line 8 local. Seven minutes and forty seconds of the express's scheduled stop had elapsed. The man in the cap began to swing a lantern.

Very quickly Parr went along the corridor, opened the door, stepped down, crossed the platform and boarded the Line 8 train. The Budapest-Vienna express had already begun to move, steam billowing from the stack above the engine boiler. Soon it picked up speed and hurtled from the Györ station.

Seconds later the Line 8 local lurched and was underway.

Parr bolted the door of the cubicle in the men's room at the Sopron station an hour later. He placed the briefcase on the lid of the toilet, hung the green loden cloak on the door hook and undressed down to his underwear. He began to shake with cold. Working fast, he unbuckled the bulging briefcase and removed wide-wale corduroy hiking knickers, red flannel shirt, anorak, worn leather boots. After he dressed, he transferred the manila envelope from the inner pocket of the cloak to the zip pocket of the anorak, along with his billfold, passport, and return bus ticket. He heard a toilet flush, and footsteps on tile, then the door, then silence. He opened the cubicle and stuffed city shoes, suit and loden cloak into the rubbish bin near the door.

Outside, the snow falling heavily now in the night, he

walked to the Ibusz office on the cobbled square near the fire tower and gateway to the inner town. The driver was just switching on the headlights of the idling bus.

"Vienna?" a voice called. Parr walked faster.

A dozen or so Austrian tourists left the Ibusz waiting room and walked through the snow to the bus. Sopron, just across the border in Hungary, with its Roman statuary, winding cobbled streets and fine baroque buildings, was a popular day excursion from Vienna, even in winter, especially on a Sunday.

Gideon Parr looked at his watch. He was feeling smug. A late dinner at Sacher's, a good night's sleep at the Bristol, the Vienna-Frankfurt morning flight, then the TWA Super Constellation for the States. First thing Tuesday morning he'd walk into Prestridge's office with the envelope. With the ghost of Josef Stalin on a platter, all carved up. Over the hill, my ass, he thought, and he chuckled.

"Hello, Gideon."

He turned, startled by the voice, surprised—if only momentarily—that it should be hers. She wore a trenchcoat and a mannish hat, its brim pulled down against the snow. He couldn't make out her face in the darkness. But the voice he knew. She sounded almost sad.

Inside the lighted bus the driver was looking down at him inquiringly.

She was flanked by two big men wearing leather jackets and caps. In a quick move so coordinated it seemed rehearsed, they came forward and pivoted and were flanking him instead of her.

The driver looked at them a long moment, then pulled on the lever that shut the door. Diesel engine roaring, the bus backed away from the sidewalk. It turned and Parr watched the red taillights receding until the snow and the night and the bus's own exhaust swallowed them.

They walked him past the lighted plate glass windows on either side of the Ibusz office to where a large black sedan waited at the curb. An American model a few years old, it looked huge on the streets of Sopron, Hungary. It was the sort of car so commonly used by the AVO that people often referred to the secret police as *amerikai*.

They got in, the woman in back with him, the two leather jackets in front. The rear wheels churned snow, then found traction. They began to move. Large snowflakes exploded out of darkness at the windshield.

"Give it to me, please," she said, speaking in German. Again he sensed the sadness in her voice. He unzipped the anorak pocket and gave her the manila envelope.

"Tell me," she asked, "why did you risk your life—for that? They say you haven't been well."

He thought. He had never really answered the question for himself; never even asked it.

"A thing like that," she said. "It can't remain secret. A month, two. Surely by summer. The whole world will know."

"I had to know first," he said after a while. "I had to get it. It had to be me."

"Yes," she said. "I suppose it did."

They had left the town behind, were driving along a narrow road bordered by tall reeds whipped by the wind.

She lit two of the black-tobacco cigarettes she always smoked, her fineboned face and the pale eyes visible for an instant. She gave him one of the cigarettes.

"And now?" he asked.

She shrugged. "Three years ago at Zhdanovsk in the Azerbaijan S.S.R., thirty miles from the Iranian frontier, the Russians erected a small power station on the river. Near the power station they built a radar tower. They assembled prefabricated barracks, bulldozed a runway, and began excavation for underground facilities. You know what happened?"

Gideon Parr's face felt flushed. He knew. He said nothing.

"Eight Iranians run by the CIA were rolled up along with two Soviet citizens, including a school teacher in Zhdanovsk. Flies to honey, moths to flame. The mysterious installation had no other purpose."

"And the envelope?"

"No, no. That's genuine. You haven't read it?"

Gideon Parr said that he hadn't. He knew he never would.

"So," she said, dropping the cigarette on the floor, stepping on it. "They only knew it would be somebody big, the resident for Hungary, perhaps. But I knew it would be you." She laughed, a sudden false note that silenced her for seconds. Then she said, "Fool! Why didn't you stay in America? What am I going to do with you?"

"Oh, I figure the same as with the resident, if it had been the resident," he said calmly. "A safe house, an interrogation team."

"They'll break you."

"Given enough time, they'd break anyone. I know that."

"Still, you'll fight them, won't you? You'll resist every step of the way. That will only make things worse for you. But it's the way you are, isn't it?"

"Maybe," he said. What he was like no longer mattered.

"How sick are you, Gideon? Gid?"

"It's nothing."

"They said your heart—"

"I told you it's nothing."

"They'll wring information from you like water from a sponge. Let them. After a few years in Vorkuta they'll release you. That would be the end of it. No one would stop you from going home."

"I could never go home."

"Because you'll be shamed? Surely you're not still an idealist, Gideon. Do you believe you're any better than we are, or we any worse than you? Does God support your side? Or history ours?"

"I could never go back."

"Then a life of anonymity in Russia, or the DDR if you prefer."

They were just words, spoken neither for his benefit nor for hers, spoken only for the two anonymous men in the front seat. He knew that she knew him too well to expect him to take the suggestions seriously. He wished he could see her face. Or touch her lips. Or feel her remembered body against his own.

"A position with the Ministry for State Security in Berlin," she said brightly. "That's the answer. I could arrange it. A new life, a small office of your own, translations, nothing strenuous, a fine way to spend your declining years. What could be more welcome after a life like yours than the prospect of a little boredom?"

The big car slowed before a curve on the snow-covered road, its headlights raking the tall marsh reeds. Beyond the marshes was a lake—Lake Fertö, he remembered; once it had been his business to know this terrain—salt, shallow, fed by subterranean springs, a bird sanctuary, the great Rust storks, herons . . . All but its southern shores Austrian territory.

He lunged hard against the door, clawing for the handle, tumbling out an instant before the car accelerated into the curve. Something ripped in his shoulder as he rolled over and over across the snow-covered road and into the reeds and through thin new ice into frigid water, knee-deep when he could get to his feet.

The car skidded to a stop twenty yards further along the road. He saw the beam of a flashlight and heard the two men's voices carrying above the clatter and whisper of the reeds in the wind. He turned his back on the road and at first he panicked, beginning an awkward blind run, frantically parting the thick unseen stalks of the marsh reeds as he plunged on. He slowed to a walk, boots making sucking sounds in water and mud, and wondered if they

11

could hear him. He decided the clatter of the reeds would cover any sound he made. He walked steadily away from the road. He thought it was away from the road. After a while he knew it was impossible to keep moving in one direction. There was no point of reference. But at least the water had deepened to mid-thigh. That must have meant he was approaching the lake. When does a marsh become a lake? he thought wildly. Was he in the lake? He could wade north to Austria. He could . . .

Just how the hell would he know when he'd crossed the frontier? His thighs parted thin ice. He wondered how long it would take him to freeze to death. He saw faint light and turned. The flashlight was behind him, not close, but it panicked him a second time into running awkwardly, heavily, through the water, reed-stalks snapping against his upflung arms. He had been in Washington too long, a desk jockey going soft; she was right, he'd been a fool to come. The betrayal they had discussed was not, however, the worst one. The worst betrayal was of yourself. He was middle-aged, his heart was diseased, he was here where he shouldn't be, and he would never leave. That was the way out for him, of course. She had given him his way out, such as it was—just as he had once done for her. Life, what was left of his life if he gave in, would be intolerable. She had known that much about him even before he had.

Calmly then he ran, floundering through the deepening water where marsh became or did not become lake. For an instant he felt a spurious sense of well-being, his shoulder hardly hurting at all, Vienna and Frankfurt and Washington ahead of him through the clattering reeds if only he could keep going a little while longer.

She got out of the car. The night air felt good. It was snowing hard. Not a flicker from him when she had dismissed the contents of the envelope with mild contempt, not a flicker when she had taunted him with the mysterious installation at Zhdanovsk.

He hadn't known what was in the envelope. And that meant the Americans did not know.

She heard the two men returning, and waited for them to speak.

"Dead, major. He's dead."

"You shot him?"

"We found him floating facedown in three feet of water."

She brushed snowflakes from her cheek, warm like tears.

2

After the children's evening prayers at the settlement village school, Deborah would spend an hour with them telling Bible stories and answering questions. Especially questions, how these Yemenite children could ask questions! Two thousand five hundred years in a feudal ghetto locked in by the desert and mountains of southern Arabia, their Jewishness kept alive by a miracle, the Yemenite Jews had survived. But to fly from their primitive ghetto to Israel, which they had never heard of, in airplanes, which they had not known existed—how had they survived the shock? More than most, the Yemenites were People of the Book. And wasn't it there, in black and white, for their rabbis to read to them from Isaiah? "They that wait upon the Lord shall mount up with wings as eagles."

The wings had been American DC-4s; the Yemenites had come, possessionless but unafraid, in fulfillment of biblical prophecy.

They could sing the Psalms in ancient, not modern, Hebrew and in that dead language, Aramaic. Even the Arabic so many of them spoke had an almost feudal sound to it. Deborah was fluent in the language, which was why she came on her motorbike every afternoon, racing south after work along the eucalyptus-lined road from Tel Aviv to

13

the settlement village. She generally told them stories in modern Hebrew, but their questions were invariably in Arabic. Daddy Sam wouldn't approve. Definitely not. "What's the matter?" he would say. "English isn't good enough for them? Hebrew, I mean." His own Hebrew was questionable at best. He spoke no Yiddish. His English was American, subspecies New York, or rather Brooklyn, where he had been born and raised. Deborah had an acute ear for languages, a nimble tongue that could dance from one to another.

"So Jacob's mother made him look like his brother Esau," Deborah said that Sunday evening in March, "and fooled their father Isaac into giving his blessing to him instead of Esau."

"I thought Isaac was blind. So how could Jacob fool him by looking like Esau? How could Isaac see him?" asked Eliahu, a ten-year-old with olive skin, almond eyes, and a smile so open and guileless it could make you weep with joy.

"Well, I meant *feel* like Esau. By wearing the skin of a goat."

"Esau was a goat?"

"Stop that, Eliahu. You know what I mean. Esau was hairier than Jacob. Anyway, it was much later when Jacob ran away, still fearful of his brother's anger. In a dark canyon in the desert one night . . . does everybody know what a canyon is?"

They all knew what a canyon was. "Would someone turn on the light, please? Ibrahim?" The day had been balmy, almost springlike, but now at dusk the temperature had plummeted back to late winter in moments. "And shut the windows at the bottom?"

Ibrahim was the smallest of the fifteen Yemenites in the schoolroom. He had a clubfoot and he liked to do things like working the light switch or shutting the windows. He hated the clubfoot. But when he helped out, he was useful, he was just like everyone else.

14

"Well. In a dark canyon in the desert one night he wrestled with his own soul, which appeared in the guise of a mysterious stranger."

"His soul? A soul is like air. Poof! How can you wrestle with a soul?"

"That's a good question, Eliahu," Deborah said, wondering how to answer it.

"And anyway," the almond-eyed boy continued, "what's this? His soul in the guise of a mysterious stranger? He had visions?"

"It isn't meant to be taken literally," Deborah said.

Blank looks were exchanged around the room.

"I mean, if his conscience was bothering him bad enough, he might *imagine* himself wrestling with a mysterious stranger."

"Meshugge," said Eliahu, who obviously had picked up some Yiddish in the six months since his arrival at the settlement village. "That's what he was, *meshugge.*"

"Well, anyway, after that Jacob was called Israel—"

"Called Israel, like the country? You mean he changed his name, Miss Brodsky?" Naomi asked. That much at least should give them no problem, Deborah thought. From Prime Minister Ben-Gurion on down, the taking of heroic-sounding Hebrew names was a common enough thing. Not Daddy Sam, of course. He was Sam Brodsky from Brooklyn, and he figured if that had been good enough for Flatbush Avenue and the U.S. Army, it was good enough for Dizengoff Street and the Israeli Army.

"He was *called* Israel. He didn't necessarily change his name himself."

"Who called him Israel?"

"The scribes, the unknown people who wrote the Book. Israel . . . do you know what it means?"

"It means here. It's the name of the country," said Eliahu, as if it were a dumb question.

"Well, yes. But it means 'he who fought with God.' "

15

"The name of the whole *country?*" said Aaron.

"God?" said Eliahu. "I thought it was his soul he fought with." Eliahu's smile then had the faintest touch of mischief. "Or a mysterious stranger or something. Maybe I'm wrong, Miss Brodsky."

"When we discuss things like this," Deborah explained, "there isn't always a right and a wrong. Things can be interpreted one way or they can be interpreted another. Wise men even—"

A window shattered, and a brilliant flash of orange fire blazed against the night darkness. Something went *slam-slam-slam* very fast. The door burst in. For a single instant Deborah saw figures in the doorway. Then, with a short burst from a submachine gun, the overhead light was shot out.

"On the floor!" Deborah cried in the darkness. "Everybody!" She hit the floor herself, between the desks, before the unused blackboard, and the terrible sound of submachine-gun fire was so loud now it had to be more than one gun. Even so, she could hear the screams. In a muzzle flash she saw a contorted face and then no face, Eliahu, she thought it was Eliahu, the face shot away, the room dark again, the air acrid with cordite. Another muzzle flash and down crashed the wall map, Israel, barely twelve miles wide at its waist, no Israeli more than twenty miles from a terrorist knife or gun, the Arab assassination squads creeping north from their sanctuary in Gaza. A final burst of fire, two, from different corners of he classroom —there had to be two of them, two at least—and then she heard more glass shattering and they were out the window. Voices shouted, footsteps pounded, a siren wailed. Deborah felt a weight on her back, warm, still, wet, drenching her, more blood than a child's body could possibly hold. Deborah fainted.

She answered the questions the man from Military Intelligence asked her. She was of no help to him, though,

16

and anyway he was a lieutenant and diffident. Daddy Sam was a major, after all. Two gunmen, three, four, a hundred—what difference did it make? Eliahu was dead, and Aaron and Naomi and all the others except Ibrahim, who would lose a leg, the one with the clubfoot. She visited him in the hospital in Tel Aviv and on the first day he was silent. On the second day he said if he had to lose a leg, he lost the right one. On the third day he said he was wrestling with his soul or maybe with God. He said that timidly but in earnest. He said when he grew up he was going to kill all the Arabs he could find, and he wouldn't wait for them to come to him, he would go looking for them.

Deborah returned for just one day to work at the State Radio Studios, Kol Israel. That day she read the news in Hebrew, Arabic, English and French. Gaza had been shelled in retaliation for the terrorist raid on the settlement school; the British, as perfidious now in Cyprus as they had been a decade earlier in Palestine, had deported Archbishop Makarios from the island. What did it matter? What did any of it matter now?

Deborah Brodsky was wrestling with her soul too. It was no mysterious stranger. On the surface at least it was Daddy Sam. Major Brodsky came back from wherever it was he had been—Shin Beth did not exactly announce his arrivals and departures—on the Wednesday morning after the massacre at the settlement village school.

"Baby. Oh, Jesus, baby. I didn't know. I just heard."

Deborah almost thought she was going to smile. How many other officers in the Israeli Army, Intelligence Service or not, would use the name of the Christian deity, even in vain?

But she could not smile. Her face broke and she started to cry, really cry, for the first time since it had happened.

She clutched Daddy Sam around the waist, her hands barely meeting behind his back. He was six feet four inches tall and broader now than when he had played basketball for a school called L.I.U. Second team all-American forward, whatever that was. She held him, just held him. He kissed the top of her head. He gave her his handkerchief and she blew her nose, hard.

"Baby," he said, "you're pretty even when you're crying your eyes out. Blow again."

Obediently, she did. Sam tilted her chin up and kissed her cheek. He needed a shave. His khaki pants and shirt looked slept in.

He made coffee. He was the world's firmest believer in the restorative properties of coffee, this huge American-Israeli who had adopted her after their arrival in Israel ten years ago.

"Shouldn't you be working?" he asked.

"I tried. I—it's too soon, that's all. I don't want to do anything yet. I'm so tired, Daddy Sam. All I want to do is sleep."

Ten years ago the psychiatrists had warned him about that. Almost as soon as they settled in Tel Aviv, she began to sleep. And sleep and sleep. Twelve and fourteen hours a day. Sleep is her refuge, Mr. Brodsky, they told him. Israel still isn't real to her. We have seen this among other survivors of the death camps—the camps, and then the DP centers, and for some, detention behind British barbed wire on Cyprus. Now they are free, free to *decide*. And they're afraid to. So they retreat into sleep, the psyche postponing the need to act. Under certain extreme conditions it can even develop into catatonia, but I think in your child's case we needn't worry about that. Perhaps an occasional relapse when she feels threatened or has undergone a particularly stressful experience. But Deborah's mind is lively, and her test profile is encouraging. She *wants* to be involved with life. Your job is to encourage that.

"Work helps, baby," he said now. "Believe me. I know."

"Maybe tomorrow."

Alone, they spoke English. It was the only language

18

Daddy Sam really felt at home in.

She could talk to him, she could open up. To him and to children and to no one else. At Kol Israel they called her the Ice Maiden. She wasn't. She wasn't. She didn't want to be.

"Ben-Yehuda, a skinny lieutenant? He the guy you saw?"

"Yes."

"Brave, dumb and necessary, like most Sabras. I don't like it that they sent Ben-Yehuda."

"What difference does it make?"

"He's a paper-pusher. They sent him so someone could fill out the forms. It means they don't know a goddamn thing and don't expect to learn any more."

"You mean they won't even try to find the people who—"

"Try? Oh, they'll keep it open officially. But practically, what can they do? One more isolated incident . . ."

"I see." She felt like the Ice Maiden then. She wanted to.

"Hey, baby, what are you looking at me that way for?"

"Isolated incident—is that all those children were?" She was shouting. "You're no different from the rest. They're just a report on paper to you, something to be filled out, filed and forgotten."

Suddenly she bowed her head. "I'm sorry, Daddy Sam. I know it's not your fault, I just . . ." Her voice choked and he drew her into the shelter of his arms.

That night she dreamed about the concentration camp for the first time in months. A child hardly older than Eliahu or Naomi, she was being marched to the gas chamber and then the tall woman with the pale eyes came and . . .

Saturday was *Shabbat,* but she phoned the number anyway from a pay phone on Dizengoff Street. A Hassid in black coat and broad-brimmed black hat, with greasy beard and sidelocks, shook his fist at her. She gave him the Ice Maiden look and he kept on walking.

The number rang twice before it was answered, long

enough to wonder if he would remember her. It had been more than a year ago.

His voice said, "Yes?"

"This is Deborah Brodsky," she said tentatively. "Maybe you don't remember, but we met at Kol Israel, the studio canteen, last January."

"I remember," he said, and then Deborah was no longer tentative.

"I'm ready," she said. "I'm ready now."

Part One

Chapter One

1

He was in no hurry to leave the bus station when his shift ended. For two hours he drank beer in the station buffet with a pair of cronies, and he stayed for dinner. But when he finally left, he was alone. Southard buttoned his raincoat and followed.

For the first fifteen minutes it was easy, but as his quarry walked north toward the Danube Canal, traffic thinned out and they passed only an occasional pedestrian. Southard crossed to the other side of the street and dropped back a full block.

A misty rain fell on Vienna; the streetlamps wore haloes. The bus driver, Oskar Kunschak, paused to light a cigarette before crossing Marxergasse. He turned and cupped his hands as the match flared. Southard slowed to keep enough distance. You do not accost a man at eleven o'clock at night in the rain on a deserted street without alarming him. Southard wanted Kunschak at his ease, ready to talk.

The bus driver resumed walking. He was tall, his normal stride as long as Southard's, and he hurried now. That and the cigarette probably meant he was nearing his destination.

Goal gradient, Southard's ex-wife would have said, in the jargon of her profession. They had scorned each other's work, Janet on moral grounds, he because he doubted you learned about people by running white rats through

Skinner boxes. They had been divorced two years and those rare times he tried to picture her, her face blurred with others. That was understandable. But he hardly remembered what seven-year-old Suzie looked like, either. He carried no pictures.

It should have been simple, once he was based in Washington, to see his daughter. His work frequently took him to the Agency "farm" in Virginia, not far from where Janet taught college. He could easily have picked up Suzie for lunch at one of the nearby colonial restaurants or for a drive to Jamestown and a ferry ride. But Janet claimed such impromptu visits were bad for the child emotionally, and contrived to keep them to a minimum. She said all visits should be scheduled, knowing he could schedule nothing.

Somewhere ahead, Southard heard the moan of a barge horn. They weren't far from the Danube Canal. Beyond the bus driver, the street seemed to end in a wall of gray mist.

Oskar Kunschak vanished. Southard crossed the street diagonally, almost running. Three dark doorways, four. And then a light and a small sign that said Löwen Keller. Southard opened the door and went down steep stairs. He parted a heavy curtain and entered a room with a service bar on one wall and a dozen small tables. Bare of decoration except for a half-life-sized Christ leaning from His cross in one corner, the cellar was immaculate. The natural wood tabletops glowed a dull gold as if they had been sanded that morning. The barman was drawing beer from the two taps, letting it overflow a pair of liter steins. He brought the steins to two women with hard faces and their shoes off. He said something and they laughed reluctantly, their eyes not on the barman but on Southard. The barman went over to the patron's table with its little metal *Stammtisch* sign. That was where Kunschak sat. The barman shook his hand and they laughed and talked and the barman offered snuff, which Kunschak took, sniffing it hard off the back of his own hand and sneezing appreciatively. The barman went to the bar and returned with a green bottle and two wine glasses. Southard was about to sit at another table when the telephone behind the bar rang. The barman listened and put the receiver down and went to the table where the two women without shoes sat. He spoke to one of them. She made a face and pointed to her feet. He shrugged and went back to the phone.

By then Southard was seated at the patron's table. His sudden appearance there startled Kunschak. By custom, only friends of the proprietor sit there, even if the table is unoccupied and all the others taken.

Southard wore a tan raincoat and no hat. His sandy hair, short but not crewcut, was wet and plastered to his head. His blue eyes studied Kunschak's face. His own face might have been conventionally handsome except for the constrained, almost angry set of the mouth and jaw. To Kunschak he looked maybe thirty years old and German. He was thirty-eight and Virginian.

Kunschak tilted his cap back. "I don't know you, do I?"

"You're Oskar Kunschak. I bring you greetings from Herr Jochl." Southard's German was excellent, but it was not the speech of Vienna and was certainly no Austrian dialect.

The barman came out from behind the bar but paused when he saw where Southard was sitting. He looked at Kunschak, who shrugged. Southard's back was to the barman; he did not turn. He half-expected the man to join them until Kunschak poured red wine from the bottle into the two glasses and ungraciously nudged one across the table at him. Southard relaxed.

"Prosit," Kunschak said, drank the quarter of a liter in three thirsty gulps and refilled his glass. Southard drank off half his wine. It was harsh but good. Kunschak lit a cigarette and gave Southard a sour look. "How is Josef these days?"

"His arthritis—what can you expect?"

Recognition had been established.

It did not make Kunschak look any happier.

He poured the rest of the wine for both of them. He had a long face, long nose and long upper lip. The upper lip was beaded with sweat.

"What do I call you?"

"Beck will do," Southard said. "A week ago Sunday evening in Sopron a man about my size, older but not old, was one of your passengers. Or, he was supposed to be. He never got on the bus."

"Shit, I might have known," Kunschak said.

"He was wearing either a green loden cloak of a black anorak and corduroy knickers."

"It was the anorak and knickers," Kunschak said wearily, "just like I told Jochl. Three times I answered those questions, maybe more. So what was it he forgot to ask?"

"You talked to Josef Jochl? Personally?"

"Didn't I say so? Last week, Tuesday I think."

"What did he look like?"

Kunschak's eyes narrowed. "You're supposed to be his friend. You tell *me.*"

"Oskar." Southard leaned forward. "You know and I know that Josef Jochl is just a name. Anybody could be using it. Had you met this man before?"

"Well, no," Kunschak pulled on his long jaw. Southard waited. Kunschak stubbed out his cigarette and said, "Okay. Thin guy, not tall. Freckles. Short hair going gray. Careful dresser. Forty, forty-five." A pause. "One thing I'll tell you, the way he walked, he never had arthritis."

Southard nodded. "You're a good observer."

"I used to be a cop. Vice squad. I quit, though, didn't care for the company—Reds every last one of them. I wasn't political before that, but they made me anti-Communist fast." Kunschak grinned. "All you have to do is work with those pricks. They're in traffic too, and the prison system. The Russians put them in right after the war, mostly in political and criminal branches, and a lot of them got to be permanent civil service so they couldn't be fired. Then the Reds lost control back in '50. Vice and the prisons and traffic is where their boys got dumped. Twenty more years Austria will have to live with them. You know our traffic cops got the worst reputation of any in Europe? Fucking storm troopers," said Oskar Kunschak. He gave a disgusted shake of his head, then looked past Southard to the bar. "Alois, another bottle!"

The wine came and this time Southard was quick to put a hundred-schilling note on the table.

"Keep your money in your pocket," Kunschak protested. "I like a man who listens."

"No, this one's mine." Southard filled their glasses. "Tell me about it."

"That Sunday? There isn't much to tell. He was there, in the anorak and knickers. He was going to board the bus."

"Did he take your bus into Hungary that morning?"

"Look, the bus was crowded. I'm not sure."

"All right. You said he was going to board."

"Yeah, but he's hanging back, letting the others get on first. I'm about ready to pull out, when a car stops on the far side of the Ibusz office. The car, the Hungarians call them *amerikai*, and the bastards who drive them too. You know what they mean by that?"

"Yes."

"Okay, then you know nobody'd want to get involved with them. So I'll say it before you ask. Sure, I knew he wanted to get on the bus. And I could bet they weren't going to let him. And I knew he had something I was supposed to carry across the border for him."

"How did you know?"

"Well, either he had it or the person who did never showed up. I was supposed to find it in the map case under the dash. An envelope. I know the border cops, the Hungarians. I've been on the Vienna-Sopron run so long

I'm part of the scenery. I'm the last man in Austria they'd search. Anyway, I figured it was him, the way he let the rest go ahead. I wasn't told who, just what and when."

"How was the word passed?"

Kunschak rubbed his long nose. "Somebody called," he said, his hand muffling his words. "From Jochl. I didn't recognize the voice."

"This was on the phone?"

Kunschak became surly. "Don't you understand plain German?"

"Not so loud," Southard said. "And don't start lying to me now."

Vienna station used a different recognition code for the telephone. Kunschak obviously didn't know that.

He shoved his chair back from the table and half-stood. His face was flushed. "Who are you to call me a liar?" The two women were watching him; so was the barman.

"I'm Jochl's boss," Southard said tightly. "The man who missed your bus wound up dead. Now sit down and shut up."

Kunschak slouched down into his chair. The angry color slowly left his face. "Jesus," he said. "I'm sorry. I didn't know. But what could I have done?"

"Who told you the man with the envelope would be on the bus?"

"All right," Kunschak said. "All right. It was a boy named Istvan Varady."

Southard breathed easier. Kunschak was no agent reporting to a case officer. An occasional courier, an occasional cutout, he was peripheral to Vienna station's operation. Southard did not know how Hackler, an incompetent like Warren Hackler, was able to control him effectively. He only cared that Hackler could. So that *he* could.

"Istvan's just a kid," Kunschak said earnestly. "He's my half brother. Leave him out of this."

"I can't," Southard said truthfully. "How do I see him?"

There was more sweat on Kunschak's upper lip and he brushed at it distractedly. "The tourist pavilion at the head of the Neusiedler See. That's where you'll find him most afternoons this time of year."

"Where is he the rest of the time?"

"That's a good question," Kunschak said. "I wish I knew. That kid worries me."

"You were telling me about the AVO car," Southard said. "It pulled up just before you took the bus out."

"There were three of them. Two big fellows in leather jackets. The third was a woman."

"A woman?" It was unusual.

"I'm telling you what I saw. She had on pants and an unbelted coat and a Tyrolean hat, but there's light coming from the office window and I can see she's wearing lipstick and her hair's down over the ears and tucked back. She stands like a woman too. The men move in on him, one on either side. Very professional. I've got my hand on the door lever. I see what's happening, I *know* what's happening. I admit it. I admitted it already. They're the AVO, the secret police. I pull the lever and shut the door. What else can I do."

"Did they say anything to him?"

Kunschak exhaled a long breath and shook his head slowly. The memory disturbed him, as if shutting the door on a man he didn't know had been an act of betrayal.

"What else could I do?" he repeated softly.

"Did you hear anyone speak to him?" Southard persisted.

"What? Speak?" Kunschak's eyes opened wide. "Sweet God! I should have remembered that, but Jochl didn't ask. The woman," he said. "It was the woman."

"Tell me."

"That was why he stopped. He was about to get on the bus when she spoke to him."

"What did she say?"

"Hardly anything. Just hello—hello, and then his name."

"What name?"

Kunschak shook his head. "I don't remember."

"How did she sound? Angry? Coy? Threatening? Businesslike? Did she sound like she knew him? Or only knew his name."

Kunschak removed his visored cap. He rubbed the red line it had made across his forehead. "She sounded, I don't now, just sort of—flat. Remember, the bus is idling. She's talking loud enough so he can hear her, but I'm not so close. Wait a minute. The name, it was an odd one. Or maybe it wasn't even a name at all. *Geben*. She might have said *geben*. 'Hello, give?' That doesn't make sense."

"Gideon? Was it Gideon?"

Kunschak pulled at his jaw. "It could have been. Sure. Maybe that was it. Gideon."

Southard leaned back. The bits of information he had pried from Kunschak were few, but solid. He knew that one of the people who took Gideon Parr was a woman, and that she had called him by name. Possibly she knew him on a first-name basis, but not necessarily. Cops anywhere will first-name you to gain an edge. She had known him, though.

Kunschak suggested a third bottle of wine. Southard said no. "But many thanks. You've been very helpful."

"You're going to see Istvan tomorrow?"

"I have to."

"When you see him, tell him from me—" He sighed. "No, don't bother. He never listens anyway."

Two men came into the cellar bar, both flashily dressed under damp, open raincoats. They looked around. One of the women hooked a stiletto-heeled shoe with her toes and swung it slowly, appraising the two men. The one with the mustache immediately began to smile at her. He nudged his companion in the ribs. The woman glanced at Kunschak. He shook his head once quickly.

30

"Vice squad," he told Southard as the men stood at the bar and ordered beer. "I'm useful around here. I can spot them better than the ladies can. They depend on me."

Southard put on his raincoat.

"Say, are you interested in one of them?" Kunschak asked suddenly. "I can arrange it. The blonde really puts her heart in it."

Southard declined this offer too.

As he parted the curtain at the foot of the stairs, the two women joined Oskar Kunschak at the patron's table.

The blonde, two hours later, was in the bedroom of a top-floor walk-up on Wassergasse. The flashily dressed man with the mustache, naked now, lay on his back while she straddled him, leaning forward, her breasts hanging. His eyes were shut and he had a look of pained pleasure on his face. Her eyes were open and she looked bored. She rode him up and down mechanically. His hand came up and twisted in her hair, pulling her head forward and lower, shifting more of her weight to her plump hands, which gripped his shoulders. There was a sucking sound where their bodies joined and her movement was now forward and back as much as up and down, but just as mechanical. He said "ahh" three times, each time more drawn out. She waited a polite few seconds and then climbed off him and off the bed in one quick dismounting motion, like someone familiar with horses who doesn't like to ride.

While she was on the bidet he said, "You're really good. You're wonderful, you know that?"

She soaped up. He paid well. For information too.

2

Southard parked his rented Opel in the village of Neusiedlam See and walked down to the dock at the head of the lake. He saw three large colorful posters mounted on the side of the boathouse. On one were rows of animals—a weasel, a marmot, a fox, a hedgehog, a rat which was awesomely large if painted to scale, a beaver. But whole rows were unfamiliar, like animals from some other planet. He did not bother to read the names printed in German and Latin. He looked briefly at the bird poster and the fish poster.

It was warm at the edge of the dock, windless, the sun bright on the shallow saltwater lake. A fish jumped and submerged, leaving ripples in the murky water. A fat man in the small party of tourists near the end of the dock pointed, and the little boy with him, in lederhosen, tugged his sleeve and begged him to make the fish do it again.

Tied up alongside the dock were half a dozen freshly painted skiffs. The elderly uniformed caretaker pointed to their flat bottoms, then to the lake as he told the tourists that the maximum depth was two meters. The lake was 1.8 percent salt, fed by underground springs. Thirty kilometers, he said, to the far end in Hungary, where they call it Lake Fertö. He said the lakeshore shifts, sometimes whole kilometers, when the winds blow long and hard—an exaggeration, Southard thought. The eastern shore had a palace that once belonged to Empress Maria Theresia, the man continued, a reed-free beach, salt marshes and reed forests and finally, around Illmitz, real flat *puszta*. You might as well be in Hungary, you practically were—not, he added with a smile, that he was recommending it. "Come back next month when the boats go out," the old man urged. "Then you'll really see the lake. There are even windmills in Seewinkel."

The travelogue had ended abruptly on the promise of windmills next month. The old man shook hands and accepted coins with feigned surprise and reluctance as the tourists filed off the dock.

Southard walked past the row of newly painted skiffs in

the water below. Another skiff, still needing paint, sat on its flat bottom on the dock. A slender girl wearing tight shorts and a skimpy halter knelt in the skiff near the rearmost thwart, filling a sprung seam with caulking compound. A boy about her age, which Southard estimated as nineteen or twenty, reclined in the prow. He wore swimming trunks and a blissful expression on his face, which was tilted up at the early April sun.

"When the boats go out, does she do the rowing too?" Southard said.

The girl looked up at him with a quick friendly smile. She was blonde and lovely, the boy dark and handsome. Tanned, as they would be soon, they would be a god and goddess.

"Nobody rows," she said.

"We use poles," the boy explained, sitting up. "The water's shallow enough. It's less work."

"We?" said the girl.

"Somebody has to sell the tickets," the boy said.

The boy did not resemble Kunschak in the slightest, but then they were only half brothers.

"Istvan Varady?" Southard said. "My name is Beck. I'm a friend of Herr Jochl."

They completed the recognition code, then the boy jumped nimbly to his feet to shake Southard's hand. "Oskar called and said he'd met you. What's with my big brother?"

"You worry him."

The boy laughed, the kind of laugh that said, as eloquently as words: if only he knew. The girl looked at each of them in turn with intense interest. Southard amended her age downward. Seventeen, he thought. And Istvan perhaps two or three years older.

"You're not much like Oskar, are you?" Southard said. "Even your name—it's pure Hungarian."

Istvan Varady took a quick tug at his lower jaw. For an instant then he did remind Southard of his half brother. "I live here now, but I went to the Polytechnique in Budapest. I grew up there."

"He's very intelligent," the girl said. "They're going to fight a war to see who gets the benefit of his brains, Austria or Hungary."

"Friedl, why don't you go up to the pavilion," Istvan said, "and get us some sandwiches? *Leberkäse* would be nice, and some beer."

"We already ate."

"Since when does that matter?"

"Then give me some money."

Istvan patted the flanks of his skintight swimming trunks in mute insolent apology.

The girl stuck her tongue out at him, vaulted from the skiff and walked past the boathouse toward the pavilion. They both watched her departure.

"She's something," Istvan said.

Southard agreed. Then he said, "Why did you leave Hungary?"

"Same reason I go back sometimes. My father's there in Budapest." Istvan spat into the water. When he turned back to Southard, his face looked older and bitter. "I feel I have to go, but I hate everything he stands for. He's an AVO officer. Are you sure you want to talk to me?"

"A week ago Sunday you gave Oskar a message."

"That a man would be on the bus from Sopron to Vienna, yes. He would pass an envelope to Oskar, and Oskar would return it to him at the end of the trip."

"Did you meet him?"

"No. I just made the arrangements. For Oskar to help him get it out; you know that part. And for the pickup in Budapest. That was handled by another friend of Jochl, the headwaiter at the Café Hungaria. A good man—he was in the underground against Hitler, and doesn't like the Communists any better."

"Who gave *him* the envelope? And what was in it?"

34

"You've got a lot of questions," said Istvan, his eyes steady on Southard's. "And they're all the right ones. So how is it you don't have the answers? Or maybe you do."

"No. No, I don't have the answers. You see, the man never got on Oskar's bus. The envelope never got out of Hungary. The man was killed."

Istvan's eyes gleamed then, flooded with tears. It was not grief. He could not have known Gideon Parr. He said savagely, "Goddamn it all to hell, the work that went into it, every step so tightly planned, and now—oh shit! Why didn't they just let me do it? Why? I could have had that envelope from Budapest to Vienna in four hours. But no, it had to be done the standard way, don't trust anybody too far, split it up. Sure! A whole chain, and if one link gives—"

Southard felt pity for the boy, for all his nameless confederates, for the outmoded, pathetic network run by Warren Hackler from Vienna. Hackler would be replaced of course. Southard wondered how long it would take to restructure Vienna. They would have to send a new station chief. Have to make each operation separate, linear: case officer to resident or principal to agent, cutouts as necessary. And no risk of a house of cards collapsing if anything went wrong. Every member of Hackler's network would have to go, on the assumption that all had been compromised. They would have to begin from scratch. Southard didn't envy the new man. Hackler should have been replaced even before the Austrian Peace Treaty went into effect last year.

"Listen," Southard said, "the dead man was my friend. Someone in your net betrayed him. Will you help me learn who it was?"

The boy thought it over. "You know the name Miklos Manyoki? He's Minister of the Interior for Transdanubia. In February he went to Moscow with the Hungarian delegation to the Twentieth Party Congress. The Hungarian delegation stayed two weeks. Miklos Manyoki stayed three."

35

"How'd he manage that?"

"Dumb luck. He fell on an icy sidewalk and broke his leg. They put him in hospital in Moscow for eight days."

"Where is he now?"

"Budapest. The Kobanyai Street Medical Center. Hungary's best, naturally. Manyoki is a party official." Istvan Varady smiled. "He's also one of us. A committed Communist, sure. But he'd give his life to throw the Russians out of Hungary.

"Manyoki somehow got his hands on the document in Moscow during that extra week. On the night of 24-25 February, after the official end of the 20th Party Congress, Khrushchev called a meeting. Midnight in the Great Kremlin Palace, no foreign delegates but fourteen hundred from all over the Soviet Union. I ask you, how can fourteen hundred people keep a secret? One of them passed a transcript to Manyoki."

"Where'd you learn all that?"

"A doctor at Kobanyai Street—the same man who took the envelope straight from Manyoki to the Café Hungaria."

"I want to meet him. Could you arrange that?"

"Here in Austria," Istvan asked, then made a motion with his thumb like a hitchhiker, "or on the other side of the lake?"

Southard preferred Hungary. The right kind of cover, the right kind of help from the doctor, and he might even reach Manyoki himself. He had to weigh that against the sort of cover he could expect from Warren Hackler— inadequate, if not dangerous—but there was really no alternative but to take the risk.

"I'll go in," he said.

"Good. Budapest would be better for Dr. Landler too."

"I'll let Oskar know when."

The girl was coming back along the dock carrying the cutoff bottom of a cardboard carton as a tray. It was loaded down with hard-roll sandwiches and half a dozen bottles of beer.

"What took you so long?" Istvan said. "I'm starving."

"Hungarians," the girl told Southard, "are impossible."

This time Istvan Varady did not deny he was Hungarian.

3

Warren Hackler had an upstairs office at the Embassy on Boltzmanngasse in Vienna's First District. He was a trim, freckle-faced man with burr-cut graying hair and a beautifully tailored gabardine suit. His cover, a good one if predictable, was assistant commercial attaché.

Southard had run his name through personnel before coming to Vienna. Warren Hackler had served as a captain in Army G-2 during the early years of the Occupation, working out of the Hotel Bristol. Recruited by an Agency spotter before discharge, he had spent three years at the Eastern Europe desk in Washington before being posted back to Vienna as station chief running operations for Austria and Hungary. He already had his contacts, after all.

They hadn't helped. Hackler's efficiency rating was poor. Southard wondered where they would send him next. To the Farm in Tidewater, Virginia, maybe, except that at forty-five Warren Hackler would be considered too old for the thorough retreading he needed. Southard's guess was a university; Hackler had his Ph.D. in political science. The Company would arrange tenure at a good if not first-rate college, supplementing Hackler's salary with a yearly bonus, its size dependent on how well Hackler scouted the campus for potential Agency recruits.

The universities were a major dumping ground for Company failures, frequently OSS veterans who couldn't get the hang of the new tradecraft. They were called Neanderthals.

Which, Southard reminded himself, was what some

people in Washington were already calling Gideon Parr before his heart attack. So let's give Hackler a chance, shall we?

"Sit down, Ben," Hackler said. "Is 'Ben' all right? Good. What can I do for you this time?"

Benton Southard noted the slight stress on the last two words.

After shaking hands they sat facing each other on leather sofas separated by a low coffee table.

"Some java?"

Southard declined. Hackler's use of the word *java*, the garbadine suit that fit him like a uniform, the way he stood ramrod straight while shaking hands, as if he were returning a salute, all were of a piece. Southard almost expected to see a ruptured duck, worn down by polishing, in his lapel. Like so many men desperately running to keep in place while their colleagues passed them by, Hackler must have looked back on his army career as the high point of his life.

Which, Southard reminded himself again, was a judgment he had heard passed on Gideon Parr at a cocktail party at the French Embassy in Washington a few months ago. Who had made it? Southard no longer remembered. It had seemed a cheap shot and not justified by the facts of Parr's life.

No two men could be more different than Warren Hackler, the nostalgic soldier out of uniform, and Gideon Parr, the urbane OSS veteran who'd always viewed the military with an amusement bordering on scorn. But the comparison was inevitable. Suddenly Southard wanted to get the meeting over with.

"How soon could you fix me up with paper for Hungary?"

"Well, that depends," Hackler said cautiously. "How deep a cover do you have in mind?"

"It doesn't have to be deep. Anything I can get my hands

on in a hurry."

Hackler crossed one knee over the other, arranging the trouser leg carefully to preserve the knife-edge crease. He wore clocked silk socks.

"What kind of passport are you using now?"

"American. Issued to a Curtis Beck. Current address, Milwaukee. Place of birth, Berlin."

"Say, that's good," said Hackler. "It explains the fluency in German. Business cover or what?"

"Tourist. It's all I needed for Austria."

"Yeah, sure. I can see that."

Hackler was making meaningless talk, and fidgeting. He crossed his legs the other way, again carefully arranging the gabardine. He twisted his gold wedding band. He took a small Dutch cigar from a cedar box on the coffee table and rolled it in his fingers, making no attempt to light it. "You ever try these Schimmelpennincks? Have one, go ahead, Ben. Best little cigars this side of Havana, Cuba."

Warren Hackler, ineptly running a station, lived in terror of the unforseeable. The terror was self-perpetuating. For Hackler, now, the ideal case load would be zero. No operations in progress, no errors of judgment possible. Southard knew of station chiefs just this side of a nervous breakdown who had gone six months without running an agent, without even recruiting one.

Anything that changed Hackler's day-to-day routine menaced him. Benton Southard especially menaced him. Southard had G-17 status, the same as Hackler, just right for a station chief. But Southard wasn't that. Southard was chief of counterespionage, Europe. Hackler knew by now that he was in deep trouble.

The little cigar broke in his hand. He dropped the two pieces in an onyx ashtray. Behind the bland expression on his freckled face Southard sensed a desperate panic.

If Hackler gave Southard what he wanted, without authorization, that could be the final mistake of his career.

If Hackler refused him, that could be the same.

Southard felt sorry for the man, and it angered him. It made him think of Gideon Parr a third time, measuring him against Hackler. Not that Parr had ever panicked. Not even when Southard walked in on him and the German woman in the safe house that night in Frankfurt.

The one who almost panicked then had been Southard.

Now he tossed the Curtis Beck passport on the coffee table. "Let's start from scratch—passport, Hungarian visa, business cards, a checkbook, an old letter or two. The usual package."

Hackler got up and went to the window, where he stood with his back to the room. "Where's your authorization?"

"What did you say?" Southard demanded.

"Your trip ticket, Ben. Endorsed by someone up the line. I can't go around handing out passports like free passes to the opera, can I?"

Southard stood. "Sure," he said, "kick it back to Washington or Frankfurt, why don't you? Maybe you'll get the endorsement by June."

Hackler turned away from the window. He went behind his big desk and sat. He squared the onyx desk set precisely with the edges of the desk, squared the blotter, moving each a fraction of an inch, like a compulsive housewife fussing with a picture on the wall.

"What are you so mad about?" he said.

"Just have the package ready for me by morning." Southard felt drained. Nothing he could do now would help or hurt Warren Hackler. Hackler was not the cause of his anger.

"A business connection," Hackler said, suddenly enthusiastic, a salesman now. "We'll get you a letter. The Orion Radio and Vacuum Flask Company in Budapest. They export all over Europe. They . . ."

He rambled on, a second-rater searching for a personality he had never had. Southard wasn't listening.

Even in the good days they had called Gideon Parr the chameleon.

Early the next afternoon, Southard boarded the Budapest express at the Aspang Station. He shared a first-class compartment with two men and a woman, all speaking Hungarian.

Every word Southard spoke, every gesture he made, every thought he had, every time he got up in the morning or skied down a mountain or sailed a boat or bedded a woman, every bottle of wine he opened, every joy, every sorrow, every second of his life he owed to Gideon Parr. The couplings jolted, the train got underway. He tried to recall the lean, almost ascetic face, the sudden sardonic smile that seemed to mock a courage as reflexive as breathing. But as the train entered the tunnel that would take it southeast out of Vienna he saw instead alongside his reflection in the mirror of the dark window the bland features and controlled panic of Warren Hackler.

Chapter Two

1

After six hours in the gloom of the police station, the sun-struck street dazzled her. She felt exposed, and more alone than she thought a human being could ever be. Behind the windowless mud-brick walls facing the narrow street, she was sure, lurked unseen watchers.

Stop that, she thought. You didn't come here to feel sorry for yourself. Besides, you've been through this before.

Except, of course, that the last time—the only other time—hadn't been in enemy territory. It had been comparatively safe, operating on home ground. There had been a new man at the radio station, quiet, efficient and self-contained, but with eyes that were as watchful as they were intelligent. After working at the station for a few months he had apparently decided to ignore Deborah's reputation as the Ice Maiden. At first she had guessed he must find her a challenge, although she was not entirely averse to his attentions. Not, that is, until he had found out—how? she wondered—that she had survived a Nazi death camp and oh-so-delicately tried to prod her into revealing how she had achieved this miracle. She didn't know herself, but only after the first shock of his broaching the subject, a subject no Israeli would bring up, had she realized that this man had also shown a persistent, if seemingly casual interest in Daddy Sam. With the thought that her survival of Auschwitz might put her true sympathies in question and that the man believed she, as the adopted daughter of Sam Brodsky of Shin Beth, might have access to sensitive information . . . Paranoia, that was what she'd thought it was, paranoia and perhaps shame that she could respond with no real warmth to the man's attentions. But after Daddy Sam's apartment had been broken into and virtually ripped apart, she took her fears directly to Iser Harel of the Mossad, not wanting to alarm her father unnecessarily. From there on, the romance became a sham, with Deborah, at the Mossad's instructions, keeping her eyes and ears finely tuned to the man's activities, allowing him to believe he had charmed his way into her confidence, and feeding him misinformation concerning Shin Beth's operations. It had been dangerous, of course, and it had sickened her, but she had pulled it off easily, uncovering this *fedayeen* agent with more cunning and deception than she had known she possessed. For protection, she'd had her own surprisingly accurate and quick instinct, her previous training and service with Israel's defense forces, and the presence of the Mossad's invisible men. It had been a training ground, preparing her for this. The Mossad had wanted her to continue, but she hadn't been ready. Now . . . now she was.

Her name, her new name, was Jehan Khalid. Good. Much better. Stick to basics.

The burn on her left forearm, healing nicely now after a week, itched under the bandage. She rubbed it and took a few steps along the street, seeking shadow. But the early afternoon sun blazed directly overhead. An old woman in black approached, her face veiled to the eyes. The old woman looked at her, made a sibilant reptilian sound and hurried past.

Three bearded apparitions in dirty striped robes ran wildly by, their faces contorted with pain or ecstasy, ancient Lee-Enfield rifles brandished overhead. She pressed herself flat against the mud-brick wall.

It had not been difficult in the police station at first. She was a complication the police in Gaza, Egypt, certainly did not need today. She waited three hours in a large room with a bare table, a few rickety chairs, Colonel Nasser in black and white on the scabrous wall. At the start of the fourth hour two policemen came in and asked her some questions. They wore black wool uniforms and red tarbooshes. They were preoccupied; they were nervous. She obviously was superfluous. They left and ten minutes later she was confronted by another pair of wool uniforms stinking of sweat, another pair of red tarbooshes. The same desultory questions, more or less. The men went out. She waited. She rubbed at the healing burn under the bandage.

She heard the crackle of gunfire like a distant string of firecrackers and there flashed through her mind the image of a boy, his face shot away by machine-gun bullets.

Her fingernails dug into her palms and she reminded herself that Jehan Khalid would know nothing about that. So neither could she. See how simple it was? The image went away. More police came in. What is your name? Again. Where are you from? Again. How did you burn yourself? Again. Where were you born? Again. How did you arrive in Gaza? Again. If you are Egyptian on your father's side and Lebanese on your mother's, why do you carry Israeli papers saying you are Palestinian? They pounced on that one, cleverly, when she was lulled by the ease of answering the other questions. And she looked them in the eyes and pointed out haughtily—Had Jehan been haughty? she wondered—that her father was not only Egyptian but a highly valued spy; since their papers were convincing enough to fool the Israelis for more than seven years, it would be surprising if the Gaza police could detect a flaw. Which they couldn't.

Still, though she was prepared for the questions, they made her nervous.

By ten o'clock she had to go to the bathroom. By eleven

she really had to go, was bursting with the need to relieve her bladder. She went to the door. A black wool sleeve moved, a hand gestured: back, back inside. She crossed the room to the single small window. It looked out on a courtyard, four walls, three other small windows, shutters closed, a moribund umbrella pine in a patch of dusty earth. She was contemplating a quick visit to the courtyard but just then two policemen came in. They asked questions, not very difficult questions really, repetitive questions if you got right down to it. She answered them. She thought she answered them. She had to go to the bathroom. She crossed her legs and sat and answered questions she hardly heard and one of the policemen went from the room, leaving the elderly one with the gray hair and the big gray mustache, the one who had a clipped way of speaking as if he had been taught Arabic by an Englishman.

"From Israel." He shook his head in believing disbelief.

She said something. She got up and walked to the wall where the picture of Nasser hung. It was crooked. She straightened it and came back and sat down. She crossed her legs, hard.

"I read in the papers about your father," said the gray-haired policeman with the big mustache. "They framed him, you know."

"No they didn't."

"They didn't?"

"They said he was an Egyptian spy, and he was. He lived in Israel as a Palestinian ever since '48, spying for us. He did valuable work."

"All the same, they framed him."

First, last and always, the men from the Arab Affairs Section of the Mossad had told her, remember that you are Jehan Khalid. Your father is serving a life sentence in Tel Aviv. You are the daughter of Akhmed Khalid, Egyptian spy. Jehan, you are Jehan. You think like Jehan only. You talk like Jehan only. When you do something, whatever you

45

do, whatever reasons you have for doing it, the reasons and the doing are Jehan's. Like method acting. They call it The Method. You live and think and breathe Jehan Khalid, and you *become* Jehan Khalid. No mistakes. So you minimize the danger to yourself.

Jehan Khalid had to go to the bathroom.

"They didn't frame him. It was an accident that they caught him, but they knew what he was. They just didn't know how good. They didn't learn a fraction of what he did. He's a hero." She crossed her legs the other way.

The elderly policeman studied her. He nodded decisively and said, "Come with me."

Along a dim hall and down a flight of stairs and around a corner and along another dim hall, where she had to grope her way to a door.

"In there," said the policeman.

The small cubicle smelled foul. There was a hole in the floor flanked by the cracked tile imprints of two giant feet. She set her shoes down squarely on the two giant imprints and unfastened her belt and squatted and emptied her bursting bladder in a long scalding rush.

When she came out, the gray-haired policeman averted his eyes. "My granddaughter," he mumbled, "same thing, just like you. Crosses them one way, then the other." They walked back along the hall and turned the corner and climbed the stairs. "Only human," he said. Her emergency seemed to form a bond between them.

"Be finished with you soon," he told her. "You are who you say you are, that's obvious. Take some advice? Stay off the streets today. We ought to keep you here, but we've got our hands full. And you wouldn't want that anyway, would you."

"No. But what's happening?"

"Fedayeen coming into town. You know about them?"

"Of course I do."

"Heroes," the policeman said dryly. "Like your father."

46

He had the cynicism of an old man who has seen too much, most of it bad.

Would Jehan have objected to what he said?

"It's hardly the same," she said haughtily. "Can you imagine what it's like to live two lives at once among the Zionist pigs?" Would Jehan have said 'pigs'? It sounded right in Arabic.

"No, and wouldn't care to," he said. "Listen—when we let you go, get off the streets. There's going to be trouble. Already is. The police as usual can't cope with it. Never would have happened under the British. I ought to know; served under them almost twenty years." He cleared his throat. "Fedayeen coming in from as far away as Cairo, and the Brotherhood waiting for them. Just get off the streets."

"Where should I go?"

"Anywhere, long as you're off the streets. Keep away from the Brotherhood. Keep away from the Germans. The Grand Gaza Hotel on Falastin Square ought to be safe. Turn left out of here and keep walking. Dressed the way you are, you make it worse for yourself. Khaki pants and that open shirt—you look like the fedayeen. Just get off the streets and you'll be all right, in *sha*'Allah."

"In *sha*'Allah," she said, and they were back in the interrogation room. Half an hour later she was out on the street and the three bearded men were rushing by, brandishing rifles.

Her name was Jehan Khalid. Now she even had temporary identification papers to prove it, issued by the Gaza City Police.

Her eyes grew accustomed to the sun. The street was unpaved, unimaginably filthy, and that brown stream flowing sluggishly along one side, foul-smelling, was a sewer, and what that man hunkered over it was doing was defecating—no more than twenty yards from where children were playing at the edge of the stream. The children wore rags, and their faces had odd leprous-looking

47

patches on them. As she approached, the patches on the children's faces seemed to move, darkly, obscenely green, changing shape. She realized they were swarms of flies feasting on open sores, scabs and pus.

Her name, her new name, was Jehan Khalid.

She clung to that. Clinging to that, all else would follow. In *sha*'Allah, if God wills it.

Two old men with unkempt beards were following her. When she turned, one of them shouted, his face twisted with that mixture of outrage and desire that the puritanical male so often directs at the fallen woman, the loose woman, the whore.

She walked on. She had been told to expect this. Gaza was a conservative city, the last stronghold of the Moslem Brotherhood, its morality that of the Koran. Women went out, if at all, heavily robed and veiled. Her snug khaki slacks and the short-sleeved shirt open at the throat were an affront. But Jehan, the Jehan constructed by the Arab Affairs Section of the Mossad, would wear khaki.

Something hurtled past her head and struck the mud-brick wall. Chips flew, stinging her cheek.

She walked faster. She had been told, ironically, that safety would be found among the fedayeen. Find them? Not necessary. They would find her. News of her solitary arrival aboard the motor sailer *Yallah*—home port Haifa, Israel, stenciled boldly on the transom—beached at dawn on the sand west of Gaza City, would have reached the fedayeen as soon as it reached the police. Sooner, perhaps. But the fedayeen would wait until the police had interrogated her.

A stone struck her shoulder and old men's voices lifted in spiteful triumph behind her. She bit her lip and faltered, then decided that Jehan might run, that Jehan would not allow fear to catch her in indecision, in inactivity. She broke into a run, her shoulder throbbing with each step. She bit her lip again.

Had Jehan been a lip-biter?

Her name was Jehan Khalid.

This cover, according to the Arab Affairs Section of the Mossad, was excellent but not foolproof. To establish foolproof cover takes time. And all they had was a week.

In a way, they told her, Jehan Khalid was a gift from the sea.

The body of the real Jehan, daughter of a spy from the Mukhabarat al-Aam—Egypt's General Intelligence Agency —who was arrested in Tel Aviv in December 1955, had washed ashore three months later on the beach near Haifa, victim of either accidental drowning or suicide. The living and dead Jehans had been born within two months of each other. That the resemblance between them was super- ficial—a certain dark-haired, dark-eyed prettiness—hardly mattered. The real Jehan's mother had died years ago and Jehan had spent the time from late 1948 until her own death ten days ago in the heavily Arab Israeli city of Jaffa, where she and her father passed as Palestinians from a village destroyed in the war. Jehan's youth had been spent in Beirut. Mossad resources there could uncover no known relatives, and the same was true in Cairo. The real Jehan, during her father's long double life in Israel, apparently remained in ignorance of his espionage activities.

From the Mossad briefing:

. . . *the situation in Gaza. The Moslem Brotherhood traditionally control the city, the fedayeen the desert and the coastal plantations. Brotherhood armed forces are commanded by the German Wehrmacht veteran Joachim Griem (also known since 1951 by his Moslem name Haj Rashid Ali Krim), the fedayeen by the Husayni twins, Maryam and Sulayman.*

Real control of the city over the last few weeks has slipped into the hands of the fedayeen. A confrontation with the Moslem Brotherhood can be expected at any time. Mossad resources in Cairo predict the fedayeen will win.

[N.B.: The attempt by a Brotherhood fanatic to

assassinate Colonel Nasser gave the army an excuse to throw unofficial support to the fedayeen. But in point of fact, when Nasser turned to Russia for military aid, the rabid ex-Nazi Griem-Krim became a liability to the regime, and the Brotherhood an embarrassment. Our resources believe the fedayeen or the Russians will liquidate Krim. But given his following among the powerful clergy, they may well try to discredit him first.]

Until the split between the fedayeen and the Brotherhood, the Husayni twins helped train terrorist squads at the base near Khan Yunis under the command of Griem-Krim. That base we have destroyed.

Your mission has three objectives:

(1) To locate the new fedayeen base.

(2) To confirm the presence there of Russian training cadre, and to determine their numbers.

(3) To evaluate the probable consequences for Israel of a fedayeen victory over the Moslem Brotherhood.

You will exercise care in dealing with the Husayni twins; both are known killers. Establishing acceptable contact with them should be easy. Your credentials are admirable. They are eager for recruits and will seek you out. Contact will be facilitated by your sale of the yacht Yallah; the fedayeen extort a cut from every substantial transaction in Gaza, and the Yallah should bring seven to eight thousand Egyptian pounds. . . .

She had no trouble outdistancing the bearded old men—a turn, twenty running strides into a deserted alley, another turn, alleys twisting into alleys, an occasional small courtyard, the smell of ancient garbage. Soon the alleys were wider and beggars sat in the dust and then the beggars gave way to merchants who sat cross-legged near grubby cloths heaped with dates, slices of watermelon, and flat round breads, all crawling with flies. She turned onto a street with stalls and pushcarts shaded by tatters of awning. Donkeys brayed, the sound at once aspirant and clanking.

An old car came from a sidestreet, three boys on the running board, dressed in khaki with bandoliers across their chests and carrying sleek new automatic rifles. The car did not stop as the three boys, none more than sixteen, jumped off and walked to a pushcart heaped with half-rotten fruit. The fat man behind the cart, who an instant before had been hawking watermelon slices and pomegranates, now stood by and watched without a flicker of expression as the boys overturned his cart. The muzzle of one boy's sleek new automatic rifle indented his fat belly and he stood there and took that too, face now white but still expressionless under his dingy headcloth. Then, planting his feet wide, the boy swung his rifle at the head of the stoic merchant, making a meaty sound, and the fat man fell down with blood spurting from his nose and teeth flying from his mouth as if he were spitting out small yellow stones. He sat on a mound of rotting fruit, blood now streaming from flattened nose and broken mouth, and never made a sound. In no hurry, the three boys went after the choking cloud of dust left by the car that had brought them.

Her name, her new name, was Jehan Khalid.

She reached Falastin Square and saw the piled sandbags, the iron shutters bolted over shop windows, the jeeps and six-wheeled scout cars and armed young khaki-clad figures everywhere. She kept walking, as if she belonged exactly where she was, going where she was going, until she saw the sign that said Grand Gaza Hotel, where, finally, two men barred her way with rifles.

Not that they were particularly wary. Her khakis served almost as a uniform.

"I'm Jehan Khalid," she told them.

The sentries studied her with that bored, amused contempt for the stranger so common to the Arab city-dweller.

"Get someone," she said peremptorily. The haughty

51

persona she had given Jehan and the Ice Maiden herself prevailed. One sentry disappeared into the hotel and returned with a short, plump man wearing a dirty red-and-white-checked headcloth and rumpled khaki shirt and trousers so ill-fitting they looked borrowed. He needed a shave and he smelled. He had protruding eyes, a broad hooked nose and fleshy lips above a receding chin. A leather gunbelt girdled him low around his thick middle, the holstered automatic resting against his plump thigh. "Allah, I thought you'd never get here," he said.

Maybe he'd mistaken her for someone else.

"Didn't they tell you in the police station to come straight here? Lady, the streets are dangerous. You could get killed." The plump man had a wheedling voice. "*Yallah,*" he said, and started into the hotel.

The boat? What did he know about the *Yallah?*

"Come on," he said impatiently. "*Yallah, yallah!*"

In Arabic *yallah* meant "let's go." A nice cute name for a boat. He was telling her to come with him.

They went together into the deserted lobby.

"I'm cousin Yasir," he said. She gave him a blank look. "Husayni," he told her more impatiently. "Like my cousins the twins? Surely you've heard of *them?*"

"Yes, of course I have," she said.

Her name was Jehan Khalid.

2

In Tel Aviv that same afternoon Sam Brodsky stormed into a small office in the government quarter of Ha Qirya and shouted: "Well, Jesus Christ, it's about time! What kind of crap is this? You've been avoiding me all week."

The diminutive man behind the desk imperturbably stood to shake Sam Brodsky's hand. Sam was immediately reminded, as he always was when he saw Iser Harel, of his youth in Brooklyn and a pair of comic-strip characters called Mutt and Jeff. The discrepancy in their sizes was the same. Sam Brodsky, former L.I.U. basketball star, was six feet four. Iser Harel, forty-three-year-old commander of the Mossad and by extension chief of all three Israeli intelligence services including the Shin Beth, in which Major Sam Brodsky served, was all of four feet ten inches tall. He was bald, he had piercing blue eyes, he never wore a necktie, he never stood on ceremony, he never played favorites. His Mossad subordinates feared him and loved him. The mostly British-trained officers of Shin Beth tended to underestimate their nominal superior, this Latvian refugee who had come up through the ranks of the Haganah to become its intelligence chief before Ben-Gurion asked him in 1951 to organize the Mossad. Sam Brodsky was smart enough not to make the usual Shin Beth mistake. But he was mad.

"*Shalom,*" Iser Harel said calmly.

"*Shalom,* my ass! Where is she?"

"Once I was out of the country for three weeks and my wife Rivkah goes to Ben-Gurion and says, 'Where is he?' She pleads with him. You know what the prime minister says? 'Rivkah, believe me, if I knew where Iser was, I'd tell you. That man never tells me anything.' "

"Meaning you don't know where she is, or you won't tell me?"

"Meaning calm down, Sam. I was away on business, I'm back, I got your message, you're here. What can I do for you?" Iser Harel's English was fluent but accented; it was the only language Sam Brodsky trusted.

"Tell me where you sent Debbie."

Iser Harel said calmly, "Gaza."

"Gaza?" Sam leaped to his feet and made a lunge at the door as if he wanted to knock it down.

"Where do you think you're going?"

"Gaza," said Sam Brodsky

Iser Harel lowered his voice. "You wanted to see me. Now don't waste my time." Hardly more than a hoarse whisper, the words nevertheless stopped Brodsky. Harel never shouted. When he whispered, you paid double attention. "I can give you ten minutes, Sam. So stop acting like a big balloon-ball baby and let's talk."

"Basketball," Sam growled, but he sat down again.

"Ever since last September," Iser Harel said, "Egypt has been getting Russian arms through Czechoslovakia. Not just tokens—a massive military buildup."

"I know that," Sam began.

"Let me finish. Two hundred modern warplanes. MiG-15s, some of the newer MiG-17s, Ilyushin-28 light twin-jet bombers. Twice that many tanks—Soviet T34s, BTR scout cars and self-propelled SU100 artillery in addition to—"

"Cut it out, will you? You said ten minutes."

"They have also sent 'advisors' to train the fedayeen. And they've helped the fedayeen gain the upper hand over the Moslem Brotherhood. Do you know why?"

"Sure I know why. It's my line of work too," Sam pointed out impatiently. "The Brotherhood, they're fanatic Moslems and they won't go near Communism. The fedayeen are younger, willing to take a chance on anybody who helps them kick the West out of the Middle East, and us into the sea. The fedayeen'll play ball with Moscow. It's as simple as that."

"Whenever anybody says 'it's as simple as that,' right away I get suspicious. Nothing is as simple as that." Harel sighed. "A war machine for Nasser, equipment and training for the terrorists—"

Sam looked at his watch. When Iser Harel said ten minutes, he did not mean ten minutes and five seconds. And Sam knew only too well how he operated. Facts. He flooded you with facts, often peripheral, sometimes irrelevant, and then he told you what he wanted to tell you, and then your allotted time ran out. But Iser Harel was the *memuneh*, the big boss. After his one outburst, chewing long seconds from the clock, Sam suffered in silence.

"—operating out of not just Gaza, but Syria and Jordan too. Over two hundred civilians have died at their hands in the past year. It isn't safe for women to go to market or children to school—"

"Please, Iser—where is she?"

"I told you. Gaza. When you found the base outside Khan Yunis, Dayan destroyed it. Where is their new base?"

"Not in the Gaza Strip. If it was, Shin Beth would know."

"But you haven't been able to find out where?"

"No. Not yet," Sam admitted.

"Your Debbie will find it for us."

"Debbie? She's a child, she's had hardly any training, she—"

"She's twenty-four years old, she's served in the defense forces, she did a surprisingly competent job of exposing that fellow at the station . . . She's not exactly helpless, Sam—and I don't have to tell you how well motivated she is or why."

"Motivated, sure. But I could give you twenty Shin Beth people her age tomorrow. Why Debbie?"

"She speaks English and French fluently."

"English and French? So what?"

"The top fedayeen, a fraction of 1 percent, are educated fanatics. The rest, rabble from the camps. So fluency in Western languages is a rarity. And for reasons unknown to our resources in Cairo, the Russian advisors are searching for linguists."

"So Debbie's a linguist. That doesn't make her an intelligence agent. She knows nothing—"

"Sam, you're wasting your own time telling me how helpless she is." Iser Harel picked up a sheet of paper and read: "Brodsky, Deborah. Active service Defense Forces 1952-54. Basic training, etc., etc. . . . Firearms, rifle:

marksman. Firearms, pistol: expert . . . Unarmed combat: general proficiency . . . Advanced training Military Intelligence School 1953, assigned to interrogate terrorist raiders infiltrating from Syria and Lebanon, etc., etc. . . . Reserve rank, sergeant, Military Intelligence."

"Iser, does it say she became a schoolteacher when she got out? A teacher, Iser . . . and a radio announcer. As for that other business, it was pure luck, child's play."

The diminutive Mossad chief looked at his watch. "If you want to waste your time talking about that, it's okay with me. You have less than three minutes left."

Sam groaned inwardly and shook his head.

"Young Arabs who speak fluent English, French, German. What do the Russians want with them? We think Debbie can get the answer. And I think you underestimated her, though I understand it's only out of concern. We haven't sent her in unsupported, Sam, our resources in Cairo know of her mission. The station chief himself is her control."

Sam remembered something suddenly. "The Auschwitz tattoo on her wrist," he said. "Jesus Christ, Iser! The concentration camp number!"

"A burn. It leaves a scar."

"But even a moron—"

"Keep in mind, Sam, only Auschwitz used the tattoo. The other camps put the number on your clothing, right? And there weren't many survivors of Auschwitz. She's the only one we've ever sent in. So they have no reason to be suspicious of a burn."

"She has no reason to be there. She's a kid, an untrained kid. What does she know about tradecraft?"

"Sometimes tradecraft doesn't help, sometimes it gets you killed. If you spot a tail, say, or cover your moves too professionally, you arouse suspicion. But a kid like Debbie, an ex-soldier, competent but no tradecraft, she'll act normal."

"Normal. In Egypt. Alone . . ."

"If she's scared, that's a plus too," Iser Harel pointed out. "A young Arab girl starting fedayeen training—being scared is normal."

The observation was sound but not comforting.

"You'll keep me informed?"

"No," Harel said. "I wouldn't keep God informed unless He could demonstrate a need to know." Iser Harel rose, all four feet ten inches of him. "I'm afraid that's it, Sam. *Shalom.*"

After Sam left, Iser Harel leafed through the file on Sam's adopted daughter. It was a good, thorough job—but it barely touched on one point. Even the little Mossad chief and Sam Brodsky had discussed it only glancingly.

Debbie was the survivor of a Nazi death camp.

Not only that, she was a young survivor, having spent her twelfth to fourteenth years in that most notorious of all Nazi death camps, Auschwitz.

And not only *that*, there were the rumors about her survival, strange tales. The Mossad's chief psychiatrist had told Iser Harel of three or four people in Israel who wouldn't go near Debbie, even now, more than ten years later. They called her the ghost. The Mossad had never followed up. No one had actually accused Debbie of collaboration with the Nazis and, even if someone had, she'd been a child then. Under the circumstances, no organization serving the best interests of the Israeli people would have taken the matter further. Israel had learned the hard way, in a decade of trial and error, how to live with its thousands of death-camp survivors.

In 1951 Iser Harel had asked the Mossad psychiatrist to draw up a profile of young death-camp survivors. The word *young* was crucial; the Institute needed young people. Already in Tel Aviv alone, the Mossad employed dozens of such survivors. They were dedicated, hard workers.

The psychological profile, when it was finished, disturbed Harel. Not unexpectedly, it contained much social-science jargon, but several concrete points came through.

The typical young death-camp inmate, placed in a constantly life-threatening environment (how Iser Harel hated the jargon!), developed as survival techniques mental patterns which often diminished the sense of self and distorted perceptions of time and place. Harel's translation: *These kids had to go a little crazy, in order to stay sane.*

Of the several neurotic-psychotic symptoms to which the survivor was prone, the most serious was neurasthenia, paranoia and, in rare cases under extreme stress, catatonia. Harel's translation: *Some of them are nervous wrecks, some feel they've been persecuted (!), some just can't face life anymore and, if I've got this one right, unplug themselves and wind up like vegetables.*

In later life, various psychological, social and physiological manifestations could be anticipated, but insufficient time had elapsed to develop that profile beyond mere speculation. Divorce, drug or drinking problems, nervous breakdown, ulcers, high blood pressure, heart disease were among the possibilities. Or: *It's too early to tell what will happen to the young death-camp survivor when he gets older.*

In their twenties, a larger percentage of them than was to be found in an equivalent sample of the general population were withdrawn, suspicious, watchful, self-sufficient.

The last part needed no translation, and it was the only part Iser Harel liked. Withdrawn, suspicious, watchful, self-sufficient — that was the ideal deep-cover agent. Against it, Iser Harel had to weigh the jargon of diminished sense of self, neurasthenia, paranoia and catatonia.

Conclusion: Death-camp survivors could make great agents — unless they went nuts.

Harel had interviewed Debbie before sending her to the

Mossad camp in the desolate country of the Horns of Hattin for a week's briefing, and of course also when she had come to the Mossad a year or so ago with her suspicions about her amorous coworker at the State Radio Studios. An attractive woman of twenty-four, Iser Harel decided, except for the coldness. The psychiatrist told him she was normal in the various tests—Rorschach, T.A.T.—and she was a sweetheart with children, and, apparently, genuinely close to the man who had brought her from a DP camp to Israel ten years ago, Sam Brodsky. But the warmth ended there. What a waste, Harel thought. Where she worked they called her the Ice Maiden.

At the Horns of Hattin they had been pleased with her: a tremendously quick study. But, Iser Harel reflected unhappily, the Horns of Hattin staff had been pleased with the other two, a pair of young Mossad probationary officers they had sent into Egypt under good cover some time before sending Debbie. In less than a month the first, wearing the traditional purple cap, black shirt and red trousers of those condemned under Egyptian law, had been hanged at a military base outside Alexandria on the northwestern edge of the Nile Delta. The body of the second, his genitals violated, was found one morning on the Seine embankment near the Pont Neuf in Paris.

Iser Harel hadn't been putting Sam on. The two unfortunates were professionals, if new at their work. But sometimes a relative amateur could accomplish more. And live to tell of it.

Sometimes.

Had he been a religious man. Iser Harel would have spent a moment praying for Deborah.

3

"Allah akbar, Allah akbar, Allah akbar! Ashadu an la

ilaha illa-llah, ashadu anna Mohammedarrasulullah! Hayya'alas-sala!"

The muezzin's wail floated over the rooftops of Gaza in the last full daylight of the afternoon. Allah is great, Allah is great, Allah is great! Bear witness that there is no god but Allah and Mohammed is his Prophet! Come to prayer!

Cousin Yasir groaned. Prayer wouldn't help. It was too late for prayer, as it always was when you flung yourself in desperation on a prayer rug, prostrate, facing Mecca, to submit yourself to the *qadar*, the divine will, or to dwell on the Ninety-Nine Most Beautiful Names of God. Very efficacious.

Well, thought cousin Yasir sourly, very fine-sounding anyway.

There was the Protector, the Strong, the All-Powerful, the Compassionate. . . .

Compassionate to both sides? Yasir could see the armies marching against each other throughout history, Saladin and the Crusaders, Turks and Greeks, Axis and Allies; imams and priests on both sides exhorting the faithful to heroism, and God, whatever god, guiding their right hands to victory.

One chance out of two, God's side lost.

And what if it was the selfsame God? The All-Knowing and Merciful, to mention two more of the Ninety-Nine Most Beautiful?

If the Ikhwan, the Moslem Brotherhood, were fanatically devout, the fedayeen often stood accused of indifference, sometimes of impiety, occasionally blasphemy.

Who had time for God?

Who did God have time for?

Yasir, alone, was occupying the sitting room of the only suite in the Grand Gaza Hotel, one floor up. The windows afforded a glimpse of Falastin Square through intricate grillwork. Maps covered the low round copper tables, empty bandoliers and cartridge belts hung on the backs of chairs, two AK-47 assault rifles stood propped in a corner near an ornamental screen of white filigree. Yasir's battered old briefcase rested innocent-looking on a brocaded cushion on the low divan. Inside were acid-and-wire timing devices, fulminate of mercury percussion caps—and enough plastique to demolish two or three buildings the size of the Grand Gaza Hotel.

Far more than enough to blow up Krim's headquarters in a restaurant out beyond the cemetery on Omar al-Mukhtar Avenue. Which would have been Yasir's assignment if everything hadn't gone wrong.

Everything had gone wrong.

Yasir put down his pen, shoved the paper aside, and took out his *sibha*, his prayer beads. He moved one of the large amber beads. First, fifty fedayeen, armed to the teeth, had somehow disappeared en route from Cairo in modern Soviet trucks. He moved another bead. Second, the Ikhwan had fired treacherously on an ambulance clearly marked with the Red Crescent, the machine-gun bullets igniting the vehicle, killing its driver and detonating its cargo of hand grenades and 7.62-mm ammunition. Another bead. Third, if Allah knew where they came from Allah wasn't saying, but hundreds (well, dozens anyway) of Brotherhood fanatics had materialized out of nowhere screaming the greatness of Allah and attacking fedayeen strongpoints around the city, dragging the self-sacrificers into the streets, beating them with lead-weighted bamboo sticks and sending them on their way limping and moaning toward the desert. Fourth bead, the Husayni twins had left their command post (this suite at the Grand Gaza Hotel which Yasir had since, on what he hoped was a temporary basis, commandeered) and hadn't been seen or heard from since shortly after noon. Where were they? Did even Allah know? Were they fleeing back toward the delta? Or dead? Did Krim have them? He wondered if Krim had raped Maryam Husayni before cutting out her tongue, plucking out her

61

eyes and pouring acid into their sockets. Krim certainly would have raped Maryam if he could, before he killed her. Ever since the early days at Khan Yanis he had wanted to rape her, because it was clear she wouldn't let him do it any other way. The final bead: gunfire closer all the time, and a handful of desperate fedayeen who hadn't left the city waiting in the lobby of the Grand Gaza for a miracle. You didn't need von Clausewitz's *On War* to predict the outcome.

Not that you could dignify the day's events with the word *war*. It was more like Chicago, Yasir thought—gangsters with tommy guns and red Indians with tomahawks fighting for control of the city. And the police, just when you needed them, conspicuous by their absence.

There was a lull in the rifle fire outside. Yasir, a methodical if nervous man who followed orders until there were no more orders to follow, took up his pen and resumed writing. He finished the bill of sale. It was work any clerk could have done and by now inconsequential besides, but it was something to do with his hands, like the prayer beads.

This morning, only this morning—why had he been so convinced the German was finished? Not to mention the Moslem Brotherhood, all of whom could recite the Ninety-Nine Most Beautiful Names backwards. In their sleep.

No less a personage than Yasir's mother's cousin Haj Amin al-Husayni, the old grand mufti of Jerusalem himself, still supported the Ikhwan, still backed the German. To be quite fair, not just the German Krim. The Germans, plural. Any Germans as long as they were Nazis. Somewhat difficult to find these days, although less so in Egypt than elsewhere. The mufti, when Yasir was a child of ten, had left Jerusalem a step ahead of the British police and spent the war years in Berlin. Yasir carried a photograph of his elderly relative, not so old then, taken fifteen years ago with the Fuehrer himself. He had often thought of getting rid of the photograph. But an opportunist waits as often as he leaps. Maybe he'd better hold onto the photograph a while longer. True, the last he knew, the mufti was out of favor, under virtual house arrest in Cairo, but that could change. What was happening right here in Gaza could change it.

His cousin, Haj Amin al-Husayni, the grand mufti of Jerusalem. Once that counted for something.

His cousins, the Husayni twins. The mufti was their distant kinsman too. They despised him.

They weren't too cordial to Yasir either. Maybe that was the trouble. Allah, but they were a pair of snobs! Educated in Switzerland and France, how they looked down on him with his degree in civil engineering from King Fuad (now Cairo) University. If they hadn't been so insufferably superior. . . .

The Grand Gaza Hotel. Safest place in the city, Yasir. So Yasir obediently held the fort.

He briefly envisioned Krim with enough hashish in him to make raping Maryam Husayni inevitable.

The girl Jehan came in. She had caught her long hair up and pinned it back, but a few strands had escaped and hung down limply. Her face gleamed with sweat and there was a smudge of soot on one cheek. She looked haggard.

"Well?" he said. She had come here, sailing her fine yacht from Haifa to the Gaza coast, to join the fedayeen. She was still unaware that the yacht was forfeit; the Husaynis would force her to sell for a pittance. He had accepted her tacitly into the fedayeen, putting her to work as his eyes and ears downstairs. Like the Eyes and Ears of Persia's Great King Cyrus, what a fine ring that had to it! She even seemed to know what she was doing—accurate information, concisely reported, almost as if she'd had military experience. Of course she must have helped her father in Jaffa or Tel Aviv or wherever the Israelis captured him.

The girl sank heavily onto the divan. "Eight men in the lobby," she said. "They have rifles but they're useless."

"They're brand new Russian AK-47 assault rifles. What do you mean, useless?"

"Not the rifles. The eight boys down there. They're frightened out of their wits." She poked absently at her straggling hair, then pulled out the pins, shaking the hair loose. "And you've got no one outside in the square."

"What do you mean, no one?"

The girl ignored his second question. Like the other it was more lament than question anyway. "The Ikhwan are setting up a machine gun where Omar al-Mukhtar Avenue enters the square," she said.

"That close? They can't be."

"Maybe not, but they are." The girl stretched until her shoulders creaked. She put her elbows on her knees and rubbed her face hard with both hands, as if she were washing. She stretched again and yawned.

The Ikhwan machine gun on Omar al-Mukhtar Avenue began to fire suddenly, a long stuttering burst.

Yasir had to do something, anything, to calm his nerves. He pulled out his prayer beads but thrust them impatiently back into his pocket. Why let Allah have the satisfaction? He gave the girl the bill of sale he had written in his beautiful script for the yacht *Yallah*, which, shortly after dawn, the police had impounded on the coast west of town.

The girl began to read. " 'As Allah is my witness, I, Jehan Khalid, accept as payment in full for the title free and clear to the motor sailing vessel *Yallah*, former port of registry Haifa, Israel, the sum of five hundred (500) Egyptian pounds, receipt of which is hereby—' What is this?"

"You can read, lady, I assume you can write. Sign it."

"It's a ridiculous offer. The *Yallah*'s worth twenty times that much. I need the money to live on."

Yasir forgot the machine gun on Omar al-Mukhtar Avenue. He warmed to the bargaining. "If you're with the fedayeen, you need no money to live on. My cousins are generous to pay you anything."

"Generous! And I thought the Jews were thieves! You know how much that boat is—"

"It's worth what my cousin Sulayman Husayni says it's worth. You won't find another buyer. What about a thousand? Here, I'll make it a thousand." Yasir reached for the bill of sale.

"No." The girl dropped the paper on the floor, put her feet up on the divan and stretched out full length.

"Fifteen hundred?" Yasir tried.

The machine gun began to fire again, hammering steadily for several seconds. Bullets clanged resonantly as they ricocheted off the iron window grille.

Yasir tried to picture Falastin Square and the point where Omar al-Mukhtar Avenue entered it. He was sure, he was almost sure, that the angle of fire was too acute for bullets to penetrate the grille.

Unless the Brotherhood had repositioned their machine gun. It began to hammer again and the resonant clanging resumed at once. Yasir sat on the floor and whimpered.

She turned on her side facing the back of the divan and drew up her knees. A shudder ran through her body.

It had been all right while she was bargaining with the sweaty little fat man who called himself cousin Yasir. It was easy to assume the role of Jehan. Amusing, almost. The fat man was funny—when he wasn't terrified. She was certain Jehan would have got the better of the bargain.

She remembered the Horns of Hattin. *You are Jehan. You think like Jehan only. You talk like Jehan only. Whatever you do, whatever reasons you have for doing it, the reasons and the doing are Jehan's. You live and think and breathe Jehan Khalid. So you minimize the danger to yourself.*

The machine gun stuttered to a stop.

Minimize the danger?

Bullets could kill Jehan as easily as anyone else.

She lay there, knees drawn up, hands clasped around them, gripping hard. Her body went rigid for an instant and then she relaxed, and exhaustion rolled over her like waves on a beach. My God, thirty-six hours without sleep, she thought. But it was only half a thought, dimly there, dimly realized, and it was slipping away from her. She buried her face in the angle made by the brocaded cushions of the divan and saw herself shuffling forward with the others—Ten minutes left to live? twenty?—not caring because there is no way to care when there is nothing to do but suddenly the pale eyes came and she went where she was taken until it was safe to go back to the barracks but the other inmates shunned her and the second time it happened they began calling her the ghost and said she must have done terrible things to be singled out like that for survival and she tried to explain but how could she when she never knew the reason herself. . . .

She lay there in the strange room in the hotel in Gaza and let the exhaustion take everything away from her.

It wasn't until two hours later that the machine gun on Omar al-Mukhtar opened up again. Yasir had waited for a miracle—well, for the Husayni twins anyway. Now he stood to one side of the window and peered anxiously through the grille. In the dark of early evening tracer bullets streaked across Falastin Square. This started an exodus from the lobby. Yasir saw khaki-clad figures rush out to zigzag in the direction of al-Wahda Street, where they vanished. The machine gun went silent and Yasir saw a truck's headlights moving up Omar al-Mukhtar. It rumbled into Falastin Square, a second pair of headlights close behind.

Yasir had seen enough. He left the window and crossed the room to where the girl lay sleeping. He shook her shoulder. She stirred and mumbled something incomprehensible in her sleep. It sounded almost like a foreign language. Yasir shook her shoulder again, more urgently. She turned her face back to the divan.

"Lady!" he cried, shaking her a third time. "Please, lady!"

This did not even disturb the rhythm of her breathing.

Talk about waking the dead—

He'd be dead himself if he didn't get out of there. Probably do better on his own anyway. The girl was so deeply asleep she might as well have been drugged. It wasn't as if he owed her anything, after all.

Yasir grabbed his briefcase and one of the rifles in the corner and ran downstairs. Outside, in his awkward waddling run, he crossed Falastin Square in the direction of al-Wahda Street. . . .

Haj Rashid Ali Krim, the ex-Nazi and former Wehrmacht warrant officer, face streaked with sweat and dust, hair the color of a wheatfield at harvest, lips parted in an exultant grin, was the first to enter the hotel.

Chapter Three

1

Halfway across the Danube the bridge divided, one fork continuing west to the hilly Buda shore, the other going north to Margaret Island. Southard walked the few hundred yards to the island and past the entrance to the Pioneers' Stadium, shut until later in the spring, to the first of several soccer fields.

Parting the Danube for a distance of one and a half miles, Margaret Island was Budapest's playground, a country resort in the middle of a city of two million people. Despite the raw day and the dark clouds scudding overhead in the stiff wind, their swift-moving shadows almost black on the choppy leaden gray of the river itself, the island gave the city a livable, human dimension. The roadways and paths were crowded with people going nowhere in particular, doing nothing in particular. They looked happy.

Southard watched the soccer game in progress. The players were young. When the blue team scored a goal the few dozen standing spectators applauded politely but the players went wild on the field, jumping, embracing, flinging their arms high. After joining in the applause, Southard removed the Danube steamer schedule from his coat pocket and studied it, the glossy paper fluttering in the wind.

A man near him said in German, "They don't have full

service until May 15, you know."

"Apparently my travel agent in Munich doesn't know that."

The man stuck a cigarette in his mouth and searched vainly in his pockets for a match. Southard took out a box on which was printed *Hotel Royal, Lenin Boulevard 40, restaurant, café, nightclub* and struck a match in his cupped hands.

They fell into step together. Southard placed his companion in his late thirties or early forties. Short and stocky, he wore a mustache small by Hungarian standards and a worn topcoat of that odd color found in Eastern Europe that is neither pink nor tan.

Tall winter-bare oaks lined the path. Along the borders men in blue smocks were on their knees carefully setting out bedding plants in the recently turned earth.

"Good to meet you, doctor. How's your patient with the broken leg doing?"

"Quite well. He's leaving the hospital this afternoon."

"I'm glad to hear that. Then I'll be able to see him?"

"I think it might be arranged. Where are you staying?"

"The Hotel Royal."

"Of course." Apparently Dr. Landler had forgotten the box of matches used as recognition. He sighed, then smiled. "Nothing but first class for you rich capitalists." He told Southard: "He'll be spending a night or two at his sister's apartment. It isn't far from the Royal. Our young friend Varady can show you."

"Istvan? Is he here?"

The doctor smiled again. "Often."

"I don't like it," Southard said.

The doctor seemed offended. "Istvan is trustworthy, I assure you."

"That's not the point, Dr. Landler. You all know each other." But it wasn't Landler's fault, and it wasn't Istvan's. Warren Hackler's cumbersome, insecure network could jeopardize them all. Probably it already had.

"I'm sorry," Dr. Landler said. It was obvious he didn't understand. Southard let it go.

They walked in silence for a while on the main roadway toward the north end of the island. After a while it split and split again into ever narrower paths and they were in a rock garden with Japanese dwarf trees and lily ponds. They crossed a tiny ornamental bridge.

"Did you get a look at what Manyoki brought back from Moscow?"

"Of course." Landler indicated a rectangular dimension with his hands. "An envelope. This size."

"No, I meant did you read it?"

"I had no opportunity."

"Would you have?"

"Certainly." The question seemed to surprise Landler. "Why do you ask?"

There was no reason, except to confirm the perilous laxness of Hackler's network. And that wasn't Southard's chief concern here. But he did not like the feeling that Landler's answer gave him.

"What about Manyoki's sister? Will she be there?"

"I expect so, yes."

"Tell me about her."

"Spinster. In her late fifties. Lives alone. She works as a court stenographer for the Ministry of Justice."

Beyond the rock garden loomed a huge water tower and the bridge that connected the northern end of the island with Buda and Pest.

"It would be better if I could see him somewhere else," Southard said.

"That isn't possible. They've just put him on crutches and he's not young. Please try to understand."

There was nothing else Southard could do, except not see Manyoki. "Yes, all right, doctor."

"At six, then. The Hotel Royal café."

At six-fifteen Southard and Istvan Varady were walking through rush-hour crowds along the Grand Boulevard. Unlike the hills of Buda across the river, downtown Pest was flat and lay shrouded now in mist rolling off the Danube. The turn-of-the-century architecture, the soot-blackened stone, the brooding mansard roofs, the sidewalk arcades, all receded surrealistically into fog and dusk. Trolley bells clanged and blue sparks shot from the overhead wires.

Istvan wore a trench coat too small for him and a snap-brim hat. He walked with a springy step, glad to be at Southard's side, glad to be involved. He looked very young.

"What did you think of Dr. Landler?"

"A nice guy."

"He's a Jew." Istvan pursed his lips and blew. "My father hates the Jews. I mean really hates them, the way the Nazis did. The AVO—shit, they're no different from the Gestapo."

They turned a corner into a residential street. The noise of the boulevard faded behind them. Through the mist Southard saw trees, their cut-back branches thick and gnarled, spaced evenly along the sidewalk. Only a few cars were parked on the street. A stately woman in a fur stole came by walking a dog that was all coarse black hair and legs. You couldn't see the eyes at all.

"Here it is," Istvan said. "This is the place."

They entered the small lobby of what looked like a townhouse converted into apartments. There were six brass nameplates. One said: Manyoki Eva—2-ik emelet.

The narrow staircase turned back on itself three times to climb two floors, each landing dimly lit by a feeble candle-shaped bulb. A brass plate on the door immediately off the landing repeated the name Manyoki Eva. Southard stood listening at the door but heard nothing. He could see a thin line of light underneath.

Istvan tugged at the bellpull.

The door opened swiftly and wide on a small foyer with a

gilt mirror filling the opposite wall. A woman of about sixty with a pinched face stood in the doorway, her narrow back reflected in the mirror. Southard's own reflection looked large and menacing, not at all as he had hoped to appear. Istvan was a schoolboy in a snap-brim hat.

"*Guten Abend. Ist hier schon der Herr Minister Miklos Man—*" Southard began, and something in the apartment thumped and an old man's voice cried:

" *'Raus! Eilen Sie! Der AVO—*"

The voice stopped. Heavy footsteps pounded in the apartment. The last thing Southard saw inside was the woman's face, confusion on it, fear perhaps, her mouth open and one hand rising to it. Then he pulled the door shut and grabbed Istvan's arm and plunged down the dim stairway. From the first landing he looked back and saw in the light at the top of the stairs two bulky silhouettes.

Down another flight, Istvan at his side. Stairs and landing shook.

They raced stumbling into the lobby, where a large man in a black leather coat blocked the doorway. Southard ran straight at him and a big hand, cupped but not clenched, slapped at Southard's ear. It was intended to rupture his eardrum. He ducked under it, driving at the man's middle with his shoulder. He could smell the leather of the coat as the man folded over him, breath rushing out in a prolonged exhalation. Southard straightened quickly, grabbed a leg and flipped the man heavily on his back. He brought a heel down on the face and felt bone and cartilage give. The man made a choked mewling sound.

Turning, Southard saw the two men from the apartment with Istvan at the foot of the stairs. One man had forced Istvan facedown on the floor, an arm levered between his shoulder blades. The other was scrambling to his feet. Southard started back, heard voices calling outside, stopped. He would be caught along with Istvan. It would mean the end for Landler too and anyone else in the

72

Hungarian network—the fruit of Warren Hackler's incompetence fully harvested. Southard ran through the open doorway into the mist and collided with a trench-coated figure. They went down together and he could feel the softness and faintly smell the perfume. In the rectangle of light spilling from the lobby she saw her face. The shock of recognition froze him there for an instant, her pale blue eyes staring directly into his eyes, fine droplets of mist glistening in her blonde hair. She cried out and tried to hold him but he broke away and ran and then, finally, there was gunfire, two shots. The German woman cried out again, more sharply. He kept running past bare gnarled trees toward the lights of the Grand Boulevard that shimmered in the mist. They did not shoot again and he thought they would not. The German woman wanted information. She could not know that he had none to give her.

The stately woman with the dog that was all coarse black hair and legs was coming back in the other direction. She watched Southard running; the dog barked and tugged at its leash. The lights of the Grand Boulevard were close now, bright in the mist off the Danube. Horns blew and a trolley-bus clanged its bell. A car accelerated up the residential street behind him but he turned the corner and became part of the late rush-hour crowd.

Getting out of Hungary would be another matter.

2

He called from a booth in the lobby of the Palace Hotel on Rákóczi Street, a few blocks from his own hotel, the Royal. He had no idea what hours Dr. Landler kept at the Kobanyai Street Medical Center. A woman's voice answered, the words incomprehensible, the tone bored.

"Darf ich Deutsch sprechen?" Southard pronounced the

73

German words slowly and with emphasis. "I must talk to Dr Landler. An urgent matter."

"Dr. Landler has gone for the day," the bored switchboard voice said in German.

"Wait, please. Can you tell me where—"

"It is not permitted," said the bored voice.

"Then can you reach him? Could you telephone for me and give him my number? It is most urgent, Fräulein."

"Your name is?"

Landler had to be warned. He was probably compromised already. Southard couldn't chance the name Jochl, though; the name would finish Landler at once, if his phone was tapped.

Southard remembered their conversation on Margaret Island. The doctor was intelligent but so literal minded. Would he make the connection? Southard said, "My name is Reich." It was German for *rich*.

"Herr Reich?"

Southard spelled it, then read the six-digit number to the switchboard operator. "I will wait at the phone," he said. "I cannot thank you enough, Fräulein. You could be saving someone's life."

He waited ten minutes, hunched over the phone as if still using it, fingers on the disconnect bar. He wished he had a cigarette. In the field in Eastern Europe he avoided smoking. How you smoked could give you away. Eastern Europeans smoked like oral erotics, sucking greedily at cigarettes in cupped hands. . . . All right, he told himself, enough of that. He knew that tension made you squander thought. It could be as dangerous as panic.

He had to warn Landler and then he had to start moving. It was the first rule you learned. When in trouble, move, and keep moving.

On the first ring he lifted his hand from the disconnect bar. "Yes?"

"Herr Reich?"

"Hello, doctor. You remember me? We met at Margaret's today." It would have to serve for recognition.

He could sense the relief in Landler's voice. "Indeed. How can I help you, Herr Reich?"

"Our young friend is very sick. He and the old man we were visiting. Both of them."

"Fatally sick?"

"I hope not. But our young friend cannot move. I was with him and so were you," Southard said. "I'd better warn you it's contagious. You are very likely to come down with it. Take measures to protect yourself."

"Yes, I will do what I can. Are you all right?"

"For the moment. Can anything be done to help our young friend?" Landler said after a pause, "His father is a specialist, you know."

Southard wondered if that was why there had been no gunfire until after they had taken Istvan Varady. He had early ruled out the possibility that Istvan had betrayed Parr—too obvious, and the boy was a young idealist, a rebel, not a professional agent. Istvan's father would not go easy on him; he couldn't afford to. But neither, Southard hoped, would Istvan be pushed to the limit.

"Well, you'd know more about that than I," Southard replied.

"For yourself, I would advise a change of air, if you have been exposed. An old-fashioned remedy, but sometimes they are best. Can you leave where you are calling from?"

Southard said that he could. He wondered what Landler was driving at.

"Good. That's splendid. It is now, let me see, seven-thirty exactly," the doctor said. Southard was amazed that only an hour and a half had passed since he had met Istvan Varady at the Hotel Royal café.

"Seven-thirty," Southard repeated. "Right."

"You know where our elderly friend was staying until this afternoon? Can you meet me there?"

"I don't want to expose you any further," Southard said. "There's a chance you haven't caught it. But I've already come down with it."

"Nonsense. I am a doctor; it is my work. One hour from now. Will you be all right until then?"

"I can't let you—"

"What nonsense, what utter nonsense. Eight-thirty but no later," Landler said. "There is a delivery entrance at the rear. If you had to get sick, your timing could not possibly have been better. *Auf Wiedersehen*, Herr Reich."

At a bus shelter on Lenin Boulevard, Southard studied the map. Kobanyai Street was in a northern industrial suburb of Pest, here on the east bank of the river. A number five bus would take him close enough to walk the rest of the way to the medical center. He did not like involving Landler any more, but the doctor had already involved himself. Southard would be there at eight-thirty.

Tatters of mist drifted past the streetlamp like smoke. As he climbed on the bus Southard hoped the fog would last at least until he got to Kobanyai Street. Already it had helped him get away from the German woman. He felt the shock again, as strong as when he first recognized her.

He had come to Hungary to learn why Gideon Parr died. But the German woman belonged in another place, another time.

3

They drove west out of Budapest on National Route 1 toward Györ. From there the most direct way to Austria was straight on Route 1 to the border crossing at Hegyeshalom, but the hospital van never took that road and of course it never went as far as the frontier.

It was a Volkswagen minibus, painted white with a huge red cross on either side. Dr. Landler was driving.

"They must have a watch on the airport," he said, "and the railroad and bus stations. The roads too. But they expect this van to make the northern Transdanubia run on Thursday nights. As I said, your timing was good."

Equipped with an incubator and a refrigerator, the van would stop at clinics and pickup points in Hungary's westernmost province, collecting laboratory specimens to be processed at the Kobanyai Street Medical Center—blood, sputum, urine, feces that required analysis too complex for the limited provincial facilities.

"Do you know Istvan's father?" Southard asked.

"I know him." Landler's voice was cool. Southard recalled what Istvan had said about his father's anti-Semitism. "By now he'll have been told his colleagues have Istvan."

"What will he do?"

"I stopped trying to predict what bigots would do a long time ago." Landler wore glasses for driving, and he adjusted them higher on the bridge of his nose. "Or even what human beings would do, any human beings under any circumstances." Landler shook his head. "I'm a doctor, I'm expected to understand people. The only thing I understand is that they're incomprehensible."

The road was empty, the moon obscured by high clouds. At a town called Bicske twenty-five miles from Budapest Landler made his first pickup at a pharmacy, coming out with two small lockboxes, one for the incubator, one for the refrigerator.

Landler resumed driving. "Pharmacist there," he said, "man name of Toth, served as a medic with the Hungarian Army in the Ukraine during the war. It was a slaugher. His two brothers, both infantrymen, were killed. Did that cure Toth?"

"Cure him of what?"

"Militarism. Every generation needs a good war, he says, to cleanse the soul, and just when you decide he has some arcane religious reason for this lunacy, he tells you he's an atheist. People," said Landler, driving through the darkness. "Or take me. I survived under the Nazis by curing junior officers of venereal disease picked up from nice Hungarian girls, cured them so they could go out and round up more Gypsies and Jews. Now we have the Reds, and people still disappear in the middle of the night—for me anything else is automatically better. So I do things for Jochl."

"Forget Jochl," Southard said. "Jochl is all finished."

They drove for a while in silence. Then Landler asked, "Is it really free, in the West? I mean, if there were such a thing as free will, could it be exercised? Could *you* exercise it? Quit what you're doing, for example?"

"I believe in what I'm doing. I believe it's important," Southard said, vaguely angry. He knew his anger had nothing to do with Landler.

"But could you quit tomorrow?" the doctor persisted.

Southard said that he could.

A lateral gust of wind struck the minibus and it veered sharply to the right. Landler fought the wheel for a moment. "But did you ever really think of doing it? Quitting? Just like that?"

Southard said, "I'm thinking of it right now." He had not anticipated saying that.

Landler sighed. "Because of what happened tonight?"

Southard said nothing. He did not want to talk about it.

"It's hard for me to believe Istvan will betray us. I've known him for years."

"But that's just it, don't you see? You all worked together, knew each other, real names and addreses. And now they'll roll you all up, one big happy family. Goddamn it!"

"Please," the doctor protested, "you are not responsible."

"No? I knew what shape the network was in when I came. That didn't stop me from using it. I had to find out something."

"And did you?"

"Not yet," Southard said.

The van slowed at the entrance to a town. This time Landler stopped outside a small clinic. As he climbed down from the van, Southard added softly, "But I will."

When they were moving again he said to Landler, "Tell me about Manyoki."

"He's an interesting case—the Hungarian paradox. High in the party, all the perquisites, and he still supports the system in spite of its corruption. But the corruption comes from outside. From Russia. What does a man like Miklos Manyoki want? Just what I want, or Istvan. We want the Russians the hell out of our country. They bleed our economy dry every time theirs needs a transfusion. They take our uranium from the mines near Pecs and ship it to Russia. They call that war reparations, as if it was our idea to join the Nazis. We could sell that uranium on the open market for hard currency. What do we want? We want a better standard of living. We want to fly the Kossuth crest from our flagstaffs instead of their hammer and sickle. We want to be free. I'll tell you something—Manyoki said in the hospital that there would be revolution. Here in Hungary. In Poland, perhaps in East Germany. Before the year is over. Manyoki was convinced of that. He might have been one of its leaders. Now they'll kill him."

A car came up behind them, dipping then raising its lights. Landler played a short ululating salute on the van's siren. The black and white police car passed them and dipped its lights briefly again. Southard thought he saw a hand wave in greeting when the two vehicles were parallel.

"They're from the barracks in Tatra," Landler said. "I make these runs every now and then, when the regular driver can't for some reason. I don't mind doing it. Driving through the night a man can think."

"Why is Manyoki so sure there'll be revolution? Does it have something to do with what he brought from Moscow?"

"Maybe. I don't know. Maybe he just sees things clearly. After all, the days of empire are ending. The British have lost theirs, the French are finished in Indochina and what they're doing now in Algeria corrupts them and cannot last. Only Russia has a true empire now. From East Germany to Vladivostok. But it too must end. One spark, just one somewhere in those twelve million square miles, and there will be a firestorm. We Hungarians could strike that spark. We are a proud people."

Landler laughed then, a lonely, mocking sound in the night. "Listen to the Jew talking of what a proud people we Hungarians are."

"What will you do now?" Southard asked.

A resigned shrug, and for a while only the sound of the van's short-stroke engine. Then, "What can I do? I have a wife, a small child. Our home is here. Perhaps they won't make the connection between Istvan Varady and me."

"They'll make it," Southard told him bluntly.

He stared at the stocky doctor in the near darkness. The age-old dilemma of the Jew in troubled Central Europe, he thought. Patriotism was a danger, roots could kill. So could pride or success.

"How many people in the Jochl net do you know?"

Landler thought for a while. "Well, ten anyway."

"Good God," Southard said under his breath.

"Shall I warn them?"

"Sure, if you don't use the phone. If you don't see them in person. And if you assume their mail will be opened."

Landler whistled softly. "Then what *can* I do?"

"Take your family and get out of Hungary."

The doctor did not reply. They had said all that could be said. Landler knew the danger to himself and his family but the mere knowledge was not enough. Some men were like that—the greater the degree of peril, the more they refused to acknowledge it. Like thinking: all men die, of course, but not me; or if me, then not this month, not this year;

from day to day I am immortal. It was understandable to think like that. Especially for condemned men, and the very old. And also for the most recklessly successful agents Southard had ever run.

Gideon Parr had been like that. So he had gone into the field, here in Hungary, six months after the coronary thrombosis that had almost killed him.

Did that make Parr a fool? Or a hero? Or just a human being?

4

A stretch of poorly surfaced road, the cobbled streets of a town, its huddled gabled houses looming in the dark, a five-minute stop. Places called Kisber and Bakony and Kapuvar. There was a village called Dad and a town called Papa. Midnight came and went, the wind blew stronger, the temperature dropped ten degrees. Southard drifted off to sleep and dreamed about the sea and awoke thinking he could smell it.

Dr. Landler was shaking his shoulder. He could hear a rustling, clattering sound that he could not place. He thought he still smelled the sea. The van was parked, engine off, lights off, on a dirt track.

Landler produced a flat bottle. *"Barack,"* he said. "It will warm you." His hand was trembling with cold when he thrust the bottle at Southard.

"Take a drink yourself."

"Very well. A small one." Landler pulled the cork and drank. He passed the bottle. Southard took a swallow of the fiery apricot brandy.

"A wind like this," said Landler, "and the whole lake shifts. So you have a problem. Only the southern part is Hungarian, but the frontier is irregular. Three miles north of here on the east shore lies Austria. If there *is* an east shore in this wind."

Southard climbed from the van. The cold wind buffeted him. The saltwater smell was stronger: Neusiedler Lake, where he had first met Istvan Varady. There were no stars. He could see almost nothing.

"What about the west shore?" he asked Landler after he climbed back in the van.

"The water will recede there, but it's almost nine miles to the frontier."

"Is the lake patrolled?"

"Theoretically, but they won't be out on a night like this."

"Is there barbed wire? Guard towers? Anything like that?"

"Five miles east of the lake, at Andau. Between Andau and the lake is marsh. That is barrier enough. On the west side north of Sopron there are watchtowers."

"I'll try it here," Southard said. Only three miles and no guard towers was preferable, even if the lake had overflowed its basin.

"It won't be easy, either way. Too bad Istvan didn't leave the skiff."

"Is this where he crosses?"

"Just ahead of us. But usually the girl Friedl brings him and goes back."

"I thought he carried both Austrian and Hungarian passports."

"The skiff is better when you are taking fugitives across," said Landler.

Something pounded on Southard's side of the van, a hand slapping against metal. He dimly saw a figure through the glass. The hand pounded on the window then. A voice shouted over the rustle of cattails and clatter of reeds in the wind. Southard opened the door.

The girl said, "You better have brought something to drink or I'll freeze to death."

She wore a hooded oilskin raincoat. Southard helped her climb up between them and gave her the bottle of *barack*. She tilted her head back and the hood slid off the blonde hair as she drank. Southard thought again how pretty she was, and how young. Her throat worked smoothly, swallowing, and she wiped her mouth.

"It is good to see you again, Dr. Landler." Friedl looked at Southard and then expectantly into the rear of the van. "And you are the man who came to see Istvan on the dock." She was smiling, and talking quickly and steadily, as if she wanted to avoid asking the question that had to be asked. "Istvan didn't want me to come. There was no telling when, he said. I told him I would be here tonight from midnight. And tomorrow the same."

"I didn't know that," Landler said. "We—had no chance to talk."

"Why not? What happened? Where is he?"

Landler looked at Southard.

"Is he all right?" Her small hands grasped the doctor's arm. "Tell me quickly. Please. Is he alive?"

"He's alive. The AVO have him. His father has been informed," Landler said.

For a while the girl said nothing. Then, "Please give me another drink." She took three long swallows. "Is he hurt?"

"I was with him when the AVO came," Southard said. "He was not hurt then."

"And you got away?" It was a cruel question, the way she asked it.

"Yes," Southard said.

"I'm sorry, I didn't mean that the way it sounded." She asked Landler, "Will his father do anything for him?"

"I don't know. We can hope."

"Please, another drink."

She drank. Then she said, "Was it important, what you were doing?"

Landler immediately said, "Yes."

"Were you successful?"

The men looked at each other. Southard thought of the German woman. Her presence there was significant in a way that Southard did not yet understand. He said truthfully, "I went there trying to learn something. I learned something else—possibly of greater importance."

She gave him the bottle and he drank and gave the bottle to Landler, who finished it.

"The skiff is just beyond the end of the track," she said. "The way the wind is blowing we'll be at Illmitz in less than half an hour. Twenty minutes. Already the lake has overflowed and flooded the lowlands there."

Landler got out with them and walked the hundred yards to the water. On either side, reeds rustled and clattered frantically as if trying to escape the wind. It blew so hard that even in the darkness Southard could see whitecaps on the black water.

He shook Landler's hand. "Take care of yourself." He had to shout to be heard, his mouth close to Landler's ear. "And warn the others if you can find a way."

Friedl had anchored the skiff offshore. Southard could just make it out, straining at its anchor rope. He waded into the freezing water, knee-deep, and got hold of the rope. He braced himself and pulled, then Landler was helping him bring the skiff closer. Friedl hugged Landler quickly and climbed aboard.

Southard told Landler, "Get your family out while there's still time."

Clambering aboard with the anchor, he did not hear Landler's answer. Friedl, standing in the prow, began to pole. The skiff rocked and Southard dropped to his haunches against a thwart. The girl kept her balance like a tightrope walker. Southard doubted he could have done it. The wind on the broad transom sped them across the lake, Friedl using the long pole now on one side, now the other, to correct their course.

After ten minutes Southard saw a glow. It grew steadily brighter, then separated into points of light which became a string of streetlamps and an occasional window. Twenty minutes from the time Southard brought the anchor aboard, the skiff scraped bottom and he was wading in icy calf-deep water dragging it toward shore.

"We are in Austria," the girl told him when she climbed out. "It is all right now. You'll be safe here."

She threw the anchor overboard again and struck off toward the lights of Illmitz, leaving him to follow. They slogged through shallow water, then soggy marsh. The lights of the town were close and the ground solid when she suddenly pitched forward onto her knees.

He was beside her instantly, trying to raise her. "Friedl?"

"Why?" Her small fists beat helplessly against her thighs. He could barely hear her voice, thin and tight like a stretched metal wire. "Why did it have to be Istvan?"

Chapter Four

1

Haj Rashid Ali Krim entered the Grand Gaza Hotel followed by three Ikhwan warriors in their traditional striped robes and headcloths. Krim stomped across the abandoned lobby exultantly.

With a few dozen Moslem Brothers using elderly Lee-Enfields and a pair of museum-piece machine guns, old Hotchkiss 8-mm relics he'd picked up cheap from a retired foreign legionnaire, he had sent the Russian-equipped fedayeen streaming from the city in absolute-fucking-terror. No fight in them at all once the Brothers came out into the streets crying *"Allah akbar!"* and attacking. A few hours ended the whole shooting match. Brotherhood casualties: one killed by a sniper in the cemetery, two wounded.

Only possible outcome, of course. Good German leadership, the *Führerprinzip* still valid ten years later, against the Russian-trained fedayeen. The rout couldn't have been more total if the Husaynis had ordered it themselves.

It had been almost too easy. Krim flipped like a page in a book from exultation to let down. He was always doing that. It wasn't just the hashish. It had begun before that, way back when his brother died. Thirteen goddamn years ago in Berlin, and all because of a cock-teasing little Jewess who. . . .

86

Gaza meant Israel, or at least the road to Israel, the Gaza Strip pointing like a dagger up the coast to Tel Aviv. It meant that Nasser would have to relent, no longer blame the Ikhwan (and certainly not Krim) for the attempt on his life by a Brother who also happened to be a madman. It meant that money, and gleaming new weapons still coated with Cosmoline, would flow into the hands not of the fedayeen but of the Ikhwan. It meant that terrorist attacks on Israel, from now on, would be Ikhwan attacks. It meant that Krim would command the forces that, in *sha*'Allah, one day would drive the Zionists into the sea.

The page had flipped again. Krim went exultantly to the reception desk, palmed the bell hard, laughed, and turned to see Heini and Rolf coming in. Krim was up a little on hashish, but not too much. Still every inch in control. Could bear to be sitting somewhere with a *nargileh*, though, puffing away. The part of him which was Arab could, at least; the part which took the pilgrimage to Mecca seriously. The German in Krim—Joachim Griem, Berliner—would have preferred some whisky. And a woman.

Heini rubbed his tanned, shaven head. "Quiet out there," he said. "The cemetery, Falastin Square, there's nobody."

"Is that so," said Krim, his voice lazy.

"Sure, all you have to—"

"How's about you take a half a dozen of the Brothers and do some patrolling? The cemetery, back along Omar al-Mukhtar, up al-Wahda Street. Then get some of those sandbags away from the shops and set up the machine gun in the center of the square. You think you can do that, Heini?"

"Night patrol?" Heini said. "Well, you know the Brothers when it comes to dark."

Krim looked at him. "Isn't that too fucking bad."

Heini exchanged an uneasy glance with Rolf. They had

seen Krim like this often enough before, some hashish in him but not so much that he was slow on his feet or in his head. He was in that state of mind where his languor could give way in an instant and with no provocation to a murderous rage.

Heini tried once more. "I still think—"

"Don't," Krim told him.

With his wheat-blond hair worn somewhat long, his smooth pink and white complexion that would never tan, his baby blue eyes, the silky blond beard on his chin—Krim had the appearance of a twenty-year-old innocent. Heini and Rolf knew that he had served with the Afrika Korps from the day in February 1941 when Rommel came ashore at Tripoli with the Fifth Light Armored almost until the end came for the Korps at Cap Bon more than two years later. So he had to be in his early thirties anyway.

The one word *don't* was all the warning they'd get. Krim was weird sometimes; no predicting what he would do. Heini and Rolf, former SS Totenkopf concentration camp guards, sometimes wished they'd joined the foreign legion instead of throwing their lot in with Joachim Griem.

When Krim could hear Heini shouting orders outside, he told Rolf, "Take a few of the Brothers and give this place a shakedown. I don't want any surprises."

The only surprise he got was the girl.

Krim drew a cane-back chair up to the brocaded divan and looked down at the girl. She was sleeping so soundly he figured at first she'd been drugged. Then he saw the smudges of exhaustion under her eyes and he could smell the woman scent of her faintly in the khaki blouse, its underarms ringed white with salt. She was beat, just beat. Fedayeen, if the khaki meant anything. He knew the fedayeen had begun recruiting girls; Maryam Husayni wasn't the only one.

He wondered why they had left her behind, then

shrugged. Typical, he thought; when they hightail it out, Arabs don't exactly wait for stragglers.

Krim reached into his pocket and fingered his pipe. Should he? Hell, why not — he had earned it.

Soon the sweet-acrid hashish smoke mingled with the faint woman smell of the sleeping Arab girl. The combination excited him.

Dark and attractive in the expected Semitic mode, hair that appeared black but, he was sure, would glint auburn in sunlight, high cheekbones and a small nose with the slightest elegant suggestion of the sharp-bridged stereotype somehow enhancing her sexuality — she reminded Krim of someone.

He wondered what color her eyes were. Brown, but that kind of brown that was flecked with green, hazel it was called. He was willing to bet on it.

He examined her face. There was no real resemblance, of course, just superficial — the one a Jewess, the other an Arab. Both Semitic, after all; a racial type, weren't they?

Except for the pretty Jewess, his older brother Klaus would have been forty now.

When Klaus was invalided out of the army toward the end of the *Sitzkrieg*, the phony war, it was only May 1940. The first real battle in the West, at a place in France called Sedan, and Klaus loses an arm. Typical of Klaus-Albrecht Griem. If he'd survived the summer of '43 they'd probably have put him back in uniform. He was a high school teacher and he lived with his wife Lise in Berlin-Charlottenburg. That was where they got involved with the Uncle Emil organization.

The Uncle Emil organization hid Jews. U-boats, they were called. A week here, a month there, shuttle them around; it was a question of where ration books could be found for the food to keep them alive. The members of Uncle Emil worried about staying alive too. The penalty for harboring Jews was death.

His brother Klaus. Son of a bitch, how about that, his own brother?

Joachim Griem gets his first leave in more than two years, ten days before his assignment to the Lichterfelde Cadet School, and goes to the big walled villa in Charlottenburg, the inheritance of his sister-in-law Lise.

He no longer remembers how he found out, but after three days he knows there are Jews living in the cellar. A young couple called Müller. Twenty-year-old Joachim, hating Jews neither more nor less than the next man, is curious. Goes down to the cellar wearing his field gray, and of course that scares the shit out of the Müllers. Relax, he says, I'm the brother. It turns out Frau Müller is a little cock-teaser. Well, maybe not intentionally. He just has this thing about Jewesses—the dark alien eyes, the full breasts, the firm little ass on that Frau Müller.

Krim glanced down at the sleeping Arab girl, watched the rhythmic rise and fall of her breasts against the khaki. There was a bandage on her forearm.

Three times in his army career Joachim Griem waited on line at a whorehouse, the line going up the steep stairs one fuck at a time, three times he went in and got out so fast he hardly felt himself come off, three times he cleaned himself the way they explained in the health lecture, and that was sex.

The Jewess was twenty-three, maybe twenty-four. Anna, Anna Müller—not even a Jew name.

Two days he works on her. He has to get her upstairs, away from the husband. How? He doesn't remember. Food, maybe? But anyway they're upstairs and at first he can't get his eyes off her and then he can't get his hands off her, but she's fighting him, she doesn't want it, and he starts to rip at her clothing and he forces her down on the sofa in the smallest of the three sitting rooms, the one facing on the rear garden, cuffing her around a little as he spreads her legs with a knee and he's inside her when Klaus walks in on them.

Before you know it they're fighting—the last thing he wants is to fight his one-armed brother, but a man's got to defend himself, right? And then all of a sudden Klaus staggers back and goes down, his head striking the slate skirting of the hearth with one awful moist smacking sound.

At first Joachim goes crazy, doesn't know what to do. Murder is murder, isn't it, even in wartime?

He spends a few minutes compulsively tidying the room, putting everything in order, even returning books, magazines to shelves, even emptying ashtrays into the hearth.

And then he knows what has to be done. He locks the Müllers in the cellar storeroom. He calls the Gestapo.

"This is Sergeant Joachim Griem, Twenty-first Panzer Division, on leave before assignment to Lichterfelde. I must report that I have just killed my brother. He was a traitor to the Reich, I regret to say. Harboring Jews in his own house. Yes, they're still here." He gives the address in Charlottenburg.

The sister-in-law comes home just as the Gestapo is about to leave with the terrified Karl and Anna Müller. He avoids her by going out the back way, through the garden.

Joachim Griem leaves with nothing but the uniform on his back. Soon he starts to whistle "Lili Marlene." The linden trees are in full leaf on the Charlottenburger Chaussee, dark and regal in the sunset. Joachim has always loved beautiful things. . . .

Krim, surprised, saw what his hand was doing. It was stroking the sleeping Arab girl's breast, stroking it the way you stroke a cat. The nipple stood erect under khaki cloth. Krim drew his hand back as if he had burned it. Then the girl made a sound in her sleep and stirred, stretching, the contours of her breast changing with the movement of her arms. Another little cock-teaser, he was willing to bet.

When she woke, she saw a blond man with blue eyes and a shy smile. He was sitting on a chair drawn up close to the divan. In one hand he held a pipe loosely; hashish smoke hung in the air. She saw maps still strewn on the low copper tables, cartridge belts draped over the backs of chairs, a rifle propped in one corner near a lovely white filigree screen, a sheet of parchmentlike paper on the Oriental carpet.

Cousin Yasir's ridiculous bill of sale, she remembered now, and her own utter exhaustion while he stood there trying to strike a bargain with her. She'd never felt so wrung out in her whole life. She remembered, more or less remembered, stretching out on the divan. After that it was like falling off a cliff.

She sat up. The blond man stood quickly as if she had startled him. He glanced down at himself and turned away, even more quickly. The back of his neck went red. He moved around the room tidying things like a compulsive housekeeper, gathering the cartridge belts and piling them in the corner, carefully folding the maps. He stopped for the sheet of paper on the carpet.

When he spoke, it was in a stilted, pompous Arabic with a faint accent. "I do hope you are feeling quite recovered now?"

"There was nothing wrong with me. Just out on my feet."

Her own tone of voice, she hoped, sounded light, but she was wary. With those blue eyes and that blond hair it was obvious he was no Arab. She hadn't needed to hear him talk to know that. German—he had to be one of the Germans with the Brotherhood. Possibly the one called Krim himself.

He placed the stack of maps neatly on one table, edges aligned so they looked like a book, and straddled a camel-saddle stool, facing her and frowning at the sheet of paper as if he had trouble reading Arabic. "It seems to be some kind of bill of sale," he said in a perplexed tone. "For a boat, of all things."

"I can explain that. The boat belongs to me. I came here in it earlier today and — is it midnight? Yesterday, then. In the middle of everything, there was this fat little man named Yasir who wanted me to practically give it away." She was aware of speaking rapidly, inanely, the words spilling out. She was more than wary now. The friendly looking blond man made her nervous. Because he was German?

"Then that means your name is Jehan Khalid."

"That's who I am, yes."

He got up with a quizzical smile on his face and she saw the scar, bone white, a thin puckered line from left cheekbone to the corner of his mouth, his badge of honor earned at a university dueling society in prewar Germany. He looked Aryan, even without the dueling scar.

Looked Aryan — how silly! Let's do without the racial stereotypes, she told herself. She'd seen plenty of blond, blue-eyed Sabras on kibbutzim in Israel, all looking more Aryan than this scar-faced fellow and twice as tough.

"It says here that the port of registry is Haifa, Israel."

"Well, yes. That's where I came here from."

He raised an eyebrow and the quizzical smile became incredulous. "You're an Israeli?"

"Of course not. What would I be doing here?"

"What were you doing in Israel?"

"Living there. My father was a spy."

"For Israel? I'm afraid I don't understand."

"For Egypt *in* Israel. We lived there more than seven years. I attended school in Israel. I even learned to speak Hebrew." Nervous laughter. Why was she talking so much?

"And where is your father now?"

"The Shin Beth caught him and he was tried and sent to prison. For life."

"Why did you come here?"

"How could I stay in Israel?"

"You have a home here?"

"No, but I'm Egyptian. Even though I grew up in Lebanon, and then in Israel."

His questions were more sharply put now, and more unsettling, than those the police had asked her.

"Why didn't you go back to Lebanon then?"

"I have no one there."

"Have you anyone here?"

"No. I came to join the fedayeen."

He burst out laughing. "You picked the wrong day to join the fedayeen." The laughter seemed to relax something in him. "I'm sorry," he said, "I shouldn't be firing questions at you like this. Forgive me."

He really did sound contrite. She searched for a friendly answer. "It's all right, I understand. You just don't like talking all around a subject the way we Arabs do. I'll bet you often wish we had a little of your German directness and efficiency."

"What makes you think I'm German?"

She would not give a German, even a friendly one, the satisfaction of knowing she had resorted to a racial stereotype. "Well, the dueling scar," she said.

"Oh, yes?"

"The sabre scar, on your cheek there. From a university dueling society, am I right?"

"From a shrapnel wound at El Alamein in 1942," he said. "And how, precisely, do you know about dueling scars, Fräulein?"

"I just know. Everybody does."

"Were you in Germany before the war?"

"No—no, I've never been to Europe."

"You had relatives there?"

"Relatives? No, how could I—"

"But you know all about dueling societies and sabre

94

scars, don't you?"

"I—I must have read about that somewhere."

His lips parted in a faint but infinitely superior smile. "Everything you've told me is a lie. I don't know what your name is, but it isn't Jehan Khalid. And you're no more Lebanese than I am."

"Egyptian." She stood, her face flushed. "I was born right here in Eygypt."

"That too is a lie." He grasped her wrist. "You are a Jew."

"How dare you call me a Jew!"

His laugh was soft but infinitely superior, like the smile. "Fräulein, please. For the past two minutes I have been speaking German and you have been answering me in German. You were born in Germany, were you not? From your accent I would say Berlin."

He was still holding her wrist. She tried to pull away from him and the bandage came loose. The burn was covered by the shiny pink of new scar tissue.

"Dueling scar?" he asked.

She said nothing.

"I didn't realize little Jewesses belonged to dueling societies in prewar Germany," he said.

Still she said nothing.

"Was it Auschwitz?" he said. "They tattooed the number on the left forearm in Auschwitz, I have heard. So you survived Auschwitz and you went to Israel and grew up, and the Mossad sent you here to Gaza. Is that correct? Why did they send you, Fräulein? Please don't misunderstand—I have nothing, absolutely nothing against Jewesses. But it is my business to know about Israeli spies."

She was finished, it was all over; less than twenty-four hours and they had her.

"Sit down," he ordered, grasping her arm harder, hurting her. "Tell me about it."

She should have seen it happening—the friendly smile

95

and then the clever questions and the switch to German that took her unawares and his cool deduction that she'd been in Auschwitz, was Israeli, had come here to spy. Had he suspected her from the start?

The police had accepted her story. Cousin Yasir had even chided her for being late. The Arabs had given her no trouble.

It had to be a stinking no-good German renegade.

She gave a choked, wordless cry of frustration, twisted free and lashed out at his face. Three lines appeared, as livid as the scar before they filled with the blood her fingernails had drawn. She backed away but he grabbed both her arms and pulled her against him hard. She tried to break free a second time. His eyes were intent on her, and yet oddly remote, as if all this had nothing to do with her even though he was holding her tighter now, forcing her backward. When she tried to raise a knee between his legs he shouted, "Jewish bitch!" and clubbed the side of her head with his fist, spilling her on the brocade cushions of the divan, one big arm holding her down while he unbelted her khaki trousers, then hit her face again, a contemptuous backhand swat, when she tried to get out from under him and there was no way she was going to do that until he was through with her but it really wasn't her after all so she could lie there while he raped someone else.

It would have made no difference to Jehan Khalid that the man raping her was German.

3

Her senses returned to her one at a time. She squinted against the brightness of the overhead light, closed her eyes, opened them again; she looked around warily for the German, but she was alone in the room. She smelled the hashish smoke, heavier than before, sweet and acrid. She

96

heard a roaring sound that made no sense at first. Then she knew it for the rush of water into a tub.

She hurt most between the legs, which was to be expected: the German had used her brutally. But she hadn't realized how he'd battered her face. The left side of her mouth felt swollen, her cheek numb, the side of her head tender when she explored it with her fingers. She hurt even more when she sat up. The dizziness came in quick waves and she almost blacked out again.

She slumped forward, head down, elbows on bare thighs. Sitting like that, she could smell his seed on her. Her right elbow rested on wetness.

She opened her eyes and saw the shiny mucoid streak on her thigh.

She picked up the bandage the German had torn off her and scrubbed her leg. She touched the spot with her fingertips. It was still sticky. She scrubbed at it again until all traces were gone.

Except for the rest of it, inside her.

The rage came then, finally, and she sat there and let it shake her.

The rush of water in the adjacent room stopped. She heard splashing.

He was bathing. The German was bathing. Having sullied himself on the body of the dirty Jewess, the Aryan would now use scalding water and strong soap. . . .

She got up and belted her pants. She could hardly manage the buckle because her hands shook so. She tried a few deep breaths. Cold sweat beaded her forehead. She thought she was going to be sick. She waited that out; the nausea retreated. Her shirt was torn straight down the front, the buttons nesting in their holes with incongruous neatness a scant inch from the long sharp rent. She tucked it in as best she could.

She crossed to the hall door and tested it: locked.

She moved over to the filigree screen and stood looking at

the Russian assault rifle propped in the corner. An AK-47, inferior to the Czech Model 23 and the Uzi—she had trained with all three—but serviceable, the curving handle-shaped magazine that fed its thirty-round load into the breech just in front of the trigger guard. . . .

More splashing inside.

She picked up the AK-47. The rage told her to kill him, kill him now.

She forced herself to think.

The German knew everything—who she was, what she was. It was his business, he'd said, to know about Israeli spies.

She would be killed, unless she killed him first.

And if she did?

Apparently the fedayeen had lost. If so, that ended her mission with them—and her refuge, too. What was she left with?

She had come in as Jehan Khalid, and no matter what had happened in Gaza, if she was going to get out she had to get out as Jehan Khalid.

You are Jehan. You think like Jehan only. You talk like Jehan only. Whatever you do, whatever reasons you have for doing it, the reasons and the doing are Jehan's.

What would Jehan have done? No, that was the wrong question; she knew what had to be done. Would Jehan have been capable of doing it?

In the Arab world the punishment for rape was death. But that was the punishment for adultery too, and rape was seldom reported because in the public mind the two crimes tended to blur. No woman, certainly no young unmarried woman, would ever acknowledge she had been raped. Rape and seduction, was there a difference? The marriage prospects of a rape victim would be no better than a reformed prostitute's.

Jehan, knowing all that, would. . . .

She turned the AK-47 over and checked the magazine to

make sure it was loaded. She propped the assault rifle back against the wall.

Would Jehan?

Never mind Jehan. Jehan only had to explain it later.

Deborah had to kill the German now.

She picked up the AK-47 again, hefted it. The short 7.62-mm cartridge meant a manageable weight. Manageable recoil too, something a woman could handle. . . .

She knew she was stalling. She had lost the first fierce rage, and without it she was not sure she could do it.

She fitted the solid beechwood stock to her shoulder. Trigger and trigger guard were outsized to accommodate a gloved hand in cold weather.

Her hands were trembling.

She had to make the rage come back, make herself feel it all again. The smell of his seed on her . . . the shiny mucoid streak on her thigh . . . the rest of it, inside her. . . .

She set the AK-47 on automatic, then lowered it. It felt more comfortable at her side, and it was easier to keep her hands steady. She crossed to the inner door and opened it quickly, both hands back on the rifle before the door had swung wide.

She saw a large bedroom, two beds, a big old free-standing armoire, a deep-bordered carpet in whites and blues. There was a small window facing an interior courtyard. The room was dimly lit by light coming from the partially ajar bathroom door.

She went through the bedroom. She felt calm now and very, very competent.

She pushed the bathroom door open, not hard.

He was just climbing out of the tub, his pale white body gleaming wet, a fluffy white towel held in both hands.

His mouth and eyes opened wide. He began to straighten.

She held the AK-47 low against her right hip and felt it jolting against her. He might have screamed, but all she heard was the rifle.

The first short burst caught him where he had violated her and lifted him. The second burst spilled him back into the tub, one arm dangling over the side. Ropes of red like fronds of an exotic plant turned the water pink.

She walked back through the bedroom to the sitting room of the suite. In the hall outside she heard running footsteps. Boots thudded against the door, the jamb splintered, the door slammed open. Two men stood there. One, the one who was completely bald, swung the muzzle of his short-barreled submachine gun to bear on her. He was quick but she was quicker.

She had more than half the thirty rounds left in the AK-47.

Heini and Rolf died before the looks of shock and terror had quite formed on their faces.

4

The message reached Iser Harel forty-eight hours later through the diplomatic pouch of a Western European country which maintained a legation in Egypt and an embassy in Israel. After decoding, the message read:

To: DIRECTOR MOSSAD
From: STATION CHIEF CAIRO
Subject: FEDAYEEN-IKHWAN CONFRONTATION

As anticipated, trap closed on Ikhwan early this morning in Gaza when fifty Fedayeen with Russian heavy arms and transport struck from the south at dawn. Ikhwan were already disorganized and leaderless as Joachim Griem with subordinates Braun and Rauschenbach died prior to

Fedayeen counterattack, apparently assassinated by Fedayeen infiltrators in their headquarters.

With Gaza secured from Ikhwan, anticipate increase in Fedayeen raids up coast.

Still no word from agent Raven. Has she been infiltrated into Gaza? Please advise.

Chapter Five

1

The ruins of the Adlon Hotel stood not a hundred yards east of the Brandenburg Gate. In the courtyard of the bombed-out building squatted an ugly barrackslike structure, like a toadstool in a rotting tree trunk. This was the new Adlon, all that East Berlin's Russian masters would grudgingly provide to replace what had once been the favored rendezvous of high functionaries of the Nazi regime.

Incongruously, sleek black chauffeur-driven cars drew up one after another to the ruin, bringing functionaries of the Communist regime to lunch in the bleak courtyard building.

Erika Graf came on foot.

Except for the dazzling white granite Russian Embassy, Unter den Linden was still a wasteland of weed-grown lots and crumbling walls. The city's Red masters had moved its center further east to the Alexanderplatz and the architectural excesses of Stalinallee, leaving a no-man's-land a mile wide confronting West Berlin.

To shift the capital's focus one mile, Erika knew, symbolized the ease of the switch from Nazi to Red dictatorship. For a generation East Berliners had lived and died under rigid totalitarian control. The prevailing ideology was largely irrelevant.

Erika Graf's long stride took her past the row of official

cars and into the barrackslike building in the Adlon courtyard. She climbed the single flight of stairs to the crowded, noisy restaurant with its proletarian-rustic decor.

"A table near the window for the comrade major?" the headwaiter Fritz asked eagerly. A table near the window would give Erika a view of the crumbling carapace of the once deluxe hotel. "Or perhaps the comrade major would prefer—"

"Colonel Kossior is expecting me."

Fritz's eyes clouded but his deeply creased parchmentlike face held onto the smile. Fritz was not young and the tides of history had swept him straight from black hooked cross to gold hammer and sickle. He still regarded Russians like Colonel Kossior as the enemy.

"Zu Befehl!" he said with a perfunctory heel-click, and led Erika toward the colonel's table.

She unbelted her trench coat as she followed. She wore a simple gray wool dress and no makeup and she stood two inches under six feet tall in flat shoes. Her blonde hair was drawn back into a bun and covered by a green Tyrolean hat with a jaunty feather. The overall effect was supposed to be sexless, even mannish. Erika often wondered why she bothered. The trench coat only emphasized her Junoesque figure, and the severe hairstyle drew her skin taut over finely modeled cheekbones, accentuating the challenge of pale blue eyes and the controlled sensuality of mouth. Every man in the Adlon restaurant, Colonel Dmitri Platonovich Kossior possibly excluded, wanted to unpin the hair, meet the challenge of the eyes, make the sensual mouth lose its control. Erika Graf, at thirty-two, knew the impact she had on men. It had served her in her work often enough.

A busboy took Erika's coat while the Russian pushed awkwardly to his feet.

"How nice to see you, comrade major!" Kossior said effusively. "It *is* major these days?"

A nod from Erika and a smile she hoped wasn't too

forced. "I must have done something right for once. How are you, Dmitri Platonovich?" Name and patronymic, no rank. She wanted to evoke the easy informality of their last meeting.

That had been three years ago, in the aftermath of the East Berlin riots of June, 1953. While the headwaiter seated her and Kossior ordered drinks, Erika appraised the Russian.

He still looked like a middle-level bureaucrat mired in his undemanding station in life. He wore a rumpled blue suit; its baggy trousers, she was sure, would break sloppily over his shoes. His straw-gray hair was thinning, his eyes looked vague and uncertain, and his round pink face wore a lugubrious bloodhound expression. Short and plump, he appeared the most unprepossessing of men and certainly no threat to Erika. She knew better. Dmitri Platonovich Kossior held the rank of full colonel in the Chief Intelligence Directorate, the GRU.

They made small talk while he tossed back his vodka and Erika chased a sip of Schinkenhäger with a long swallow of beer. Kossior, with uxorious pride, showed Erika photographs of his wife and three daughters in Moscow. The wife, as plump as Kossior, was an English translator with Glavlit, the state censorship organization. Dmitri Platonovich Kossior himself spoke five languages fluently, one fewer than Erika, and he practiced a harmless Anglophilia which stopped this side of politics.

After the waiter brought him another vodka, Kossior turned abruptly to the business at hand.

"Moscow can now account for the movements of every foreign delegate after the official close of the Party Congress. Almost all of them left Russia by the evening of February 24, but some fifteen remained, either by prior arrangement or with approval for reasons such as ill health. Only one actually paid visits to Miklos Manyoki at the Kremlin Clinic, but between visits he was seen in the company of at least five Warsaw pact delegates and a Frenchman. This confirms the testimony given by Manyoki in Budapest."

"I was there for his session of interrogation by the AVO," Erika said. "He couldn't wait to talk—a low threshold of pain." Three years ago she might have spoken those words contemptuously, but now there was a touch of pity in her voice.

"You'd have done better to stay for the rest," Kossior said dryly. "Even those reprocessed Gestapists might have been less zealous in the presence of a woman. As it is, Miklos Manyoki is of no value to anyone. He's dead."

"Dead? I'm sorry to hear that. If I'd thought—but you see, the AVO didn't want me there, intruding. And they seemed to consider Manyoki a harmless ideologue, as I did."

"I wouldn't exactly call him harmless. You *did* read the Manyoki document?"

"It's a long way from writing it to implementing it."

"Implementation," said Kossior, "is precisely what we now must—What will you have, my dear?"

The headwaiter had materialized at Kossior's side, pad and pencil poised.

"The assorted cold cuts, then the saddle of hare, please. And another light beer."

Kossior repeated her order to Fritz. "Cucumber salad and boiled carp for me," he said. "Mineral water, Apollinaris if you have it. And black bread."

"Black," said Fritz with icy correctness, "is the only kind we have."

After he left with their order, Erika took out a cigarette. Kossior lit it for her.

"Your 'harmless ideologue' was a persuasive man," he said impatiently. "Even from a hospital bed he was able to set up contacts and plant his seeds of treason over a wide field. The go-between, and the five Warsaw Pact delegates we know he met with, were subsequently picked up in their native countries and interrogated. Of the six, four had become converts to Manyoki's counterrevolutionary proposals and by the time of their arrest were already seeking converts of their own. Two apparently declined to work with Manyoki but on the other hand chose not to betray him."

Kossior mentioned no nationalities, named no names. Erika had not expected him to. She asked, "How did Manyoki learn so quickly of the Khrushchev speech?"

Kossior shrugged. "Fortunately, that's the KGB's problem, not mine. It could have been anyone with access to the speech and to Manyoki after that. For example, the very next day a group of Latvian delegates was admitted to the Kremlin Clinic with food poisoning. Latvians don't like Russian domination any better than Manyoki did. One of them may have smuggled the speech out of the Great Kremlin Palace, determined to get it out of Russia. Or Manyoki, once he heard about it, could have got an authentic copy from a Russian friend, of which he had many. How he did it is irrelevant. The consequences of his treason are what matter."

Their first course came. Erika attacked the sliced sausage and Westphalian ham angrily. Kossior was manipulating the conversation, doling out his superior knowledge with typical Russian charm.

He picked at his cucumber salad and resumed. "Comrade Khrushchev was taking a calculated risk from the start. That midnight speech at the Great Kremlin Palace carried a clear message for the party in Russia. And it carried one for external consumption as well. To condemn Stalin, to call him a tyrant and mass murderer worse than Hitler, will give Khrushchev a certain legitimacy in the West. Or at least a moral breathing space. No one can reasonably expect the gulag to be cleared out overnight, after all.

"On the other hand, parts of the speech, such as Khrushchev's own complicity in Stalin's crimes, were never meant for Western eyes. At this moment Italy's Party Chief Palmiro Togliatti is negotiating the sale of a transcript of the Khrushchev speech, suitably doctored, for $250,000 to the CIA. A *Time* Magazine correspondent will be permitted to smuggle a corroborative copy out of Poland. And shortly, my dear Erika, you will arrange something similar in France—the initial move, as you'll see, in a far more complex operation."

Erika was going to interrupt, but Kossior held up a plump hand. "Let me finish, please."

"For release in Eastern Europe, the speech will likewise be edited. But even omitting our contingency plans for insurrection in the Warsaw Pact countries, it will cause a furor. Thus, we know that certain cosmetic improvements in the standard of living will be needed to defuse the situation.

"The Manyoki version, however, includes these contingency plans, right up to invasion and total occupation of Eastern Europe by the Red Army if necessary. The rest of the Manyoki package, of course, is his own blueprint for forcing the Red Army's hand—demands for free speech, for the end of one-party rule, for free and secret elections. And while you, my dear, very neatly prevented that package from reaching the West, it is surely now being circulated in Poland and Hungary."

"But what can they do about it? Strikes here and there, a riot or two—as you said, your contingency plans are drawn. They'll be quashed."

"At a price," Kossior agreed. "I needn't remind you what happened here in Berlin three years ago. Every time we're forced to use tanks and guns, we only invite the next rebellion. And what Manyoki's followers want is far worse—they want a counterrevolution."

"They'll lose," Erika said flatly.

"And so may we. Think of the reactions in the West. I don't mean the usual capitalist tub-thumping, that's nothing. But what about the Communist parties of the so-called free world? Once they see the Warsaw Pact countries resisting control from Moscow, what happens then?"

Erika took another cigarette, lit it herself. She nodded thoughtfully. "Yes, I see. One brand of Communism for France, another for Italy, a third for England, a fourth for the underground in Spain . . ."

"Precisely, my dear Erika. It would spell the end of world Communist unity. Communism itself might not survive. Perhaps your friend Gideon Parr was thinking of that the night he died. And perhaps you weren't."

"Listen," Erika said fiercely, "in 1953 it served your interests, and mine, and Gideon Parr's, to work together. As for what happened at Lake Fertö last month—"

"Yes? Tell me."

Erika and Kossior stared at each other. They both knew that ultimately they had to cooperate. The events of three years ago left them no choice—except murder. And even murder might lead to questions the survivor could not afford to answer.

"It was snowing hard. The car was crawling. Parr got out and ran. That's all that happened."

"Why did they send you in the first place?"

"I happened to be in Vienna at the time, I spoke the language, I knew the terrain."

"Not to mention the man they were sending in."

"Use your head," Erika told him. "Nobody knew who the CIA would send. Even the station chief, a mediocrity named Hackler, would have been a good catch if we wanted to learn what they knew."

Kossior dismissed Hackler with a disdainful grunt.

"Moscow has the feeling you gave Parr the option of a quick death," he said.

"A quick death by heart attack? How absolutely brilliant of me."

108

"Well, then, the option of escaping."

"But he didn't, did he? You can't have it both ways, and either way I don't like what you're implying."

Again they stared across the small table at each other. A waiter brought their main dishes. When he left, Kossior said:

"I'm not implying anything. I'm only repeating what I heard in Moscow. Trust me, Erika."

"I have to trust you," she told him.

"Friends?"

She said nothing.

"Sometimes I wonder whether you resent me because you've never been able to seduce me."

In spite of herself, Erika smiled. "I never tried."

Kossior laughed. "Friends?" he repeated.

"Yes, all right, Dmitri Platonovich. Friends."

They let the next few minutes pass in silence while they separated meat and fish from bone. Erika had finished the hare and was sipping her beer when Kossior said:

"In sum, Moscow must expect revolt in Eastern Europe, possibly in two or more countries acting in concert, probably before the year is out. And this rebellion may well lead to Red Army intervention, even total occupation." He pushed the last bit of boiled carp aside. "Before that happens, we must arrange a moral justification for ourselves."

"Moral justification? When did we ever worry about that? Besides, all the disinformation experts in Moscow couldn't put a moral gloss on naked invasion."

"You forget, my dear Erika, that morality is relative. What if the West could be edged into a position no better than our own? Say they were to engage in some piece of military adventurism, to expose themselves yet again to charges of imperialist aggression. Who then could cast the first stone?"

Kossior spoke steadily for ten minutes. He continued

talking as they went downstairs and out to the line of official cars, where his chauffeur ushered them into a black prewar Mercedes. He talked while they drove eastward, talked all the way to the Normannenstrasse and its complex of buildings that housed the MfS, the Ministry for State Security of the German Democratic Republic.

When the Mercedes stopped, Kossior was still talking, caught up in his own rhetoric. Clearly the plan excited him.

It dazzled Erika.

2

Southard drove westward from Munich-Riem Airport straight across the city, then turned north and left the lights of Munich behind. He passed through Dachau an hour before midnight and began watching for the secondary road to Markt Indersdorf, his impatience growing with every kilometer.

But he knew he had to do this Gehlen's way.

He had been delayed too long in Frankfurt already, chafing at the confinement of the warren of offices in the I. G. Farben building innocuously called Department of Army Detachment. For most of a week he had pored over dossiers, conferred with the counterespionage field chief, written reports, set in motion the machinery to search every inch of the Austro-Hungarian net for breaches and then replace it all from Warren Hackler on down.

And now, when he could finally get to Munich, he had to drive far into the Bavarian countryside to meet with the obsessively secretive Reinhard Gehlen.

Should he have gone directly to Berlin?

Berlin was the logical place to look for Erika Graf. Or was it? From her Agency dossier, Southard knew she currently was deputy for Westwork at the Normannenstrasse. Yet she'd turned up in Hungary early in

March when Gideon Parr died, and again later in the month outside Miklos Manyoki's apartment. She might not be in Berlin at all.

In 1953, when their paths first crossed, she had been there, working on internal security at MfS headquarters. After that, the dossier put her in France and Austria for most of 1954, and back at the Normannenstrasse since February of last year. Before 1953, the Agency knew little of Erika Graf. But the Agency itself was only five years old then.

In 1953, Southard was Berlin station chief. In those days he could have mobilized all the station's resources to trace Erika Graf. Then as now, anyone with the price of an *S-Bahn* ticket could cross between the Western and Russian sectors with no difficulty. The border was a sieve with agents slipping through both ways.

But none of those agents was Southard's now. He would have to work through Berlin's current station chief. And while MacReedy was a good field officer, he and Southard had scarcely met. No favors were owed, no debts awaited collection. MacReedy, a team player with a reputation for keeping his neck well tucked in, would probably kick Southard's request upstairs to Adam Prestridge in Washington.

Which would end Southard's involvement.

Prestridge, the Agency's deputy director for plans, had been an early detractor of Gideon Parr, and consequently his relations with Southard were as cool as civility permitted. Once Prestridge knew that Parr's trail led to Erika Graf, he would turn it over to MacReedy's Berlin station. And Southard would find himself back in Foggy Bottom, dismantling outmoded networks.

Instead, he had chosen to leave the protection of the Agency umbrella and step outside on his own.

From Frankfurt his call had gone through swiftly to Gehlen himself, but only to set up a meeting. Reinhard

Gehlen mistrusted the telephone. He did all business in person.

And yet, if Southard could be sure of one thing tonight, it was that he would not see Gehlen's face.

Two minutes after the fork toward Markt Indersdorf, a Citroën overtook him, slowing again almost immediately. Southard followed closely, on parking lights only, as instructed. He saw the lead car's taillights and little else. By the time they had made half a dozen turns on unpaved roads, his sense of direction was lost.

The Citroën drew up behind a parked car. It looked like a Mercedes limousine in the brief glimpse Southard had before the headlights cut out. He stopped his own car, rolled down the window and waited. Suddenly he was staring directly into a powerful flashlight.

"Out."

He got out, submitted to a thorough frisking and was led past the Citroën to the limousine. When the rear door swung open, the flashlight went out and the dome light remained dark.

Inside, Southard settled onto the glove-soft leather upholstery. He could sense, not see, the other man—the quiet breathing, the faint scent of aftershave.

The man spoke. "We've had no dealings since you were Berlin station chief. What brings you to me now?"

Reinhard Gehlen, a/k/a the Gray General, a/k/a Herr Schneider, had been a lifelong anti-Communist but, if you could believe him, never a Nazi. A lieutenant general of intelligence in Hitler's Wehrmacht, he disappeared toward the end of the war into the Bavarian Alps, along with fifty cases of papers documenting German Communism since 1920. When he offered the documents and his then small staff to the U.S. Third Army, they set him up in business in the Munich suburb of Pullach. With the advent of the German Federal Republic in 1955, Gehlen went to work for

Chancellor Adenauer. What had been the unofficial Gehlen Group blossomed into the official Federal Intelligence Service. Reinhard Gehlen's assiduously guarded facelessness was no paranoia. Hundreds of Red agents infiltrated the West as refugees from East Germany every year, and the assassin who hit Reinhard Gehlen would be set for life.

"I'm interested in Erika Graf."

"How interested?" Gehlen said.

"I want to know where she is, what she does, who she talks to and, if possible, what they say."

Gehlen let five seconds pass. "She's not in Berlin?"

The real question was: Why aren't you using MacReedy's people? And Southard didn't want to say he wasn't.

"I won't know until I get there," he said. "But even in Berlin you have contacts we don't. And she may not stay put. She's done a lot of moving lately."

"Berlin would be no problem, provided she's there."

Gehlen had not agreed to help, not yet. Southard didn't want to push him. He waited.

"If she started moving, would you want close surveillance?"

"No, I don't think so," Southard said slowly. "It's not just the manpower. With her training, there's too much danger she'd pick it up."

"Then what?"

"The travel bureau." Knowing the pride Gehlen took in it, Southard added, "You have the widest coverage, and the fastest."

The other man was dimly visible now. He might have nodded.

"Where can you be reached in Berlin?"

"I'll be at the Kempinski, under the name of Curtis Beck."

"All right. You'll be contacted there—Herr Beck." The leather sighed as Reinhard Gehlen changed position. He tapped on the glass, and Southard's door opened instantly.

Southard was about to climb out when Gehlen cleared his throat. "My condolences. Gideon Parr was a professional."

It was his highest accolade.

3

Deborah tried to think, all the way into town, how she could get away by herself, get to a telephone. Today might be her only chance.

They had crowded into Sulayman Husayni's jeep, six of them, and headed for El Mansûra to have their pictures taken. There were no cameras permitted at the base, except for the instructors' cine camera which sometimes filmed them coming up behind a victim with knife or garrote, or learning the uses of plastique and fulminate of mercury percussion caps or how to rig an innocent-looking letter bomb (cousin Yasir was the explosives expert, who ever would have thought that?), or practicing the quick, unexpected, deadly moves of unarmed combat. Once Deborah even heard the cine camera's metallic purr while, blindfolded, she disassembled and assembled an AK-47 assault rifle.

This was not their first visit to El Mansûra. They had driven in from the base on two other occasions to practice following or eluding one another, to devise safe message drops, to identify good ground for abduction, for ambush, for quiet assassination. But the instructors had been with them then, watching every move, and Deborah had not been able to shake them.

At the base they worked sixteen hours a day, sometimes eighteen. Every night for two weeks she had stumbled into her tent and flung herself on the cot so exhausted she never remembered waiting to fall asleep, and all too soon it would

114

be that time before dawn when you could just distinguish black thread from white, and it would begin again— running five miles in an hour with a sixty-pound backpack and an automatic rifle; or crawling on your belly, the ubiquitous rifle in your hands, across the field of young cotton and over the ridges that protected the seedlings and through the silt-laden ditches and canals; or the hours on the firing range; or unarmed combat with the wiry little instructor who, sooner or later, would say: "No, no, not the fist! What's a fist? A loose bag of bones and if you hit something hard like a jaw you will hurt the fist more than the jaw, yes? You have elbows and knees and the heel of your hand for hammers. You have the edges of your hands, held so, for cleavers. And unless you are naked in the middle of the desert, you have objects to strike with—a pencil for gouging or a comb for raking, hot liquid in a cup, a belt buckle or a shoe heel or a nail file, a necktie, a hatpin, a tobacco pipe. Especially where you are going and how you will be dressing, you always have weapons." Men twice his size would try to use those weapons on him and he would disarm them and hurt them just enough to show they had much to learn, and they would learn, the girls too, herself and Maryam Husayni.

Maryam, darkly beautiful, was the most Arab-looking of them all, but Maryam said that did not matter because she had been educated in Europe and, anyway, could pass for Provençal or Italian. Maryam preferred the speed of the knife and the garrote to the rigors of unarmed combat. Deborah recoiled from the idea of killing with her hands, but she made herself show as much blood-lust as the others.

Her skills came back rapidly. At first she wondered how fast Jehan Khalid would learn, but then she decided to hide none of her competence. Jehan's father, the master spy Akhmed Khalid, could have taught her. Jehan had to equal and even excel the others, or she might be dropped from the group. The Russian-trained group, just as the Israelis had suspected.

When she had entered the Special Group under the wing of the beautiful Maryam, the instructors were dubious. Now they were enthusiastic. It was a matter of language, language and appearance; no training could give any of the others the aptitude that Jehan Khalid had for French and English and German. Dress Jehan like a Frenchwoman and Jehan would *be* a Frenchwoman. Of them all she was the most European-looking, they said. The languages, the appearance, the *style*—all ultimately were more important than the weeks of training she had missed.

So was her proven ability to kill, but they did not tell her that.

Like her, the twins Maryam and Sulayman Husayni had languages and they had style. And like her, they had missed part of the Special Group training. They had been too busy commanding the fedayeen, setting their trap for the Brotherhood, for the German Krim and his lieutenants, the trap they had sprung the night Jehan Khalid killed all three of them, doing their work for them while they raced into Gaza from the desert with their fifty missing troops after waiting patiently for Krim to succumb to Aryan overconfidence.

She remembered sitting there on the floor, the rifle across her lap, wisps of gunsmoke still drifting in the air, when the Husayni twins walked in on her and the three dead men, and if she'd had the strength or the will she might have raised the AK-47 and sent a burst in their direction, but she just sat there and they took the rifle away from her and she cried and it was the best thing she could have done because, from that moment, Maryam Husayni was Jehan Khalid's protector.

They had let her sleep all the next day, but by nightfall the three of them were in a car speeding along the coast road past Khan Yunis and El 'Arish and the Roman ruins of Pelusium and then south to cross the Suez Canal at

Ismailia, and from there El Mansûra and the base were not far.

Soon, the twins told her, the training would end and those who qualified would be sent to other places, where they would learn and serve, learn by serving, and they would work for the *ferenghi* so when they returned they would be ready to terrorize and decimate and finally annihilate the Zionists.

Listening to them, seeing the fanaticism in their eyes, Deborah had a sudden chilling vision of what they would do to her if they found out she was not Jehan Khalid.

But mostly she was too busy to brood and once or twice there was even something to make her laugh, usually cousin Yasir, who was so good with explosives and so bad at everything else, cousin Yasir, who desperately wanted to be a member of the Special Group but who looked like what he was and would always be, a soft stout unshaven Arab with a prow of a nose, a weak chin, no linguistic flair despite the English and French he had studied at Cairo University, no skill at all in unarmed combat and a blubbering terror of the infiltration course with its exploding grenades and live machine-gun fire; cousin Yasir, who stood alone at the entrance to the base watching the jeep leave for El Mansûra the day the survivors of the training went to have their pictures taken, cousin Yasir knowing at last what the others had known from the beginning, that he would be left behind.

When they had finished with the photographer, the six of them walked along the dusty main street of El Mansûra, three abreast, looking like students on a holiday. Outside a dingy café Sulayman Husayni decided to treat them all to a cool drink of sherbet. He commandeered the only large table, sending the occupants off protesting feebly, and called for the proprietor.

Deborah waited, rehearsing her words, until a frightened little man in a tarboosh set their drinks before them.

117

Taking a slow, appreciative sip, she pushed her chair back.

"Excuse me." She hoped her voice sounded normal, was convinced it did not. "I was meaning to get some skin lotion. All that desert sun—I won't be a minute."

She walked away in no hurry, as if she hadn't far to go. But when she saw the sign she lengthened her stride. The labyrinthine streets of the bazaar separated her from her destination.

HOTEL DAMIETTA, All Comfort, 500 meters

"All comfort" was an exaggeration, she was sure, but a hotel had to have a public phone, which was more than could be said for the tiny shops of the bazaar. She hurried along the street.

Maryam overtook her just at the entrance to the bazaar.

"Darling Jehan! Of course you're right, we have to start thinking about our appearance. Let's explore the souks together, and buy all sorts of things to make us beautiful."

Deborah managed a smile as Maryam fell into step with her. Perhaps, if she could get the Palestinian girl absorbed in some merchant's wares, she could still slip away.

But Maryam would not pass one stall, one tiny doorless shop, without asking Jehan's opinion. Was this gold bracelet really tasteful? Was the silver-threaded scarf too Oriental-looking?

When Maryam led the way into a perfume shop hardly bigger than a closet, Deborah felt a surge of hope. The white-haired merchant eagerly unstoppered vial after vial of scent like a conjuror and thrust them close for approval—myrrh, jasmine, a dozen others. Maryam was entranced, tilting her head to one side, her eyes half-shut, as the merchant touched her wrist delicately with the glass stoppers. Deborah edged toward the door. It was so easy to get separated in the crowded bazaar, after all.

Sulayman Husayni stood outside. "Come on," he said,

"the others are waiting. It's time we got back."

Maryam came to the doorway. "I think you should have the second one, Jehan. It's right for you. The other scents are too—"

Sulayman glared, and Maryam stopped. When he strode off toward where the jeep was parked, she ran after him, slipping her hand into his.

He looked back. Deborah-Jehan followed.

The twins were always together, she thought, almost like lovers. Some at the base joked that Jehan Khalid had come between them, though never so Sulayman could hear. Sulayman had a temper and his slenderness was deceptive; it was said that in an all-out fight with the instructor of unarmed combat, Sulayman would win.

"What was she doing all this time?" he demanded.

"Leave her alone, it's all right."

"I asked you what she was doing."

"Remembering what it's like to be a woman. What's wrong with that?"

A few minutes later the six members of the Special Group drove north in the jeep through the cotton fields of the Nile Delta toward Damietta Mouth. Deborah saw tall white triangular sails on the water and rows of women in black crouching over the cotton seedlings like crows. The jeep turned east on an unpaved road along a canal hardly wider than a ditch. The canal smelled of brackish seawater, they were that close to the coast.

Deborah did not look for landmarks. She knew them all now, for what good it did. She had no way to tell anyone where she was or where she was going.

4

On the morning of Monday, April 9, Erika Graf took Colonel Kossior to the Ministry for State Security's technical center at Freienwalder Strasse 12. A high wall topped with barbed wire and with watchtowers at each corner surrounded the grimy brick buildings. The MfS Freienwalder Strasse facility resembled a prison more than the laboratory and factory complex it in fact was. Housing scientists and technicians, some of them defectors from the West, Freienwalder Strasse 12 produced spook equipment. Not just the Ministry for State Security but the Russian GRU used its products—miniature cameras and microphones, wiretapping devices, weapons that looked like cigarette cases or lighters and contained such exotics as curare and prussic acid sprays lethal at close range in three seconds.

Erika Graf and Colonel Kossior were met at Documents Section by its director Richard Quast. A stooped man whose tortoiseshell glasses magnified his eyes enormously, Quast never used the word *forgery*. His products were so good you couldn't tell them from the real thing. Quast had begun his career shortly before the rise of the Nazis to power, mass-producing new identities for German Communists.

At Freienwalder Strasse, given a week he could deliver a package of papers that documented an entire life—passport, driver's license, police ID and social security cards, even so-called pocket trash. His assortment of visas and entry and exit stamps was the world's most extensive; virtually no country, no frontier post, no port of entry was missing. Much of Quast's material came from passports photographed at East German border points behind frosted windows while their owners submitted to a quarter-hour of bureaucratic delay.

Kossier explained what he wanted, and when.

Quast whistled.

The Russian gave him an envelope containing six photographs and a sheet of information compiled in neat boxes. With slender purple-stained fingers Quast spread the small glossy prints on a low table. He studied them. He flexed the print paper. He lit a bright lamp and peered at each print in turn, Kossior at his side.

Erika stood behind them. Taller than either man, she could look easily over their shoulders. She saw ID-sized photographs of four young men and two young women, none of them blond, none fair-skinned, but only two noticeably Arab-looking.

Erika's breath caught. She closed her eyes for a moment, and told herself it had to be imagination. It simply could not be the same girl. There wasn't even any real resemblance. Of course, she would have changed, would be the same age now as the girl in the photograph. But the other one, the girl from the nightmare time, had been undernourished, emaciated even. She couldn't have survived. It was just the eyes and perhaps the bones of the face that. . . .

The men had bent closer over the table. "—but still of usable quality," Quast was saying. "Let me see that data sheet. Age, height, weight, eyes, hair. What's this entry?"

Kossior flipped the nearest photograph facedown. "The European languages the subject commands. This one, for example." He noted the number penciled on the back, and traced that line across the data sheet to a box with the notations ENG, FRA, DEU.

"Ah, yes. She speaks English, French, German," Quast said, "Clear enough."

"I require at least three sets for each subject, Herr Quast. The usual package. If some show fewer than three languages, duplicate nationalities as needed."

"But Wednesday," the older man protested, his magnified eyes looking from Kossior to Erika in apologetic dismay.

By then Erika had regained her composure. "Wednesday noon," she told him, "and there will be something extra in it for you, Herr Quast. Shall we say—one thousand *West*

German marks?"

"Ever for one thousand Westmarks I cannot guarantee perfection by Wednesday noon," Quast said. Then he added with a faint, self-satisfied smile, "However, I alone will be able to tell the difference."

Erika's smile was satisfied too. She could almost forget that she had seen a ghost.

5

Sam Brodsky sat in the apartment on Dizengoff Street in Tel Aviv, drinking his sixth cup of strong dark coffee. Dusk had fallen, but Sam had lit no lights. He got up and paced to the window and looked out and sat again in darkness. If there was anything, anything at all, Iser Harel would have called him.

No, he wouldn't. He'd said he wouldn't tell God Himself.

Sam checked the number in his pocket diary. It was several months old. Maybe it had already been changed.

Sam paced to the window again.

Iser Harel disliked being disturbed at home. But Sam Brodsky was at home, and Sam Brodsky was disturbed.

He picked up the phone and called the private number.

Rivkah Harel answered, then muffled the mouthpiece. Iser came on the line. "Sam, I've been meaning to—"

"You've heard from her?"

"Sam, listen, we both know an agent can't always make contact right away. That's why I said I wouldn't inform you, so you wouldn't worry if—"

"Iser, do you know how many days it's been?"

"I know. I'll call you as soon as I have anything."

Sam Brodsky drank another cup of tepid coffee. He sat in darkness. If he turned on the lights in the apartment, the photographs of Debbie everywhere he looked would only make him feel more helpless.

122

Southard called from a pay phone at a café a few doors up the Kurfürstendamm from the Kempinski.

"Curtis Beck here," he said.

The voice, the same one that had reached him at the hotel and told him what number to call, began without greeting. "Major Graf returned to Berlin on March 31. Since then her only contacts were routine ones with colleagues at MfS headquarters, with one exception. On Wednesday she lunched with a GRU colonel named Dmitri Platonovich Kossior at the Adlon, where the colonel is registered. Since arrival he has conferred with Graf at the Normannenstrasse headquarters daily. And this morning Graf and the colonel together visited another MfS facility at Freienwalder Strasse 12. This is their technical center. Do you know it?"

Southard said that he did.

"They met there with Richard Quast of the documents section. The nature of their business has not now been ascertained. We will keep you informed."

Southard stood for a minute holding the dead receiver.

The phone call indicated that Gehlen had penetrated the East German Ministry for State Security itself. Nothing about Reinhard Gehlen surprised Southard.

The surprise came in the information he transmitted.

Erika Graf, Southard himself, and now Kossior—three of the five key figures from the 1953 operation were back in Berlin. The missing two, Gideon Parr and Leonid Golovin, were both dead.

Chapter Six

1

When Joseph Stalin died at 9:50 P.M. Moscow time on March 5, 1953, four days after a massive cerebral hemorrhage, he was in his thirtieth year of power.

Absolute dictator of the Soviet Union since 1924, he extended his rule after the Second World War over Eastern Europe as well.

He elevated an economic doctrine which bore him to the status of a universal religion, with himself as god.

He built a secret police apparatus that could reach into any factory, any collective farm, any household from the Elbe River in Germany to Big Diomede Island in the Bering Strait.

He cultivated terror as a way of life and mass murder as a way of death.

Then he died.

Throughout his monolithic empire, unrest spread, an unrest based on hope. The tyrant was gone; since things could not get any worse, they had to get better. A generation that had mortgaged itself to a dubious tomorrow began to dream of a better today.

This was truer in the German Democratic Republic—East Germany—than elsewhere.

East Germans could travel relatively freely to the West. They could see for themselves the contrast between the two Germanies. They could listen to West German radio, read

Western periodicals, stroll like poor country cousins past the glitter and wealth in the shop windows of West Berlin's Kudamm. They could even, with a minimum of personal danger, escape permanently to the West by boarding a train or, in much of Berlin, by simply stepping across the border.

More than 20 percent of East Germany's population did just that. Most were young professional people and technicians, many were Berliners. Berliners hadn't liked Hitler much, either.

Still, until three months after Stalin's death, those who stayed behind in the East German capital were docile.

Then in late May the East German Politburo approved a 10-percent increase in work norms for every industry in the country. The workers faced longer hours at no increase in wages—already painfully low as an East Berliner could see after a short ride on the *S-Bahn*. For two weeks the ferment grew.

On Tuesday, June 16, construction workers marched in protest from Stalinallee, East Berlin's showpiece boulevard then under construction, to the gleaming white granite Russian Embassy on Unter den Linden. The Politburo swiftly revoked the 10-percent increase in work norms. The workers dispersed. The crisis seemed averted.

It wasn't.

A dreary rain fell the next morning when East Berliners began assembling at first light on Unter den Linden. Peasants in from the surrounding countryside were joined by students from Humboldt University at the eastern end of the great boulevard. The construction workers led the way, the resonant shuffle of their wooden clogs pounding like an insistent drumbeat.

Shortly after noon the mob reached Potsdamer Platz, where Russian, American and British sectors of Berlin converged. Fights broke out with the Volkspolizei, and Communist officials who tried to speak to the mob were dragged down and beaten. Banners appeared demanding free elections and free political parties. At 2:00 P.M. flying squads of helmeted Russian soldiers with submachine guns marched against the crowds. They began firing when the huge Russian flag atop the monumental six-columned Brandenburg Gate was torn down and replaced by West Germany's red, black and gold ensign. Then the Red Army, led by T-34 tanks, swept the streets.

By nightfall it was over. Downtown East Berlin was littered with broken glass, bricks and paving stones, smoking heaps of rubble. The rain began to fall again, washing away the pools of blood in Potsdamer Platz. Twenty Berliners were dead, and almost two hundred wounded.

Within days Moscow was accusing West Germany and the United States of inciting the riots. Two Soviet armored divisions occupied the city under martial law; one hundred fifty Volkspolizei fled to the West, many with their families; four "agents provocateurs" were executed; thousands were jailed. And Brigadier General Leonid Golovin of the KGB flew in from Moscow to begin assigning the blame.

In a system that considers itself infallible, scapegoats are a necessity.

Any nation's intelligence services compete with, and therefore denigrate, one another. The CIA takes the attitude: "What the FBI doesn't know won't hurt it." In Britain, M15 views M16 as clubby, old-school tie and effete; M16 thinks M15 uneducated, lower class, crude.

The infighting is fiercest when the intelligence services duplicate each other's functions, so often the case in a police state. Russia's KGB serves itself first, the party second, the government third. The GRU answers to the Red Army and the government. Among their many activities, both run foreign intelligence operations. The rivalry is sometimes bloody and the KGB usually wins. It has this advantage: at every level of command, its agents infiltrate all government and military organizations in the Soviet Union, including the GRU.

The usual advantage did not help Leonid Mironovich Golovin in Berlin in 1953.

General Golovin's duty—to find traitors—was unquestioned. Since the Communist system is by definition infallible, any breakdown must be blamed on human failure.

In Berlin Golovin unhesitatingly sought this failure in the two customary places—the rival GRU and the local intelligence service, the East German MfS. Both should have predicted the Berlin riots in June. Their failure constituted not incompetence but treachery.

Golovin attacked them from within.

By August the MfS was taking apart the woodwork at the Normannenstrasse, searching for double agents. By September Golovin's witch hunt had paralyzed the GRU's German operation in Wünsdorf.

Colonel Kossior, then GRU chief at Wunsdorf, called a desperation meeting with his MfS opposite number.

The plan they evolved was Byzantine, but their first move was simplicity itself. They sent an emissary to Frankfurt, where Gideon Parr then ran counterespionage for the CIA in Europe.

The emissary they chose was Erika Graf.

2

Southard never learned, that September or later, whether Gideon Parr and Erika Graf were already lovers before she was sent to Frankfurt.

He did know, the moment he turned his key in the lock and walked into the living room of the safe house on Frankfurt's aptly named Grafstrasse, that his arrival was

127

poorly timed. Somehow the signals had gotten crossed.

Parr and the woman were lounging on a sofa before the fireplace, sharing a bottle of Sekt, the local champagne. Both wore dressing gowns. Both were barefoot. Parr's eyes were closed, the woman's only half-open. She was smoking a black-tobacco cigarette. Her blonde hair fanned across her shoulders. Her cheeks still had the flush of recent lovemaking.

She looked up, her free hand moving unhurriedly to the front of her ice-blue silk robe, pulling it closed over bare skin.

Parr rose smoothly. "Hello, Ben. You made better time than I thought. Come in, come in, don't stand there gaping."

Southard remained just inside the door, wondering what to say. He knew Parr, in his early forties, was a bachelor and bon vivant with a reputation as strong as Allen Dulles's own for appreciating gourmet food, vintage wines and beautiful women. And the woman was certainly stunning. But here? Yet Parr was calmly saying:

"I don't think you two have met. Ben, this is Erika Graf."

Southard recognized her, of course. Her photograph in Berlin station's growing file on MfS personnel did not do her justice, but he knew her. Probably she knew him too. They nodded.

She stood now, her head on a level with Parr's. "Is he going to be stuffy, Gideon?" she said. "Should I put some clothes on?"

"No, no. I'm sure he's delighted with you just as you are."

Erika dragged deeply on her cigarette. "If he isn't, he will be once he knows why I'm here." Her pale clear eyes sparkled. She was enjoying herself, enjoying the puzzled look on Southard's face.

"Believe it or not, Ben, Captain Graf has come on business," Parr told him. "She's here on behalf of the

Normannenstrasse."

"And on behalf of Colonel Kossior of the GRU. A minister plenipotentiary, you might call me," Erika said.

"That's why I sent for you," Parr said. "Captain Graf proposes something rather—unusual. An interagency collaboration."

"Hands across the border." Erika laughed softly, and so did Parr.

Southard looked at her, then at him. "All right, you've had your fun. Now will someone let me in on the joke?"

"Ben," Gideon Parr said slowly, "they're going to make us a present of General Golovin."

Ten days later, Gideon Parr was pacing back and forth in Southard's office at the American Consulate in Berlin, studying an enlarged aerial photograph. He handed it to Southard, walked over to the map on the desk, and pointed.

"The whole street isn't very long. She said halfway. That makes it about here."

The two men stood together over the map. They did not know how Erika and her GRU ally Colonel Kossior would deliver Golovin. They knew only that it would be done on the Prinz-Albrecht-Strasse, a barren strip between the Russian and U.S. sectors of Berlin, and that it would be tonight.

"Fifty yards from the pile of rubble that was once Gestapo headquarters," Parr said. "Golovin ought to feel right at home. They call him the Russian Himmler, did you know that?"

Southard knew. He also knew Parr was just talking to break the tension. In fifteen hours, with luck, they'd have one of the KGB's top officers in their hands. Already the best CIA interrogation team was in Germany, waiting for them at Camp King in the Taunus Mountains. Parr must have known that too, but still he asked.

"You hear from King? Everything all set?"

Southard nodded. "Gid, look. Their part of the bargain is to hand over Golovin. Their only part. After that, we're welcome to wring anything out of him we can, anything to blow the KGB sky-high. That's what they want, right?"

"Sure, you know how they—"

"But do they want Golovin to blow their own operations too? Christ, Gid, he's been taking the Normannenstrasse apart brick by brick for three months now, and he can quote chapter and verse on the whole Wünsdorf set up. Where does that leave Kossior and Graf, once we get our hands on him?"

Parr looked steadily, appraisingly at Southard. Finally he nodded. "I was almost beginning to think that would never occur to you. It occurred to *them* right at the beginning. So how do you think they plan on getting around it?"

"They'll hand him over alive. But they won't let us take him out of Berlin alive."

Parr waited. Then he smiled slowly. "You're close, Ben. But *they* won't kill him. They'll leak word to the KGB that Golovin's defecting. His own people will do it. That way, we have no complaints about Kossior and Graf not keeping their end of the bargain. Cute, isn't it?"

"Gideon." Southard spoke his friend's name softly.

"Yeah, kid?" Parr's manner was offhand, his speech colloquial as it usually was with Southard, as if to emphasize the difference in their backgrounds. But Southard knew that Gideon Parr, self-taught or no, was a cultivated, urbane man who dined frequently with the Dulles brothers and who was much prized on the Washington cocktail circuit when he was in town. For the first time Southard found Parr's lowbrow pose patronizing.

"I was just wondering. How much of this were you planning to tell me? If I hadn't asked."

"Would have depended on where you were tonight," Parr said. "Gehlen's giving us three cars and eight people, and I brought a man from Frankfurt—Texan named Wilkins, you know him?—to handle Golovin personally. Where would those arrangements leave you?"

"I'm going out with them," Southard said quietly.

"Still? After all we've just been saying?"

"That's where I'm going to be," Southard said.

They were, Southard thought they were, old friends. Gideon Parr had gone straight from the OSS to the two-year experiment of the Central Intelligence Group to the present CIA, and he had brought Southard, ten years his junior, along.

"Well, you've answered your own question, haven't you? If you were going out there tonight—and I figured you would—then I had to tell you all of it, didn't I?" Suddenly Parr was grinning the infectious grin that Southard knew so well. "But Jesus Christ, Ben, give me some operating space, will you? Maybe, just maybe, it won't turn out the way anybody over there expects."

Southard and Erika Graf would have three minutes. During that time, no military patrol from either sector would go near Prinz-Albrecht-Strasse. The time was set for 11:45 exactly. Southard arrived from the west end of the street in a four-door DKW with a Gehlen agent at the wheel and the CIA-man Wilkins in back. The other two Gehlen Group cars slid into place, with four Gehlen people in the lead car and three in the sweep car. Erika Graf's Volkswagen minibus appeared at the east end of the street a few seconds later.

In the moonlight the huge piles of rubble that had been Gestapo headquarters and the ethnological museum lay like thick impasto on the ruined canvas of Berlin.

Southard saw four figures approaching from the parked minibus.

Golovin, in civilian clothing, could walk—but only just. They obviously had drugged the sixty-year-old KGB general. A man on either side was helping him along, Erika Graf a few paces behind them.

Southard should have seen the problem then, but he was too eager to get his hands on Golovin.

The transfer on Prinz-Albrecht-Strasse went without a hitch. A minute and a half after the minibus appeared, Golovin was in the DKW and they were driving southeast along Stresemannstrasse toward Tempelhof Airport, where a CIA proprietory Air America C-47 was waiting to take them to Camp King.

The convoy was making good speed, but Southard was not happy with the directness of the route. Gehlen didn't normally operate that way. Then suddenly he had something else to worry about.

Golovin came out of the drug just as the DKW was crossing the Landwehr Canal.

"Well, if it doesn't look like our boy is wide awake," Wilkins observed in mild surprise. Southard heard movement behind him and Wilkins said. "Easy, easy now, boy," exactly as he might have spoken to a balky stallion.

At that moment the DKW accelerated into a sharp abrupt left turn that took it on shrieking rubber along a narrow street past two parked cars facing out. A second left turn brought it to a dead end at the edge of the canal, where the driver cut the ignition.

Southard heard a grinding crash somewhere behind them. He figured that meant the sweep car had been taken out.

Then it came to him. He had assumed the moment of maximum danger would be on Prinz-Albrecht-Strasse, when the transfer was made. It would have been—if a smooth operation had not been in the interests of all sides.

The last thing the KGB wanted, short of losing Golovin outright, was a shootout with the Gehlen Group at the frontier. So they would wait.

How long?

That would depend on Golovin. Maximum danger would come when the drug wore off. He was bound to create a diversion, however small.

He had come out of the drug unexpectedly fast, and that was when the Gehlen driver had abandoned their route.

All as if the KGB knew what drug Golovin had been given, knew the precise dosage, knew exactly at what point the effects would wear off.

Southard drew the Walther PPK from his clip-on belt holster just as the Gehlen driver opened his door. "Hold it!"

The driver dove out of the car, rolled over twice and came up in a crouching run.

Southard heard shouts and saw lights bobbing up and down behind them—men with flashlights, running. The lights winked out. A submachine gun began to hammer, muzzle flash bright even in the moonlight.

Southard aimed for the legs and shot the Gehlen driver, who screamed and pitched forward and down. Assuming they got out of this—at the moment not a safe assumption—he wanted the driver alive.

The rear window of the DKW shattered as the submachine gun fired another burst. Shards of flying glass exploded like shrapnel through the interior of the car, and Southard felt something sting his cheek. Wilkins had rolled down the rear side window and was leaning out to return the fire blindly when a bullet slammed him against the backrest of the front seat. Golovin was clawing at the door on his side of the car, streaming blood from a scalp wound.

Then he was out on the street and running, keeping low, zigzagging away from the canalbank.

Several submachine guns let go at once and Southard saw muzzle flashes erupt some distance behind the car, and in front from the direction of the canal.

The crossfire sent Golovin jerking back and forth as first one, then another stream of bullets hit him. The Russian's legs kicked high. His arms semaphored. He spun and dipped and rose and whirled like a top toward the curb, where a final hail of bullets cut him down.

In the sudden silence Southard could hear the ringing in his ears and the pounding of his heart and the pulse of fear throbbing in his throat. The trap had been sprung, the driver paid, Golovin caught in crossfire, Southard a dead man if he got out of the car to run and a dead man if he stayed inside.

He heard a scraping sound. The Gehlen driver was dragging himself away, clawing at the cobblestones and crawling along with broken-insect slowness. A wind blew off the canal and Southard could smell gunsmoke now. He watched the Gehlen driver. The man was dragging himself toward Golovin's corpse, as if safety lay in that direction. He moaned. He was moaning continuously by the time he had dragged himself the length of his own body. One leg stuck out at an impossible angle, the knee obviously shattered.

Southard wondered what they were waiting for, why they didn't get it over with.

He touched his face, his hand coming away darkly wet. He groped for the steering column. The driver had taken the ignition key. It really didn't matter. He wasn't going to drive anywhere. He was boxed in.

He heard the crackle of submachine guns further off now.

The lead car, returning?

A voice shouted, "Hey, Ben! Get the hell down here! Ben, hey, Ben!"

Gideon Parr's voice. But where?

Southard opened the door on the driver's side.

Three things happened at once.

A submachine gun stuttered, closer, and he could see the angle of a brick wall lit up by the muzzle flash.

The Gehlen driver had turned over on his back, gripping an automatic with both hands and pointing it at Southard.

His hands shook, which might make a difference. Southard would know in a split second. By the time he could bring the Walther to bear, the wounded man would get off two or three rounds.

Southard almost shot the figure that materialized in front of the DKW's radiator grill.

Gideon Parr cried "Ben!" and the Gehlen driver fired once, missing, before Gideon Parr shot him dead.

Southard ran after Parr to the embankment. Ricocheting bullets threw sparks from the cobblestones and when both men whirled to return the fire, running backwards then, Southard could see the sparks stitching an erratic line along the cobblestones toward him. A sledgehammer blow struck his right side and tumbled him onto his back, and he saw Parr's face, and then Parr lifted him in a fireman-carry for the remaining few steps to the embankment, and the movement shifted the bullet so that he wanted to cry out against the pain.

There was a three-foot drop to the well of a motor launch, the man waiting below not getting a firm enough grip on him when Parr let go. His side, his whole right side below the ribs, seemed to rip open then.

The motor launch throbbed and vibrated with power. When Southard lost consciousness it was already hydroplaning, prow high out of the water.

3

It was a Gehlen Group safe house and a Gehlen Group doctor. He stayed ten days. He had lost a lot of blood and the bullet had shattered a rib and deflected downward to puncture the liver, just missing the hepatic vein. They gave him plasma and then whole blood and glucose and antibiotics intravenously, and by the time he could sit up and have visitors and take food by mouth he was in that odd receptive state that convalescents reach when they realize they are going to live but don't yet feel well enough for anything else to matter.

In that state of indifference, he listened to Parr talking, and Parr said: "Here's the way they did it. They gave Golovin Demerol, a hundred milligrams to dope him up. Then when they took him to Prinz-Albrecht-Strasse, they administered the antidote, five milligrams of nalline. With exact dosages, you can predict to the minute how long it will take a healthy person to come out of it. So I studied a map. The KGB had to make their move right around the time you were crossing the canal. Two options, I figured. Either they block the bridge at both ends after you're on it, or your driver doubles back to the canal as soon as he can. In a fast launch we could cover either possibility."

Parr also said: "Your driver was the key. They bought him, of course. Or maybe he'd already been planted in the Gehlen Group."

And Parr said: "We lost Wilkins and they lost the driver," while Southard listened in that receptive stage of convalescence, not sure if it was Parr's first or second visit, and Parr said: "Golovin, good Christ, you saw what happened, he must have taken a hundred slugs."

He also said: "Graf and Kossior beat us, kid, but we were lucky. It could have been bad. It could have been everybody, the army, Allen and the older brother, maybe Ike himself, screaming for our heads, except what can they prove? That Wilkins got caught in a firefight between the KGB and the Gehlen Group? Not one fucking thing else. Which is why we used Gehlen's people, if you hadn't guessed."

Finally Parr said: "Gehlen owes us. Mark it in your book, kid, for when you need it. He was a Nazi, and there's a war crime in his past. Eight years he was in the party, early even for an ambitious Wehrmacht officer without Prussian connections. Golovin was ready to quote party card number, date, the works. The MfS and some of his own people were opposed. Discredit Gehelen, they said, and you'd put the MfS out of business too. Because Ghelen has his own names and card numbers. Hell, chances are any trained agent in either Germany over the age of thirty was once a Nazi, and probably Gestapo or SS. Still, Golovin was going to blow the whistle on Gehlen. So it all worked out neatly."

There were questions Southard did not think to ask in the early days of convalescence, and afterwards, every time they met somehow wasn't the right time to ask them and finally a time came when it was too late ever to ask them. He owed all the rest of his life to Gideon Parr.

The questions went, would have gone:

Why did they tell Parr about the Demerol and nalline? So he could study his map and hire his launch and stop the KGB from killing Golovin? But Kossior and Erika Graf wanted Golovin dead. And weren't the Demerol and nalline just the sort of specific detail meant to sidetrack Southard and thereby finesse the unanswerable? All they had to tell Parr was: the bridge crossing the Landwehr Canal. Parr never intended getting Golovin out alive. Then what *was* he doing?

File that one for the moment.

Why had Parr used Gehlen people instead of the CIA? He'd answered that: so the Agency's hands would be clean if anything went wrong. It was logical, and the only thing wrong with it was that Reinhard Gehlen, like Kossior and Graf, would stay in business only if Golovin died.

File that one too.

Whatever Parr did, mightn't the operation have been blown anyway by a KGB plant in Kossior's headquarters? Golovin had been in Berlin for three months and he'd hit Wünsdorf with the kind of witch hunt that made Joe McCarthy, back in the States, look like a bashful census taker standing at the door with his hat in his hand. So even if Golovin didn't have a man in the GRU before he got to Berlin, and that seemed unlikely, by the time of the operation half the Wünsdorf staff would be stomping on one another to exculpate themselves from the treason of failure. Everyone must have figured that out, Parr included. Yet Parr had gone ahead with an operation that had little chance of success from the start. Why?

To save Erika Graf's neck?

Then what about you? Southard asked himself. You didn't exactly shout no at the top of your voice, either, and you knew most of it. Whose neck were *you* trying to save? Well, no neck. But there was the glory dream, wasn't there, the biggest espionage coup of the decade, the chance to deliver Golovin?

Southard's own *mea culpa* would have to be as loud as Gideon Parr's.

Still he kept coming back to Erika Graf.

Parr and Erika.

Chances are any trained agent in either Germany over the age of thirty was once a Nazi, and probably Gestapo or SS.

Erika Graf?

And had Golovin known it?

Erika Graf, not just a scapegoat to keep the myth of Communist infallibility unblemished, but a former Nazi with war crimes buried in her past?

Did that explain why Parr had sent Wilkins to his death, and Southard almost to his, only to come galloping in like the cavalry? He was, after all, Gideon Parr, and if anyone could have it both ways, wasn't he the man to pull it off?

The questions were always there, whenever he saw Parr, but the right occasion to ask them never arose in those first months, possibly because he didn't want to learn the answers as Parr himself saw them. Then one day Parr got the big job in Washington and Southard moved up to Parr's old slot as chief of counter-espionage for Europe, and they spoke on the phone frequently but saw each other seldom, and those were no questions you could ask on the phone. And when Parr was struck down by an almost fatal coronary and Southard flew to Washington to see him, it was certainly no time to ask.

And that was the last time they'd met.

Southard liked to think this: Maybe Parr had set up the operation to save Erika Graf's life and maybe in some way that Southard would never understand it was even worth saving, but the fact remained that if Parr hadn't showed up that night he, Southard, would not be around to ask or not ask the questions that remained unanswered and possibly had no answers he wanted to hear.

Part Two

Chapter Seven

1

Willi Tiefel stared at the blonde. Willi considered himself a connoisseur, and the blonde was really something.

She was a bottle of '49 Schloss Johannisberg *Spätlese*. She was a pair of soft hands caressing Willi's lower back, which ached now from too much schnapps chased by too much beer last night at the meeting of Willi Tiefel's singing club. She was an improbable A over high C. Willi had never heard an A over high C. He had never seen a blonde like this.

Willi worked as a baggage handler at Tempelhof Airport. The day was gloomy, too cold for the second Wednesday in April, with a low slate-gray overcast and the runway lights on at two in the afternoon. The blonde leaned over to set her two valises on the low scale. Her trench coat fell open, displaying cleavage. Willi, ever the connoisseur, amended his '49 Schloss Johannisberg to a *Trockenbeerenauslese*. The girl in Pan Am blue tagged the luggage for Hamburg, and then Willi lifted the two valises, his gaze lingering on the blonde, fixed at chest level.

The sudden backfire of an igniting engine startled the blonde. Her head came up, her hair swung back to reveal her face clearly under the broad-brimmed hat. Willi stood holding the valises, still staring.

Willi Tiefel knew the blonde.

Not personally, of course. But he had seen her

photograph and Willi was good at faces.

The Pan Am girl said. "Have a pleasant flight, Fräulein von Weber."

So her name was von Weber, her destination Hamburg. Willi repeated the information to himself silently.

He placed the valises on the luggage cart and told his partner he'd be right back, it was his kidneys, the schnapps and beer last night. Willi hurried toward the men's room, then beyond to the telephones.

And the travel bureau began to write its ticket on Erika Graf.

For Horst Rossbach, concierge at the Hotel Vier Jahreszeiten on Maximillianstrasse in Munich, it was a day like those golden days before the war. For most of his sixty years Rossbach had taken vicarious pleasure in the conspicuous consumption of the guests at Munich's most luxurious hotel. Since the war there was too little of it, the fatherland only lately back on its feet, profiteers and parvenus emerging from the ruins to blink uncertainly in the bright light of the new Germany. But once in a long while appeared someone like the tall beautiful Margit von Weber, who had swept through the lobby that morning, someone with style, taste, breeding. Rossbach could not place her branch of the family, which he assumed from her accent was Prussian, but he knew Margit von Weber's social caste. He could tell just from her shopping habits. All day, from the most elegant and exclusive of Munich's shops, the uniformed boys had been arriving.

"Package for Fräulein von Weber."

"Kindly have this delivered to Fräulein von Weber."

"For Fräulein von Weber, please sign here."

At four that afternoon she returned to the hotel, hatless now, her blonde hair sparkling with raindrops. Horst Rossbach had her key ready in his hand and a cordial but deferential smile on his face as she came to the desk. Then he had his first close look at her, and with it his perfect day ended.

He would make the telephone call, of course. Business was business, he could use the money. But he felt a profound sadness.

At the filling station outside Ventimiglia, the last on the Italian Riviera before the border, the attendant was whistling. It was a balmy April day, and he was in love with life. The whistle dropped to one steady sustained note when he saw the car pulling in, a silver Mercedes gull-wing roadster. It rose abruptly again when he got a look at the Teutonic beauty behind the wheel.

She rolled the window down and fanned three gas coupons. "Use these up, then stop."

Fairly good Italian, he thought. Of course, she could be deaf and dumb and still earn him ten thousand lire for one phone call. But seeing her now, twice as gorgeous as in the photograph, he suddenly wanted a personal bonus. A smile, perhaps a little flirtation . . .

What the hell, he decided, it's spring, it's the land of *amore*, what can I lose?

"Some car you have, signorina." With his best smile. "So perfect, in fact, it's almost good enough for you."

She lit a cigarette, looking past him straight at the *probito fumare* sign.

"Won't go far on thirty liters, though. You don't think maybe you ought to get more?"

"No."

"Must be you're not going far, then. Let me guess. Heading for Monaco?"

"Isn't everybody?"

"They will be, once they know you are." Another smile. She blew a plume of smoke and turned toward him. "Clean the windshield.

"Check the battery.

"Check the oil."

He shrugged and picked up the bucket and sponge.

He wished he were rich and famous as well as young and handsome. He wished he were the kind of guy that got invited to the royal wedding in Monaco. Not that Grace Kelly had anything on this big blonde Kraut. Too bad she wasn't more friendly, though.

When he finished, she handed him the coupons. No tip.

"Arrivederci, bellissima."

He watched her drive off along the Mediterranean coast toward the French frontier, where clouds billowed and roiled about the first range of pre-Alpine foothills. The brilliant spring sunshine was deceptive, the steady wind from the west a sure sign of rain.

He smiled. Millionaires got rained on too.

Reinhard Gehlen slipped the last paper back into the dossier and tapped his desk in satisfaction. The travel bureau was his baby, and once again it had not let him down. For loose surveillance, there was nothing like it.

The day after Southard's request, the photograph of Erika was already being shown to auxiliary agents throughout Europe. They worked in the continent's airports and railroad stations, along its highways, in the hotels and restaurants of its principal cities. They were baggage handlers and ticket sellers and stewardesses and postal clerks, bartenders, waiters, doormen, taxi drivers. They were even, occasionally, travel agents. They were local police and "friendlies" in cooperating intelligence services. Some few were junior opposition agents moonlighting.

The advantage of these auxiliaries was that they knew nothing. They did not know each other. They did not know, beyond their own cutouts, who had ordered surveillance or why. They did not know when they were being tested, so they were generally reliable.

But the best part was that the subject knew nothing

either. The travel bureau stayed in place. Only the subject moved, followed by reports, preceded by alerts, watched over by a net that could not be shaken because it could not even be seen.

Reinhard Gehlen reached across the dossier for the telephone.

The limousine pulled away from the curb before Southard had settled into the soft leather seat. All around the passenger compartment shades were drawn, so he could not see the streets of Munich, but he could hear the hiss of tires on the rain-slick pavement. As before he waited for Gehlen to speak.

"Your bird's come to roost in France. On the most glittering stretch of the Riviera, complete with her gull-wing Mercedes and her chic new wardrobe." Gehlen chuckled. "Whatever she's up to, she's doing it in high capitalist style."

"Still calling herself Margit von Weber?"

"Yes. She's at the Réserve in Beaulieu-sur-Mer for a few days. She told them she didn't know how long."

Southard barely considered calling on the Agency's French resources for close surveillance. It would take too long to mobilize enough manpower, even if he could justify it. Besides, the minute he checked in, Washington would hit the roof. He had come too far now to quit empty-handed.

"Who do you use in France?" he asked Gehlen.

"Depends. There's the SDECE. Naturally we always keep a channel open to them, but frankly they're a poor choice."

That was exactly the Agency's attitude. The French intelligence service played its own unpredictable game.

"Who else?" Southard asked.

"Well, *le Milieu*, of course."

"Of course." It amused Southard that both Gehlen and the Agency preferred doing business with the French underworld. "Get them onto her right away, will you? And tell them I'll be on the first flight tomorrow."

"Who pays?"

Southard did not answer.

"Your credit isn't endless, you know." Gehlen sighed. "I'll make the arrangements."

2

Venturino exchanged his chips for crisp new ten-thousand-franc notes and crossed the Cercle Privé to the roulette table. Ari was just leaving his usual place to the left of the croupier. You could set your watch by Ari. A dapper man with a saturnine face and sleek black hair, Ari sat down at midnight and rose precisely six hours later, signaling the beginning and the end of the serious gaming in the Monte Carlo casino.

Venturino punched the smaller man's shoulder. "Win any of your own dough?" he asked in his deep voice. Giovanni Venturino was tall and broad in a midnight-blue dinner jacket, and at forty-nine his face was still stamped with the menacing good looks and ageless virility that had always drawn women to him. In America, Giovanni Venturino would have been called a millionaire sportsman; in Monte Carlo he was known, more accurately, as a retired boss of the Union Corse, France's Mafia. Now he had friends in *le Milieu* and friends in *le tout Paris,* and the Hollywood crowd who had come over for the wedding all knew him.

With Ari he walked through the gallery from the Cercle Privé to the American Room with its blackjack and craps tables. Venturino held Ari's elbow lightly, but it was difficult for the big man to do anything with a delicate touch and it almost seemed he was forcibly evicting the Greek from the room.

When they crossed the American Room to the bar, the barman was ready with filled glasses. *"Bon soir*, Monsieur Onassis, Monsieur Venturino."

Onassis drank Dom Perignon, Venturino a glass of Patrimonio, the deep red Corsican wine stocked by the casino for him.

"How can you drink that stuff?" Ari asked.

"Like mother's milk," Venturino said. "Good for the digestion."

"Maybe I ought to try it. The kid's been giving me an ulcer. Before I got his royal okay to buy the casino, you know what I had to do? I had to get him a boat to play with."

By "the kid" Ari meant Prince Rainier III of Monaco, and the "boat" was the royal yacht *Deo Jovante II*, which, at week's end, would take Prince Rainier and his bride Grace Kelly on their honeymoon.

"All I did," Ari complained, "was save the Société des Bains-de-Mer, not to mention the whole fucking principality, from bankruptcy."

Venturino grinned. His teeth were large, white and uncapped. "Sure, Ari, you're the most altruistic guy I ever met. You should remember that line about the boat, though. The reporters will love you for it."

"They already love me, I'm a billionaire."

Venturino punched the Greek's shoulder again and crossed the central hall to the Renaissance Room to see if Tolo was still there. She was, her back to a darkened craps table, engaged in conversation with Porfirio Rubirosa.

"No, I mean it," Rubirosa was saying.

"That'll be the day."

"I am," insisted Latin America's premier playboy, "absolutely, categorically through with women. Life is difficult enough without them. I am here to gamble."

"Say that once more, and I'll quote you."

Porfirio Rubirosa slipped an arm around Tolo's back. She wore a three-tiered skirt of turquoise and white, a yoked bodice and a single strand of pearls. The full flaring skirts hid what Venturino considered the best pair of legs on the Riviera. Tolo had a stunning body. He had seen her often enough oiled against the sun on the apron of the pool at Thierry de Cheverny's villa on Cap Ferrat. But poor Tolo, Venturino thought, her face was definitely unmemorable. With a face to match the figure, she might not be a working journalist digging for items about the jet set. She might be one of them.

"Of course," said Rubirosa, his hand reappearing at Tolo's side and sliding lightly up to her breast. "I am prepared to make certain exceptions."

Tolo brushed idly at the hand. "Go win some money," she said, and when Rubirosa, left with a flashing display of expensively capped teeth, Venturino moved forward to join the girl. Then he changed his mind and stepped back toward the most active roulette table, where an old woman with a face textured and colored like a crocodile's belly had attracted a crowd with her winning streak. Venturino didn't want to see Tolo after all. Tolo was not a winner. Tolo had no future whatever.

Venturino went outside and around to the sea side of the great slab of terrace on which the Casino of Monte Carlo stood. A stiff breeze blew, and he turned up the collar of his dinner jacket. At least it wasn't raining. The overcast sky was beginning to lighten, the dawn impending—it was an hour familiar to Venturino ever since he'd run contraband to and from Italy when he was a kid who owned a single pair of shoes cut from old truck tires.

That threadbare kid had come a long way. From petty smuggling to power in the Union Corse to a raffish respectability. From the bleak hills of Corsica to the glitter of Monte Carlo and Gstaad, London and Paris. From

150

village virgins and waterfront whores to international beauties. To Margit von Weber.

He wondered how long she would stay on the Riviera this time. He knew for as long as she was here, he would devote himself to meeting her demands, in bed and elsewhere. And he would do it gladly.

He might have done it, he thought, even without party orders.

Giovanni Venturino, millionaire sportsman, had been a secret member of the Partie Communiste Française since the war. Three years with the Résistance in the Massif Central had politicized him. To be anything but a Communist in France in 1945, he believed, was unthinkable.

He met with Maurice Thorez right after the war. Thorez, secretary general of the party, was both lower-class and lowbrow, but he was shrewd.

"What the shit do you use for brains?" was his greeting. "Walking right in the front door. Jesus!"

"Because I'm in the Union, you mean? Don't worry, I'll quit." Venturino thought that Maurice Thorez couldn't risk being seen in the company of the Union Corse. But he had it backwards.

"The fuck you'll quit, I need *le Milieu* contacts. You stay in. Just as long as it takes you to get rich. And then you'll go legitimate. You may not have noticed, but some of these society types get a thrill out of rubbing shoulders with the underworld. You can exploit them for us. A lot of people do other people favors without knowing who they're helping out, if you get what I mean."

Venturino got what he meant.

"About the party. You want in, you're in. But no meetings, no card, no friends who are known PCF members. For now you're *le Milieu* and if I need a hit man or a drug dealer or the best call girl in France, I'll know

151

who to ask. And don't come near me again until I send for you."

Venturino did as he was told.

The Berlin blockade came, and the Cold War, breaking up the Popular Front in France and thinning the ranks of the PCF. Venturino's faith, as strong as the religion he'd rejected, forged in the war years in the pine forests and mountains of the Massif Central, never wavered.

When Thorez said it was time to cut his ties with the Union Corse and become that odd phenomenon, the socialite ex-gangster, Venturino was amazed at how easy it was. He had a rough charm. His amatory exploits generated the right kind of gossip in the right places. There were plenty of people glad to sponsor him. No one now would remember that among the first was Thierry de Cheverny, the man who had everything including a seat in the Chamber of Deputies—the second-ranking seat of the PCF. But Giovanni Venturino the lowborn gangster appreciated the irony of gaining an entrée into polite society through de Cheverny the highborn revolutionary.

One day a man who might have been Russian came to see him, and Venturino found he was not finished with *le Milieu* after all. He put the possible Russian in touch with some people he knew in Marseilles. In the next few months several leaders of the PCF's intellectual wing, challengers of the hard line of Thorez, died. And Venturino, the indispensable broker, knew he had graduated from living in one hazardous netherworld to living in two.

Now he walked back around the eclectic white extravagance of the casino, signaled to the parking attendant, and mounted the sweeping stairway. Inside, he found Margit von Weber in the opulent European Grand Salon playing blackjack at twenty thousand francs. He waited until the deal was completed, then moved to her side.

152

"No hurry," he said, "but the car's ready whenever you are."

She turned, the skirts of her champagne-colored bouffant gown rustling. In high-heeled satin shoes she was almost Venturino's height. "You're psychic. I just lost my last chip."

He took her arm the way he had taken Ari's, but she disengaged. He didn't explain that he meant nothing possessive by the gesture. He knew better than to try.

The Bentley came to a feather-soft stop at the foot of the stairs just as they emerged. They did not speak until they were in the car and had driven past the Hôtel de Paris and down to the harbor and behind the rock of Monaco where the toy palace stood and then west past Fontveille to the deserted lower corniche, the coast road. It began to rain, and he started the wipers.

"Any problems getting them set up?" she asked.

"No. I found a place for them in Villefranche. It's handy, about fifteen kilometers from here, five from Nice. No other houses close, and a big walled garden around it. The villa's nothing special, but it was short notice."

"After where they've just been, they won't complain." She didn't say where that was; he didn't expect her to. Whoever they were, he had no need to know. So he had more sense than to ask.

"Stop the car," she said.

He did better than that. He drove off the highway onto a narrow track at Cap-d'Ail. She came into his arms fiercely, her mouth hungry on his as they drew together.

She was using him, of course, as he had used women all his life. It didn't bother him at all. He was using her too.

Giovanni Venturino didn't believe it was any different for anyone else. They just said it was.

Chapter Eight

1

Three days of waiting, of isolation, of incessant rain—it all got on Sulayman Husayni's nerves and he took it out on Deborah.

She did her best to encourage him.

Late Monday morning she sat, feet propped on an ottoman, in the dingy salon of the small villa in the hills above Villefranche. She was reading a book from the meager collection on the recessed shelves to the left of the hearth when Sulayman came in. He removed his raincoat, shook water from it, and took a folded newspaper from an inner pocket. He gave Deborah a meaningful look—hers was the only comfortable reading chair in the room, hers the only decent reading light.

She stretched her legs, crossed them at the ankle, and ostentatiously ignored him.

Sulayman angled a chair near the window and struggled with the damp pages of the newspaper. He scanned headlines for a minute, then snorted in disgust. "How can they call this news?" he said. "Listen."

Maryam, in slacks and a roll-neck sweater, came in from the kitchen and leaned against the doorjamb, smoking a cigarette.

"Ben-Gurion," her twin brother read, "refuses to accept a cease-fire. Ben-Gurion refuses to allow fixed UN positions on the Gaza border. Ben-Gurion refuses . . ."

154

Deborah stopped listening to the words, though she heard the vitriolic tone. What choice did the Israeli prime minister have? With the Moslem Brotherhood defeated, the fedayeen would make Gaza City their staging center. A string of UN bases on the frontier would not check fedayeen terrorist raids, only Israeli counterstrikes. Unless the fedayeen were neutralized, Ben-Gurion could not bow to world opinion. And no one in Israel knew the location of the main base at El Mansûra. Deborah hadn't had even the slightest opportunity to relay this information. It had been so easy to fall in with the fedayeen, to discover their main base as she'd been instructed to do, but so difficult to pass the information on. Between their intensive training, Maryam's protective friendliness, and Sulaymen's watchful eye. . . . Was he merely jealous of her friendship with Maryam, she wondered, or was there also suspicion in his attitude? No, there was too much sulkiness; adored and adoring brother displaced in his sister's affections.

Sulayman tossed the copy of *Le Figaro* aside and began to pace. Eight steps from the window to the tiny foyer and back. "If we were in Gaza where we belong," he said, "we'd be up to our eyes in work. How long do we have to sit around here waiting?"

Maryam dragged on her cigarette. "As long as they want us to," she said calmly. "They trained us, they equipped us, they helped us against the Brotherhood. Now they expect something in return. But don't forget this is training too, Suly. When we go back home, we'll be—"

"Fully operational, like the latest weaponry. Sure, we've heard it all ten times. I still don't like the idea of doing their dirty work for them."

"But we will. So they keep on training and equipping us. And so, later, they stay on our side. You want to fight with Lee-Enfields held together with baling wire like the Ikhwan? Against Israeli tanks?"

Sulayman grumbled something and continued pacing, eight steps to the foyer and back.

The salon was like all the other rooms in the villa, small and gloomy and tastelessly furnished. But at least it no longer smelled musty. When they arrived, the first thing Deborah saw was patches of greenish mold creeping up the damp whitewashed walls. She left the twins exploring, opening and closing doors, while she lugged armloads of olive wood from the garage and foraged for tinder. By the time the twins had unloaded the Peugeot, Deborah had a roaring fire going.

That was Friday, the end of the long journey from Cairo's Almaza Airport via Rome to Nice. After clearing customs, Sulayman Husayni went to a coin locker and returned with a set of keys and an Air France flight bag. Outside the terminal, he left Maryam and Deborah under an overhang while he darted through the rain to the parking lot and came back in a gray Peugeot 303 sedan. He drove confidently through the traffic of Nice to the lower corniche and east to Villefranche. He consulted no maps, asked directions of no one. Half an hour after leaving the airport he turned up the steep lane through the pines to the villa.

There they found a stocked pantry, plenty of bedding, firewood, a few books—all they needed while they waited.

For what?

Deborah didn't ask. She had asked Sulayman about the keys and flight bag and received a look of icy superiority for answer. She wouldn't give him the satisfaction again. Nor would she risk seeming too curious.

Now he stopped pacing and pointed. "What's that junk you're reading?"

Deborah kept her eyes studiedly on the book.

Maryam sat on an arm of the sofa, lighting another cigarette. Like her brother she was dark, but they looked no

156

more Palestinian than Provençal. They were the same height, Maryam somewhat tall for a woman, her twin brother just under middle height for a man. Both had the refined features common to their branch of the big Middle Eastern Husayni clan, so different from cousin Yasir's coarseness. Maryam wore her flowing sable hair combed behind her ears to emphasize the great dark-brown Husayni eyes. At first glance her face seemed flawless, until you saw the slightest hint of the Husayni receding chin and the trace of petulance on the lips. Sulayman, with the same features, was almost too pretty.

He stood over Deborah and pulled the book from her hands. "Françoise Sagan, *Bonjour Tristesse*. Improving your mind, are you?"

Deborah snatched the book back. "It's a very sensitive story about a girl and her father."

" 'Sensitive,' " Sulayman mimicked. "It's decadent, that's what it is. Decadent and frivolous and French."

"That's right, French," Deborah said, seizing the defense he offered her, the defense Jehan might have made. "It's written in good French, modern French. And I'm getting more out of reading it than you are out of grumbling half the day in Arabic. You never read anything but your precious newspaper."

"There's nothing around here fit to read."

"Maybe not," she said, "for someone of your elevated tastes." That wasn't Jehan; it was pure Deborah.

The petty arguments had been building for three days. Sulayman turned to Maryam and shouted, "Would you get your little protégée the hell out of my hair?"

Deborah flounced to the foyer and took her raincoat from its peg. "I'll get out of your hair. I'll get out of the whole house. I'm going for a walk."

Sulayman would have disputed that too, but his sister said smoothly, "That's good, Jehan dear. You need the fresh air. If you hurry, you can pick up a bread for lunch before the bakeries close." She added sweetly to her brother, "I gather you forgot?"

Sulayman glared at Maryam. He picked up the newspaper, sat in the chair Deborah had vacated, and began turning pages.

In the foyer Deborah slid the strap of her bag over her shoulder and eased the doorlatch up. She held her breath until she was outside the villa, outside the high surrounding walls.

She walked quickly, almost ran, down the steep lane through the pines. The tile roofs of Villefranche were below her, then spreading out before her, then higher than her line of sight. Less than fifteen minutes after she left the villa she stopped a passerby on Avenue Albert Ier.

"The post office, monsieur, could you tell me where it is?"

First street on the right, two blocks, *voilà*.

She passed a bakery and retraced her steps. The bread—better get the bread now. Didn't bakeries shut at noon?

There were three customers ahead of her. The first only wanted a bread, but the next selected pastries, one for each member of the family, consulting with the old woman behind the counter. Deborah shifted from foot to foot. What time did the post office shut? Noon also?

Finally it was her turn. "A baguette, please."

She waited while the old woman shuffled on carpet slippers to the bin where the breads stood on end and scrutinized the thin, crusty loaves before withdrawing one. She glanced at her watch as the old woman made change. Almost noon. She tucked the bread inside her raincoat and ran outside.

As she pushed through the post office door, a man in a blue smock approached from the other side, carrying a cardboard sign in the form of a clock.

At the telephone desk, a woman was just removing her headset. *"Oui?"*

"The Paris directory, please."

The woman pointed to a shelf. "But hurry. Technically, we are now closed for lunch. That is to say, *my* lunch."

Deborah hurried. She found the directory and scribbled on a scrap of paper the number of the Israeli Embassy in Paris.

At the desk, the operator was buffing her nails. Deborah laid the paper before her. "This number, please. PCV to the Office of Personnel Coordination."

"PCV *and* person-to-person?" The operator dropped her nail buffer in a drawer and slammed it shut. "Come back after lunch."

"I—can't."

"And *I* can't spend my entire lunch break putting your call through. I'm sorry." She stood, not looking sorry at all.

"Wait, please! It's important. I'd be extremely grateful if you could help me." The operator raised an eyebrow, waiting for Deborah to say more. It took a moment for Deborah to understand. Then she fumbled in her bag and found a one-thousand franc note. "If you'd just try."

The woman resumed her seat and her headset. "Your name?"

"What?"

"Your name, your name. For PCV, I must have the name."

She hesitated. She could not use Deborah, nor Jehan. Should she use the name on the French passport in her bag?

"Well? If I am to ask the receiving party to accept the charges," said the woman with exaggerated patience, "it is required by regulations, not to mention by simple logic, that—"

"Corbeau, Mademoiselle Corbeau." It was her code name, Raven, in French.

Deborah, watching the woman plug in a cord and open a key, realized the name mattered only to the operator. According to her briefing, if she found herself in any country with an Israeli embassy or legation, she had only to ask for the "Office of Personnel Coordination" to reach the Mossad. She could have said the Queen of Sheba.

Deborah waited by the shelf of directories. The man in the blue smock came by, leaning on a wide push broom, rearranging cigarette stubs and scrap paper on the floor. The operator went back to buffing her nails. After ten minutes she began to speak into her headset. Then: "Booth number one, mademoiselle. And please try to be brief."

Deborah caught up the receiver and said breathlessly in Hebrew, "Office of Personnel Coordination?"

"Yes, how may I help you?" The man's voice sounded impersonal, efficient.

"Can you transmit a report to the Institute for me?"

"Of course. What routing?"

"Division II." It was the Mossad's largest, the Division of Arab Affairs.

She thought the man sighed. "You wouldn't care, miss, to be a bit more specific?"

"That's just it, I can't. You see, I was sent into Egypt last month but I had no chance to report to Cairo and now I've landed in France without a control and I'm lucky to know how to reach *you* let alone—"

"Never mind," he said briskly, "We'll just send it straight to the top and let them sort it out. What's the message?"

Deborah took a deep breath. It was hot in the booth. She swung the door partially open. The operator was staring at her. The man with the push broom stood near the street door smoking.

"My code name is Raven, reporting to Divison II from Villefranche on the Côte d'Azur, where I arrived on Friday in the company of the twins Sulayman and Maryam Husayni."

"Miss," said the voice in Paris, with an overtone of amusement, "you need not speak so slowly. I'm not transcribing in longhand. You've been recorded since you came on the line."

"Oh. Yes, of course," Deborah stammered. "Well, then —

"I reached Gaza City as projected on the morning of 24 March and established contact with the fedayeen just before their decisive confrontation with the Ikhwan. From there I accompanied the Husaynis to the fedayeen main base in the Nile delta near El Mansûra. It is, as Khan Yanis was, a training installation, and a supply depot as well. Its increased distance from the frontier makes it less vulnerable to attack, but correspondingly less threatening as a terrorist staging center."

The man in Paris cleared his throat softly. It was not for Deborah to give opinions, only information. Evaluating it was the job of Mossad specialists in Tel Aviv.

"During my two weeks at El Mansûra, I was given intensive training in a specialized unit, and thus could make only sporadic observations of the base as a whole. The Russian instructors, while apparently few, were accorded great deference. I could not determine the quantity of matériel. Smaller weapons from side arms to assault rifles were in generous supply. I saw scout cars and self-propelled guns but no tanks." Deborah's words gained strength and precision as her tongue adjusted gladly to speaking Hebrew. She gave general observations on El Mansûra, then went on to describe the Special Group and its training. "I have not been told our mission here in

161

France, but I understand that our two teams of three—the other went, I believe, to Paris—are not the first sent out of Egypt by the Russians. These European missions are represented as experience in the field, the culmination of training. But they are evidently also repayment for Russian aid—Sulayman Husayni calls it 'doing their dirty work for them.' He and his sister have no Communist sympathies; their only loyalty is to the fedayeen.

"That's all I have now. I'll try to learn more from Maryam, who regards me quite warmly. Sulayman does not, as I am neither a male nor a Husayni, yet he accepts me because—"

The man on the other end cleared his throat again, but Deborah went on. "—in the battle for Gaza City, it was I who at their headquarters shot and killed the three Germans who led the Ikhwan." She said it firmly, as though she had done only what had to be done. She said nothing about the rape. Rape was a detail of no interest to the Mossad, like personal opinions.

The voice in Paris held a new note of respect. "What support can we give you now? Do you want a ticket home?"

She hadn't expected that.

She thought of Daddy Sam, big and shambling and bearlike, and the ache of missing him almost made her say yes right away. She could see the two of them sitting over endless pots of coffee in the kitchen of the apartment on Dizengoff Street while they talked of the work they now shared. Except that if she went back, they would no longer share it. She would once again be reading news for Kol Israel, a trivial job that could be done by thousands of others in that multilingual land. And she would be telling bedtime stories to bright-eyes Yemeni immigrant children who would

162

never grow up unless —

She shifted the receiver to her other hand and rubbed her sweat-slippery palm on the lining of her coat.

"No, no need. I don't think I'm under any suspicion, not so far. The present mission may not turn out to be very important, but the connection with the Husaynis will be. I'll call you again when I can, and unless you have other orders for me, I'll go on as before."

When she left the booth, the operator already had her coat on, and the man with the push broom stood by the door, ready to unlock it.

The operator gestured toward the shelf of directories. "Don't forget your bread."

Deborah tucked the baguette back inside her raincoat and hurried after her. The blue-smocked man let them out with a murmured, *"Bon Appétit."*

Cutting west toward Albert Ier, Deborah wondered what to tell Sulayman if he asked about the missing thousand francs. She could not have spent that much in a café. Perhaps she could say she gave them to a beggar. Charity was a duty in Islam.

She wondered next, climbing through the pines, whether she had told the Mossad everything important. Only when she was almost at the villa did she realize the phone call had told her something too, something about herself.

She was in for the duration.

2

Sulayman brought two gnarled, heavy olive logs in from the garage. He poked at the embers under the firedogs and placed the logs on top.

"Where the devil is she? What's taking her so long?"

163

"She's gone for a walk, that's all. The way you two have been bickering, I'd think you'd be glad to have her out for a while. Why don't you relax? It's a long time since we could sit down with a real drink and not feel we were breaking Koranic Law."

Maryam herself sat with her legs tucked under, sipping a tall Camparisoda.

"We're not here on a pleasure trip, you know. And she just makes it worse. We're going to have our hands full with her."

"I don't think so. Considering what she's gone through, I think she's coming out of it remarkably well. You must have seen the change in her."

"It's the change in you I don't like."

Sulayman went to the bar and poured Scotch over ice in an old-fashioned glass.

"Oh?" Maryam's voice was soft. And dangerous.

"You were always a born leader, even more than me. You wanted to take charge, give orders, get things done. But now you don't seem to mind how long they keep us sitting here and waiting, as long as you can play nursemaid to poor little Jehan."

"So that's it. Now we come to it."

Sulayman drained half his Scotch. "Come to what?"

"Suly dear, I know you. All right, maybe I have been babying Jehan. But the quicker she's back to normal, the more she can pull her own weight."

"And how can you say when she's normal? Actually you don't know the first thing about her."

"We know this much. We know she can kill."

"To defend herself against rape? That's hardly the same as killing on assignment."

"Not defend, avenge. And she didn't stop with Krim, remember. When we walked in there I had the feeling she was a hair's breadth away from shooting us too."

"Wonderful. So we have a compulsive killer on our hands. A homicidal maniac."

"Oh, come on, Suly. First you say she's one thing, then another."

He finished his Scotch and crossed to the sofa where she sat. "Maybe that's the point. I don't know who she is, and neither do you. The least we should do is check her out a little more thoroughly, instead of just accepting her at face value."

"The police in Gaza accepted her papers, didn't they? Besides, I'm sure our Russian friends must have verified her background. She'll be all right," Maryam said. "Don't worry about it."

"She'd better be, with all the time you've spent sheltering her under your wing."

"Instead of smoothing *your* ruffled feathers?"

She reached for her twin's hand. He shook free irritably.

"Suly dearest," she said gently, "you're not jealous of her, surely?" Again she reached up for his hand. This time he let her draw him down to sit beside her.

"We're the Husaynis. We were born together, we'll always be together." She rested her head on his shoulder, and felt the tension leave him as he began to stroke her long lush hair. "Nothing will ever change that."

3

Southard's flight touched down at Nice-Côte d'Azur Airport a few minutes after noon. Tarmac and sky were dark with rain and the Mediterranean could manage only a dull pewter color.

Traveling with a single carry-on suitcase, Southard was through to the arrivals rotunda ten minutes after landing. He bought a pack of cigarettes and a *Paris Herald-Tribune* at the newsstand and started for the exit.

"Here, let me take that."

The man who fell into step with Southard had a raincoat folded over his arm and wore a cheap gray suit that looked, like most ready-made clothing in France, half wool and half cardboard. He was a nimble little man with protuberant ears and eyes like small black marbles. As he reached for the suitcase, which the Gehlen people had supplied with stickers from the Hotel Kempinski in Berlin and the Zum Ritter in Heidelberg, he said:

"I'm called Le Matou. Welcome to the sunny south coast."

In the parking lot he tossed the suitcase into the back of a tan Deux Chevaux. The seats of the tiny car bounced and swayed on interior springs as Le Matou drove along the coast into Nice and threaded through the traffic on the Promenade des Anglais.

"What have you got for me?" Southard asked.

Le Matou removed one hand from the steering wheel long enough to kiss the fingers and open them as if releasing a tiny bird to flight. "She is a Valkyrie, that one. They don't make women like that in France."

A horn blared. Le Matou narrowly avoided a black Jaguar with British plates. He shook his fist and cursed steadily for thirty seconds in an argot Southard couldn't understand. Then he made a definitive statement about British drivers and buggery, accepted a cigarette, and returned to Southard's question.

"Give me an hour or so, my friend, and I'll have more. Unless they hit a problem, the morning team won't report in until they've eaten."

"Any problems so far?"

"Of course not," said Le Matou, as if offended. "We are very competent, none better. It is just that we have yet to establish her routine."

Le Matou parked the tiny car in a space that hadn't seemed large enough for a motorcycle. He dialed the time on a cardboard clockface and stuck it inside the windshield. "From here we walk. What do I call you, my friend?"

"Beck."

Le Matou repeated the name, "German, are you? I'd have guessed English or American."

"Would you? Don't tell me my accent's that bad." Southard reached behind the seat. "I'll take the suitcase."

Southard crossed the drafty, high-ceilinged room and opened the French windows onto the balcony. Three stories below, the narrow street of shops in the heart of Nice's Old Town was quiet, business suspended for lunch, the displays of merchandise that spilled from the tiny shops covered now by awnings and tarpaulins. A block away the bells of Ste. Réparate struck one. An occasional pedestrian hurried by under an umbrella; the street was too narrow and crowded for cars.

Southard unpacked quickly and spent a few minutes skimming the *Paris Trib*, then changed his suit coat for an old wool sweater. He decided against shaving. He went downstairs and out past a row of mailboxes with no names on them and back inside the yellow stucco building's ground-floor café. Between the hour and the rain, it was mobbed with shopkeepers still wearing their aprons and men dressed in electric blue work smocks and in cardboard suits like Le Matou's and women in dark dresses and carpet slippers. The women were overweight and slovenly. The men were small and quick, gesticulating as they talked, touching each other frequently for reassurance as they conducted their business over coffee or red wine. They seemed more Italian than French: they were Niçois.

Southard took the café's copy of *Nice-Matin* from the rack near the cash register and found a vacant chair, sharing a small table with a fat man eating a huge round sandwich from which black olives and rings of onion fell whenever he squeezed the bread to get his jowls around it. Southard browsed the local news for five minutes until the lone harried waiter appeared. He ordered a carafe of red wine and whatever his companion was having.

"One *pan bagnat* coming up."

The wine came first. Southard drank one glass, poured another and finished the newspaper. He leaned back and listened to the din around him, too loud to distinguish conversations.

He wondered what it would be like to lead a normal life, to commute to an office, return every night to his wife in the suburbs, raise a couple of kids, join a country club and the PTA. He wondered if Gideon Parr had ever had such thoughts, growing sentimental over a life he'd never had.

He reached for his wine again. There were always a few moments like that in a new place, before it became real, before he could feel involved in why he had come.

The waiter with his *pan bagnat* arrived at the same time as Le Matou, who growled at the fat man, "Stuff the rest of that down your maw and beat it."

The fat man gave Southard a reproachful look for having such friends, but in ten seconds he was on his feet, retreating, still chewing. Le Matou took his chair.

"Either fear or love, nothing else works. Me, I don't much inspire love." He grinned. "Except with women."

Southard moved his sandwich aside and waited for Le Matou to report. His appearance had brought Southard back into himself. He was here, he was now; he felt almost grateful.

Le Matou hunched himself over a glass of draft beer, shaking his wet head. "People come here for the weather, now that's a joke, eh?" He saluted Southard with his glass and drank.

"So. About your lady friend. She calls herself Margit von Weber. Drives a silver gull-wing Mercedes 300SL with Hamburg number plates and enough luggage to suggest it's no weekend visit."

"Your people get a look at the car registration?"

Le Matou nodded. "Either the papers are superb fakes or La Weber owns it. Passport looks genuine too, according to the desk of the Réserve in Beaulieu, where she's staying. Says she's a West German citizen, born in Silesia, thirty-two years old, no distinguishing scars or marks." Le Matou laughed. "I wouldn't mind checking that part myself."

He picked up his empty beer glass and went to the bar, where he leaned over and worked the tap himself. Southard lifted the top of his big round sandwich and inspected the contents, which included hard-boiled egg, black olives, four kinds of raw sliced vegetables and two kinds of fish. Le Matou, resuming his chair, said, "Ought to be anchovies *or* tuna, not both. Everything's getting corrupted nowadays."

Southard glanced up, ready to acknowledge the joke, and saw that Le Matou had intended none. He said quickly: "How far have you been able to follow her movements?"

"We've had some reconstructing to do." Le Matou made it sound like a reproach. "She's been here all weekend. Seems she's been on the phone a lot with real estate agents, and out looking at villas. She doesn't seem to mind where—right here in Nice, as far west as Cannes, and all the way past Monaco to the Italian border—as long as they're real villas. I mean big, expensive, private places. She's looking for a furnished rental."

"For how long?"

"The rest of the year, more or less. The summer's going to be the problem, especially August. The first week of *les grandes vacances,* they turn the whole N7 south from Paris into a one-way street leading right here," Le Matou said. "But she'll find a place, the kind of dough she's offering. Jesus, don't some people have it all? She was first in line when they were handing out looks *and* money."

"She been seeing anybody but real estate agents?"

"Yes indeed, she leads a very full social life. Parties on Cap Ferrat, gambling at the Monte Carlo casino until dawn, the usual. Her escort, most of the time, is a sort of ex-colleague of mine named Venturino. He's what they call socially presentable. You know how it is, a bigshot in the Union Corse goes legit, and all of a sudden he's a socialite?"

Southard said he knew how it was.

"Last night, though, she was out for a while without Venturino. She drove up alone in that gull-wing roadster of hers to a little village in the hills near Vence. You know the area?"

"Not at firsthand. Isn't that where Picasso lives?"

"No, he's closer to the coast. You're probably thinking of Marc Chagall," said Le Matou, surprising Southard with his knowledge. "Chagall lives in St. Paul de Vence. It's painter country all around there. And it was a painter La Weber had dinner with, an American named Kip Chaffee. Not quite Picasso or Chagall maybe, but the galleries eat up—" Le Matou looked at Southard speculatively. "I think I just struck a responsive chord. You know this Chaffee?"

Southard wondered what involuntary flicker Le Matou had detected. Then he wondered why he bothered to wonder. He and Gideon Parr had remarked it often enough, how much the professional spy and criminal had in common. And Le Matou was tops in his line.

"Know him? Only by reputation," he said blandly. Kip Chaffee worked for the CIA.

Le Matou shrugged. "So it's none of my business. Anyway, that brings us almost up to date. She got up late today, true to form, and came into Nice. Last report was she was having a drink, and probably lunch, with the journalist Marie-Claude Tolosano." Le Matou showed his hands palms up on the table. "And there you are, my friend."

Yes, here he was. But where was that?

He had traced Erika Graf from the death of Gideon Parr to the arrest of Miklos Manyoki in Budapest to her meetings with Kossior in Berlin to her current gaudy impersonation on the French Riviera, and he was getting less and less hopeful that every step was linked. Her contacts with the GRU colonel could just have marked the end of one assignment and the beginning of another. After all, the Russians often employed MfS agents, especially in the West, just as the CIA used the Gehlen Group; both liked to keep their own people out of the trenches. And for work in the West, the Russians could hardly come up with a home-grown product to match Erika Graf.

Nothing she had done since leaving Berlin had an obvious explanation, least of all her meeting with Chaffee. Southard could not imagine how she had an acquaintance, let alone business, with him. But Chaffee was a further indication she had moved on to something new. Southard had used the last of his credit with Gehlen on a wild goose chase, and if he didn't check in soon with the Agency he'd have no credit left there either. He already had an enemy, or at least an antagonist, in Adam Prestridge.

". . . you to decide which, if any," Le Matou was saying, "but if you share the aversion to Communists of our mutual friend in Munich, you might think Tolo merits a watchful eye."

Southard had been thinking his own thoughts, none of them pleasant, but now he paid full attention. "What did you say?"

"That as the journalist Marie-Claude Tolosano is a known member of the Partie Communiste Française—"

"Tolo. You said Tolo."

"But of couse. That's how she signs her columns. Tolo."

Southard felt the smile building on his face.

He went to the newspaper rack, took down *Nice-Matin* from where he had replaced it just twenty minutes before, and flipped to the remembered article.

It was a gushing exercise in name-dropping, recounting gown by gown and course by course the dinner party given the previous night by Prince Rainier's sister Antoinette at her villa in Èze. Another half-page was devoted to flash-lit photos of celebrities leaving the villa. The Gregory Pecks, the David Nivens . . . there it was, the shot of a French politician Southard had recognized and a woman he hadn't. The caption read, "M. Thierry de Cheverny, Député for the Alpes-Maritimes, with your own Tolo."

Thierry de Cheverny, whose power in the Partie Communiste Française was second only to that of Maurice Thorez. Thierry de Cheverny, who had been in Moscow with the French delegation to the 20th Party Congress.

Southard had his connection.

Chapter Nine

1

For six centuries the ancestors of Prince Rainier III had reigned over Monaco, ever since a medieval member of the House of Grimaldi had bought the tiny principality from Genoa. But if they reigned, they did not always rule. The tides of history washed turbulently over that rocky corner of the Mediterranean coast, and it was invested in turn by France, Spain, even Sardinia. Independence came only after the defeat of Napoleon in 1814.

Independence meant no taxes, and no conscription into the French Army. However, the Treaty of Paris provided that Monaco, should its prince die without issue, would revert to French rule, French taxes, the French draft, possibly even French bad manners. And to the dismay of his Monegasque subjects, Rainier III, into his early thirties, was still savoring life as a bachelor.

Until he met Miss Grace Kelly of Philadelphia and Hollywood.

From that point, the script could have come from MGM; the bride's studio did in fact furnish the wedding gown. Now the Kellys of Philadelphia were in town, half of Hollywood with them, and on Wednesday, April 18, Grace Kelly would become Her Most Serene Highness Princess Gracia Patricia of Monaco.

On Tuesday it was still raining.

Few native Monegasques objected to this meteorological

faux pas. They were used to it; it generally rained in April in Monaco. But this April it rained intermittently, sometimes inordinately, for five straight days before the wedding. Tempers grew short. A certain amount of complaining was heard.

The aged novelist W. Somerset Maugham, living on nearby Cap Ferrat, complained forthrightly of the damp and the cold.

Randolph Churchill, Winston's son, complained with a sniff that he hadn't come to Monaco to mix with riffraff like the Kellys of Philadelphia.

King Farouk, ex-monarch of Egypt, complained vigorously when a palace envoy intimated it would be gauche for his Albanian bodyguards to wear their flamboyant uniforms anywhere within the principality's 368 acres.

Conrad Hilton, representing President Eisenhower, complained that Monaco was not an appropriate site for a Hilton hotel.

Clementine Paddleford, food columnist of the *New York Herald-Tribune*, complained that she was kept waiting eight hours for an audience—with the palace chef.

Prince Rainier complained about the press photographers.

The press photographers complained about Prince Rainier.

Maree Pamp, bridesmaid, and Mrs. Matthew McCloskey, guest, both of Philadelphia, complained that jewelry worth six and forty-eight thousand dollars respectively was stolen from their rooms in Monte Carlo's fashionable Hotel de Paris.

Jewel thieves from *Le Milieu* complained that, with the rain, hotel guests spent too much time in their rooms.

The police complained of overwork.

Tolo's complaint, voiced to Thierry de Cheverny over a

cup of black coffee, was the bitter resumption of an argument begun the night before.

"You're getting tired of me."

"Ridiculous," said Thierry de Cheverny.

They sat side by side, theatrically careful not to touch, in the large canopied bed (Madame de Pompadour had slept in it) in the master bedroom of the de Cheverny *mas,* a forty-room Provençal-style villa not far from the medieval village of Èze perched on its rock spire fifteen hundred feet above the Mediterranean a few miles west of Monaco.

"Then you must be in love with someone else."

De Cheverny sighed. "This has nothing to do with love. Or even sex."

"Everything has something to do with sex."

"I only said I thought we shouldn't see each other for a while."

"And *that* has nothing to do with sex?" Tolo placed cup and saucer on the night table and swung her feet off the edge of the bed. Below the plain face and tousled no-color hair, her breasts were perfect, high and firm, with hard little nipples centered in unpuckered tan aureoles. "Tell me what it has to do with then."

"You're upset."

"I am not upset!" shouted Tolo. "You will know when I am upset!" She gestured effusively with raised arms. The perfect breasts lifted, jutted, flared. "I will make it clear when I am upset!"

Again de Cheverny sighed. Seeing Tolo like that, it was difficult to proceed logically. "It has to do with my career. And with yours. We are both in considerable jeopardy."

"Must you sound so dramatic, Thierry? They're only a political party."

"Don't be naive, *chérie.*"

Tolo went barefoot across the floor to pull the windows inward and push the shutters out. Sunlight burst into the room. "Look at that," she marveled. "It's completely

175

stopped raining."

"How can you stand there talking about the weather?"

"I'm making more sense than you are." Tolo stood silhouetted against the morning brightness, her arms crossed under the perfect breasts.

"You don't understand how furious Thorez is," de Cheverny tried to explain. "When I got back from Moscow, I thought the mood of the party was shifting, that they were ready to try a few baby steps without holding onto Mother Russia's hand. But I misguessed badly. When those articles of yours were published, Thorez can have had no doubt who leaked the information to you. There's no telling how the party will choose to deal with me."

"Come now, they don't have purges here. Besides, they wouldn't dare do anything to you. You're Thierry de Cheverny."

"Perhaps you're right. If they don't need me, they need my name. They do not, however, need yours."

While he was speaking, Tolo had begun to dress. With that glorious body covered, it was easier to say the cruel words. He spoke to the sad, plain face.

"We mustn't be seen together; it would only remind them. I'll have to spend more time in Paris mending fences. And you, my flower, will be well advised to give up the political columns and let them forget you ever tried to rise above your station as a society-page scribbler.

"Above my station . . . society-page scribbler!"

Tolo retrieved Sevres cup and saucer from the night table and hurled them at him. They struck the headboard. The crash of china was followed by other sounds—her howl of anguish, the tattoo of her heels in the corridor and on the stairs, the roar of her car's engine in the courtyard below.

From the window, Thierry de Cheverny could have watched her drive off. He stayed in bed.

At noon they left the Peugeot in the Fontveille parking lot and made their way into town on foot. It was a brilliant day, a technicolor day, the air washed clear, the sky azure, the sunlight golden, the red and white Monegasque flags lining the road flapping stiffly in the breeze. The streets of Monaco were clogged with cars and the sidewalks with pedestrians. Souvenir vendors hawked their wares on every corner.

The man called Giovanni was waiting for them just outside the cliffside gardens of St. Martin. He gestured in the direction of the Oceanographic Museum. "She's in there."

They strolled along the shady paths toward the museum, Sulayman in earnest conversation with Giovanni, the two girls behind.

As they neared the main entrance to the building, Giovanni stopped them. "She should be coming out that doorway in just a few minutes. I'll let you know."

Inside the building it was almost impossible to hear, or even to move. The main gallery of the Oceanographic Museum had been converted into a press center for the two-thousand-odd reporters and photographers who were in Monaco for the wedding, and it seemed to Tolo that a good quarter of those were there right now. As they moved toward the exit together, she spoke directly into the ear of her blonde companion. "At least tell me who it is I'm to meet."

"You'll find out tonight. If you keep the appointment, that is."

"Of course I will," Tolo assured her. "But why so mysterious?"

Margit von Weber shook her head and smiled. "I didn't let you down the last time, did I?"

For answer Tolo smiled back.

The last time had been close to two years ago. Margit von Weber had spent four months on the Riviera then, her only previous visit that Tolo knew of. With her obvious wealth and beauty, she was soon seen in all the right places with all the right people, an accepted part of the footloose international set that wintered on the Côte d'Azur when they weren't skiing in Gstaad or St. Moritz. Covering their antics for the society pages of *Nice-Matin* was then Tolo's full-time job.

It was Margit von Weber who gave Tolo her first hard-news break, a break that opened up the chance to do some straight reporting, even political writing, and ultimately brought her to the attention of Thierry de Cheverny. Though Tolo received the German woman's lead with initial skepticism, she followed it. She dug into the background of a nightclub bouncer who was stabbed to death one night in Nice. The police knew little about the victim and less about who killed him. Tolo solved one of those questions at least. She discovered that the dead man was Günther Pohl, once deputy commander of Auschwitz.

Tolo had a scoop.

The day her by-lined exclusive made the front page of *Nice-Matin*, and was picked up by everyone from Agence France Presse to the international wire services, Tolo tried to call Margit von Weber to thank her, but she had left France. Now she was back, promising another break in Tolo's career just when she needed it most.

They made their way past the model of the whaling boat inside the main entrance of the museum.

Tolo was beginning to suspect that the mysterious Margit von Weber might just turn out to be the biggest story of all.

"That's her," Giovanni said. "Here she comes."

"The tall blonde?" Maryam asked. "How attractive she is!"

178

"No, the one with her, the little mouse," Giovanni said.

Not twenty feet away, the two women walked past them through a crowd of newspapermen.

Deborah did not see the one Giovanni called the little mouse, once she saw the tall blonde. Though the pale eyes swept past her indifferently, Deborah's heart began to pound.

She had told herself that, returning to Europe, she might stir painful memories. But this, how could she have expected it? It would have been a shock even if she had been in Germany to see a woman so much like the other one a decade ago—the same height, facial contours, coloring.

Deborah closed her eyes but the picture grew stronger and for a moment she was a child again, hysterical with the fear of dying.

She forced herself to breathe deeply. When she opened her eyes she was once more a twenty-four-year-old Mossad agent, and the woman she watched walking away was a tall blonde she had never met.

"Until tonight then," Erika said as Tolo climbed into her car and raised the visor to which her press card was clipped. Tolo waved and Erika watched her drive off.

She turned toward the entrance of the museum, but they were gone.

How much, she wondered, would a face change in eleven years? Her own had, and she'd already been an adult then. If the Jewish child had survived Auschwitz, how much would she resemble that pretty Arab girl? Erika had let her eyes slide right over the girl, but the image was still in her mind, and she could not shake the feeling of recognition.

Nonsense, she told herself. It was only a week since she had seen the girl's photograph in Quast's office; of course the girl seemed familiar. All the rest was just overwrought nerves.

Being on the Riviera reminded Erika how long it had

been since her last vacation.

3

Le Matou and Southard sat at a sidewalk café overlooking the port, gazing out past the swaying masts of smaller boats to Onassis's gigantic yacht. Southard was drinking a *pastis*. Le Matou drained his beer.

"It's Venturino I don't understand," said Le Matou with a frown. "The two women went there and met, obviously by arrangement. But Venturino went there too, and then carefully *didn't* meet them."

"Also obviously by arrangement," Southard said.

"How's that? When he showed up with those three kids, I'd have sworn the point was to get them together."

"It must have been," Southard agreed. "But the introduction was one-sided. When the German woman and Tolo came outside, they barely glanced around, but those three kids took a long look. Who are they, anyway, *Milieu?*"

"If they are, they're not local. They looked like they could come from Corsica, though."

Southard finished his drink and lit a cigarette. Le Matou signaled the waiter, but Southard shook his head.

"Whoever they are, Venturino brought them so he could point out one of the women to them, after he'd set it up with the other one."

"You mean," said Le Matou, "The von Weber woman had Venturino finger Tolo, and the three kids are going to tail her or something?"

"Sure. But there's the other possibility. Venturino knows both women—it could be Tolo set it up, and the German is the target."

Le Matou's small dark eyes blinked in the bright sunlight. "But why?"

"Maybe he has reasons, like us, for wanting to know just

what she's doing here. It's a long shot, I'd say, but worth considering too."

Le Matou nodded thoughtfully. He didn't speak for several seconds.

"You have a commendable mind," he told Southard, "for a foreigner."

4

"Then you get rid of the guns," Sulayman told Deborah.

He had been talking steadily for twenty minutes, relaying instructions ever since his return by bus from Monte Carlo.

"We meet at the parking lot in Fontveille, drive into Nice and leave the car in a garage for Giovanni to pick up. Then we spend the night at a hotel and take the morning train to Paris."

Sulayman took three rolls of banknotes from the blue Air France flight bag, each fastened with a rubber band. "A hundred thousand francs each," he said, distributing the money. "Enough to reach Paris and live a few days in case there's trouble and we have to separate."

"Why should there be trouble?" Maryam asked her brother.

"There shouldn't. This is just in case. Now, if we do separate, get to Paris the best way you can. Go to the Café Rotonde on the corner of Raspail and Montparnasse between seven and closing. A man will come around every hour or so selling windup toys. You buy one, say it's for your nephew Giovanni. He'll be there every night till Sunday if necessary. If you're delayed beyond then, go to the Egyptian Embassy and contact the Mukhabarat people the standard way."

The chances of anything going wrong, Deborah thought, were minimal. The purpose of the meticulous details of rendezvous was to prevent them dwelling on what they

181

would do tonight.

Sulayman reached into the flight bag again and casually tossed Deborah a Beretta 935 automatic. She caught it virtually by reflex, checked the safety, gripped it by the barrel, extracted the clip from the butt, placed the pistol on the table and held out her hand for the box of 7.65-mm ammunition. When Sulayman slapped that in her palm she loaded seven rounds, picked up the Beretta, slammed the clip back into the butt and stared defiantly at him.

Sulayman handed an identical weapon to Maryam and began to load a third. All of them had done it a hundred times blindfolded at El Mansûra.

Doing it now, seeing them do it, made everything finally real to Deborah. They had been chosen, trained, sent here as a fedayeen hit team.

This time, of course, she would only be the backup member. She wondered whether they had given her that assignment out of kindness. Or because they didn't trust her. Or just to be selfish.

Chapter Ten

1

The crowd milled ten or twelve deep behind the roped-off section of the waterfront, but Southard found Le Matou where he had been told to look, near the east end, the seaward end of the Quai des Ètats-Unis. It was eleven-thirty. The little man stood behind the last uneven row of spectators, gazing skyward, his face reflecting the almost continuous display of light bursting above. In the time it took Southard to recognize him, he turned an eerie green, blue, red, pulsating yellow. Then the sky went dark.

Southard heard the rushing noise and then the collective *aaah!* from the crowd and then the loud crack that signaled the next display. Soon it sounded like an artillery barrage overhead and looked like the Northern Lights. Clouds of smoke drifted down carrying the smell of gunpowder, to be dissipated by the cold onshore breeze. On the waterfront itself spun huge hissing pinwheels of fire. The crowd said *aaaaah!* again as brilliant multicolored fountains of light showered the sky, each spawning a different-colored starburst. The hissing pinwheels on the waterfront became a cascade of golden light. Roman candles whizzed skyward on steep trajectories, burning orange trails through the night. Red and white parachute flares drifted down in tandem toward the royal yacht, the *Deo Jovante II*, bouncing the Monegasque colors off its hull. The crowd applauded and so did Le Matou.

"I'm still a kid when it comes to fireworks," he said.

Southard watched the sky burning. "What?"

Le Matou laughed. "You too, eh?"

For an instant Southard had been back in Tidewater, Virginia, on a long-ago Fourth of July, when he was still young enough to believe that the whole world celebrated Independence Day.

"Here's the situation," Le Matou said. "I've got a dozen people circulating in the crowd. One of them spotted Margit von Weber and then lost her, but she's around. And two of my *copains* have been sticking like glue to the Tolosano woman since nightfall."

"Where is she?"

The sky rattled and shook and slid toward the sea in a tide of silver and gold.

"What did you say?" Le Matou shouted.

"I said, 'where is she?' "

"Right there behind you, at a third-row table outside the café. My *copains* are at the table behind her."

"What about Venturino and his three pals?" Southard asked.

"No sign of Venturino. And believe me, my boys would know him even in a better disguise than yours."

Since arriving, Southard had supplemented his old sweater with a cheap cloth cap and espadrilles. The trousers, though his own, needed pressing. If he was not exactly disguised, he no longer stood out as a foreigner.

"But would they know the other three?" he asked.

In the dying golden glow Le Matou shrugged. "What kind of description could I give? I'm not sure I'd recognize them myself. Would you?"

The three, Southard recalled, were of an age, early-middle twenties; dark, as if they'd cultivated their tans all winter; Mediterranean types, maybe *pieds-noirs* up from

Algeria; a vague impression of healthy good looks. The taller girl resembled the boy strongly. But Southard's eyes, like Le Matou's, had been on the principals — Erika Graf, Tolo, Venturino.

"Maybe not," he said, "unless all three were together."

He turned, scanning the tables outside the Café des Flots. In the eerie light he could not pick out the plain, unmemorable face of Tolo.

Why is she here? he asked himself. As the society reporter for the big local paper, she ought to have no time to draw a breath tonight from dusk to dawn. She must be waiting here at Erika's behest. Could she conceivably be working with Erika?

No, Southard decided, but she might think she was.

He had spent the late afternoon digging through back issues of *Nice-Matin*, reading the political columns signed *Tolo*. Her commentary had a breathless quality, ten parts Walter Winchell to one part Walter Lippmann. Innuendo and speculation substituted for hard fact. Tolo dropped political names like a society writer adrift on the editorial page. Her questions were phrased to suggest the answers, and they took on added interest for Southard after the return from Moscow of her lover Thierry de Cheverny. Everything was still vague and unsubstantiated — 20th Party Congress . . . Khrushchev's secret midnight meeting . . . distressing fate of Hungarian delegate Miklos Manyoki . . . danger here in France of slavish pro-Russian attitude among Neanderthals in the PCF — but by the latest column Tolo was becoming, for her, almost specific. Too specific, it seemed, for the tastes of Mother Russia, and her slant too critical of Russia's party line.

Southard regretted briefly that Tolo could not be warned. But that would only alert Erika. She would accomplish whatever she wanted in some other way, and much less openly. Southard had to learn what he could now while Tolo, innocent bystander, victim of her own naïveté, took her chances with Erika.

Corruscating streaks of fire spanned the sky. Le Matou watched, his neck craned. Southard touched his elbow. "Point her out to me." He turned back toward the tables outside the café, five rows of them flanked by plate-glass partitions to protect the patrons from chill breezes. As the Frenchman raised his arm, the sky darkened.

With a single great burst of light over the harbor, an enormous explosion so strong that Southard could feel the shock wave in his ears, it was over.

The tightly packed spectators moved back from the edge of the quay. They eddied around Southard and Le Matou and began to stream west along the broad promenade. Southard saw the flare of matches and lighters, smelled burning punk. Hand-held sparklers traced patterns in the night. There was laughter and singing. The first few firecrackers were thrown in the general direction of the sea. The professionals had finished. Now it was amateur night.

A hurled cherry bomb went off just outside the café, sounding exactly like a gunshot. In mid-cry a woman's scream broke on a note of nervous laughter. Southard pushed his way through the surging crowd.

The café was brightly lighted from within now and the lamposts along the edge of the quay had come on. Someone lit a string of firecrackers and tossed it, the explosive bursts coming at close intervals like sustained rifle fire.

Near the plate-glass wall at the west end of the third row of tables, Southard recognized Tolo.

2

Tolo was drinking Marie Brizard anisette and black coffee. She felt a bit nostalgic, but philosophical too. Thierry de Cheverny, with his wife and children, with his demanding political life, with his roving eye, could never have lasted. Such liaisons never did. It would have ended, if not today, then next week or next month. Tolo had to look at her career now, and Margit von Weber could save it.

The German woman had been reticent, but Tolo had drawn from her enough to form certain conclusions. That Margit von Weber worked for the Bonn government as a Nazi-hunter; that certain as yet unnamed politicians here in France dealt in counterfeit papers for fugitive war criminals, if the price was right.

Tolo would have another exclusive.

Margit had said immediately after the fireworks, but in this crowd punctuality would be impossible. Tolo was virtually certain that when Margit did appear, she would not be alone. That would explain the odd choice of rendezvous. Margit was bringing someone who wanted to talk, who *would* talk to Tolo, but who wished for the time being to maintain anonymity.

Tolo raised her hand, and for once it worked for her the way it always had for Thierry de Cheverny. The busy waiter came right over. Tolo smiled up a him and told herself she must stop thinking of Thierry de Cheverny.

"Madame?"

"The same, please. Coffee and Marie Brizard."

Those were the last words she ever spoke.

She was aware of two men at the table behind her rising quickly, one of them shouting, both of them reaching for her. Time seemed to hang on the shout and the sudden movement. She saw a figure outside the plate glass—no, two figures, both pointing at her. Just standing there and pointing in the hanging moment of time, why were they doing that? One of the men from the table behind her grabbed Tolo's shoulder and tried to tumble her off her chair. Tolo resisted. She thought the waiter was coming back. He was a big man. He would help her. Tolo struggled to her feet. The plate glass exploded. Tolo's brain said, scream. But she did not have enough time left for that.

Southard was running before the glass shattered, before the first shot was fired. He had seen the two figures approaching the other side of the plate glass where Tolo sat but by then it was already too late. Even Le Matou's men right behind her could not save her once she resisted them. Southard saw the glass go first, then the four muzzle flashes. It was a boy and a tall girl, two of those he had seen with Venturino. The boy kicked in the plate glass and then they fired. Kicking the plate glass was clever. The bullets might have drilled neat holes, leaving the glass intact. The shattering glass created instant panic among the patrons of the café. Gunfire alone would not have done that, not tonight, not after the fireworks. People rushed from their chairs, some pushing toward the interior of the café, some trying to leave the terrace. Southard thought all four bullets hit Tolo. His view was blocked for an instant, but that didn't matter. He already knew which way the killers had gone. Seeing Tolo die would not have helped. He shouted, "*Viens, Matou!*" and pushed through the crowd.

Now more people were coming toward the café than leaving it. Southard fought against a solid phalanx of them, but that didn't matter either. The killers would face the same problem. Knowledge of violence always moves through a crowd impossibly fast. Southard heard more firecrackers. He heard a police whistle and, further off, another. He did not think the killers would outdistance him, not with the sound of the whistles coming from ahead of them. Even if they could run in this crush, they would not. Running, they might be stopped.

Suddenly he was free of the worst congestion, still surrounded by milling revelers but able to move, able to see. Someone lurched into him from behind. A hand fastened on his arm.

"Are they there?" Le Matou gasped. "I lost them about a

minute ago."

Southard, taller by a head, scanned the quayside promenade. At first he thought he had lost them too, but then he spotted them, closer than he expected. They had attached themselves to a knot of people around a man firing Roman candles at the water's edge. They stood, apparently absorbed, while the shrill of police whistles came closer. But as soon as the two *flics* went jogging by, the boy took the girl's hand and they moved off again.

Twenty yards behind, Southard and Le Matou kept pace easily. Most people were going in the same direction. One, a tall woman in a raincoat and kerchief, hurried westward almost parallel with them. Southard was too intent on keeping the pair ahead in view to notice her.

Which was why she did not notice him either.

4

Deborah shifted the blue Air France flight bag on her shoulder and stepped back closer to the building, a small restaurant shut for the night, two hundred meters from the entrance to the place Ste.-Dévote. It was not crowded here, away from the quayside, now that the fireworks were over. The mob was breaking into groups of three, four, half a dozen. A larger group, between Deborah and the water, had gathered around an accordionist. She heard "La Vie en Rose" and "Valentine" and "La Seine," and she thought: I have become a murderer; in Gaza I did not feel this way when I killed three men myself, but the woman tonight was innocent, and I helped to plan and carry out her death, and I am as guilty as the Husayni twins, who did the shooting.

To Jehan that would mean nothing; it was why Jehan came here. So think like Jehan, *be* Jehan.

It didn't work, not now. She was Deborah.

189

For one bad moment she thought she would walk away, just walk away and phone the Office of Personnel Coordination in Paris and tell them she couldn't go ahead with this, she was finished, they'd better send someone who didn't care.

But then she remembered the last afternoon of what she now thought of as her normal life—riding her motorbike south from Tel Aviv on the highway bordered by great eucalyptus trees, the Yemeni children listening to her story of Jacob and Esau, the mischief in Eliahu's eyes, and then the machine guns—*that* was the slaughter of innocents. Set beside that grotesque bloodletting, anything she might have to do could be explained, excused, expiated. . . .

Suddenly Maryam and Sulayman were there.

They greeted her, first the girl then her brother, in the effusive French style, a hug, a kiss alongside her right cheek, a kiss alongside her left, and when Maryam did that she heard the faint sound of a zipper and felt the increase of weight in the flight bag, and when Sulayman did it the weight came first and then the zipper sound, and they were gone, and she had three guns.

Erika Graf stood motionless on the pavement, her fists jammed into her coat pockets, watching the guns being passed.

The transfer was accomplished with the same precision as the mission itself. The two young Arabs lingered near an accordion player at the quayside, looking neither watchful nor hurried, until the timing was just right. Then they moved off to meet the third one, the smaller girl, with a convincing show of surprised delight, well done and not overplayed. Moments later they separated again, the smaller girl walking away from the quay, the other two dashing across the corner to catch a bus, swinging aboard just as it picked up speed.

Very professionally done, Erika thought, no doubt about it.

She had seen all she came for, yet she found herself following the lone girl away from the port and the crowds. The girl walked fast but nonchalantly, swinging her free arm, the flight bag tucked against her side. Erika studied the relaxed stride, looking for anything familiar.

There was nothing. She really had to stop letting a chance facial resemblance haunt her. The body movements told the true story. The Jewish child had been nervy, skittish, taut as a tripwire. Erika had often enough followed her about at Auschwitz, followed her three times to the very doors of the gas chamber. . . .

The Arab girl walked, loose-limbed and confident, around the corner and out of sight.

5

When Southard saw the three coming together, he touched Le Matou's arm.

The Frenchman grunted. "Now if they'd just stay put somewhere long enough for me to get some help, maybe we could—*merde*, they're splitting up again. Now what do we do? Follow the original pair, or split up ourselves?"

Southard watched the pair take the decision out of their hands by sprinting for the bus and swinging aboard. With Le Matou he set out in pursuit of the girl on foot.

They hadn't gone far when the Frenchman said, "We've got her now. She's heading into the Place Ste.-Dévote. Once she's past the corner, she's bottled up."

Southard saw what he meant. The floodlit Place Ste.-Dévote led to a church, as the name implied, but it was no ordinary city square. On either side rose a sheer precipice, flanking the little church and converging behind it in a dark and narrow chasm. High overhead ran a huge railroad bridge, its utilitarian arch seeming to encase the chapel in an incongruous niche.

Suddenly Southard held Le Matou back, but the Frenchman smiled. "Don't worry about that pair of sots." Two drunks stood near a corner of the church. One tilted his head to drain a wine bottle, staggered a few paces and hurled the bottle to shatter in the darkness of the gorge. The other urinated copiously against the church wall. Then they reeled noisily toward the center of the square.

After a moment's hesitation, the girl ignored them and approached the church door. Southard thought she would go in, but she moved off to the left along the stone façade and followed the side wall. In seconds she was lost in shadow.

"What's back there?" Southard asked Le Matou.

"Just a path leading nowhere. She's got to come out this way."

The drunks were coming back, arguing, their stumbling footsteps loud.

"Better follow her anyway."

Southard himself ran around the other side of the building, his rope-soled shoes almost silent on the cobblestones. When he reached the back, the girl was just coming around the other corner. Flat against the wall he watched, straining to see in the near darkness behind the church. The girl walked swiftly a few steps along the path leading nowhere, then stopped. Southard could make out the shape of bushes on either side.

He had half-expected someone else to be waiting. There was no one. The girl simply shoved the flight bag into the shrubbery bordering the path and turned away.

From his belt Southard drew the Browning 9-mm automatic Le Matou had provided for him. He stepped in front of the girl, wanting to surprise her, but she was quick. She spun just outside his grasp, sidestepped, ducked, and came up swinging the flight bag. Southard turned a hip into it, keeping his hands free so that when momentum brought them together he got both arms around her, one circling her from behind and the other prodding her side with the gun. "All right, that's enough," he said.

Inside his tightening grip, her ribcage expanded with indrawn breath. She was going to scream. Deliberately, and despite the threat of the gun at her ribs. He felt an instant's admiration as he raised his arm, ready to silence her. Then he did not have to hit her after all. A train clattered onto the railroad viaduct and no matter how loud she screamed no one could have heard her.

By then Le Matou was there. The girl stopped struggling, now that there were two of them.

"Let go of her," Le Matou said.

Southard looked at him. The Frenchman waited, his face impassive. Southard released the girl.

Calmly and with precision, Le Matou brought his right fist up and clipped the side of the girl's jaw. The blow was harder than it looked. The girl's knees sagged. Southard was almost too startled to catch her.

Le Matou retrieved the flight bag. "How else do you think we'd get her out of here, by begging her to behave herself?" he asked, shaking his head. "You Americans, sometimes you baffle me."

They were walking around the side of the church, Southard carrying the unconscious girl.

Le Matou halted him with a hand on his shoulder. "That's far enough. No one will come around here, but if someone should, hold her as if you are making love. With that one it would be no chore." Le Matou lit a cigarette. "I'll be ten minutes, five if we're lucky. One of my *copains* ought to be at a café in the next street. We'll bring a car. I'll come back here and help you carry her out."

Southard nodded.

"And, Monsieur Beck? If she wakes up while I'm gone . . ." Le Matou brought his hands together sharply and walked off.

The girl was just beginning to stir when he returned.

193

They gave her forty-five minutes beyond the hour set as the maximum permissible delay. The Fontveille parking lot was almost empty by then, and they could not simply stay there. They tried the railroad station on Rue Grimaldi, but there were no more trains until morning, and the waiting room was deserted. They walked. People were still promenading, the occasional firecracker could still be heard, traffic still flowed west along the N559 out of Monaco. They crossed the highway and walked below the Jardin Exotique. The streetlamps were bright there, but that didn't matter. They looked like any other late-night revelers, some of whom, Maryam tried to tell her brother, would rove the streets and promenades of Monaco until breakfast. "The same as we're doing," she said. "She'll come later. There's been some kind of delay, that's all."

They were then crossing the N559 again, returning for the third time to the parking lot. It was better than before. A few fireworks enthusiasts were now using part of the broad tarmac expanse as a proving ground, and thirty or forty people had gathered to watch. Two policemen looked on with tolerant smiles.

"Later?" Sulayman said. "How much later? If she isn't here by now she may not come at all. Anything could have happened. She could have been caught with the guns. The police could be interrogating her right now. She'd talk. You know she would."

"You're being unfair, Suly. We can't just desert her."

"She knows what the arrangements are. She has money. Stop worrying about her."

"I *am* worried."

Sulayman gave his sister a venomous look. "We should have left her in the house in Villefranche. Or better yet, back in Egypt."

They had reached the Peugeot 303. Sulayman unlocked

the car, got in behind the wheel, leaned across the seat to open the passenger door. Maryam stood there, undecided. Her brother started the engine. He leaned across the seat again and rolled down the window. "Well? Make up your mind. Are you going to come with me—or wait for her the rest of the night?"

Forty-five minutes later Maryam was waiting at the window of a room in the Hôtel Univers on Avenue Jacques-Médecin in Nice. Twin beds, sink, bidet, no bathroom. Three suitcases, including Jehan's. Sulayman had gone to park the car in the garage Giovanni had specified.

Maryam hated when she argued with her brother. It was a new thing. She supposed she was to blame more than he. It was Jehan, the almost motherly sense of responsibility she felt for the girl. But it would be foolish to let that spoil what she and Sulayman had together.

They were closer, closer in every way, than other people, closer even than other twins. From childhood they had shared a special existence—their mission foreseen by the grand mufti himself, their education rigorously supervised, their superiority daily confirmed. And now they were fulfilling their destiny, alone together, as they were meant to be.

She heard the door. Sulayman came in.

She stayed by the window, smiling in mute apology. After a long minute his great dark Husayni eyes answered the plea in hers, his thin Husayni lips softened and he raised his arms.

As they came together in the center of the room, she tried to remember how long it had been. Six weeks? She thought it was six weeks since last he had held her as he was holding her now, since last they had shared the special Husayni excitement, the high of killing in fulfillment of their mission, the alone-together exaltation afterwards—six weeks since they had returned across the border to Gaza and spent the night in a mud-brick hut in the desert after the raid on the school south of Tel Aviv.

Chapter Eleven

1

Her passport was French, issued in the name of Hélène Girard. Birthplace Algiers, Algeria. Home address the same. The passport was two years old and contained Belgian, Dutch, German and Swiss entry and exit stamps. Hélène Girard was a student, twenty-three years old, eyes brown, hair dark brown, one hundred sixty centimeters tall, forty-nine kilos in weight, no distinguishing marks or scars.

The passport photograph, marred by the embossed République Française stamp, showed Hélène Girard to be a pretty girl, her small nose slightly aquiline, her cheekbones high and sharply defined, her long hair framing an unsmiling face staring straight at the camera. Hélène Girard was not smiling now, either.

The murder weapons, three identical prewar Beretta 935 automatics, lay beside the empty flight bag on the dresser. Two smelled of gunpowder, the two with scorched barrels and only five shots left in their clips. One smelled of gun oil and contained the full seven rounds.

Hélène Girard sat on the edge of the bed in the large high-ceilinged room on the top floor of the yellow stucco building around the corner from the church of Ste.-Réparate in Nice. She was hunched forward with her arms folded across her breasts and she still wore a light blue raincoat. It was cold in the room at four o'clock in the morning. Southard had been questioning her steadily for more than an hour. He had learned little more than what the passport told him about Hélène Girard. Now he crushed out his cigarette and resumed.

"Where are the others now?"

"I don't know who you mean."

"The ones who used the guns. Are they Algerian too?"

"I don't know. I don't even know who you mean. Who are you? What do you want from me?"

Instinct told Southard to answer the girl Hélène Girard's question, one way or another. He looked at her, huddled on the edge of the bed, holding her own arms. Her chin rested on her chest so that she seemed to stare up defiantly at him. But in asking her question, she had jerked her head up and he realized she was trembling. With cold? Perhaps. But more likely she held her head that way and gripped her own arms so he wouldn't see how nervous she was.

"Let's say I'm someone who didn't want Marie-Claude Tolosano to die."

"Marie—I never heard the name."

"Marie-Claude Tolosano," Southard repeated patiently. "The woman you killed."

"I didn't kill anybody."

"No, but your friends did and you helped them. Why did they kill Tolo?"

"Tolo—oh, I see. Tolosano. The woman who was shot."

"How do you know she was shot?"

"You just said—"

"I said she was dead. Not shot."

The girl glanced toward the guns and said nothing.

Southard got up and walked over to the dresser. He looked at the guns for a while. Then he picked up the roll of bank notes and tossed it. "A hundred thousand francs. You sell yourself cheap. Who gave you the money?"

"Nobody. It's my money. I got it at the bank."

Southard shrugged and flipped the roll of bills back onto

the dresser. "Why did your friends desert you?"

No answer.

"What were you doing in the place Ste.-Dévote?"

No answer.

"You were leaving the guns for someone, weren't you? Whose guns are they?"

"I don't know."

"You carry around three guns, two of them murder weapons, and you don't know who they belong to?"

No answer.

"Was it Venturino?"

"Never heard of him."

"Was it the German woman?"

"What German woman?"

"The one who was with Tolo this afternoon. Margit von Weber."

"I don't know anyone of that name."

"Or Erika Graf?"

"No."

"Did the German woman pay you to kill Tolo?"

"I don't know any German woman."

"When were you in Germany?"

"I've never been there."

"Never in Strasbourg?"

"No."

"Never on the Friedrichshafen-Romanshorn ferry?"

"I never even heard of it!"

Southard opened her passport, found the page. "Entry, 16 June 1954, Strasbourg. Exit, 24 June 1954, Bodensee ferry, Friedrichshafen to Romanshorn, Switzerland."

"Oh. Oh, yes. The Bodensee. Of course I remember."

"You're not Hélène Girard, are you?" Southard said.

"Of course I am. Hélène Girard."

"Where'd you get this passport?"

No answer.

"From the German woman? From Erika Graf?"

"I don't know any Erika Graf! Why do you keep talking about Germany? You're not German. You're not French either, not with that accent. What are you? American?"

Southard's instinct now told him to switch to English, and to ease up for the moment. "You're pretty good at languages, aren't you?"

"You *are* American. I thought you were." That seemed to make a difference to her; he could not tell why.

"That's right. How did you know? You haven't been to the States, not on this passport anyway."

"No."

"You have American friends?"

"My—yes, I have friends."

"Where?"

No answer.

"Where do you come from?"

"Algiers."

"Why did you kill her?"

"I told you. I didn't kill anyone."

"How many people have you killed before tonight?"

A pause. Chin tucked hard against chest. "None."

"When did you first meet Venturino?"

"I don't know any Venturino."

"You were with him near the museum at noon. Giovanni Venturino."

"Giovanni?"

"Giovanni. Giovanni and you and the two who did the shooting."

"If you say so."

"And Tolo was there with Erika Graf. What was Erika's part in it?"

Another defiant look. "Why don't you play this game by yourself? You're the one who knows all the answers."

"Did she give you the money?"

"No."

"The passport?"

"No."

"The guns?"

"No."

"Did you get the guns from Venturino?"

"No."

"Where did you get them?"

No answer.

"Who's Erika Graf?"

"I don't know."

"Margit von Weber?"

"I don't know."

"Erika Graf?"

"I told you I—"

"Venturino?"

"I don't—"

"Hélène Girard?"

"I don't know, I don't know, I don't know!"

2

And that, she thought, feeling nothing but the weariness, seemed to take care of that. She watched the man get up and open the door and say something to someone outside. He came back and offered her a cigarette, which she declined. She watched him smoke one himself, leaning against the dresser. He was tall and he wore a bulky sweater and slacks. His sandy hair was short but not crew cut. He had blue eyes and they looked like nice eyes even while he was hurling the questions at her, but she thought his mouth was hard. His mouth made him look angry. He was thirty-something, maybe thirty-five, she decided. A baritone voice, and he spoke a different kind of American from Daddy Sam's. But that was New York City, and Daddy Sam always said New York was a whole different country with a whole different language.

The door opened and the little man with big ears and dark close-set eyes came in with a round tray. The smell of coffee filled the room. The little man gave Deborah a curious look, then he set the tray on the night table, glanced at the tall American and went out.

"Have some coffee, go ahead."

It was a soup bowl of a cup with no handles and she was still shaking. She had to raise it to her lips with both hands. The cup was hot and the coffee very strong.

"Now that we know who you're not," he said, and smiled, "maybe you'll tell me who you are."

She warmed her hands on the bowl-sized cup and sipped, looking over the rim at him. Don't take the smile too seriously, she warned herself; he doesn't mean the smile. But it changed his face. The hardness and the anger were gone. He was, when he smiled, a handsome man. As if that had anything to do with anything.

He said nothing else then—a technique familiar to her from her interrogation training with the Israeli defense forces. Giving her time to consider. Time to consider what?

Who was he, anyway? Obviously not police, since he wasn't even French. He wasn't, apparently, working with the police either. Yet he knew about her mission, in some ways more than she did, and he opposed it. If he knew why she and the Husaynis were here, then maybe he knew they had been trained at El Mansûra by the Russians, and sent here by them, and it was really the Russians he opposed. What would that make him?

Some kind of American agent?

But maybe he wasn't. Maybe he just wanted her to think he was. Maybe it was an elaborate double-switch, to test her. Had Jehan Khalid ever really been accepted? But if she wasn't, why would they send her to France?

He must be American. Everything she knew about language said he was. But she herself could speak perfect French and Arabic, couldn't she, not to mention German?

Did he *look* American? Well, not if Daddy Sam did. But American males weren't all huge, shambling, bearlike former basketball players.

She watched him finish his cigarette and pour himself a cup of coffee. He still said nothing. He didn't even seem to be paying close attention to her. From the big free-standing armoire he took a suitcase and opened it. His bulky, shapeless sweater was folded and packed, replaced with a suit coat and knit tie. He kicked off his rope-soled espadrilles and put on cordovan leather shoes. The cap he had worn outdoors was tossed into the armoire along with the espadrilles. With each change of clothing he looked less European.

He was American, she'd bet on it.

Bet what? Her life, for example?

All right, he was American. So what? Most Americans, according to Daddy Sam, were pro-Israeli. But Sam Brodsky was a Jew, after all, and maybe most of his friends in the States had been Jewish. Maybe he didn't know the other ones very well. Besides, he had always added a caveat: oil. When it came to oil, Americans were like the rest of the world, maybe worse. The Americans had spent a fortune developing Arab oil fields. So some Americans weren't necessarily anti-Israeli, they were just pro-oil. Even Truman's secretary of state, General Marshall, a great man, counseled the president in 1947 against recognizing the emerging state of Israel. Oil was the hard fact of the future.

Daddy Sam thought the current secretary of state, John Foster Dulles, was no less a pragmatist. And wasn't Dulles's brother Allen head of American intelligence? He was probably the boss of this blue-eyed man who was now leaning against the dresser again, his hands in his pockets, whistling tunelessly.

Could she trust him? *How* could she trust him? All he had done so far was manhandle her, hold a gun on her, abduct her to this place, and. . . .

"My name is Deborah. What's yours?"

3

Le Matou got them a car at the Gare Routière, a four-door Renault rented in the name of Curtis Beck, American, and at ten-thirty that morning they were on their way. The Israeli girl had had less than five hours of sleep and by the time Southard drove out of Nice and picked up the road at Cagnes-sur-Mer that headed inland on the first leg of the six-hundred-mile drive to Paris, the girl was fast asleep at his side.

Which could have meant that she completely trusted him, or only that she was exhausted.

Her story bordered on the fantastic. Southard was inclined to believe every word of it for the simple reason that no one could have made it up.

Besides, fantastic or not, much of it checked out.

The Agency knew that the Mossad had been trying to locate the new fedayeen main base after Moshe Dayan leveled Khan Yunis. The Agency had a dossier on Sulayman and Maryam Husayni, young leaders of the Palestinians and known terrorists. And finally, the Agency had been getting diffuse reports that the GRU was experimenting with non-Russian teams for foreign, particularly European, operations—making Colonel Kossior a plausible link to Erika Graf.

The girl Deborah did not know the name Erika Graf, but when she described the blonde woman outside the Oceanographic Museum, it was Graf she described. It was the only time Southard had to press her. It almost seemed the thought of the German woman frightened her; she would not say why.

Shortly before noon Southard parked on the boulevard

Victor Hugo in Grasse. The girl awoke immediately and smiled at him. "Where are we?"

"Grasse. Last big town in a while," Southard told her. "The country gets pretty desolate after this. I thought you'd want to buy some stuff."

They got out of the car. She had her hair tied back in a pony tail. Dark brown, the passport said, but the sunlight brought out auburn highlights. She walked to the overlook near the statue of Victor Hugo and gazed down over the sloping valley and low ranges of hills below the town. "What a lovely view!" she exclaimed. There was a look of real pleasure on her face, as if the view were an unexpected gift. "I'm glad we didn't fly."

Southard hadn't wanted to take the slight risk that the Husaynis or their confederates would be watching the Nice Airport. And this way Le Matou would have plenty of time to substantiate the excuse for her delay, so that the Husayni twins would accept her late return with no questions, or at least no suspicion.

"No great rush to get to Paris?"

"I'm not afraid, if that's what you mean. It's just that for the first time since all this started, I can forget about playing a role and relax."

Southard looked at his watch. "Better go get whatever you'll need for the next two days," he said. "The shops close at noon."

"Two whole days," she said softly. "Could we take the back roads?"

Southard smiled. "That's the general idea."

He lit a cigarette and leaned against the rail of the overlook. She started off, then hesitated. "Thank you," she said.

He watched her cross the main street, feeling uncomfortable with her gratitude. The two-day drive to Paris would be stolen time for him too, because at the end of it he knew he would fly back to Washington and face the consequences of his disappearance. He wanted these two days as much as she did.

The route Napoléon climbed steeply out of Grasse. At Castellane in a restaurant on the edge of the swift-flowing Verdon River they ate an omelette and salad and a crisp loaf of bread and shared a bottle of white wine. After Castellane the road twisted through the wild country of the pre-Alps, white granite summits bare under a hard blue dome of sky, torrents thundering through gray gorges, the occasional stunted green scrub of the *maquis* the only sign of life.

"It's a wasteland," Deborah marveled. "I thought Europe was a garden compared with Israel, but this is every bit as desolate as the Horns of Hattin."

"Wasteland was what I thought when I first saw it, too. That was during the war, 1944."

"Here? What on earth were you doing here?"

"Well, not here exactly, a little further north. A town called Digne. It was after the landings on the Riviera. I parachuted in to arrange a supply drop for the Maquis. You'd still have been a schoolgirl in pigtails—what were you, about ten at the time?"

When there was no answer, he turned and glanced at her face. It had a pinched, closed look. Finally she said, "I was twelve in 1944."

He got it then. For some reason he'd taken her for a Sabra, a native-born Israeli. She wasn't.

"I'm sorry, I didn't realize. You were here in Europe, weren't you?"

"Auschwitz." Her voice sounded brittle. "I was a child prodigy. Or so they told me. The violin. They had a band at Auschwitz, did you know that? A band to play for the new arrivals when they tumbled out of the cattle cars and, if the SS thought you were good enough, a chamber group to perform for the camp bigshots. I was lucky. There was an SS Hauptsturmführer named Kerrl. He was in charge of such things. He put me in the chamber group. Within six months my mother was gassed, but I was still alive. Alive! I used to play at dinner for Kerrl. After dinner sometimes. And then suddenly I wasn't a little girl anymore. He started trying to seduce me. Not rape, seduce. That was important to him. Herr Kerrl was a cultured man. He wanted to introduce me gradually into maturity. And I was his ungrateful little Jewess. I said no. I couldn't. He was repulsive to me—he was German. I pulled away when he touched me. And he didn't insist. I knew he was angry. Still, I thought it would be all right. They made me hold my hand in the hinge part of the door in Herr Kerrl's office, my left hand that did the fingering on the violin. Herr Kerrl himself shut the door."

Her voice stopped. He could find nothing to say. His war had merely been dangerous.

He had planned a mid-afternoon break in Digne, a few minutes' walk along boulevard Gassendi, a drink on the place de la Libération at a café whose proprietor had been in the Maquis. But he drove right through.

It was as if she read his mind. "You could have stopped," she said.

"Stopped? What for?"

"You wanted to, didn't you? To see your old friends from the Resistance? You should have."

"It doesn't matter. It was all a long time ago."

They were driving northwest across the high white desolate *garrigue* country above Digne. Ten minutes of silence built, twenty. He was very conscious of her presence beside him in the little car. He wanted to touch her. He wanted to touch her left hand, where they had done that to her. He wanted to do something to please her. He wanted to make her smile. He remembered, as they approached the great rift of the Durance Valley where the town of Sisteron huddled on the river's edge, exactly where to park. They got out of the car. He didn't have to say anything. The wind was fierce, and unexpectedly cold. The enormous rock of La Baume rose across the river from the town, the granite strata running almost straight up from the sky-reflecting water of the Durance to the dome of the sky itself. Her hand opened and he reached out for it. Her left hand. He held it gently. The wind blew so hard it brought tears to her eyes. She turned toward him.

"You look like you're crying," she said.

"I thought *you* were."

"Perhaps I am. It's so beautiful." She moved closer, sheltering from the wind in the circle of his arm. "It looks like a building block left there by the giants after they finished making the mountains. See? They left it and the wind blew it over."

"They left it there to hold the sky up."

"Hold me," she said. "Please hold me."

4

They reached Le Vieux Moulin at ten that night.

It was an ancient stone building off a secondary road in the foothills west of Lyon. Southard had phoned ahead, and two rooms were waiting for them. Madame Odette had kept the kitchen open and a table was set near the window in the small high-ceilinged dining room. Outside the window in the angle of the L-shaped building, startlingly close in the moonlight, Deborah could see a waterwheel.

"It really is a mill," she said.

"Used to be."

"What were you doing here during the war?"

"It's a complicated story. We were supposed to make our way to Switzerland, Gideon Parr and me. Allen Dulles was assembling a staff for the OSS in Bern. We holed up here for a while. Parr had a badly sprained ankle. Madame

Odette's son was fifteen then and he wanted a piece of the war. He was with the Maquis when they blew up the bridge over the Rhone at Givors. The Germans came looking for him. Parr was able to travel by then. We took the boy with us. Two weeks later we were in Switzerland."

Madame Odette brought the country pâté, cut two thick slices and left the crock on the table. She was a stout, red-faced woman. "The way he talks, it was nothing. But they saved Étienne's life. He's a doctor of medicine now." Every time her eyes met Southard's Madame Odette grinned. It was as if she still couldn't believe he was real.

"And Monsieur Gideon?" she asked.

Southard looked at her. "Gideon's fine," he said after a while. "He has an important job in Washington."

"But yes, one could tell he would be important."

When Madame Odette left, Deborah asked, "Wasn't he the one you told me about, your friend who died in Hungary?"

Southard nodded. "Why tell her? Why spoil it for her? She hasn't seen either of us since the war. She doesn't expect him to come."

Madame Odette returned with the wine. "Romanée Conti 1947," she said reverently. "The last bottle in the cellar."

She fussed over them, readjusting the single yellow rose in its slender vase, examining the utensils on the side table as if she'd never seen them before. She kept glancing at Deborah. It had been that way ever since they drank an aperitif with her in the tiny bar.

"You are quite certain the rooms are all right?" she had asked them, and, "You did say two rooms?" She quickly added, "I only wanted to be sure. My hearing isn't what it once was."

Deborah remembered how he had carefully not looked at her. After a moment he grinned at the woman. "Is that why you gave us rooms with a connecting door? You always were resourceful, Madame Odette." They laughed together, and Deborah wondered whether she was expected to laugh too. But then he had reached under the table and found her hand for a brief reassuring touch.

Now he was holding her hand again, on top of the table. Deborah was almost sure she would say yes—if he asked her, she would say yes. She thought he was going to ask her.

"Tired?" he asked.

"No! I mean, no."

"It was a long drive. Tomorrow ought to be no more than eight hours. We'll get an early start."

"Yes."

"The real scenery's behind us anyway."

"Yes."

Deborah heard herself with dismay, responding only in monosyllables.

In the car, during the long drive after Sisteron, she could not seem to stop talking. She had wanted him to know her, all of her, in one day. She told him about the displaced persons camp and Sergeant Sam Brodsky. She told him how Sam, fed up one day with all the red tape and waiting, got leave from the army and commandeered some trucks and took Deborah and fifty other Jewish refugees south to Italy and arranged for the boat and at the last minute went with them because he wanted to see them through all the way to Israel. He ran the British blockade with them and stayed a week and then he went away and came back as a civilian and just stayed.

She told Southard about her life in Tel Aviv and her work at the radio station, and she was even able to talk about that terrible evening at the school south of the city.

Now she couldn't seem to talk at all.

Madame Odette sailed out of the kitchen with the rack of lamb and the little pale green beans called flageolets. She poured the wine and carved the meat and served, and this time she left right away.

Deborah hardly tasted the food. She toyed with her wine glass, twirling it by the stem, holding it up so the light played in the rich translucent Burgundy.

He raised his glass and clinked it against hers. "*L'chaim*. Did I get that right."

She smiled. "Just right."

"Madame Odette must like you. A lot of people say this is the best wine in the world."

"I believe them."

He looked at her plate, almost untouched. "Will you want dessert? Coffee?"

"No, thank you." Her voice sounded unnatural to her. "I mean, perhaps Madame Odette would like to go to bed."

"Perhaps you would, too." His eyes were steady on hers. They were gray now, with only a touch of blue.

Deborah met his gaze, then faltered. "But the wine is only half finished. It would be a shame . . ."

"Unthinkable. So we have two choices. Finish it here. Or finish it upstairs."

Deborah's eyes came up again, and she managed to keep them from wavering while she slowly drew the napkin from her lap and laid it on the table.

There was a fireplace and sometime during dinner Madame Odette had found time to light it. Firelight flickered on the ceiling and on the fleur-de-lis wallpaper and the ancient oak furniture. Deborah heard his breathing and her own and the wind outside and the rattle of icy rain against the windows. But it was snug in here, in the big old four-poster bed with her head on his shoulder and their bodies barely touching under the covers.

It was all right when their bodies touched like that. It was good. She felt warm and protected and safe. As long as she was careful not to move and rouse him, she could almost pretend the other part had been all right too.

She had wanted to be everything for him. She had

wanted to be bold and playful, a hoyden. She hoped he would like that. She had wanted to be artful and alluring, a courtesan. She thought he would like that. She had wanted to be tender and loving, a woman. She knew he would like that.

She had been the Ice Maiden.

He knew just where he was, as he always did, the moment he woke. He lay still, careful not to move, then he spoke softly. "Deborah? Debbie?"

"I'm awake." Her voice was muffled in the pillow.

The fire had burned down to embers. She lay on her side, her back to him. He felt her shoulder stiffen to his touch.

"Easy," he said. "I just wanted to be sure you were okay."

She let out a long breath. "I'd feel better if you weren't so nice about it. Why can't you get mad at me, the way I deserve?"

"Come on now. Don't be so hard on yourself. You were tired and overwrought, that's all."

"No, that's not all."

"It was my fault. I should have known it was too soon for you."

He meant it was too soon after they met. And he meant, more than that, it was too soon after what happened to her in Gaza. But she gave a forced laugh and said: "Too soon? I'm twenty-four now, Ben. How can you call that too soon?"

He didn't answer. He just closed his eyes, as if he could shut out her words along with the dying firelight. He had misjudged her more than once already, but this time there was no way he could undo it. It had never occurred to him that, with the glaring exception of her rape and the fedayeen spy she had exposed at Kol Israel, she was an innocent—an ill-used innocent—in matters of sex. He tried to think whether his approach might have frightened her, what he might have done differently if he had known. If he had known, he would have done nothing at all.

When he opened his eyes she was lying on her back, her arms out of the covers, her hands tight fists at her sides. "I'm sorry," she said after a while. "I really thought it was going to be all right. I thought, with you, I could relax and just . . . let it happen. I was so sure."

He found her hand, her left hand, gently uncurled the fingers and kissed the palm. Then he turned her to him and held her. He thought she would pull away. She didn't. She clung to him hard. He could feel her tears on his bare shoulder.

"It's no use, Ben. Please don't waste any more time on me. I wish I could be like other people, but I'm just not. When they made me, they left something out."

She came awake in the pale dawn and found herself alone in the bed. A faint warmth remained where he had been lying. She let her hand rest there, remembering how he had held her in the middle of the night. There had been a moment then when she might have pulled away. But her anguish was stronger than her shame, and she had let him comfort her.

He came in from the other room. He was already dressed. She watched him build up the fire, then cross to the window and stare fixedly out, and a wave of pain swept her.

Please God, she thought, don't make me fall in love with him. Don't make me fall in love with anyone. I'm no good for anything like that.

5

In Paris late the next afternoon Southard phoned Harry Sullivan, the Agency station chief at the American Embassy, and told him what he wanted.

"No problem. I know some of their people. Give me an

hour and call me back," Sullivan said. "Meanwhile I've got a question of my own, Ben. Where the hell have you been? They've got an alert out on you all over Europe."

"That's the other reason I called. Would you get me on the first plane back to the States?"

Southard phoned Nice next. Le Matou was expecting his call. "It will cost Gehlen four hundred thousand francs. But that includes a police report, the genuine item. It's cheap at the price, believe me. Here's her story."

Over drinks at a café on the rue de Rivoli, Southard repeated it to Deborah. Rush-hour traffic clogged the street, and pedestrians hurried by under the arcades, sheltered from the April drizzle. "You probably won't have to get that specific," he said. "But those are the details, and if they're checked out in Nice even the police will confirm them."

Southard had already phoned Sullivan back. An Israeli named Kaplan would meet them at six-thirty, less than five minutes from now.

"You didn't have to contact my people. I could have done that myself."

Originally, Southard had planned to do it as assurance she was no imposter. Now he just wanted to see her safely in. It was only a gesture, he knew. She'd be going out again, back to the fedayeen, in a few hours.

"Ask them for an around-the-clock panic number."

"All right. I will."

"And take care of yourself."

"I will." Their eyes met. "When are you flying to Washington?"

"Tonight, eight-thirty."

"Well," she said, and smiled. It was a pert, pretty smile, but remote. "Then I guess this is good-bye." She turned her head away quickly, as if she were looking for Kaplan.

He said, "Here in France they say *au revoir*."

She faced him, her eyes bright with tears. "But we're not

French, and it's no good pretending."

A portly, balding man with a white carnation in his lapel looked at their table, saw how the copy of *Le Figaro* was folded and said. *"Bon soir. Mademoiselle Corbeau, je crois?"*

"Oui. Bon soir, Monsieur Kaplan."

He seated himself in the third cane-backed chair at the small table and nodded curtly in Southard's direction. "You have the Institute's thanks, sir." His impatience for Southard to leave was barely disguised.

Southard rose. Deborah held out her hand and gave him the pert smile again. They shook hands like newly met strangers saying a casual farewell.

Southard stepped into the street and walked in the rain outside the arcades so that if he looked back he would not be able to see her.

Part Three

Chapter Twelve

1

As the black Chaika limousine sped away from the Kremlin, Dmitri Platonovich Kossior could hear the bells in the Ivan the Great tower brazenly tolling. It was noon on Saturday, June 16, and Colonel Kossior was already late. He tried not to show his impatience. General Shalin was a hard man to hurry. But as chief of the Central Intelligence Directorate of the Soviet Union, the GRU, he was also hard to fool.

General Shalin leaned forward and spoke to his chauffeur. "I'm going to Znamensky Street. After that take the comrade colonel where he wishes." Then the general, a graying man of sixty, settled back and chuckled. "Let me guess, Dmitri Platonovich," he said, "It's your wife."

"Well, actually it's my daughter Irina," said Colonel Kossior uncomfortably.

The Chaika limousine raced along the central VIP lane of Arbat Street away from Red Square. Traffic policemen waved buses, trucks and the occasional car out of its speeding path.

"Of course. A school interview, now I remember. I received a letter—MIMO, wasn't it?" said General Shalin.

Kossior did not ask his superior officer what sort of recommendation he had written for Irina. Shalin said, "Stop worrying. She'll be accepted. You don't have any enemies on the Central Committee—not yet, at any rate."

"I'd prefer to keep it that way."

Again Shalin chuckled. "Wouldn't we all," he said.

"The meeting went well, I thought."

"It went beautifully, for all that means. At the moment we have Comrade Khrushchev's ear and the KGB doesn't. But how long, my dear colonel, can that last? The system permits them to spy on us, not the other way around."

The Chaika cut across three traffic lanes and pulled to the curb at 19 Znamensky Street. When the chauffeur opened the door Shalin remained seated. "Khrushchev was impressed with you, I could tell."

Colonel Kossior was unsure what reaction Shalin expected. He tried a self-deprecating smile. "I'm pleased you think so, comrade general."

"On the other hand, this project increases our vulnerability to KGB attack. And General Serov is a merciless opponent."

Colonel Kossior wondered whether Shalin would describe himself differently. Like Serov, he confronted with the same ruthlessness the enemy in the West and his rivals here in Moscow.

"See that you give Serov no opportunity," Shalin warned. He stepped from the limousine and walked quickly past the sentry box into the courtyard of GRU headquarters.

"The Institute for International Relations," Kossior told the chauffeur.

Two hours later Kossior was lunching with his daughter Irina at the Armed Forces Officers Club. As a field grade officer and a graduate of Frunze Academy, Russia's West Point, Kossior was entitled to use the smaller and more luxurious of the club's dining rooms. The hour was late enough so that they were given a window table with a fine view over the Moscow River.

"Oh, father, I'm so happy," Irina said. She was a pink-faced girl of eighteen who wore an unfortunate blue polka-dot dress that accentuated her dumpy figure. "I never thought they'd take me."

Kossior patted her hand in a pleased, paternal gesture. Irina was bright but not deeply intelligent. She would likely have been rejected by MIMO, the Moscow Institute for International Relations, unless her father pulled strings.

"Well, you see," he beamed, "you had nothing to worry about."

MIMO would open new vistas for Irina, give her access to the Western world. She would, of course, serve the cause of international Communism in the process, but which was primary Kossior couldn't say. The paradox did not trouble him. The *vlasti*, the elite privileged class at the top of the soviet pyramid, accepted as their right such perquisites as frequent trips out of the country. Their preference for foreign assignments had nothing to do with ideology. Nobody seriously considered Moscow any better than an overgrown village, or the Soviet way of life anything but provincial. The luxury the *vlasti* enjoyed in the decadent West was a privilege made all the sweeter by a knowledge of moral superiority.

The luxury the *vlasti* enjoyed at home they took for granted.

With their fresh caviar Colonel Kossior drank chilled Stolnichaya vodka and Irina a glass of dry white wine from the Crimea. Sturgeon and roast pork would follow, and then a sweet with their coffee.

"I will devote myself," said Irina with eighteen-year-old certainty, "to the plight of the underprivileged classes in the former colonies of the imperialist powers."

Kossior smiled. "Is that a quote from your interview?"

While Irina had been interviewed, Kossior had seen the head of admissions for MIMO. The dip in Irina's grades during her third year at the gymnasium had been glossed over, explained away. The man had a son, a lieutenant in the army but no graduate of Frunze Academy, who wanted a career in the GRU. *Blat,* influence, was a two-way street.

"Of course I said it, father, but not just because it was expected of me. I really *want* to work in the underdeveloped countries."

How to tell her that concern for the welfare of the downtrodden, while admirable, led to no advancement? How to tell her the African and Southeast Asian backwaters were only for second-raters, and real careers were fashioned in the decadent West itself?

He decided not to try. Opportunism had to be learned, and idealism unlearned; at eighteen Irina was too young. He envied her.

Khrushchev gave twenty minutes that evening to Lieutenant General I.A. Serov, chief of the KGB. When they had concluded their business, a smile wreathed the first secretary's procine face.

"We have a saying in the Ukraine," he said. "Only the son of a peasant can truly appreciate palace intrigue. You understand?"

Serov said nothing. Khrushchev often spoke in pithy aphorisms and he expected no answer.

"Bulganin came up through the army," Khrushchev went on. "In any power struggle, he would naturally favor the GRU over you Chekists."

Marshal Bulganin was prime minister of the Soviet Union; Khrushchev was first secretary of the Communist party. They ruled in tandem, equal partners. Serov judged that with the party apparatus under his command, Khrushchev was more equal than his colleague.

"And yourself, comrade?" Serov asked.

"Because I'm a party veteran? That doesn't guarantee I'd support the KGB. Look at three years ago—but then, you must have been as glad as I was to see Beria executed. After all, you got his job."

Again Serov did not reply.

"With Beria's people gone, the KGB no longer shits on its own doorstep, is that what you'd tell me?"

Serov still said nothing, but he smiled slightly.

"Why should I favor either side? I favor success," said Nikita Khrushchev, his small eyes all but disappearing as he grinned. "I have here, for you to take back to the Lubyanka, a transcript of the tape made earlier today while General Shalin and his operations chief Colonel Kossior were here. I would value the KGB's views."

"Views?"

Khrushchev shrugged. "Then we'll see. You and Shalin want the same things, after all."

"Yes," said Serov solemnly. "The destabilization of the West."

Khrushchev smiled at him. "And each other's heads."

2

The pilings creaked and shifted in the water as the ferry nudged its way into the slip. Soon the ramp clanked into place and passengers filed down from the observation roof to the car deck.

Suzanne Southard tugged at her father's hand. "Please, daddy, hurry! If we don't hurry, we won't be the first car off."

Southard let himself be pulled between the two rows of cars. His Chrysler was first in line on the left. "Well," he said, "we've got one chance out of two. Those aren't bad odds, Suzie."

"We ought to be first. It's only fair. We got on first."

Suzanne, seven years old, her long blonde hair windblown, got into the driver's seat of the Chrysler and slid her small hands along the wheel. She peered grimly through the spokes. "I'm ready."

"Hey, make some room for me."

His daughter slid over, reluctantly giving up her pose as chauffeur. Southard started the engine and they were waved off the ferry.

"See? I told you it was only fair," Suzanne said, as if that had been obvious all along to everyone but Southard.

The Chrysler clattered across the ramp.

"Where are we going?"

"Nowhere."

"My mother says you always have to have a goal in life," Suzanne said coolly.

"Sure, but not every day."

"Well, that's what she says."

"See all those fields out there?" Southard pointed. "Peanuts."

"Peanuts? Honest?"

"Acres and acres of peanuts, uh-huh."

"How many jars of peanut butter grow on an acre?"

Southard admitted he didn't know.

"I'll bet my mother knows. She knows just about everything."

"I'll bet she does," Southard said.

"Are you going away soon, daddy? My mother says you're going back overseas."

If his ex-wife knew that, Southard thought wryly, then she knew what was in store for him better than he did. Flying to Washington, he'd drafted a long report which started with the bus driver Kunschak in Vienna and ended with the Mossad's Paris man Kaplan. Adam Prestridge, the deputy director for plans, had been in the Far East, and rather than let the report gather dust on his desk, Southard had sent it upstairs to Allen Dulles. Seven weeks of resounding silence followed.

Southard spent the time shuffling papers in Foggy Bottom and running retread seminars at the Farm in Virginia. He got back in touch with his agents in both political parties in Germany and in half a dozen parties in

France, including the Communists; he authorized payments to newspaper editors in a score of European cities; he evaluated reports from Spanish policemen and Italian film stars, from businessmen, military officers, barge captains, university professors, border guards, whorehouse madams. But Southard had the veteran fieldman's impatience with desk work. At the erstwhile brewery in Foggy Bottom, at the overflow offices in the so-called temporary buildings of World War I vintage, the desk work too often became an end in itself, the reams of papers eliminating personal contact, burying facts, obscuring results. Adam Prestridge and Gideon Parr epitomized the difference between the deskman and the fieldman. Southard found the thought disquieting: Prestridge had survived.

"Daddy? Are you really going away soon?"

"I don't know, doll."

"My mother says so."

"Well, maybe she'll be wrong just this once."

"Oh, I hope so," Suzanne said.

Thursday and Friday each week Southard had spent at the Farm. Granted, he was the Agency's expert on restructuring the dangerously obsolete networks into cellular groups and linear operations, but the seminars could have been conducted by the Farm's resident staff. Unlike Adam Prestridge, Southard disliked pontificating. The only benefit of the seminars was the weekly Saturday visit with Suzie. Since it was on a regular basis, Janet couldn't claim he was disrupting their daughter's schedule.

They drove into the village of Surry, its main street full of Saturday bustle. "Anybody around here want some ice cream?"

"Oh boy!"

While Suzanne was demolishing a two-scoop pistachio and chocolate cone, Southard browsed a copy of the *Washington Post*. In the presidential suite at Walter Reed Hospital, the paper said, Dwight D. Eisenhower continued his good recovery from emergency abdominal surgery the previous Saturday. In Mississippi, the paper said, Senator Eastland vowed that integration would never come to the South—a vow Southard saw nothing on the streets of Surry, Virginia, to refute. "Engine Charlie" Wilson over at the Pentagon, the paper said. Presidential alter ego Sherman Adams, it said. It said Billy Graham. It said Floyd Patterson. It said peaceful coexistence. It said that in the Suez Canal Zone the last British forces had withdrawn, ending a three-quarter-century occupation. It said Nasser and Ben-Gurion, and Southard thought of the Israeli girl, dark and slender—

"Daddy?

"Sorry, doll. What did you say?"

Suzanne was dabbing neatly at her lips with a napkin, an unexpectedly womanly gesture. "Can I have another?"

"Better not. You'll spoil your appetite for dinner."

"So? My mother won't notice, she'll be getting ready to go out."

"Still, it isn't good for you."

Suzanne sighed dramatically. "My mother always says you spoil me, but you never *do.*"

"Let it go, Suzie, okay?"

As they walked back to the car, Southard tried to remember when Suzie had developed the grating habit of saying my-mother-this and my-mother-that. Then he realized he had started it himself. Probably Janet did it too, referring to him not as daddy or even as Ben but as your-father. Still, theirs was as "civilized" as divorces came.

In the car, Suzanne said, "Can I start it?"

Southard took his hand off the ignition. "Okay, but let go as soon as it kicks over." He worked the accelerator while his daughter turned the key.

"Where are we going now?"

"Ferryboat."

"We just came from there."

"It's the only way back to your mother's—to your house, unless we go all the way around through Newport News."

"Do we have to go back already?"

"I promised I'd get you home early."

A sigh. "Sometimes I don't like it there so much."

"Sure you do."

"When you were a little boy, did you like school?"

"Sure."

"Did you like having to do everything your mother said?"

"Well, I guess she knew what was best."

"Hmm. Do they have ice cream on the ferryboat?"

"Afraid not."

Suzanne watched the peanut fields for a while. "Do you have a girl friend, daddy?"

"Nobody special."

"Not even me? Aren't I special?"

"Sure. Very special."

"I love you, daddy."

"I love you too, doll."

She drove beside him, turning an imaginary steering wheel and working imaginary brakes, until they reached the river. Southard pulled to a stop in the ferry line behind a car with D.C. plates. An ice cream truck was parked alongside.

"There, I told you!" Suzanne cried.

He bought two chocolate pops.

Suzanne nibbled hers, staring across the river. "Why do we always have to say good-bye?"

"Not always, Suzie. For every good-bye, there's a hello."

"Yes, but the good-byes last longer."

"Well then, let's not say it anymore. I'll teach you how to say until-we-see-each-other-again, the way the French do."

Suzanne copied his pronunciation with a child's natural gift for mimicry. She climbed onto the hood of the car and sat there waving her empty ice-cream stick and repeating *"au revoir, au revoir."*

He stood behind her, watching her small blonde head bobbing, and then he looked out over the river and saw instead the dark head of the girl in Paris who would not say those words.

3

The window of Adam Prestridge's office looked out over the Watergate barge and bandshell to a wide sun-dazzled stretch of Potomac and the green Virginia shore shimmering in haze. A sultry, almost tropical heat had settled over Foggy Bottom this final day of spring. It was not yet noon and the temperature already had climbed past ninety.

Southard stood by the open window, rumpled seersucker jacket slung over his shoulder, shirt clinging damply to his back, tie loosened, collar button open. Adam Prestridge was on the phone, his precise, arrogant drawl dominating the conversation. The phone had interrupted them three times.

"I can't authorize that," Prestridge said. "Sorry, James, that's it." His voice was regretful, but as he hung up the smile he gave Southard held no regret at all. He seemed two people.

Adam Prestridge was a slender, silver-haired man of fifty-five, impeccably turned out despite the weather in a dark raw-silk suit of Italian cut. The heat seemed not to touch him; even his boutonniere was unwilted. He affected rimless pince-nez, which he now removed from the bridge of his nose.

"Where were we?" he asked blandly.

The drawl, product of Choate, Harvard and the eastern establishment, gave nothing away. You learned what the deputy director for plans was thinking when he told you. If he bothered to. Prestridge preferred the impersonality of

226

memoranda and directives to the give and take of discussion. Discussion implied that more than one viewpoint was worth considering.

"The Manyoki document," Southard said.

"Yes, of course. The so-called Manyoki document. Now correct me if I'm wrong—I've only had time to give your report one quick reading—but I seem to recall you never actually saw it."

"No, I never saw it."

"And you haven't spoken with anyone who did read it, have you? Only that doctor—Landler, was it?—who didn't actually read it but only spoke with Manyoki about it. So even the existence of the document may be questioned. Our only certain knowledge is that poor Parr *believed* he was getting a transcript—the only transcript available—of Khrushchev's secret speech denouncing Stalin. And even there Parr was wrong. The transcript was hardly unique. We bought one from Palmiro Togliatti, though I must say I opposed paying him two hundred million lire for anything, and a *Time* correspondent brought one out of Poland, and Kip Chaffee recently came up with one in France. It's already three weeks since we made a composite of those transcripts and leaked it to the *New York Times*. So if that's what Gideon Parr died trying to get his hands on . . ." Prestridge shook his head, a sad dismissive gesture.

"On the other hand, according to your report, he stumbled on this so-called Manyoki document as well—which includes Soviet plans to invade and occupy Eastern Europe in the event of insurrection, not to mention Manyoki's blueprint for forcing the Red Army's hand. If its authenticity could be confirmed—" Prestridge shook his head again. "But he's dead, Ben. Parr's dead, and Manyoki too. There isn't a shred of substantiation. The new man in Vienna is good, and he's turning up nothing. There's nothing from the Soviet bloc either. There's nothing to pursue."

"Not on paper, no. That's why it's got to be done in person."

"And just where did you have in mind? You came up against a dead end in Hungary, the same in Austria. As for Germany, I resent what you did there and so does Allen. You damaged the Agency's image by going to Gehlen. And what did you come up with? Another dead end in France."

"Don't tell me Erika Graf's a dead end. She was there when they killed Parr."

"Nobody killed him. They released the body to Vienna. We did a thorough autopsy. Gideon Parr drowned, apparently after a heart attack."

"So okay, it was his heart. But if a man's already had a massive coronary, there are plenty of ways of causing the next attack."

"Why would Erika Graf want to do that? Parr would have been more valuable to them alive, wouldn't he?"

Southard knew he'd walked right into that one. He couldn't justify what he'd said without challenging Gideon Parr's motives in the Golovin operation, something he was still unwilling to do.

Suddenly the deputy director for plans smiled. "Well now," he drawled, "of course. They worked together in 1953 in Berlin, didn't they?"

"That's irrelevant, Adam. It was three years ago, another operation."

"I wonder."

"Gideon and I were both debriefed," Southard said, his voice flat. "The transcripts are on file. Read them."

Prestridge shrugged impatiently. "So your stories agree."

Southard waited ten seconds, then said, "I'll forget you said that."

Prestridge's lips made a thin bloodless line, like a surgical scar. "Yes, I suppose you're right. I retract it. Will you resume, please?"

Southard let out a long breath and spoke. "Erika Graf

was in Sopron when Parr died. She was in Budapest when the AVO took Manyoki. She was in Monte Carlo when the Palestinian hit team shot the Tolosano woman. Now, those incidents are connected. What isn't clear is how they're connected to East German interests."

"Maybe they're not. I hardly need remind you," Prestridge said dryly, "that we ourselves use Reinhard Gehlen from time to time."

"That's what I'm getting at. It's the only thing that makes any sense. She had to be working for the GRU."

"For the Russians, perhaps. But why the GRU and not the KGB?"

"In the first place, the KGB lost ground in the Beria purge, and the GRU's been expanding their Westwork operations. Second, their Westwork chief, Kossior, has worked with Graf before. And finally, the camp in Egypt where the Palestinian terrorists were trained sounds very much like a GRU operation."

"All right, I take your point," Prestridge said impatiently. "But I fail to see a connection between Manyoki and the killing in Monte Carlo."

"Manyoki stayed in Russia after the close of the 20th Party Congress in February, one of a handful of foreign delegates who did. Another was Thierry de Cheverny, the French Communist deputy, who is known to share Manyoki's distaste for taking orders from Moscow. They could have had, and probably did have, contact. De Cheverny's mistress was a journalist, and she published articles closely reflecting Manyoki's views, and she wound up equally dead."

"I thought you never saw this Manyoki document. How do you know his views?"

"From Noah Landler. He was Manyoki's friend as well as his doctor, and they had long talks every day after Manyoki got back from Moscow. The things he told Landler—his speculations on the effects of de-Stalinization in the bloc

229

countries, and the potential for insurrection—might have been outlines for the pieces Tolosano published in *Nice-Matin.*"

"Well," Prestridge said, "some of that's iffy, but for the sake of argument—the GRU through an East German agent used a Palestinian hit team to silence a second-rate French journalist. Just where do you want to take that?"

Southard forced himself to ignore the sarcasm. "I want to take it to its conclusion. I want to go back."

"I can't authorize that," the deputy director said with an almost affable smile, his voice touched with regret, the same odd combinaton Southard had noticed when Prestridge was on the phone. Southard wondered whether Gideon Parr had been given the same affable no in March. He asked: "Why not?"

"Haven't you learned a damn thing since Gideon Parr died? You mounted an operation on your own, you failed to check in, you squandered credit with Reinhard Gehlen and gave him a distorted picture of Agency discipline. It was a near thing whether you'd be asked to resign."

"Was it a near thing for Parr too?"

Prestridge looked back at him steadily. "I shouldn't speak ill of the dead, is that it? Well, let me tell you about Parr. He never got over the glory days of the OSS. He never could comprehend that in intelligence work an organization will accomplish more than an individual. If you want to run a surveillance operation on Kossior and Graf, it would probably be a waste of time. But if you do run it, run it from here."

Prestridge stood, the sunlight streaming through the window glinting on his pince-nez, the incongruous smile curving his lips. "That's it, Ben. I'm running late as it is."

4

Allen Dulles's usually sunny disposition was undergoing a severe test.

The director of Central Intelligence sat in a leather lounge chair in his book-lined study in the big house on Highlands Place, his left foot propped on an ottoman. This latest attack of gout was excruciating. He could not bring himself to follow the diet his doctor prescribed, prohibiting alcohol and all the rich foods he so enjoyed. So now he took cortisone and colchesine. The cortisone produced in Dulles a state of extreme tension, the colchesine brought waves of nausea. The sixty-three-year-old CIA director was maintaining his cultivated air of bonhomie with visible effort.

Southard watched him select a pipe from the rack on the desk. The hand that held the match wavered once, then steadied. Beads of sweat appeared above Dulles's gray mustache and on his forehead. His eyes looked vaguely troubled behind round wire-rimmed glasses. His teeth clamped hard on the stem of the pipe and Southard knew the pain was very bad then. He waited as Dulles prolonged the pipe lighting until he could speak normally.

"You never cared much for desk work, did you, Benton? Well, confidentially, that makes two of us." He patted his face with a folded handkerchief and managed an approximation of the well-known Santa Claus laugh. "Ho, ho! If you can believe Clover, the only thing that keeps me behind a desk is this godawful gout."

Allen Dulles puffed on the pipe, scowling at Southard through the blue smoke. "How old are you, Benton?"

"Thirty-eight."

"Mmm, yes. Old enough to decide what you want to do when you grow up." He said it with calculated levity. "You're a brilliant field officer, I needn't tell you that. As good as they come. As good as Gideon Parr at his best, but that's no accident, is it?"

Southard did not answer. He watched Dulles reach for his handkerchief again and dab at his forehead. His face looked gray. He said, "I blame myself for his death, you know."

"Sir?"

"I should have stopped him from going."

"He was doing what he wanted, wasn't he?"

"It wasn't his decision to make. Good Lord, Benton, at his level he knew every secret in the Agency. You can't let a man like that go into the field. Gideon Parr was my friend, yet when I learned he was dead, I thanked God. Why? He might have been captured instead. He might have blown operations all across Europe, and caused the death of who knows how many of our best agents.

"And that, may I say, is why your little disappearing act left us in a state of acute panic. We had to draw up contingency plans to withdraw your more vulnerable people, to change all our European codes. We even had plans, if you had been captured, to try to rescue you, which seemed unlikely, or to terminate you.

"Well, none of it happened, Benton, but it could have. And if you are willing to run that risk," Dulles said slowly, "we cannot afford to. Let me put this as plainly as I can. Your days as a fieldman should have ended when you took over Parr's job, and I guarantee you they are ended now. I don't mean you'll be chained to a desk in Washington; you'll go abroad as your work requires. But there will be no more cloaks and daggers, no more dark alleys. If any man in your position were to go out on his own, we would have to deal with him as a potential controlled enemy agent."

Southard didn't need it spelled out. He could think of more than one OSS precedent ordered by Wild Bill Donovan or by Dulles himself. Termination of an asset was acceptable procedure if the asset insisted on becoming a liability.

Dulles relit his pipe. "Enough of that. Time to look on the bright side. You've got a fine career ahead of you. One more promotion, and from then on it will be with the advice and consent of the Senate. I'd guess you'll have a deputy directorship by the time you're forty and then—who knows? I won't be around forever." He turned his pipe and pointed with the stem. "But, Benton, for your own sake, try to accept the change of direction gracefully. The wise ballplayer knows when it's time to hang up his cleats and take a job in the front office."

Dulles reached for his cane, and Southard stood, understanding that the interview was over. The director insisted on hobbling to the door with him.

"It was Gideon Parr, ironically, who used to warn against the superman syndrome. Yet he let it destroy his career. Don't let it destroy yours too."

Chapter Thirteen

1

The Cleveland Park section of Washington reminded Major Sam Brodsky of the borough of Queens in New York, where he'd played college basketball for L.I.U. Connecticut Avenue could have been Queens Boulevard and the streets climbing steeply from it could have been the best residential neighborhood of Forest Hills. The houses were set back behind carefully tended lawns and shaded by fine old trees, cars were parked in every driveway and along every curb were late-model Chryslers, Lincolns, Caddies. A teenaged girl came gliding by following two taut leashes, two strutting Afghan hounds. She smiled at Sam Brodsky, a faintly embarrassed smile, as if Afghans were an overly bold declaration of personality for Cleveland Park. Forest Hills had been a conservative neighborhood too.

Sam Brodsky expected to feel a wave of nostalgia. He didn't. He was homesick—for Israel.

"I see why we parked down on Connecticut Avenue," Iser Harel said, shaking his head. "So many cars—and they're as big as tanks."

"A two-ton car in every driveway and a spare at the curb," Major Sam said. "The American dream."

The diminutive Mossad chief, taking two steps for every one of Major Sam's, was wearing as suit and a tie of a subdued pattern. Sam had never seen him wear a tie before, and the discomfort showed on Harel's face as he ran a finger between his collar and the pinched skin of his neck.

Major Sam was carrying a briefcase. Iser Harel was empty-handed; his memory was legendary.

If he left empty-handed, Major Sam wondered, would it mean war?

The Dulles house, half-timbered stucco, stood at the top of Highlands Place. They watched a man in a seersucker suit come down the flagstone path, timing his progress to avoid the water sprinkler sweeping over the close-cropped lawn. As they were about to pass each other, Iser Harel said, "Good evening."

"Evening," Major Sam echoed.

The man nodded perfunctorily. He was somewhere miles away.

So was Sam Brodsky then. He was thinking of Debbie, alone in Paris—no, not alone, in the middle of a clutch of Arab terrorists in some squalid apartment on the Left Bank. He was sure it was squalid, even though Iser Harel wouldn't tell him so much as the address. All he would give him was condensed versions of her reports, three so far, and so condensed that nothing specific was left. "Why do you want details, Sam?" Iser would say. "If you knew what she was doing, you'd only worry more. Believe me, she's doing just fine."

They continued up the flagstone walk, timing their progress to the sprinkler's high sweeping arc as the man coming out had done.

Iser Harel gestured with a tilt of his bald head and said, "Benton Southard. Chief of their European counter-espionage desk."

"Yeah? Know him?"

"Only from his picture. You ought to look at the files more often, Sam."

Iser Harel was uncanny. It wasn't only that he never forgot a face. He never forgot anything.

Sam Brodsky was a man who could forget his own phone

number. And he did go through the Mossad's rogues' gallery periodically. But what would he ever have to do with the CIA's chief of counterespionage for Europe?

2

After dinner, Allen Dulles hobbled with his guests into the study. He busied himself for a while with his pipe, then suddenly pointed the stem at Major Sam. "Got it!" he said. "Madison Square Garden, 1936, '37 maybe? You played forward for St. Johns."

"Close enough. It was L.I.U."

"All-American, weren't you?"

"Only second team, sir."

Iser Harel contrived to look bored. He wasn't. Major Sam Brodsky, former American, former all-American, was unique among Israeli intelligence officers. Though dinner had been awkward, with desultory small talk, basketball now broke the ice. Iser Harel listened to their talk of jump shots and foul shots, hook shots and lay-ups, charging and dunking, all of it incomprehensible and just what he had hoped to hear.

Finally Dulles said, "And now you're an Israeli. How did that happen?"

"It's kind of a long story. When I was in the army in Europe after the war, I took a bunch of Jewish refugees from a DP camp to Palestine. Then I came home, got out of the army, went back, stayed."

"Miss the States?"

"Sure. Who wouldn't? But Israel's home now. It's hard to explain—it's like a chance to tame the American frontier all over again."

Dulles chuckled, but then his smile became forced. He took out a folded handkerchief and mopped his forehead. Behind his round wire-rimmed glasses his eyes closed briefly. His gout's bothering him, Sam thought; like Iser Harel he carefully avoided showing that he noticed. It was a while before Dulles spoke.

"Well, Mr. Harel, what's the view like these days from Tel Aviv?" he said, and Major Sam Brodsky knew the business of the evening had begun.

Prime Minister Ben-Gurion, in response to Britain's final withdrawal from the Suez Canal Zone, had sent out his big guns. Golda Meir, the canny foreign minister, flew to London because Anglo-Israeli relations were at a low ebb and all her diplomatic skills would be needed. Shimon Peres, secretary general of the Defense Ministry, flew to Paris because Franco-Israeli relations had never been better. Iser Harel, director of the Mossad, flew to Washington because Israel would gladly trade information for ordnance and Allen Dulles was known to admire the crack Israeli intelligence service.

"Our Arab neighbors are convinced that America's policy in the Middle East is dominated by international Zionism," Iser Harel said, spreading his hands palms up, smiling. "We only wish they were right."

"And the Israelis?" Dulles asked.

"Tel Aviv believes," Harel said smoothly, "that many factors influence U.S. policy in the area, but that *primus inter pares* is the matter of oil."

"We don't need Arab oil, Mr. Harel," Dulles objected. "We're the largest exporter of petroleum in the world."

"You are now," Iser Harel said. "But a Mossad study suggests that the United States will become a net *im*porter of oil sometime during the next decade. Except for offshore, and possibly Alaska, you can expect little in the way of new oilfields. Saudi Arabia, Iraq, Iran, the emirates—this is where most of the world's oil will come from. All are Moslem countries, and all Arab but Iran. We fear that U.S. foreign policy will increasingly be dictated by the politics of petroleum."

237

"We're also worried," Major Sam said, "now the British have pulled their troops out of Suez, that Egypt will take over the canal itself. Would America let them do that?"

"According to the British, Egypt would be incapable of running the canal," Dulles said, fending off the question.

"The Mossad thinks otherwise," Harel told him. "Suppose we are right. What would the British do?"

There was a pause. Then Allen Dulles said, "Well, the CIA is looking into that right now."

"So is the Mossad," Iser Harel said.

Both men smiled.

"The early indications," Iser Harel said, "are that Britain is militarily incapable of returning to the canal zone in force."

"Our first studies indicate the same."

"Is that good news or bad news?"

"As a matter of policy," Allen Dulles said, "the United States rejects the use of force in the Middle East."

"Clearly, Mr. Dulles, Israel wants peace too. But Israel may not have a choice. Major Brodsky?"

Sam looked up from the notes he had taken from his briefcase. "Two things are going on in Egypt right now that look particularly unpeaceable. One is, the fedayeen are stepping up their terrorist training. When General Dayan knocked out their base at Khan Yunis—I guess you know about that?—they had to get out of Gaza, and the terrorist raids stopped. But that may not be such a blessing in the long run. Because they've got a new base, and it makes the old one look like a Boy Scout camp. They've put it back in the Nile Delta at El Mansûra, where we can't hit it with retaliatory raids. They've got real cadre, not just a few Nazi war criminals but Red Army officers, and they're turning out terrorists on an assembly line. Our assets in Egypt say they've got seven hundred fedayeen in training."

"That many?" Dulles said it quietly, but Major Sam thought he was surprised.

"Unfortunately, yes," Iser Harel said. The little man was scowling fiercely. He fingered the knot of his tie. He seemed to be considering something. Finally he said, "Mr. Dulles, would you mind if I removed this ridiculous thing?"

Dulles laughed and waved a hand in invitation. Iser Harel took off his tie, stuffed it in a pocket, and sighed.

"El Mansûra, seven hundred," Dulles said, scribbling on a pad.

"You could always verify that with a U-2 overflight," Harel suggested.

Dulles looked up sharply. "What do you know about the U-2?"

Harel shrugged. "Lockheed-designed reconnaissance aircraft. Wingspan eighty feet, a glorified glider with a single Pratt & Whitney turbojet engine. Extremely long range. Flight ceiling 101,000 feet. Conducts overflights of the Soviet Union from Wiesbaden and Adana, Turkey, with bases in Norway and Japan contemplated. The flight ceiling precludes Soviet interception. The camera equipment is superb."

Allen Dulles filled and lit his pipe. "Amazing," he murmured.

"Is it? The Institute runs a station in Bonn and one in Moscow, with first-rate assets. The Russians, by the way, will not acknowledge the existence of your spy-in-the-sky; that would be an admission that they cannot shoot it down."

"What about here?" asked Dulles.

"I beg your pardon?"

"Has the Mossad assets here?"

"Has the CIA in Israel?"

Again both men smiled.

"Major Brodsky?" Iser Harel prompted

"We were talking about the fedayeen. It won't be long until those seven hundred trained terrorists begin striking across the Israeli border in force. And it's not only at El

239

Mansûra they're training. Selected fedayeen are in Europe now; we're sure of London, Paris, Nice and Rome. They're adapting guerrilla tactics to urban conditions, sometimes coordinating with other groups of trainees—Algerian rebels, Cubans, Cypriots, like that. They're even used on actual assignments, once at least, in Monaco, for an execution. In a way," said Major Sam, "you might call it on-the-job training."

Allen Dulles winced, and Major Sam thought it was something he said. Then he saw the folded handkerchief come out to mop the forehead again.

"So that's what the fedayeen are up to," Major Sam continued, "and they're just the amateurs. The regular military in Egypt are doing even better. The Russians are pouring arms in through Czechoslovakia. By the end of the year, they'll have 200 MiG-15s and -17s, twenty-five—well, here, see for yourself, sir." He handed Dulles a copy of the Mossad's figures.

Dulles scanned the columns quickly. "These are estimates?"

"They're accurate projections," said Iser Harel. "In six months they'll be hard facts. And Tel Aviv fears the Western powers may not appreciate the danger of so drastic a shift in the arms balance."

"We'd be hopelessly outgunned," Major Sam said flatly. "Those things the Egyptians are getting aren't toys. And no matter how often they say it, they aren't defensive weapons either. The minute they think they're strong enough to smash us, that's the minute the next war starts."

Allen Dulles nodded slowly. "So the trick is not to let them feel strong enough."

"Tel Aviv sees two options," said Iser Harel.

"One of them's pretty clear," Dulles said. "A massive infusion of American arms."

Major Sam Brodsky grinned. "It just happens that we brought a shopping list." He dipped into his briefcase and came out with a sheaf of papers.

"I'd like to study this," Dulles said, extending his hand. "But remember, I'm not the storekeeper."

"No," said Iser Harel, "but you may wind up being the cashier, Mr. Dulles. You see, Tel Aviv has authorized the Mossad to offer payment in its own currency."

"Am I following you, Mr. Harel?"

"I think you are, Mr. Dulles. The Mossad deals in information of proven quantity and quality. If our American friends were to remedy our shortage of arms, we would be pleased to share information of mutual interest."

It was only a moment before the Santa Claus laugh boomed out. "I like it. I wish I *were* the storekeeper. I don't make policy, Mr. Harel, I'm only a jumped-up spook, the same as you. But I'll see what I can do." Dulles struggled to his feet. "We shall have to talk more about this in the morning, gentlemen."

He went with them to the front door and stood there leaning on his cane as they exchanged courtesies. Then he suddenly said: "You mentioned two options. American military aid is obvious. What's the other?"

Iser Harel and Major Sam looked at each other.

"Preemptive war," Iser Harel said.

3

The next morning Southard walked past the broad-beamed Chesapeake Bay fishing boats berthed on the Maine Avenue waterfront. Hand-lettered signs announced catches of bass, rockfish, porgy. There were oysters and soft-shelled crabs. A section of dock was piled high with fat green melons, one sliced open to reveal its bright pink interior. Summer in Washington meant watermelon season.

Southard passed the busy stalls of the seafood market and reached the Wilson Line's Pier Four at the foot of N Street at exactly ten o'clock. The Mount Vernon steamer was just pulling out. Southard watched David Perlmutter, wearing a Hawaiian-shirt that would have done Harry Truman proud, pan a movie camera across the wake of the departing steamer.

It was their second meeting. The first had been two weeks earlier at the zoo in Rock Creek Park.

Perlmutter put the camera in its case. He greeted Southard and they walked together toward the Capital Yacht Basin.

"She doesn't report on any fixed schedule," Perlmutter said, "but Kaplan's heard from her three times now." A tall, florid-faced man with a ginger mustache, he held the ostensible job of political attaché at the Israeli Embassy.

"She's still in Paris?"

"I guess so, since she's reporting to Kaplan. He didn't say different. But then, he didn't say much. He doesn't see the need for this, you know. If you hadn't delivered the goods personally, I wouldn't have an answer for you at all."

"Any details you can give me?"

Perlmutter raised his shoulders and his eyebrows. "She has a cold, she had her appendix out, she's having an affair with a Mongolian circus acrobat, she's six months pregnant. How the hell should I know? What's the setup, anyway?"

"No setup. It's just something we're following."

The Mossad officer waited. Then he sighed. "Okay, so don't tell me. But the guy who developed the concept of need-to-know ought to be dipped in boiling oil before they hang him."

Southard made an apologetic gesture. "Thank Kaplan for me, will you? And tell him I'd appreciate the occasional update."

"I'll tell him. He's still not wild about it."

They walked together as far as the berth of the Chesapeake Bay bugeye ketch *Colonel R. Johnson Colton.*

"A honey," Perlmutter said. "Been used as a houseboat since before the war. How'd you like to live on her?"

"Might not be too bad."

"Did you know she's the oldest listing in *Lloyd's American Register?*"

Southard said he hadn't known that.

Perlmutter shook his head. "The things people don't know about their own country."

4

The following Tuesday shortly before noon, Allen and John Foster Dulles got off the elevator at the third floor of Walter Reed Hospital. The director of Central Intelligence, his limp gone, his step springy, looked prosperous and affable, like a successful stockbroker. The secretary of state, older, taller, sterner, looked like an Old Testament prophet.

Presidential assistant Jerry Persons met them at the nurses' station outside Ward 8. General Howard Snyder, the president's doctor, was with him.

"Keep it down to fifteen minutes, gentlemen," Jerry Persons said. "Can you do that?"

John Foster Dulles had seen the president twice since his emergency surgery for an intestinal obstruction more than two weeks before, Allen not at all.

"Not that the president's health isn't excellent," General Snyder said quickly. "Make no mistake about that. He's had an extraordinary recovery. Extraordinary."

John Foster Dulles gave the doctor a brief sour glance. "Save that for the press, why don't you, Howard?"

The Dulles brothers went with Persons to Ward 8, the presidential suite. MPs in starched khakis with white accoutrements admitted them. Allen Dulles expected to see an almost West Wing bustle inside the suite. He found none. The living room, except for two nurses and two Secret Servicemen, one of them Jim Rowley, head of the White House detail, was deserted. Press Secretary James Hagerty emerged from the spare bedroom which, in the days since Eisenhower's operation, had become his command post.

He asked the Dulles brothers, "Anything in this visit for me?"

Allen Dulles looked at his brother. Foster shook his head. "Not at the moment, Jim," Allen said, managing to make the turndown sound promising.

A staff physician was just leaving the president's room. He recognized the Dulles brothers and greeted them deferentially. But that didn't stop him from saying, "Fifteen minutes, please, gentlemen."

"Why not fourteen?" Foster demanded. "Or sixteen? What is so sacrosanct about the number fifteen?"

Allen smiled. The doctor laughed uneasily. Foster led the way into the room.

Ike sat up in bed wearing a maroon bathrobe and reading a paperbound Luke Short western. He had lost weight and had an indoor pallor, but his teeth flashed and his eyes sparkled in the famous Eisenhower grin.

The Dulles brothers took only five minutes to summarize their meeting with the two Israelis. When they finished, Ike nodded and pursed his lips. "Now," he said, "I have just about exactly one question of overriding importance. Do you think there's going to be war in the Middle East?"

"It's possible, Mr. President," John Foster Dulles said. "The Israelis have a siege mentality. If they feel threatened enough, they'll fight."

"Now," said Eisenhower, "I really don't know all the details of this situation as you fellows do, but it seems to me, what's paramount here, if we don't arm them they'd be unable to, uh, this would seem obvious, I imagine, but how can they fight a war if we don't supply them?"

Allen and John Foster Dulles exchanged a brief glance. The Eisenhower garbled syntax was almost as famous as the Eisenhower grin.

"The French will arm them," Foster said.

"The danger of war is greater," Allen said, "if we don't arm them than if we do. They'd fight the Egyptians to prevent their achieving military superiority."

"Well, then, in a situation like that going on with both of them, what about the Egyptians?"

"If they thought they could win, they'd attack Israel tomorrow. Nasser's whole foreign policy is to drive the Israelis into the sea," Allen said.

"Now, I've made it as clear as I could under these conditions," the president said, "that the United States is going to, unless the circumstances are threatening to us, we are always going to reject the use of force by any of the combatants in the Middle East, and we will. What about the canal? I recall this happened earlier this month over there, that the British have evacuated their last forces, haven't they? Will Nasser expropriate the Suez Canal Company?"

"The British claim that Egypt lacks the technical skills to run the canal," Foster Dulles said.

"The Israelis disagree," Allen Dulles said.

"Now, the point of this, we are going to use every means of persuasion at our command to minimize the risk of war if Colonel Nasser actually does claim the canal, even if the British, and I don't think this is an exaggeration, are going to view the canal as a lifeline to what's left of their empire if he takes it over, but as far as French arms to Israel are concerned, our public posture should be one of criticism but privately they are going to, and we will let them, restore the arms balance if they can."

The Dulles brothers exchanged another glance. Eisenhower, Allen noted, wasn't even breathing hard.

"We couldn't stop the British," Foster said. "They

depend on the canal for guaranteed passage of oil shipments. If Nasser expropriates, Britain might well invade."

"Now, the important consideration in that case," the president said to Allen, "is to determine in advance whether or not the British, if they want to guarantee the flow of oil, are in fact actually capable of mounting an invasion, or not."

"The British *and* the French, Mr. President," Allen said. "Egypt has been sheltering and supplying the Algerian rebels, and of course France depends on the canal for oil too."

"Yes, well, then of course as you say, the French too. And I don't want to hear about it," Ike said.

"Sir?"

"Mr. President?"

"Now, the clearest way I can put this, if you learn that war is inevitable without the possibility of preventing it, none of this is for publication. The United States government, having been kept in the dark by its allies—and by Israel," the president added after a moment's thought, "would be unable to prevent a war it did not know was in the offing. Then, afterwards, and here is the crucial thing for two reasons . . . The first, this is an election year and Dr. Snyder has already given me a clean bill of health as far as running for a second term, but on the other hand your usual energetic campaign is out. So I don't want to be seen in that light come November."

Eisenhower paused for breath. This time Allen did not dare look at Foster for fear he would not keep a straight face.

General Snyder poked his head into the room. "One more minute, gentlemen."

"Now, what I mean by that, England and France are our closest allies and if we learn they are going to fight a war in the Middle East over the Suez Canal, we ought to be able to stop them, but if we can't that is not going to look good to the electorate. So, we don't know. We are a trusting people, there is no complicity on our part in duplicity on theirs. And the Arabs," said Eisenhower, "are the second reason. Hundreds of millions of dollars have already been invested in Arab oil. They're sitting on a sea of the stuff and before long we're going to need it. Now, the Arabs just like the electorate, in the event of a Middle East war we are unable to prevent, we can be holier-than-thou to the British and French after they go in. The American position, for these reasons, is that you collect the information but if we can't stop them and if Egypt takes over the canal and they invade Egypt, we are naive, we are misinformed, but morally our position is unassailable. We just could come out of this the best friends the Arabs ever had."

5

Later, the Dulles brothers lunched together at Foster's table at Chez François.

"How did he seem to you?" the secretary of state asked.

"Mentally, I'd say he's very much himself. He was committing outright slaughter on the English language, true, but I always worked on the assumption that that was intentional. It achieves the same result as dissembling, doesn't it? And it seems more honest." The director of Central Intelligence sucked on his unlit pipe thoughtfully. "He's lost some weight, of course. And he looks older."

"Five years older," Foster agreed. "And I think you're right about his way with the English language. That is one instinctive politician."

"Can you give him what he wants at State?"

Foster Dulles studied his brother's face. Of the two men, Allen was the more open and direct, and his concern showed. Foster was the more private and, when necessary, devious. His own face was expressionless when he answered. "I'm not sure that's the question. Oh, he told us what he wanted, all right." Foster shook his head and continued in his most solemn voice. "But, it pains me to say it, does that really matter? I fear we are dealing with half a president, and never mind what Dr. Snyder says. No, what's best for the country will not be decided in Ward 8 at Walter Reed, and probably not in the Oval Office."

His brother's solemnity usually preceded pontification, Allen knew; this time was no exception. "The problem is not simply whether Israel will fight, or Egypt, or how we will respond. The real problem," said Foster Dulles, "is the dissolution of the British Empire, the crumbling of the British will, their refusal to meet their international commitments. Take Indochina before Dien Bien Phu; if they'd backed us, we might have salvaged the French position. But with Eden as foreign secretary then . . . God, what a fellow! He evades issues, he's as imprecise as Eisenhower when it suits him, and sometimes he's a plain liar."

Foster's dislike for the British was, in high Washington circles, notorious. And Allen knew his brother had more and more focused that dislike on Prime Minister Anthony Eden.

"This is one time," Allen said, "the British can't afford to duck their international commitments. They need oil, so they have to keep the canal open."

"Not a very altruistic motive. But yes, they'd probably fight. And the Jewish state would fight if Russian armed Egypt too heavily. And the French would fight because Egypt supplies the Algerian rebels, and because just now for some reason it suits France to support Israel's right to exist. Believe me, the French lose no love on Israel, the British are positively anti-Zionist. Even in America, we're hardly unanimous. It's a wonder Israel came into being at all."

Foster paused while the waiter served their first course,

then continued, his voice low and self-righteous. "It would be better if it hadn't. It's a moral thorn in all our sides. The center of power is shifting to the Persian Gulf, and will stay there. The Arabs are lucky; they're sitting on an underground ocean of petroleum. Right next door, the Jews are sitting on a sandheap."

"The politics of petroleum," Allen mused, using Iser Harel's phrase. "With that, Israel already has problems enough. Do you think we'll be able to stop Nasser from causing any more?"

"On the contrary, we won't try. It would serve us best, right now, if Nasser did take over the canal."

Allen was too shocked to protest.

"Think about it. If he doesn't, what happens? Business as usual. Britain stumbles along pretending she's still a world power. France gets mired deeper in Algeria. Israel buys arms from France and goes her own way. Nasser plays off the Russians against us, and quite likely Russia winds up getting her window on the Mediterranean. Altogether less than ideal, no? But if Egypt is so gorged with Russian arms that Nasser feels he can take over the canal?"

"They'd fight," Allen said. "The British, French and Israelis would fight. And they'd be right to. The Agency already knows of a contingency plan drawn up in London by—"

"Don't tell me about it," Foster Dulles said firmly. "At least not officially. Naturally I'll be glad of any relevant information off the record. Indeed, Allen, I count on you."

"I see. You want me to find out as much as I can, and then lose the papers, is that it?"

"I want you to realize that U.S. policy will not be in the hands of a man who in the past year has had a severe heart attack and major abdominal surgery. If it were, the nation would be ill served. The president has given us his views, and we will expand upon them as we make decisions in the coming months. As events take their course, we will turn

249

them to our account, to show that we are the only true power in the West, and to demonstrate, to the world and particularly the Arabs, our clear moral superiority over the Russians."

The CIA director knew that with Eisenhower a part-time president, his brother would more than ever be making foreign policy. And what a twisted policy it was. . . .

In his detestation of the British, Foster was forgetting our traditional alliances. In his desire for Arab friends, he was forgetting the fact that oil fields, like canals, can be expropriated. In his disregard of Israel's moral claim, he was forgetting her military importance as our one loyal ally in the area, an oasis of democracy in a desert of Arab despotism. And in his dismissal of Russia's chance to profit from coming events, he was forgetting history.

And yet all of it, Allen Dulles realized with a sinking feeling, was an elaboration of what Eisenhower had said, in his own muddled way, at Walter Reed Hospital.

Foster was pontifical and high-handed, as usual, but he was no usurper of power. Far from it. He was simply considering how best to implement his president's orders.

How could the director of Central Intelligence do any less?

Chapter Fourteen

1

Istvan Varady blinked. The sunlight made his eyes water.

"Idiot! Don't cry," his father said, misunderstanding. He grasped Istvan's arm above the elbow and steered him across the sidewalk. Ferenc Varady's car waited at the curb, an *amerikai,* big and black, dwarfing the occasional Czech Skoda and Russian Chaika driving by. A block away the roadway of the Kossuth Bridge spanned the burnished mirror of the Danube.

The air was warm, the time of day late afternoon. All right, Istvan told himself, start with that. It's simple. Afternoon, because the sun is low over the Buda Hills. Summer, because the lime and linden trees are in full leaf.

Istvan stood there, letting the balmy summer breeze off the river caress his face. He was vaguely aware of people staring at him.

"Get in, get in, hurry up," Ferenc Varady growled at his son.

Shorter than Istvan but broader across the shoulder, the elder Varady wore the uniform of a captain in the AVO, the Hungarian secret police—polished black boots, khaki breeches and blouse with gleaming blue metal markings on epaulets and collar, a garrison cap low over his eyes.

Istvan stumbled entering the car.

"Stop making a spectacle of yourself, you fool."

Istvan's right knee was stiff; that and the pain in his groin forced him to move in a shuffling crouch, like an old man.

He did not want to see his own face. They had shaved him occasionally down in the Fo Street cellars, and the shaving had been painful, the straight razor scraping over puffy new scar tissue. Compulsively he had run his fingers over his face, slowly, a blind man exploring the unfamiliar topography of a country he has no wish to visit. He touched his ear now as Ferenc Varady started the car. The ear was swollen and leathery. He already knew about the nose. The nose had been broken more than once and lay flatly crushed to the left. Three front teeth had been knocked out, three others were loose, two had jagged breaks and if he was not careful he could draw blood just by closing his mouth. Scar tissue had built up over his eyes in thick gnarled ridges. The left side of his chest hurt with every breath. There was pain too, lancing his lower back, whenever he urinated, and sometimes he urinated blood.

They drove in silence. The black *amerikai* crossed the Kossuth Bridge to Pest and turned south along the river.

"Listen, Istvan, and listen carefully," Ferenc Varady said then. His voice was cold, unpaternal, hating. "This cost me more than you'll ever know. You may have set my career back irrevocably. But you're free, you filthy little traitorous shit, I got you out of there. You have twenty-four hours to leave Hungary. If you ever return, you'll be arrested on sight. And I won't know you."

Istvan sat slumped, chin on chest, listening to the hatred.

"First thing tomorrow morning, from the West Station, there's an express for Vienna. You'll be on it."

They turned onto Stalin Street, heading east away from the Danube.

"Where are we going?"

Ferenc Varady said, "60 Stalin Street," and smiled.

On Fo Street near the Kossuth Bridge was AVO headquarters for Buda, where Istvan had been held for the last three months. 60 Stalin Street was AVO headquarters for Pest.

Istvan could feel his heart pounding. He made himself look at his father. "Don't, don't take me there."

"Imbecile. I know the doctor at 60 Stalin Street. He'll clean you up for the train."

"No. Please, no," Istvan said. He was beginning to tremble.

"You ungrateful little cocksucker, we only have to get through this night together and then we're quits. You'll do as I say."

They stopped at the intersection of Stalin Street and the Middle Boulevard. A streetcar was discharging passengers who scurried to the sidewalk. Ahead Istvan saw the massive brick and plaster façade of AVO headquarters.

He groped for the door handle, his movements stiff and awkward.

With a contemptuous backhand swing of his right hand, Ferenc Varady struck his son. The blow slammed Istvan's head against the backrest and he could taste blood in his mouth. He opened the door and tumbled out of the car. Horns blew. He heard a hoarse cry from his father. He rolled over once and got to his feet and lurched toward the sidewalk.

Ferenc Varady put the car in second gear. After the theatrical cry of rage, he paid no further attention to his son.

They had been right: just the mention of 60 Stalin Street would be enough.

They knew about Noah Landler, the Jew doctor. They had got his name from Manyoki, before Manyoki died. For the time being, Landler was free.

They knew about the waiter at the Café Hungaria. Istvan had told them, the one time Istvan had weakened. The waiter was now in the cellars at 60 Stalin Street, but he was useless even after they broke him. He could give them only a description of Istvan, before Istvan's face was ruined. The waiter would be shot.

They hoped Istvan and the Jew doctor would widen the net for them. Ferenc Varady did not think so. His son would go straight to the Jew doctor, and that would be of no value to the AVO. It might reflect poorly on Ferenc Varady, though, his son and the Jew doctor.

Ferenc Varady wished his son had never been born.

Istvan went north along the Middle Boulevard until it began to curve back toward the river. His slow shuffling gait, the threadbare AVO uniform stripped of its insignia, his broken face—all attracted attention. Some passersby gave him a wide berth, others looked at him with pity. But this close to 60 Stalin Street, he was recognizable as a released prisoner. The militiamen walking in pairs on the crowded sidewalk glanced at him without interest.

He collapsed into a chair on the terrace of the Petofi Café. The sun had gone down behind the buildings across the street and in the shade it was cool. The streetcar wires were etched sharply against the sky. As the sweat dried on his body he began to shiver. The waiter came over and wiped his table.

"Could I—just sit here a minute? I can't buy anything."

The waiter looked at him. "I'll bring you some water."

When he brought it, he brought wine too, red and strong. Istvan needed both hands to raise the short-stemmed goblet to his lips. He spilled some. The waiter stood over him, turning his tray in knobbly hands. "If there is anything else I can do," he said.

"Perhaps a phone call? But I have no money."

The waiter went away. Istvan thought the man had refused him. Why should he help? Istvan finished the wine. He felt better—not good, but better. The waiter returned.

"Come on," he said, and led Istvan inside and down a flight of stairs. The telephone was on the wall outside the toilets. The waiter left a few coins on the shelf.

The Kobanyai Street Medical Center or home? Istvan did not know. He tried the home number, and Landler himself answered. Twenty minutes, he said. Half an hour at the most.

Istvan sat on the terrace outside the café again. The waiter brought him another glass of red wine. He drank this one slowly.

He felt light-headed. People floated by. A streetcar bell clanged distantly. Istvan did not know the day of the week, the date, not even what month it was. They had their own time on Fo Street. They had ten-hour days and thirty-hour days and fourteen-hour days and most nights were short and you had to lie on the hard cot with your hands outside the thin dirty cover and they said if you turned your back to the Judas hole in the door they would shoot you. They came during the long days and the short days, and at night, and they took you to the interrogation room. They beat you with the steel-cored lengths of rubber hose and they stuffed your head in a bucket of water until you convulsively filled your lungs and then they kicked you while you lay puking. Or they took three of you and made all of you stand on one foot without moving and if one lost his balance nothing happened to that one but the other two were beaten. When he told them about the headwaiter at the Hungaria he wanted to kill himself. If there was a way to do it he would have done it. He did not want to think about what would happen to the headwaiter. He himself would heal but he would always be maimed and ugly. He had seen the looks of the women on the Middle Boulevard. He thought of Friedl in Austria, blonde and beautiful, untouched by horror. He would not see her. He could not inflict himself upon her. He would see his half-brother Oskar, and Oskar would tell Friedl that he had died. That would be best, and almost the truth.

"Istvan?"

Noah Landler stood there, stocky, dark, his kind homely

face smiling down at Istvan. Landler could do that. Landler was a doctor. Landler had seen far worse than what had become of Istvan's face.

He offered money, but the waiter refused it.

His car was a tiny Fiat 500. Istvan shut his eyes. The car jounced and swayed. Riding a horse would feel like this, Istvan thought. He drifted off once or twice. Dusk was falling.

2

Dr. Landler's apartment, two blocks from the medical center, was large by Budapest standards, three rooms including a small kitchen, and a toilet and shower in a windowless cubicle. Landler had arranged for his wife and daughter to be out. A pot of soup, with boiled chicken and vegetables, waited on the stove to be warmed.

"I'll find you some clothing," Landler said. "Meanwhile get rid of that uniform. Good Lord, but it's ripe. How long have you been wearing it?"

"I don't know. What month is this?"

Landler's eyebrows went up. "July. The fifth. Now let's have a look at you."

The doctor surveyed him, naked, under a bright light. He poked and prodded. "Can you shower yourself?"

Istvan nodded. The shower flowed feebly but the water was warm. There was a bar of brown laundry soap. He scrubbed away three months' grime, then Landler went to work with bandages and tape.

By the time he finished, the pot on the stove was steaming. The smell made Istvan faintly dizzy with hunger. He sat at the kitchen table in fresh underwear and a pair of dark slacks an inch too short for him and baggy around the waist. Landler filled a soup bowl for him.

"What you need first of all is a good few days' rest. The

broken ribs are knitting. You have a slight hernia. It can wait. You'd better see a dentist fairly soon, though. Don't worry about the knee; it will be all right. The face will heal too, though you'd be more attractive if anybody'd bothered to stitch some of those cuts." Landler realized his mistake and said quickly, "The swellings will go down. Some of the scars will remain puckered. It won't be as bad as you think."

He watched Istvan eat for a while. "I think I can arrange for you to stay at the Kobanyai Street Medical Center."

"No. I don't want to stay there. Or anywhere in Hungary."

"You can be hidden, afterwards. That can be arranged too."

"Is this something you do?" Istvan asked, looking up from his soup. "Ordinarily?"

"Well, not quite ordinarily. But I do what I can."

"Jesus, after everything that happened this spring, you still take chances like that? You're crazy. You ought to get out of Hungary too."

"I'm needed here. I have to stay."

"And if the AVO took you? If they made you talk?"

"We all have to chance that."

"Please, Dr. Landler. Take your family and get out while there's still time."

Landler shook his head. "Time? It seems ages since your friend Curtis Beck gave the same advice, but I'm still here. So you see, it's all relative."

"When did you see Beck last?"

"Not since the night you were—taken. I drove him to the lake, and he went across with Friedl."

Istvan remained silent for a while. He had stopped eating. "I was supposed to go in the morning," he said then. "But my father has my papers."

"I'll see if I can get the laboratory van tonight."

Landler called and arranged it. Then, when Istvan was

asleep, he called a pharmacist he knew in Sopron. He hoped they could get the message across the lake in time.

3

Above the rustle of reeds, Istvan heard frogs croaking. A light breeze blew from the west. There was no moon and the first faint predawn light touched the sky with purple. Istvan could smell the lake.

Dr. Landler put a hand on his shoulder, gently so as not to jar the taped ribs. "Good luck to you, Istvan. I won't say good-bye, but *auf Wiedersehen.*"

"That's better. If we see each other again, it will mean you've had the sense to get your family out of the country."

"Oh, you'll come back to Hungary."

"Never," Istvan said.

"Never? That's a long time."

"When we fly the Kossuth flag instead of the hammer and sickle, then I'll come back. When Hungary is free."

They shook hands silently. As he walked down the track to the water Istvan heard the van drive off.

He saw the skiff and the slim figure waiting at the water's edge, silhouetted against the faint glow off the surface of the lake. He wanted to run. He stood rooted.

She ran. She came up the track with her hands outstretched and her voice incanting his name, and she was inside the circle of his arms so quickly that at first he felt almost like a surprised bystander. Then he felt nothing except the overwhelming nearness of her. She held him without hurting him, her lip moving up his neck, along his scarred cheek, to his broken mouth. He tried to push her away. She took his hand and led him down the track to the skiff and he did not have the strength to resist her.

He sat in the skiff's broad stern and watched the lithe movements of her body against the lightening sky as she used the pole to steer them north through the tall reeds close to shore. The eastern sky was apple green by the time they neared the Austrian village of Illmitz. He saw the string of lights on the road along the marsh as she brought the skiff in. The bottom grated on gravel and she leaped out, her blonde hair swinging in a single thick braid across her back. She turned.

He raised his hands. "Don't look at me, Friedl," he said. "Please don't."

She came closer, splashing through the water until she stood with her face six inches from his. She touched the long puckered ridge of scar tissue over his cheekbone, touched his scarred brow. She ran a finger lightly along the swollen, twisted lower lip.

"Well, that's a relief," she said. "You're not prettier than me anymore."

Her voice broke then and she was crying against his shoulder and finally, for a while, it was he who had to be strong for the two of them.

4

Later that morning at the French border station of St.-Genis six miles from Geneva's Cointrin Airport, a *douanier* named Claude Frangy answered the telephone.

"*Oui, j'écoute.*"

"Is this the St.-Genis customs bureau?"

Claude Frangy perched on the edge of a cluttered desk. "Yes, Corporal Frangy speaking," he replied in a bored voice. "How may I help you?"

"A gray Citroën 2CV, Paris plates 115NY75, has just left Geneva on Route 46 for St.-Genis."

"All right, I've got that." Frangy wrote down the number. "What about it?"

"The driver is named Madeleine Béranger. No passengers."

"Who is this speaking?" Frangy demanded.

"Mademoiselle Béranger will be smuggling into France a quantity of uncut diamonds valued at two hundred thousand Swiss francs."

Frangy heard a click. *"Allo?"* he said. *"Allo?"* He jiggled the cradle of the handset, but the connection had been cut.

A practical joke? A crank with a grudge against this Madeleine Béranger? The real thing? Frangy had no way of knowing. He did not even know if Mademoiselle Béranger —provided there *was* a Mademoiselle Béranger—was French or Swiss.

He pocketed the slip of paper with the license number, spoke briefly with his sergeant, who immediately picked up his own phone, and went outside. It was barely twenty kilometers from Geneva to the frontier at St.-Genis. Frangy wouldn't have long to wait.

He lit a cigarette and looked east along the two-lane blacktop road, squinting in the sunlight, at the French passport control booth, the Swiss control point beyond it, the tricolor and the red Swiss flag with its white cross snapping in the gusty wind. A few cars came and went. He lit a second cigarette.

It was seventeen past ten on Frangy's watch when the gray 2CV was waved through the Swiss checkpoint. It pulled to a stop at French passport control. And from where he stood Frangy could see a dark blue French passport change hands twice. Then the small gray car drove the short distance to the French customs station.

"I'll take this one," Frangy told the man on duty.

She had a gamine prettiness, her dark brown eyes large, her cheekbones high, her small nose aquiline. She wore a blue and white striped jersey and no makeup. With her dark hair caught in twin pigtails and a guileless smile, she seemed an unlikely smuggler.

Frangy saluted her and admired the snug fit of the blue and white striped jersey. "Good morning, mademoiselle.

How long have you been in Switzerland?"

"Just overnight."

"Tourist?"

"I was visiting a friend."

"Have you anything to declare?"

The word *declare* worked its magic. The girl's smile became forced, and she began to fidget. Frangy felt regret; looking at the girl, he had hoped the caller would turn out to be a crank. But his experience now told him otherwise.

"Declare? No, I have nothing to declare at all."

The girl's tongue darted out and licked her lips.

Frangy indicated the curb near the cinderblock building. "Please park over there."

A moment later he again stood outside the window on the driver's side of the Citroën. On the seat next to the girl was a large straw handbag; otherwise the interior of the car was empty. To make sure, Frangy walked behind it and looked through the rear window at the luggage space behind the flimsy back seat. Nothing.

"If you would come with me, mademoiselle?"

"What is this?"

"You are Madeleine Béranger?"

"Yes."

"This way, please."

Again her tongue darted out to lick her lips. Frangy opened the door for her. She wore a dark blue skirt and white high-heeled shoes.

"What's the matter?" she asked.

"Nothing at all, mademoiselle. Merely routine. My regrets for the inconvenience."

As they left the car together, Frangy signaled two *douaniers* who had been lounging near the side of the building. They approached the 2CV. While Madeleine Béranger was inside, they would give the car a thorough going-over.

"Empty your handbag on the counter, please."

"I insist you tell me what this is all about," the girl said.

Frangy sighed. He turned to the police matron who had arrived from the nearby town of Gex minutes before in response to the sergeant's call.

The matron, a heavyset woman with broad shoulders, stood behind the counter watching Frangy and the girl. She had hard flat eyes. Her hands, clenched into man-sized fists, rested on her hips.

"Empty it," she said.

With a shrug the girl opened the straw handbag, considered a moment, and then turned it upside down over the counter. Out spilled an open pack of cigarettes, several books of matches, a compact, two lipsticks, a tiny flagon of Chanel No 5, eyeshadow and brush, hairpins, four emery boards, an orange stick, two combs, an eyebrow pencil, a flat tin of Nivea cream, a pocket-pack of Kleenex, some rubber bands, a billfold, and Madeleine Béranger's passport.

"All that makeup," observed the police matron.

Frangy raised his eyebrows.

"And she isn't wearing any."

Frangy nodded.

The matron approached the counter and with her big hands examined the tubes of lipstick, the compact, the perfume. She dug in the Nivea cream with one of the emery boards. The girl watched her, blinking nervously. "Nothing," the matron said.

"In that case, might I go?" the girl asked, her voice excessively sweet. "If you are *quite* satisfied?"

Frangy sighed again. The girl was regaining her composure. They usually did when it looked as if they would get away.

Of course, there was still the chance the call had been a joke or a grudge. Many of them were. But the girl was following the pattern—uncertainty, fright, then relief before the body search.

Frangy nodded to the matron.

"That way," the broad-shouldered woman pointed. "In there." She followed the girl toward an office, pulling a tight rubber glove onto her stubby-fingered right hand.

The door shut behind them.

Not quite ten minutes later, the Béranger girl came out, pale and obviously furious. Behind her the police matron shook her head.

"Someone," Madeleine Béranger cried, "is going to pay for that indignity."

The matron shrugged. Frangy apologized, but not profusely. He had yet to hear the results of the car search.

"Your name?" the girl snapped at him.

He told her.

"And the name of the bull dyke?"

The matron took a step forward. Frangy got between them. "Tell her your name," he said wearily, and the matron did.

The girl swept the contents of the counter into her straw handbag and walked outside. The two *douaniers* were just leaving her car. One of them shook his head at Frangy.

"My profound regrets," Frangy told the girl.

"It's too late for that, corporal."

Frangy decided on honesty. "Please try to understand. We received an anonymous call saying you would be smuggling diamonds. What were we to do?"

"You might have tried asking me," she said, spitting out the words. "You, corporal, are a credulous fool. And that woman is a pervert. They shall hear of this in Paris."

Madeleine Béranger got into her car. "I shall deal with Jean-Luc myself," she said. "I might have known, the moment I broke with him, he would pull some filthy trick like this. But for you, a professional, to fall for it!"

She revved the engine, clashed the gears, and left Frangy standing in a cloud of exhaust.

Four days later, at the same hour of the morning, he watched her small gray Citroën approach. She spoke to the *douanier* on duty but Frangy had the misfortune to be standing outside smoking. She spotted him, pulled over, and leaned toward her open window.

"Well, corporal? Aren't you going to search my car today? Or me? Where's your bull-dyke friend?"

"Please, Mademoiselle Béranger, I was only doing my duty."

"So do it." She swept an arm to indicate herself, the straw handbag on the seat beside her, the suitcase behind. "No? Today I'm no longer a suspicious character? Today your bull-dyke friend doesn't get a cheap thrill? You disappoint me."

Frangy lifted his hands helplessly. Her sarcasm saddened him. Again he could only watch her drive away.

In Paris that night Deborah crossed a courtyard on rue des Quatre Vents near the Odéon and climbed the staircase in the far left corner.

Maryam opened the door of the apartment and quickly reached out a hand to help Deborah with the suitcase she was carrying. "You've got them?"

"I guess. I wasn't asked to open it, so I didn't."

In the kitchen, Deborah nudged Sulayman's feet until he took them off the table and lowered his copy of *Réalités*. He looked on while she hefted the suitcase onto the table, unlocked it, and lifted the lid. Then he moved. He threw aside the top layer, the folded bath towel, and looked down at the contents.

"Nice," he said.

Inside, nested in cotton wadding, were the broken-down parts of four of the Swiss army's Erma P38 Sturmgewehr submachine guns.

Militiamen with Model 41 submachine guns patrolled unobtrusively in the thick stand of birches behind the narrow shingle beach on the Moscow River twenty miles west of the Soviet capital. Everywhere were posted no-fishing signs and everywhere members of the *nomenklatura* were fishing. Their families and guests lined the broad slow stream below the bluff that held the village of Zhukovka and their *dachas*. Should any such privileged souls chance upon a militiaman, he would salute smartly and continue his vigil. Sometimes, though, others wandered into the exclusive area. The mistake was soon rectified. Unspoiled, bucolic, Zhukovka was not for everyone.

Two men were climbing the steep path from the shingle beach to Zhukovka Village on this Sunday afternoon in mid-July. Each had a fishing pole and the younger man carried a creel which held a layer of wet leaves but no fish.

The older man said, "Sometimes I wonder why I bother. I haven't caught anything all season."

The younger man nodded and said nothing. He had been tongue-tied all afternoon. It wasn't often that a junior officer was invited for the day to the *dacha* of a general, particularly when the junior officer was a brand-new lieutenant, and the general was I.A. Serov, chief of the KGB.

They reached the top of the path and skirted the western edge of Zhukovka Village, its rough-hewn log cabins backed by vegetable gardens with out-houses among the cabbages. Zhukovka looked like any of a dozen poor villages on the Moscow River until they approached the long cinderblock store and the parking lot behind it. Here were a few big Zil limousines, more Chaikas, even more Volga sedans. Chauffeurs stood in small groups talking, some of them polishing already gleaming fenders with chamois cloths. The young lieutenant had never been in the store but he knew of it. It was stocked lavishly with Western goods for members of the *nomenklatura*, the superelite of the Soviet hierarchy.

General Serov and his young guest crossed the railroad tracks a hundred yards from Zhukovka's modest station. They continued north along the narrow unpaved road and then took a lane to the left. In five hundred meters they reached a chain link gate in a green palisade fence. The KGB guard immediately opened the gate, bringing his Kalashnikov smartly forward to present arms.

The Serov *dacha*, not five years old, was a replica of a nineteenth-century hunting lodge, rough-hewn logs outside, steeply pitched roof, belfry. Inside was a staff of three KGB noncoms, hand-rubbed walnut paneling, a modern kitchen that had been flown in piece by piece from West Germany, teak and glass furniture from Finland, Swedish scatter rugs in bright sunbursts of color, a sauna, Rosenthal china in the dining room and Baccarat crystal in the large wet-bar at one end of Serov's study—twelve rooms in all, and more luxury than the young lieutenant had ever seen.

"I'm drinking Pernod," Serov said. "Is that all right?"

The lieutenant quickly said it would be fine. He had sampled the cloying yellow licorice-flavored drink at Dzerzhinsk. He did not like it but he did not for a moment consider declining.

The KGB's total-immersion academy for Westwork was located outside the city of Dzerzhinsk, two hundred seventy miles east of Moscow, not far from where the Oka River flows into the Volga. The young lieutenant, already fluent in the French and German languages, had spent sixteen weeks in the French section of Dzerzhinsk followed by sixteen in the German—2,688 uninterrupted hours in each meticulously simulated environment.

"Your orders have been cut," General Serov said. "You are going to Paris."

The lieutenant hid his elation. "Yes, sir."

Serov said dryly, "It is permitted to smile, Andrei Leonidovich." Serov was a small wiry man with reddish hair and a high forehead. Lounging in a leather armchair, he seemed surprisingly relaxed for a man whose job was the most dangerous in the *nomenklatura*. No chief of the secret police, whether called the Cheka, OGPU, NKVD, MVD, MGB, or KGB, had died in office of natural causes, with the exception of old Felix Dzerzhinski himself. Two had been dismissed in disgrace. The rest—Yagoda, Yezhov, Beria, Merkulkov, Abakumov—had been executed. Serov was now in his third year of command. His was a KGB with its wings clipped by the treason and disgrace of Lavrenti Beria. Since then the GRU had risen under Serov's rival, the ambitious General Shalin.

Serov believed it was now time to redress the balance.

He made fresh drinks and opened a folder. "Andrei Leonidovich Golovin," he read. "Born Smolensk, 1931. Seconded from Frunze Academy to the KGB, 1953. That would have been the year your father died, I believe?"

"Yes, sir," Lieutenant Golovin said. "Murdered in Berlin by the Gehlen Group."

Serov offered cigarettes, which Golovin declined, and pinched the cardboard tip of one himself before lighting it.

"Not exactly. We are now convinced," he said slowly, "that the Gehlen Group was just one of four organizations in Germany responsible for your father's murder."

Lieutenant Golovin did not speak. A knot of muscle moved on either side of his jaw. He was a tall young man, blond, fair, blue eyes; a perfect Teutonic type, Serov thought. His cover as a Rhineland German would be a natural. Languages weren't young Golovin's only assets.

"The second was the CIA. As for the third and fourth," Serov tapped his cigarette briskly on the edge of an ashtray, "you must recall that in June of the year your father died, reactionary elements in East Berlin rioted against the authority of the state and the party. We were caught unprepared due to treason in the East German Ministry for State Security and at GRU-Wünsdorf. Your father ferreted out those responsible and would have brought them to book—if they hadn't betrayed him to the Gehlen Group and the CIA."

Serov crushed out his cigarette. "It has now become distinctly possible to discredit, disgrace and punish these traitors. And that, Andrei Leonidovich, is what your Paris assignment is all about."

Lieutenant Golovin smiled for the first time, as cold a smile as General Serov had ever seen.

6

Two time zones to the west, in the first range of pre-Alpine hills above the French Riviera, it was not yet noon. Erika Graf stretched languidly, rolled over once and stood beside the bed. With its windows shuttered, the small bedroom was dim but already the heat of the day had penetrated the thick tawny colored stucco walls of the studio near the cliff at the back of the secluded property.

Erika's skin was deeply tanned, her long blonde hair several shades lighter. It was tangled now and her eyes, darkly shadowed underneath, were slightly bloodshot. To conduct an affair with a man steadily drinking himself into an early grave was hard work. Actually, he had decreased his dependence on alcohol lately because it interfered with his virility. Erika stood looking down at him and felt a touch of warmth, possibly of pity. Either was a weakness she had to avoid.

Kip Chaffee lay, naked as she was, on his side facing where Erika had slept. A long, loose, gangly redhead of thirty-five, the American was an imaginative lover when sober. If he lacked the plunging animal strength of

Giovanni Venturino, he made up for it with an ability to read Erika's moods, an ability which could leave her gasping.

Chaffee now stirred, opened his eyes and grinned one of those lopsided grins that seemed an American monopoly.

"Bloody Mary time?" he asked.

"Say, 'Good morning, darling,' " Erika suggested.

"Good morning, darling. I gather it's not Bloody Mary time?"

"Morning, lover. Let's have a dip first and then some brunch."

The trick had been to help Chaffee dry out partially, to shift some of his dependence from alcohol to her. Over the last few weeks it had come along beautifully. Weaning him from emotional to professional dependence had been the easiest part.

Erika threw open the floor-to-ceiling shutters and stood in the doorway, silhouetted against the hot glare of summer sunlight. Chaffee came up behind her, grasped her waist and pulled her against his own hardening warmth.

"Not now, lover," she said, but the dangerous weakness was there in her voice. She wanted him too, as she had wanted Venturino before him. No, more. Venturino was a stud, and their sex only a glass of cool spring water on a hot day. But Erika was fond of this skinny, freckled American and she knew her assignment meant his destruction.

She ran across the terrazzo apron to the pool that had been blasted out of the limestone shelf and dove in, hitting the water cleanly and swimming two free-style lengths before Chaffee executed a belly-flopping racing dive and beat the water to froth with an awkward but serviceable butterfly stroke.

Soon they lay side by side on air mattresses. The patio and pool were tucked into the L of the studio on the southern edge of the property, a hundred meters from the big villa itself and on the highest land above the village of

Bourg St.-Martin in the hills twenty kilometers northwest of Nice. A short way beyond the pool the limestone shelf, flat as a tabletop, ended in a sheer cliff. On its other three sides the property was girdled by a ten-foot wall of the tawny local stone. Their privacy was absolute.

Chaffee propped himself on one bony elbow. "Francine's coming back tonight."

"You think I could forget, do you?"

Francine Chaffee owned a small art gallery on rue Bonaparte in Paris. She showed her husband's paintings, among others.

"What will you do?"

"Go back to the villa on Cap d'Antibes until she leaves, I guess. Lie on the beach, go shopping, go to parties. Whatever people do."

"Listen, baby," Chaffee began, his voice troubled. Then he shook his head. "No—never mind."

"What is it?"

"Nothing. I was only thinking—you'll be seeing Venturino?"

"We're friends. There's no reason I shouldn't see him. Anyway, I don't, not when you and I are together."

"It's when we're apart that bothers me."

Jealousy was one form his increasing dependence took. Erika encouraged it. She waited a minute, then said, "Well, what do you expect me to do when that French bitch you married is here?"

"Nothing. I don't know. Whatever you want. I don't have any claims on you." He stood, all bony angles except where the muscles of his abdomen had gone slack. Self-consciously he drew a breath, sucking in his gut. Another year or two of the kind of drinking he did, the kind of life he led, and he'd really go to flab.

He went inside for a few minutes and returned wearing a terry robe and carrying a tray with a pitcher of Bloody Marys and two tall glasses. He sat on the apron, dangled his feet in the pool and poured the glasses full. He drank thirstily. She joined him, sipping her own drink slowly. It was icy but strong, half tomato juice, half vodka, too much tabasco. He ran a fingernail lightly the length of her thigh from knee to damp, matted blonde hair.

"I was thinking," he said.

"Oh? Is that what you call thinking?"

"No, I mean it. You saved my career, you know that, don't you? Jesus, what a mess I'd made of it."

"Which one?"

"Funny. Very funny," he said.

He hadn't touched a paintbrush since she'd moved in with him. His wife had been in Paris almost a month.

"What I still wouldn't mind knowing," he said, "is why."

"Why do you have to know why?"

He poured himself another drink. She knew his tolerance for alcohol was very low. A third drink and, in his own Midwest Americanism, his back teeth would be floating.

"I just wouldn't mind knowing, that's all." He quickly drank half the second drink.

"I hadn't meant to tell you until it was definite in my own mind," she said, "but—well, I might want you as a kind of job reference. If I decided not to stay with my service, that is."

"Defect? You've got to be kidding. You have it made as it is." He treated it as a joke, but she could sense he wanted to believe her, if only he could be sure she wasn't making fun of him.

A half-truth, she had found, generally made a convincing lie. "Have I? A few years ago I was involved in something that could still get me killed. I can't arrange a completely safe new life for myself. But your people could."

He emptied the pitcher into his glass. After a while he asked, "Serious?"

"Yes."

"Jesus," he said. "Let me think about it."

"Don't misunderstand. I said I hadn't decided anything."

His voice was third-drink thick. "Want to meet some people?"

"Not yet. I need some time to think it over."

"Want to tell me what kind of trouble you're in? Maybe I could come up with something."

"No, not until—no."

Kip Chaffee peered into his empty glass, and shrugged. "Want to get laid?"

"Now, that's more like it," she said, and while he was disrobing she pushed him off the apron of the pool into the water. She dove in after him and for a few moments they were a thrashing tangle of arms and legs. Finally, at the shallow end of the pool, he stood and she sat facing him, buoyant in the water, her long legs wrapped around his middle while his hands gripped her flanks and began to move her up and down.

They were like that when Francine Chaffee stepped through the double doors.

7

London!

Dmitri Platonovich Kossior experienced the guilty pleasure of a man indulging a secret perversion.

It was noon, the sun was shining but a sudden hard rain pelted the pavement of Buckingham Palace road three floors below Kossior's window in the Hotel Reubens. So typical, so delightful! Kossior watched the large black umbrellas unfurl to bob serenely down the street, almost like sentient creatures. A man on a Vespa, wearing a bowler hat and pin-striped suit, went rasping by, quite oblivious to the downpour. A high black taxi executed a tight U-turn like a toy car on a turntable. Kossior leaned out the window to look skyward. More blue than cloud cover, but the rain continued. The air sparkled with sunlight. Across the road Kossior could see through a fence the grounds of the palace where .a somewhat toothy, somewhat dowdy young woman reigned but did not govern. Governing meant Whitehall and, as he always did when he arrived in London, Dmitri Platonovich Kossior wanted to see it. Barely a kilometer north to south, from Trafalgar Square, where black lions guarded the monument to Admiral Nelson, to Westminster Abbey, where in hallowed dimness one walked on the tombstones of the famous and breathed history with the musty air.

Kossior unpacked his battered Gladstone quickly. His tan mac was wrinkled. He had an umbrella of course. The poor cut of his gabardine suit, with too-broad lapels and shapeless trouser legs, would go unremarked. No matter how the myth appealed to Kossior, not all Londoners dressed as if they were—what was the fellow's name?—Beau Brummell.

A glance at his watch told the Russian it was a quarter-past noon, a full hour before his appointment, more than enough time for a pint of bitter before proceeding along Birdcage Walk past St. James's Park and the Guildhall to the bridge.

Kossior drank his bitter in the public bar of the Keg o' Nails, noisy, crowded, smoke-filled, and so close to Buckingham Palace that he could assume many of its patrons worked there in nameless, mysterious capacities. The pint of bitter—flat, warm, heavy with the taste of hops—reminded Kossior, as it always did, of Russian *pivo*. He never could comprehend how two countries so different produced brews with the same distinctive character. He drank his bitter slowly and, in an Oxbridge English out of place in the public bar of the Keg o' Nails, discussed the weather, still raining, still sunny, not at all freakish, with a chap who wore a cap and a tweed Norfolk jacket and who smelled unmistakably of horses.

The rain had stopped by the time he reached Horse Guards Road and he stood a moment loking up at the soot-blackened Foreign Office. He furled his umbrella, then removed the paperbound copy of *A Tale of Two Cities* from the pocket of his mac. As he crossed Parliament Street to Bridge Street, he felt the guilty pleasure again as a lump rose in his throat at the closeness of the Abbey and Big Ben, Big Ben itself, surely as symbolic of all that was British as the onion domes of St. Basil's and the crenellated walls of the Kremlin were of all things Russian. He waited at the northeast corner of Victoria Embankment, at the entrance to Westminster Bridge, leaning on the railing, gazing at the opaque gray of the Thames under what was now lowering cloud cover, *Two Cities* in his left hand, the cover displayed.

The pavement by now was crowded with lunch-hour pedestrians. Traffic moved slowly past on the wrong side of the road—cars, the high black taxis, the tall red double-decker buses like every child's dream of England. For the third time Kossior felt the guilty pleasure. He couldn't help it. He believed in history as a religious man believes in God, and history had made London on its island at once the culmination and the repository of Western culture. Flawed ultimately by capitalist decadence, of course, but the Athens of Pericles and the Rome of the Caesars had been decadent too.

A chap smoking a pipe with a deep bowl and one of those almost S-shaped stems folded his arms on the railing nearby and gazed across the water. Kossior recognized him

274

at once. The file of photographs at Znamensky Street in Moscow could have served as his biography: the student at Cambridge, taking a first in history; the young lieutenant in Naval Intelligence in North Africa early in the war; the member of the British Empire newly invested for his activities when it was learned Admiral Laborde would scuttle the French fleet; the bridegroom (twice); now in his Foreign Office persona.

Kossior saw a man in his forties, tall, slender, distinguished, Savile Row tailored, clipped mustache, deep blue eyes, hair graying at the temples—altogether the establishment type personified by the prime minister himself, Anthony Eden.

The two men leaned on the railing for a few moments in the not uncompanionable silence of strangers briefly together. Then the Englishman tapped dottle from his pipe.

"Don't see many people reading Dickens these days," he said.

"No, not very fashionable, I'm afraid."

The streets of a major city, especially at a crowded time like lunch hour, are ideal for a *tref*, provided you are not under surveillance. Both men had made certain of that. They were able to move anonymously among the crowds and they could converse as freely as if they were alone. They walked together for two hours. It rained twice briefly while they strolled south on Millbank, and showed signs of clearing when they turned into Horseferry Road. It was raining again, hard, when they lost themselves in the maze of streets between Horseferry and the Vauxhall Bridge Road. That shower lasted ten minues. Umbrellas were unfurled, furled again. They talked.

The change of command at the Secret Intelligence Service could be a problem. The former head, Sinbad, had retired under a cloud after *l'affaire* Crabb. Kossior and the Englishman chuckled over that. In April when Khrushchev and Bulganin sailed to Britain on a state visit, the frogman Lionel Crabb went for a mysterious swim under the keel of their cruiser *Ordzhonikidze,* and wound up floating headless in Portsmouth harbor. So now SIS had a new chief, Dick White, brought over from M15. He had the mentality of a policeman, and was expected to use police methods internally. And he might well want to put his own people into the top slots at SIS. Kossior knew the rivalry between Britain's M15, internal security, and SIS was as potentially explosive as that between the KGB and his own GRU. It remained to be seen whether Dick White would alleviate or exacerbate the interagency struggle.

The high-flying American U-2 reconnaissance plane could be a problem. Disinformation becomes more difficult to carry off—by no means impossible, Kossior insisted, but more difficult—in the face of photographic evidence to the contrary.

The Philby experience could be another problem. Kim Philby, now strongly suspected in Foggy Bottom to be a Russian agent, had served as Washington liaison for The Firm, as SIS was known, in the early days of the CIA. The Americans then considered themselves disciples of Great Britain's spymasters. That attitude ended abruptly when MacLean and Burgess received asylum in Russia. But if the American cousins no longer looked on SIS as an infallible mentor, they at least had faith in Dick White. Besides, at CIA insistence, the liaison office so questionably served by Kim Philby had since been moved to London, and these days information typically flowed to rather than from Washington. CIA mistrust of The Firm, Kossior hoped, could be turned into a decided asset.

Within the CIA, Adam Prestridge would be an asset

too. Not consciously, of course. Fanatic anti-Communist that he was, Adam Prestridge would take strychnine and slit his throat while jumping off a tall building if he thought he was aiding the cause of godless international Communism. But Prestridge's monomania about rolling back the Iron Curtain, however outdated, however hopeless of execution, still blinded him to all other considerations. Prestridge could be counted on to play.

The last unpredictable factor was the American president. If Operation Musketeer moved from paper to parachutes, from staff conferences to landing craft, how would Eisenhower respond? He was that paradox, a supremely gifted military commander who detested war. But perhaps the vital question wasn't how Eisenhower would respond, but when.

"Oh, I can deliver," said the Englishman as they walked along the north side of the Westminster School Playground. "*Especially* after Philby. I shan't be requesting information, after all, I'll be supplying it."

In Greencoat Row he said, "The cousins like me, you see. I've cultivated that, although it's been painful at times. Since I *am* popular with them, Dick White will need me. However much he would prefer to bring in one of his policemen, I'm secure in my position."

As they walked east along Great Peter Street toward the river he said, "I assume you are to be my controller?"

"Why would you assume that?"

"Good heavens, old boy, you seem to know everything about me. To give that sort of information to anyone except my controller would be bloody irresponsible."

"Quite," said Kossior, with clipped British precision.

The man impressed him, but that was so surprise. He had been handpicked more than twenty years ago. It had been worth saving him this long.

The project which in prospect had so dazzled Erika Graf

at the New Adlon Hotel in East Berlin was now at last fully operational.

Kendall Tarrant taxied to Chelsea through the bright afternoon sunshine, telling the driver to stop where Sloane Gardens turns sharply back toward Lower Sloane Street. The red brick townhouses, the leafy green of the curbside trees, the soft blue of the sky, all gave the short, quiet street a sense of remoteness from the bustle of Sloane Square and the busy King's Road so nearby.

Tarrant had lived in the house in Sloane Gardens since shortly after the war. At the time he already thought the waiting had been interminable, but it was only half over. It was now more than twenty years since he had been recruited at Cambridge. His devout belief in a socialist world order had never wavered, but the tension, the frustration, had destroyed his first marriage.

Letting himself in the front door, Tarrant saw that the post had been collected from the floor below the slot. That meant Carol was home.

"Hello, darling," she called and came quickly down the stairs.

Tarrant's second wife was a pretty blonde not quite young enough to be his daughter. "Aren't you lovely this afternoon," he said. They kissed.

"Sherry?" she asked. "Or one of those horrid martini cocktails you've taken such a fancy to?"

"About an hour's work, I'm afraid. Then a martini would be wonderful."

"I shouldn't be surprised to hear you start talking like an American one of these days."

Tarrant followed the fiction, so common in The Firm, of a Foreign Office career. As far as Carol or their friends knew, he worked in its American section. Whitehall, if queried, would have confirmed that in vague but convincing terms.

In reality, he worked in a government office building off Royal Mint Street not far from the Tower of London, one of several used by the Secret Intelligence Service. It seemed he had worked there forever, and had only today been awakened from a kind of death.

Tarrant smiled. For once the Russians showed a sense of humor. The code name Kossior had given him was Lazarus.

Chapter Fifteen

1

Shortly before midnight on the second Thursday in July, a black four-door Alfa Romeo sedan pulled to a stop on the south side of the Piazza Matteotti a few blocks from the Porto Vecchio in Genoa. Le Matou climbed out of the driver's seat and stood stretching cramped muscles. It was a hot night with no breeze and the little Frenchman's shirt was plastered to his back.

Southard got out the other side, came around to join him on the sidewalk, and offered cigarettes. "What now?"

"He'll come or send a message. He may not expect us this soon, though. I almost don't believe it myself. Two hundred kilometers in less than—hold on, here he is now."

Le Matou reached into the car for his jacket and tossed it over his shoulders like a cloak. He was back in uniform; until the drive from Nice, Southard had never seen him in anything but the stiffly cut cheap suit.

A plump man came puffing toward them and in the glow of the streetlights Southard could see that he was sweating profusely. He said something quickly to Le Matou in Italian. His high voice and elaborate gestures seemed to upbraid Le Matou for not arriving earlier.

"Listen," Le Matou told Southard, "your friend could be in trouble. He's in a bar drunk and spoiling for a fight."

Southard reminded himself it was going to be, for the next twenty-four hours, Friday the thirteenth. "Where is it?"

Le Matou jerked a thumb. "Three, four blocks closer to the port."

"Can he drive us there?"

Le Matou spoke to the plump Italian.

"Beppo says the streets are narrow. It could be tough getting out, if you wanted out in a hurry."

"Okay, you stay with the car. Does Beppo speak French?"

The Italian himself answered. *"Mais naturellement, monsieur,"* he told Southard, as if offended by the question.

"Allons-y," Southard said and struck off rapidly in the direction Le Matou had indicated, Beppo trotting at his side.

He hoped Kip Chaffee was still in one piece. Chaffee had worried the Agency for a month, been on a bender for a week and, as Southard learned shortly after landing in Nice, slipped his Agency surveillance two days ago. If Chaffee had gone rogue, Southard was the one in the Agency he would most likely talk to. He trusted Southard.

Not surprisingly, Prestridge had made no objection to Southard's trip. It was ostensibly a routine matter—checking up on an agent shouldn't necessarily involve the cloak-and-dagger work that Southard had been forbidden—but Prestridge had been alarmed when Chaffee, among others, had started feeding him information that verified Noah Landler's version of the Manyoki document, even though neither the information nor subsequent events had, as yet, been as momentous as Manyoki had claimed they would be. If anything, Moscow was behaving in a more benign fashion than Manyoki had predicted. Nonetheless—or perhaps for that very

281

reason—Adam Prestridge, inveterate anti-Communist, was uneasy and inclined to turn a blind eye toward the real purpose behind Southard's trip.

Southard had questions to ask, not all of them officially Agency questions, that had been on his mind ever since April, when Allen Dulles had effectively chained him to a desk. Chaffee, after all, had been one of the CIA's sources on the Khrushchev transcript and had since stumbled onto a source who had supplied more information. The overriding question was just who Chaffee's source was—Thierry de Cheverny, as Chaffee claimed, or the ubiquitous Erika Graf.

The fight had moved outside the bar to the narrow cobbled street. Southard heard shouting and then quiet and then the meaty sound of fists striking flesh. A crowd ringed the contestants in the light shining through the plate-glass window of the bar. The crowd was male and enthusiastic. Southard and Beppo pushed through, Beppo admitted at once, Southard drawing hostile stares. A beefy man turned in Southard's path, standing chest to chest with him. Southard shoved past to where he could see Kip Chaffee down on hands and knees, blood dripping from his nose onto the cobblestones. What remained of Chaffee's shirt hung from one shoulder like a Roman toga. The man who had knocked him down was bare-chested and muscular. He outweighed the gangling American painter by perhaps fifty pounds. Still, his own face had taken punishment, and the right eye was swollen almost shut. Chaffee got to his feet and swayed. His fists came up slowly. The crowd drew a collective breath, anticipating the finish; Chaffee had punched himself out.

Southard stepped through the first row of the crowd.

"Fight's over," he said, raising both hands as he moved between Chaffee and his opponent. He heard Beppo's high voice saying the same thing in Italian. The muscular man looked incredulously at Southard and took his arm, trying to hurl him aside.

Southard knew it had to be done quickly. Depriving the crowd of what they had waited for would anger them. He had to do it so they would recognize it not as a new fight but as the unmistakable resolution of the old one. He rolled a half-turn with the attempt to hurl himself aside and then struck. It all took no more than three seconds, and every part of it was dirty but precise. Southard used the edge of his left hand like a cleaver, striking for the kidney. The muscular man screamed and doubled over. Southard struck with his right hand at the back of the man's neck, and as he fell Southard kicked him in the ribs.

"Are you okay? Can you walk?" Southard asked Chaffee. He got an arm around him and pulled him through the crowd to the accompaniment of Beppo's tenor voice.

"Perf'ckly all right. Din't lay glove on me," Chaffee said.

Beppo talked to the crowd, gesticulating, cajoling. Something he said drew reluctant laughter. He kept talking and sweating and smiling and backing away after them.

"Nother minute I'd of had'm," Chaffee insisted. "You're American, huh? Catch the whole thing? Dumb wop thought he—" Then Chaffee recognized Southard. "Jesus," he said. "Jesus holy Christ."

2

At one o'clock they were twenty miles further east in

Italy. The original plan had been to drive back to Nice, but by the time they got Chaffee to the car on the Piazza Matteotti, it was clear he wasn't up to so much driving. And it wasn't necessary anyway.

"Never mind," Le Matou had said. "There are places around here just as good as mine. Leave it to me."

So now Southard waited in the back seat of the Alfa beside Chaffee, who had collapsed instantly into sleep, while Le Matou pounded at the door of a large Victorian villa behind a balustraded stone wall in a sloping garden in Rappallo, a half-dozen stepped streets above the sea. Inside the villa a dog barked, deep-throated and menacing. Le Matou continued pounding and the dog continued barking until a light went on in the heavily barred window alongside the door. The window opened, and then the door, and Le Matou went in. Beppo turned in the passenger seat of the Alfa.

"Zia Lucia herself," he told Southard.

"Who?"

"Zia Lucia, she's called. A retired madam from Genoa. Runs a very discreet rest home now. You'll like her. Everybody does."

The door opened again. Le Matou beckoned to them. Southard could see a Doberman straining at a leash in the doorway behind him.

Southard slapped Kip Chaffee's face, gently at first and then harder until Chaffee stirred and waved a languid hand. It took a minute to make him understand. Then he got out of the car, his tall gangling frame seeming to unfold sectionally.

In the doorway an obese woman wearing a purple velour tent held the Doberman on a short leash. The animal growled and gurgled, paws skittering on the marble floor of the entrance hall.

"*Il sangue,*" said the obese woman. "Mussolini smells the blood. Don't you, Musso, eh?"

The Doberman barked and the obese woman whacked his hindquarters hard with a barrel stave. Then Mussolini allowed himself to be led away, twisting to look back as he went. Southard heard a door slam and a clawing sound and the Doberman whining.

Zia Lucia rejoined them. Her face was absolutely round and in the light from the wall sconces in the wide hallway her lips and her tightly drawn-back hair matched exactly the color of her vast velour dressing gown. She appraised Southard and then studied Kip Chaffee.

Her smile was totally benign. "Of course you may both stay as long as you wish," she told Southard.

"Didn't I tell you?" Beppo said. "Zia Lucia's great. Everybody likes her."

"Only two hundred American dollars a day for everything, including nursing care for your friend," said the popular Zia Lucia.

"You'll get the money," Southard told her.

She turned to lead them into the villa. Le Matou looked at Southard. "Munich must really owe you," he said.

Southard did not answer. It was Agency money this time, but he saw no reason to tell Le Matou.

3

Kip Chaffee came out of the shower a few minutes after noon wearing a large towel around his waist. The fight had marked his skinny body with purple bruises. His nose was taped and his left eye was shot with burst capillaries. He grimaced when he saw breakfast on a tray—steaming coffee and two glazed rolls.

"Jesus, how can you start the day by drinking

battery acid? Just the smell of it gives me the heaves," he said. "Can't we do better, professor? Last night Auntie Lucy mentioned nursing care. Wouldn't you say that includes the hair of the dog?"

Southard left with the tray and returned with a bottle of Stock and one glass. Chaffee had climbed into his filthy white duck trousers and sat on the edge of the bed staring out the window. The sunny second-floor room had a view over terraced gardens down to the Mediterranean. Through the open window the hum of wasps in the bougainvillea mingled with the more distant rasp of motor scooters.

"What's the matter with them in Paris anyway?" Chaffee said. He poured brandy down his throat and shuddered and sloshed more into the glass. "Can you straighten them out?"

"They don't need it," Southard said.

"Jesus, you too, professor? Don't I have any friends left?"

That Chaffee interpreted their relationship as friendship was indicative only of his need to have friends. Southard had been one of his instructors at the Farm five years ago and had come to his defense when Chaffee, an irreverent Bohemian among the bureaucrats, was in danger of being dropped from the training program.

In fact, Chaffee seemed an ideal choice for a resident, the link between a case officer and his agents in the field. Unlike a case officer, a resident had no diplomatic post or immunity, so he needed impeccable credentials to fall back on. The obvious covers were getting overused; Americans abroad complained that a bona fide business consultant or P.R. man could hardly turn around without being accused of being a spy. Other covers had to be found.

Gideon Parr pioneered the idea of using experts. The Agency's chief resident agent in West Germany now was a musicologist with an international reputation. One resident for England worked as a country-house crawler for London's most prestigious auction firm. But the expert had to be real, and recruited from outside.

Benton Southard contributed a refinement. The celebrity, unlike the expert, could be created. Once his reputation was established, to suspect the expatriate American painter Kip Chaffee of working for the CIA would be little different from suspecting that Salvador Dali worked for the Spanish secret service.

Chaffee was good in the role. He had an easy charm but he could lean on people when necessary and he was a perfectionist. Married to a Frenchwoman, he had lived in France since the war, trying to establish himself as a painter. His work was derivative—a cynical critic for the *Paris Trib* called it rendered Cézanne—but these days his canvases hung in galleries and private collections. It had taken less than five thousand dollars of CIA seed money to launch Chaffee's career in 1951, when Agency intermediaries bought eight of his canvases at his first one-man show. Ironically, Southard knew, the Agency had quietly resold them later for a nice profit.

Kip Chaffee turned away from the window. His boyish smile was almost genuine. "All I did was get documentation on Red Army plans to counter unrest in the satellites. All I did was predict the riots in Poland last month before they fucking happened. How the shit was I supposed to know that developing a source on my own would bother those bureaucratic pricks?"

"Maybe it was the way you developed it," Southard suggested.

"Hell, I didn't have to do anything, he came to me.

Why shouldn't he? We move in the same circles on the Riviera. We've known each other for years. You already know how he's been trying to shift the party off Thorez's hard line. It came to a head in April after he got back from Russia. He was leaking stuff to his mistress Tolo to print in her paper, when somebody shoots her dead. So where does that leave de Cheverny? Talking to me, that's where."

Southard lit a cigarette and said, "Is it? Since Tolo was killed, there's been considerable interest, in one quarter and another, in the doings of Thierry de Cheverny."

Chaffee's perplexed expression, like the boyish smile, was almost genuine. "What is this, some kind of a game?"

"No game, Kip. De Cheverny's seen a lot of people in the last three months, but you're not one of them."

There was a long silence. Chaffee stared into his glass, then drained it.

"I used to be a guy who could handle his booze. Not to mention his fists. Christ, I hurt all over. Every part of me hurts."

"You ought to see the other guy," Southard said.

It was obvious that Chaffee didn't remember. "Yeah?"

"The last I saw of him he was flat on his face in the gutter."

"No kidding? Well, how about that."

There was another silence.

Chaffee broke it. "I didn't quite tell the truth about de Cheverny," he said.

Southard knew he didn't have to prompt him. Once Chaffee started, he'd be eager to unburden himself. Guilt was only one aspect of it. Exhibitionism was another. It was part of Chaffee's makeup as an artist.

"Back in January on one of my regular runs up to Paris, I called on this principal agent who's a dentist in Passy," Chaffee said. "Good cover for a principal because what's more innocent than a visit to a dentist? Nobody goes unless he has to. The dentist gives me his goods and I'm delivering them to an I.R.S. auditor at the Embassy—that's good cover too. Any painter who hasn't got a Swiss bank account and trouble with the I.R.S. by the time he's thirty-five he's a fucking failure, right?"

Southard wondered if Chaffee knew the Agency had bought his first canvases.

"A fucking failure," Chaffee repeated. He took another shot of brandy. His eyes were unnaturally bright. "So I'm on the way from the dentist's to the embassy on the metro, and I have to transfer at Étoile, you know? I'm in the *correspondance* tunnel when I realize I left the briefcase on the other train. I go tear-assing back but the train's already pulled out. I tell the I.R.S. auditor and they call some people at the prefecture. But the briefcase never turns up. They try to tell me it's routine papers, low classification, don't worry about it. I know better. Since when do I handle routine stuff? It has to be important. Or what would I be doing with it?"

"Sure, I can see that," Southard encouraged him. The material *had* been routine, but for a perfectionist like Chaffee to make a mistake like that, it had to be one short step this side of the end of the world.

"I was drinking a little bit in there after I lost the briefcase," Chaffee went on. "Nothing I couldn't handle, but you know how it is when you're feeling down. Then sometime along in early spring, there's this asset that's our best link with the PCF. He's got something big, something about Thorez and de Cheverny. Only, he's holding out for more dough." Chaffee ran a hand through his red hair. "Keep in mind the asset's no free lance, he's on salary. When they start asking for more dough, that's suspicious, right? The dentist and me decide to whipsaw him. My

289

part's the bad guy. This day it's easy. The fellow really pisses me off, or maybe it's partly my hangover—you know the kind where even your hair hurts? Anyway, I lose my temper." Chaffee sighed. "They never think I know how to fight. I don't look it, do I? But what happened was I beat the shit out of him."

Southard remained silent. He knew what had happened. He hadn't known why until now.

"The fellow can't get back at me, because he doesn't know who I am. But he knows the dentist all right. He goes to the French counterespionage people. The dentist is servicing six agents for his case officer and they're all valuable assets. The French identify every one of them. By the time Paris station catches on, all six are under arrest and the dentist is in hot water with the Sûreté himself.

"My stock is at an all-time low. And then along comes this gorgeous Kraut offering to cut me in at the top. At first I think she's selling me a bill of goods. Which doesn't stop me from buying."

"When did all this start?" Southard asked.

"Around the time of the royal wedding in Monaco. At least, that's when I knew she was back on the coast."

"You knew her before?"

"I met her a couple of years ago. As far as I knew, she was just Margit von Weber, sexy, rich, a party girl. I didn't get to know her very well—maybe Francine was down then. But this time I got to know her a lot better. By the end of May, she'd moved in with me."

"She knew you worked for us?"

"I didn't tell her, for Chrisake. I don't know how she found out. For a while there I did a lot of drinking, a lot of talking, a lot of not remembering where I was when I woke up in the morning. Don't ask me how she knew. She just knew."

"You said at first you thought she was selling you a bill of goods."

"It was obvious. For openers she gives me that speech of Khrushchev's, and the word in Paris is we already have a copy or two; it's not all that much of a secret. So what's the purpose? To establish her credentials with me, to show she can deliver. And believe me, professor, she did."

When Southard started to speak, Chaffee held up a hand. "Wait, I know—your question is *why*. Well, it wasn't on account of my fair white body, even though we turned out to be kind of sensational in bed together. She wasn't giving away information and she wasn't selling it, she was trading. The thing is, she got into some trouble three years ago back in East Germany."

"What kind of trouble?"

"The worst kind for her. KGB trouble."

"That's all she told you?"

"I didn't push her. Whatever it was, she was afraid it was catching up with her now. So here it is, professor, in case you haven't figured it out yet. She's been paving the way for defecting by giving me a few tokens of good faith."

"In that case, why claim de Cheverny was the source?"

"She wanted it that way."

"Wanted you to name de Cheverny, or not to name her?"

"To keep her out of it. You can see why. There's a pattern with high-level defectors. First they just toy with it. Then it's serious, but they're still scared to burn their bridges. They live day to day, so the right time is always later, not now. Until they finally do it. But hell, I don't have to tell you."

Southard said nothing.

Chaffee picked up the bottle of Stock, his hand almost

steady, and emptied it into his glass. He looked at Southard expectantly. Still Southard didn't speak. Chaffee licked his lips and smiled and looked at Southard's eyes and let the smile fall off his face.

Southard watched the last of the brandy disappear.

Chaffee got up and went to the window. "This is a nice town," he said after a while. "A good place to paint. You ever feel that way about a place, right away know you'd be happy in it?" He stood looking out the window and listening to the silence a while longer, then turned back to face the room.

"And that's a lot of shit too. I never would have sold one stinking painting, would I? If the Agency didn't buy the first ones. Francine told me before she kicked me out. She thought it was news. But I never cared. I liked the life. Kip Chaffee, the expatriate American painter. I liked the *double* life. Man, I was flying high. A celebrity on the Riviera and up in Paris a spymaster out of Graham Greene." Chaffee was sitting on the edge of the bed then, his elbows on his knees, his head down, staring at the floor. "I didn't want to lose any of it, no matter what. Five years I went after the war without selling a painting, five years doing handyman jobs on Cap d'Antibes so I could eat, a white nigger on the Côte d'Azur. Fuck that shit. No more failure, not for this boy. Ever."

His head came up. He met Southard's eyes defiantly. "You don't think she ever thought of defecting, do you?"

"I think it was a lie she could carry off, because under certain circumstances it might have been the truth."

"I understood she was using me all along, you know that? I'm not a fool. I just didn't want it to end, any of it."

Chaffee reached for the bottle, remembered it was empty.

"Then it did end. Francine came, and everything was over. I didn't even try to go off with her, because I knew. That's why I ran." His face seemed about to dissolve. "The information she was feeding me—it was all stuff they wanted us to have, wasn't it?"

Slowly Southard nodded.

Chaffee put his face in his hands and silently started to cry.

4

Downstairs, Zia Lucia was trying to place a call to St.-Jean-Cap-Ferrat. It wasn't far, but any phone call crossing the frontier was an ordeal. She had been at it all morning.

Now she grabbed the receiver off its hook and shouted, *"Pronto! Pronto!"*

"I have your call to France, signora."

Zia Lucia settled her three hundred pounds on to the upholstered bench beside the telephone. She was wearing a pale blue tent today with little silver butterflies on it.

Venturino's voice came over the line faintly.

"I can't hear you, Giovanni," she said.

"You're coming through loud and clear. What's up, lover?" he shouted. He sounded preoccupied. Always so many irons in the fire, that one! But always the charm. Zia Lucia wistfully remembered the old days just after the war, when she'd still had a body. She'd spent a month with Venturino on Anacapri.

She still went out of her way to do him favors, but this one was easy.

"Listen, Giovanni. I had some visitors late last night.

One of them was Beppo Sangiorgio. You remember Beppo? He told me an interesting little story."

Venturino made a sound which she thought encouraged her to go on.

"Yesterday Beppo was minding his own business, so he says, when he happened to cross paths with an American, a painter named Chaffee. Now, he had heard by your private grapevine that you were interested in news of this Chaffee, so he started keeping an eye on him. This involved visiting a few more bars than Beppo usually visits in the course of a day, but no real inconvenience.

"Now here comes the interesting part. Beppo meanwhile heard through his regular channels, which is to say *le Milieu*'s network, that someone else had put out a call on Chaffee. A very urgent call. Naturally our good soldier Beppo made sure he was first with the information. The one who put out the call was your *copain* Le Matou."

"Le Matou? My *copain*? That's very funny."

"Apparently he was concerned enough about this painter to come tearing straight to Genoa himself. And he had somebody with him, another American who knew Chaffee. Between them they got Chaffee out of a drunken brawl and out of Genoa, but then it seems a question arose about what to do with him next. Here our Beppo probably deserves some credit, as he claims. Or maybe Le Matou really thought of me himself; we've always got on very well. Anyway, he was glad to leave them in my care."

"Leave who?" Venturino sounded like he was paying attention.

"Chaffee and the other American. Chaffee didn't do too well in the brawl; he can use a rest."

"What about the other one? You get his name?"

"No. He's as tall as you. Short sandy hair, blue gray

294

eyes, good-looking. Middle-late thirties. He looks smart."

"Doesn't ring any bells," Venturino said. "How long are they staying?"

"They haven't said."

"Let me know whatever you find out."

"I will."

"You're a sweetheart, Lucia mia."

"Ciao, Giovanni."

She hung up smiling. Just hearing his voice made her feel good all over, even after ten years.

She lit a cigarette, leaned back and pondered. Le Matou would be no problem. He thought Beppo worked only for him.

Chapter Sixteen

1

High heels clicked briskly along a narrow street between the Luxembourg Gardens and the Vavin metro station in the fourteenth *arrondissement* in Paris.

The girl crossed rue Notre-Dame-des-Champs and paused under a streetlamp to fumble in her large imitation-leather handbag for a cigarette. She wore bright red shoes that matched the bag, a tight black skirt, a snug red and white striped pullover and no makeup. Hers was a gamine prettiness, her dark brown eyes large, her cheekbones high, her small nose aquiline. With her dark hair caught in a pony tail she looked like a naughty adolescent new enough at her profession to regard it less as work than as play.

Except for a reasonable cut of the profits, the Paris police generally ignored consentual crimes like prostitution, but with their horror of "irregularity" they did impose geographical restrictions. In this part of Montparnasse the only permitted street was called rue Bréa southeast and rue Vavin northwest of Notre-Dame-des-Champs. The big cafés at the busy intersection near the Vavin metro were off limits, an inconvenience irrelevant now at two-thirty in the morning.

The new girl on the block took a few puffs of her cigarette, dropped it to the sidewalk and waited.

A woman's voice rose in the darkness. "What the hell do you think you're doing here?" A figure detached itself from the recessed doorway of the restaurant Dominique.

"Waiting for a friend," said the new girl on the block.

"Beat it. Wait for your friend somewhere else."

The *quartier*'s business girls, restricted to a two-block stretch of turf, guarded it jealously.

"I like it here."

The woman approached. Large, solid, busty, she was losing her battle with middle age. Her blue skirt was taut across her broad hips and shiny in the seat. Like the new girl on the block she wore a shoulder bag and shoes of red.

"I told you to beat it."

The new girl on the block smiled sweetly. "Why don't you go home to bed, mother? At your age, after all—"

Mother made a squawking sound, and said something unpleasant and imaginative in an argot difficult for the girl to follow.

A brisk tattoo of high heels approached from both directions along the street. Three more business girls materialized in the spill of light from the streetlamp.

"Who is she?" one asked.

"You don't know her either, eh?" said Mother. "All I can tell you is, she's got a big mouth."

A brief conference followed. Mother, first on the scene, would present the ultimatum.

The argot was now even more difficult to follow but the girl got the gist of what Mother said. Something of an obscene and decidedly painful nature would befall her if she did not get off the street at once. And stay off.

She smiled demurely and shook her head.

"Maybe she's too stupid to understand," one of the others suggested.

The girl smiled demurely again. "I understood the fat sow."

Mother's bellow rose two stories, and put on a light and opened a window in an apartment building across the street. A man's voice called, "Shut your foul mouth, you filthy whore!"

Mother struck a pose, craned her neck and bellowed louder, putting on another light and opening another window.

Vituperative shouts were traded by everyone up and down the block except the new girl. Who had disappeared.

Footsteps pounded along rue Bréa from the direction of the metro station and two police whistles shrilled in the night.

2

Deborah's instructions, received from the vendor of Montélimar nougat outside the Café Rotonde, had been simple. Create a disturbance on rue Bréa just after two-thirty in the morning.

She had done so, but what she did next was on her own. She ducked around the corner and into a doorway and then, when all attention would be on the policemen, crept back to the corner and peered around it.

The *flics*, with witnesses hanging from windows in every building on the block, had no choice. A token arrest of Mother and her three companions followed. The black van came, the women climbed in with one of the *flics*, the van rumbled off.

The apartment lights went out, the remaining *flic* started back up rue Bréa, and Deborah began to think nothing more would happen after all. Then two figures stepped from an alley and suddenly the policeman was lying on the sidewalk.

The two figures crouched over him, working swiftly, stripping him to his underwear. Holstered revolver, nightstick, blue uniform—all were rolled into a bundle and thrust in a shopping bag. Soon the two figures were striding off toward the Luxembourg Gardens.

Deborah slipped off her high-heeled shoes and followed.

She stayed well behind as they went along the stone-and-spike fence bordering the west side of the park. In the distance she heard the *whoop-whoop-whoop* of the siren. On rue Vaugirard the two figures crossed to a waiting car, a dark Simca sedan. Deborah hurried now. By the time the two figures got into the car she was close enough to read its license number. She thought the driver was a girl. The car pulled away from the curb and turned at the first corner.

Deborah stepped back into her shoes. She fished in her bag for paper and pencil and noted the license number.

Whoever they were, their instructions must have been simple too. Rue Bréa, shortly after two-thirty. There will be a policeman. Overpower him. Take his uniform and weapons.

She had learned less than she hoped, but at least she could identify the car they drove. She doubted it was stolen; the one she used had been purchased at a second-hand lot in Ivry and duly registered to Madeleine Béranger. She wondered if the stealing of the police uniform was no more than an exercise for that Special Group. Perhaps they would use it later. Perhaps it would be used by another group; she had yet to learn what became of the submachine guns she had brought back from Switzerland.

Paris was bits and pieces of a puzzle no single group was

expected to understand.

She heard quick running footsteps and a boy, no more than seventeen or eighteen, seized her shoulder and spun her around. "You've got no right to be here. Who do you think you are?"

Instinctively Deborah fell back on her role as prostitute. "I've got as much right as anybody. Now buzz off, sonny. It's been a hard night, and I'm going home to bed—alone."

Who was he?

He must have been watching since rue Bréa, as she was, except that he was doing it by order. Which meant he was part of the Special Group that had just driven away, or else sent by control. She should have considered the possibility.

"You were writing something," he said. "What was it?"

He spoke French well, but with his *r*'s too far forward in his mouth. Italian, Spanish? Latin American, possibly. Part of her mind catalogued that automatically, while another part braced for abrupt action.

"Me? Writing something?"

"Quit acting innocent. I want to see it." He reached for her bag, but she turned it away from his grasp. His hand closed on her left wrist instead.

"You're hurting me!" Purposely she let her voice rise.

"Give it here."

"All *right!* I'll show you. But you don't have to make such a fuss about it. I was only doing what I was told."

As she expected, his grip relaxed fractionally. She let the bag slide from her shoulder to the crook of her elbow and gauged its weight. The large flashlight inside, she thought, would give it enough heft. She moved as if to open the bag. Her hand fastened midway along the strap.

Then she swung it as hard as she could up at his face.

The new control, usually pleasant and even charming, was angry with her. "You shouldn't have struck him."

"You shouldn't have sent him," Deborah said mildly. "If he came back whining that a woman hit him, he isn't ready to be let out alone."

"You know what I mean."

"Do I? If you wanted us to show each other professional courtesy, you could throw a *soirée* and introduce us all. That would be nice, wouldn't it? Only what would happen to the competition then?"

He ignored her saracasm. "Competition? Is that why you tried to get their license number?"

Deborah opened her clutch purse and removed a scrap of paper, smoothing it on the café table. "I didn't just try, I got it. The only thing I'm not sure of is the color of the car. I think it was dark blue or black, but it's difficult to tell at night."

He raised his hands as if invoking a whole pantheon of gods, but what he said was lost in the snarl of traffic as the light on the corner changed. All she caught was the last word, "Arabs!"

"Pardon?" Deborah bristled. "What about Arabs?"

"I said that's devious reasoning, Jehan. Typical Arab logic. We tell you to help each other, and instead you spy on them."

"Not instead. I did as instructed. I always do. What I did afterwards was on my own, but you can't call it devious, not when you laid it out yourself. Take last night. It was their operation, one of them could have created the disturbance. But no, I was called in. Why? Only to bring us into contact. If I made the most of it—well, wasn't I supposed to?"

He gazed at her noncommittally.

"I know where some of them live. I could guess the nationality of some. Some I could pick out of a crowd. Perhaps some of them are doing the same with us, but we make it as hard for them as we can."

He looked at her a moment longer, then turned to flag the waiter and raise two fingers. They were drinking beer at a corner table outside the Old Navy Tabac on boulevard S.-Germain. It was the beginning of rush hour, the hottest part of the afternoon.

He was tall, blond, about her age, she thought. Attractive in a rugged, outdoors way. His name he said, was Klaus and he came from Düsseldorf. She had switched to German early in their conversation today. He probably thought she was showing off. Really, she wanted to listen to his German. It was like his French, as flawless and featureless as a radio announcer's.

Or as hers; a radio announcer was what she had been.

"What you're saying, you know," he told her conversationally, "is that in the end you trust no one."

"It's not that. We just can't take anything at face value. Not even you. Klaus is as good a name as any, but why bother to say you're from Düsseldorf? Chances are you're from a lot further east, if they make you control for this kind of operation. Even in our training camp in Egypt they sent us real Russian instructors." she smiled. "They sent us a political officer, too, to indoctrinate us. That was a joke. It didn't take him long to figure out that our politics begin and end with anti-Zionism."

"Then what are you doing here in a Special Group?"

"We're doing whatever you tell us, and you know why. All you're teaching us can be applied as well in Jerusalem or Jaffa as in Paris. We're learning how to strike at a community from inside. We've learned what sort of apartments to rent, and now to behave with the neighbors, and that idleness arouses suspicion where part-time work doesn't. We know you should master the public transportation in a strange city right away. We know how to buy cars, steal cars, hide cars, hot-wire cars and wire the ignitions with *plastique* to blow them up. We've practiced breaking and entering, and running contraband across frontiers, and tailing someone and shaking a tail. We've learned how to get through a crowd, get lost in a crowd, collect a crowd.

"It's a new kind of guerrilla warfare you're teaching us, isn't it? Where the caves of the Maquis are an efficiency flat in a residential hotel at 232 boulevard Raspail and a third-floor apartment at 47 rue de Prony and a studio on rue St.-André-des-Arts right around the corner from where we're sitting now."

The blond young man who called himself Klaus gave her a challenging look. "You do believe in taking chances, don't you, Jehan?"

The locations she had named were where three of the other Special Groups lived.

"I don't think so. Because you're evaluating us, aren't you? The best of us will go on to . . ."

"Yes?"

"I don't know exactly. I'll know when we get there. And we will, believe me. And nothing I've said will hurt our chances."

Klaus lit a cigarette and sat looking at Deborah. She watched the traffic lights change and the cars flood boulevard St.-Germain like a millrace.

"Another beer?"

"Thanks but no. Remember, idleness arouses suspicion," Deborah told him, and smiled ingenuously. She stood up. *"Bon soir*, Klaus. Thanks for the drinks."

He watched her walk to the curb and wait for a break in traffic so she could cross. She had shapely legs and a lithe stride. Madeleine Béranger, he thought, Jehan Khalid, you are really something. This was one who knew precisely where she was going and would let nothing keep her from getting there.

She was the first to intuit—or at least to mention—the wheels within wheels of their training, the first to admit spying on the others, the only one to look him in the eye as an equal.

The man he had replaced as control for the Special Groups had singled out the Palestinians as the best of the lot. He was right, but he had missed the point. The Husayni twins, even before training, had commanded terrorists in Gaza, and they would return to positions of command. But the girl Jehan, daughter of an Egyptian spy, was another story. She was subtle in a way the twins were not. She had imagination to augment her zeal, intelligence to go with her dedication. If they were the best of the groups, she had made them so.

Pity, that her very considerable abilities would destroy her.

The blond young man signaled to the waiter and placed a thousand-franc note on the table. Discredit the best the project produced, he thought, rising, and you discredited the whole project. Which, in turn, discredited those who had developed the project.

It had to be a real fiasco. It would take time, but he would work something out. He was impatient by nature but it was easy to control that now. All he had to do was remember how they had shot his father down like an animal in Berlin.

Lieutenant Andrei Golovin went to the curb and raised a hand in what seemed an indolent gesture. Even though it was rush hour, an empty taxi immediately detached itself from the heavy traffic and stopped for him. Golovin accepted it as a matter of course. Things usually worked that way for him.

4

When Deborah returned to the apartment on rue des Quatre Vents, Sulayman was on the telephone.

"Yes, of course," he was saying. He sounded pleased and excited. "No problems at all. The night train? No, I won't have any trouble making it. Until tomorrow then."

Maryam had just washed her hair and wrapped a towel around it turban-fashion. In a half-slip and bra, she was seated on a stool in front of the only good mirror in the cramped apartment, applying eye shadow. She looked at her brother's reflection in the mirror.

"What was all that about, Suly?"

"I have to go out of town for a while. Tell you about it later." He said it that way, Deborah knew, so she would feel excluded. Then he turned to face her. "Where have *you* been?"

"At a café with Klaus."

"Why?"

"Because he asked me."

"And where were you last night, while we're at it?"

"They had a job for me. I told you that this morning."

"You didn't say what kind of job."

"If they thought you should know," Deborah said, "they'd tell you."

Although Sulayman's suspicion of her had proven to be groundless, his antagonism toward her was never far under the surface. Even that day three months ago when she had rejoined them in Paris after a forty-eight-hour delay, Sulayman had greeted her not with relief but with reproaches. How could she have helped it, she protested, if

305

two drunks had accosted her in Monaco the night of the shooting and taken her hundred thousand francs so that she had to hitchhike the six hundred miles to Paris? Sulayman ought to be glad, she said, that the robbery at least occurred after she'd dropped the guns where she was supposed to. But Sulayman continued to rail at her, so Deborah stood by in injured innocence and let Maryam defend her. After that, Sulayman did not speak to her at all for several days.

The weeks that followed fueled his antagonism. In their group exercises he gave Deborah the most demanding assignments, hoping she would fall on her face. Instead she excelled; now their control contacted her directly. It had also been her idea to gather intelligence on the other groups, an idea Sulayman had opposed. Now he was forced to concede she was right.

Having to weigh her skills against his dislike—he never thought of it as jealousy—made him dislike her all the more.

Maryam usually played peacemaker.

Now she swung around on her stool, holding a pair of nail scissors. "Come here, Suly, let me trim your mustache. It's a little uneven."

Sulayman submitted while she fussed over him. His mustache was still new enough to be a point of vanity. Deborah, when she cared to be objective, admitted it changed his appearance considerably for the better. Instead of being too pretty, he now looked rather debonair, and the petulant Husayni mouth appeared sensual instead.

Maryam swung back toward the mirror, and the two of them admired the mustache together. Then she dropped the scissors in her makeup case and took out an eyebrow pencil. Sulayman's narcissistic smile became a scowl.

"What are you painting yourself like that for?"

"I'm just putting on a little makeup. Is there a law against it?"

"In the Koran there are laws against a lot of your . . . attitudes."

Maryam shrugged. "We're a long way from where any of that matters."

"But we'll be going back. Don't ever forget that."

Maryam held his gaze in the mirror until his eyes fell. He put a hand on her shoulder. "I'm sorry," he said. "I'm edgy. We all are."

Well, Deborah thought, he's even including me. Almost as if I were human.

Sulayman's long fingers had begun to massage his sister's bare shoulders and the sides of her neck.

"That feels good. A little lower. Umm, that's lovely."

The kneading became a gentle stroking motion. Maryam shut her eyes.

Abruptly, seeing Deborah in the mirror, Sulayman drew back. "That was Giovanni on the phone," he said casually, "calling from the coast."

"Giovanni?" Maryam repeated the name.

"The fellow who met us in Monaco at the museum."

"Of course," Maryam said. She unfastened the turban and began to towel her hair. "What was on his mind?"

"I'm taking the train down there, to Nice, tonight."

"Is that smart?"

"Smart? Oh, I see, you mean Klaus. Giovanni's already cleared it with him."

"Or, he told you he did."

Listening to them, Deborah could feel not only the tension—Sulayman was right about that—but the suspicion that was so integral a part of their existence. Of all their lessons these past months, the one they had learned best was distrust.

"That's right, he told me he did—and he mentioned Klaus by name."

Maryam was brushing her hair now. "How long will you be gone?"

Sulayman showed the palms of his hands. "A while, that's all he said. But it's important."

Dark Husayni eyes looked into dark Husayni eyes. "When he says important, he means dangerous," Maryam said. "Take care, Suly."

"I will. And you be careful while I'm gone." Sulayman took the brush from his sister's hand and began to brush her hair. "I'll take you to dinner before my train," he told her. "Just the two of us."

Deborah went out to sit on the staircase over the courtyard. She felt an odd sense of embarrassment, as if she had been eavesdropping on a scene between lovers.

Chapter Seventeen

1

With Mussolini on the other side of the door worrying a bone, Zia Lucia had no need to fear eavesdroppers. Besides, there was no reason why Beppo shouldn't pay a social call at this hour on a Saturday evening. They were old friends.

Outside, lightning flashed in the darkness and thunder rumbled over the hills behind Rapallo. Mussolini growled.

Beppo fidgeted in his chair. "That dog makes me nervous."

"Relax. If I tell him you're a friend, he's as harmless as a Chihuahua." Zia Lucia was reclining on a chaise longue. She wore a voluminous robe of mock-Oriental design—a fire-breathing creature in black and red sprawled on the great satin-covered mounds of her breasts.

Thunder ripped overhead in a tearing crack. Beppo's hands moved to the arms of his chair. Sheets of rain pelted the windows.

"Thunder makes you nervous too?"

"No, I'm all right. But I'm not wild about what I've been doing. Le Matou's a pal of mine."

"Of course he is," Zia Lucia said in a maternal voice. "Of course he is, dear Beppo." She selected a liqueur-filled chocolate from a box and popped it into her mouth. "You're not doing anything to hurt him, are you?"

"N—no," said Beppo doubtfully.

"Then what are you upset about? Don't you like money?"

"Everybody likes money," Beppo said.

Zia Lucia ate another liqueur-filled chocolate.

"It's just I don't like spying on him."

"You had lunch together in Genoa, and then you went your separate ways to do a few errands. What's wrong with that?"

Thunder rolled distantly and the lights in the room flickered. The sudden downpour had stopped as quickly as it started. Mussolini made a deep baying sound.

"So where did he go after lunch?" Zia Lucia asked.

Thunder rumbled faintly. The lights dimmed and went out.

That made Beppo feel better. It was only a small act of betrayal but it would be easier in the darkness.

"He took a taxi to the port."

"The Porto Vecchio. Isn't that where you ate?"

"No, we had lunch at Giacomo's. He went to the Italian Line office after lunch." Beppo could see nothing. He heard the faint, moist sound Zia Lucia made as she bit into another chocolate-covered liqueur. He heard Mussolini's teeth crunch hard on the bone.

"He's inside most of an hour. When he comes out, I wait a few minutes, then I go in and spread some money around. The girl who served him says she thought there was something odd about it, him paying cash. Not too many people do that. He wanted the tickets written while he waited, too. I guess that's why he didn't go to a travel agent."

"What were the tickets for?"

"Two first-class passages on the *Andrea Doria*, one way, sailing from Genoa this coming Tuesday."

"Where to?"

"New York, Via Cannes, Naples and Gibraltar."

"New York," Zia Lucia repeated. Beppo heard the faint, moist sound again. "You'll find some candles in the bureau to your left," she told him.

Just then the lights flickered and came on again. Zia Lucia held out a thick roll of bank notes.

It hadn't been so difficult after all.

2

Erika flew to Berlin herself. Early on the Monday morning following the conversation between Zia Lucia and Beppo, she was in the East Sector. It was a gloomy day, overcast and cold for July. The Ministry of State Security facility at Freienwalderstrasse 12 looked more than ever like a prison—or a concentration cap.

A red light glowed outside the darkroom where she was told Richard Quast could be found, a sign under it informing her that it was absolutely forbidden to open the door while the light was on.

Quast came out smoking a cigarette after fifteen minutes. His fingers were stained yellow. He smelled of acid.

"Wie geht's?" Erika asked.

"Busy. They're working me into an early grave, Major Graf. And you?"

"Busy. They're making life interesting for me."

The bespectacled forgery expert sighed. "And that sums up the difference between us." He dropped his cigarette on the floor and stepped on it. "How can I help you?"

Erika told him what she wanted as they walked to his office.

Quast removed his smudged glasses and polished them with the tail of his white lab coat. "That shouldn't be difficult. Would sometime late next week be all right?"

"Herr Quast," Erika said, "I want it now. Today. I flew here to Berlin to get it. I'm flying out tonight."

"Today?" Quast put his glasses back on and peered at her, waiting for the rest of the joke.

Her face told him otherwise.

He said, "Today is categorically—categorically—impossible. It would make no difference if your authority came from Minister Wollweber himself." Ernst Wollweber was the minister for state security.

By then they were in Quast's cluttered office. Erika pointed to the telephone. "Why don't you call and ask him?" she suggested.

Quast's second sigh was more heartfelt.

When Erika crossed over to West Berlin on the *S-Bahn* and caught the night plane from Tempelhof to Frankfurt, hidden in her luggage was a French passport issued to one Paul Faure. The photograph, taken from the files at Freienwalderstrasse, was that of Sulayman Husayni. Toward the back of the passport was a visa, apparently issued at the American Consulate in Nice, authorizing the entry of Paul Faure into the United States of America.

3

Southard unpacked his blue canvas B-4 bag in a first-class stateroom on Upper Deck on starboard side. The cabin was small but efficiently designed, the built-in furniture unobtrusively contemporary, the floral carpeting and the chintz curtain over the porthole recess mismatched in an Italian exuberance of color that somehow worked.

Southard sat on the edge of the single berth and familiarized himself with the compact, transistorized German tape recorder. Before boarding, he and Chaffee had gone together to buy it. Southard had let him select the model. His cheerful interest, Southard knew, was another good sign. Chaffee was looking forward to every part of the ocean voyage, even the interrogation.

No setting could make him more receptive than a transatlantic crossing by luxury liner. In similar circumstances the Agency often used to good effect a Catoctin Mountain hunting lodge in Maryland, and a week at Montego Bay or at the palace in St. Moritz was not unheard of. When Southard requested authorization for the *Andrea Doria* through Paris station, Prestridge himself approved the idea of a sea change.

Chaffee knew if he cooperated—and probably even if he didn't— it was doubtful he would face any charges. The Agency existed for collecting information and, unlike the FBI, regarded criminal prosecution as irrelevant if not counterproductive. Southard did not think that made the Agency any more or less moral than the FBI. But it did mean that Kip Chaffee would not resist being questioned.

It was only a first step. Once Southard had got what he could in low-key interrogation, Chaffee would be wrung dry by experts at the Farm, drugs used as a matter of course, harsher methods as needed. He had slept with, lived with, Erika Graf for weeks. Every conversation he remembered, every nuance of phrasing, even the tone of Erika's voice, had to be considered.

Chaffee would not like to hear it, but he was far more important to the Agency now as Erika Graf's conduit for disinformation than he had ever been as a loyal resident.

At noon the foghorn blew. In the companionway a loudspeaker exhorted all guests, in Italian and English, to go ashore by the gangway on Foyer Deck. Southard opened his stateroom door. A white-vested steward passed carrying a tray of empty glasses. A couple walked by, arms linked,

313

the man talking volubly, his face alight with anticipation of the voyage, the woman listening in dispirited acceptance of separation.

Southard knocked at the door of the adjacent stateroom.

"Yo!" Chaffee called and pulled the door open.

Except for the white strip of adhesive tape across the bridge of his nose, his face was unmarked. He was grinning boyishly. "Son of a bitch, nine days in this floating palace," he gloated. "She is some boat. You look around yet? I mean, the *size*. Three times already I heard the same joke, 'When does this place get to New York?' Shall we go have a drink? I found out where all the bars are. Oh, and I signed us up for the second sitting in the dining room—first is for the hayseeds, right? You ever cross by liner before? I was on the *Ile de France* before the war, when I was still too young for my parents to disown me. This is the only way, the *onliest* way. Man!"

Chaffee's garrulous good spirits were just what Southard hoped to maintain.

"Sure, let's go get that drink," he said.

Less than an hour later, tugboats slowly pulled and nudged the 29,100 gross tons of the *Andrea Doria* from her dock in Genoa to begin the westbound leg of her fifty-first Atlantic crossing.

4

Erika had the gull-wing Mercedes roadster out of the parking lot at Nice-Côte d'Azur Airport five minutes after her plane landed. Still, she knew, there was little chance of making it to Cannes in time.

The engine trouble that had delayed her flight from Frankfurt had not been cleared up until well after noon, and as the big four-propeller DC-6 swung out over the

Mediterranean in its approach pattern, Erika could see the *Andrea Doria* cutting her sleek way through the water, already well past Nice and steaming for Cannes. Erika thought an ocean liner could do about forty kilometers an hour. The Mercedes would do five times that on the straight, but the ship had neither traffic nor curves to contend with. And probably the tender would load and be ready to meet the liner before she even anchored in Cannes harbor.

That only made it a better race.

Driving fast, so recklessly fast that any emergency would severely test her reflexes, was tonic to Erika. She looked on love of speed as a predominantly masculine trait; in Germany it was. But no one had any doubts about Erika's sex.

Her acceptance of killing was different. That, she thought of as a female trait.

She no longer remembered how many killings she had ordered for the MfS. They were not something which troubled her conscience. But for an instant, driving west toward Antibes, she had a vision, cinematically clear, of the death camp at Auschwitz. . . .

She floored the accelerator pedal. The Mercedes leaped forward. It was a straight stretch of highway, with no traffic in the oncoming lane. She moved to the left and began passing cars—three, four, five—as the needle climbed. Distantly ahead, around a curve, appeared a squat Panhard sedan. In the westbound lane there was empty road beside her, then a truck halfway between her and the approaching Panhard. She could brake now or try to pass the truck. She kept her foot to the floor. The Panhard began to edge toward the shoulder. She drew abreast of the truck and, a second later, cut the wheel sharply. She missed the Panhard by inches.

The speedometer read 200.

She laughed.

She slalomed into the curve, the wind whipping her hair forward and across her eyes, but still she kept the needle close to 150. A car loomed ahead of her. She passed it blind. The road was all curves now. She used both lanes at will, straddling the solid yellow center line. The tires sang, the slipstream roared, she felt her mouth open in a rictus of terrible joy.

She did not see Auschwitz now. Her mind was clear, death defeated by taunting it, the slate wiped clean once more. She let her instincts guide the car, and thought of Benton Southard.

There was nothing personal in it, or was there? She was doing her job, he was doing his. Both of them were professionals.

He was with Chaffee now, and that alone made him a danger. He would understand more than Chaffee realized he was telling. But until they reached Washington, the danger was confined to the two of them, and could be repaired. It *must* be repaired. Otherwise Southard and Chaffee would destroy the project Colonel Kossior was counting on so heavily.

It was incidental, she told herself, that Southard was digging into the death of Gideon Parr, incidental that he might in the process learn too much about Erika Graf. Of course it was.

What did her reasons matter anyway? No one would ever call her to account. Shipboard was the ideal setting. A killing at sea could go completely unnoticed. Even if it didn't, the country of registry, Italy, would have jurisdiction. The authorities in New York would never dream of detaining two thousand potential suspects. It would be a nightmare.

When the highway entered Cannes, she turned left and cut down to the boulevard de la Croissette. It was longer but faster, and from there she could see whether the ship was in. It was. She could see the sleek black and white liner anchored about a mile offshore.

Ahead at the end of the palm-lined promenade the Victorian bulk of the municipal casino totally hid the baldly functional Gare Maritime.

Erika slid to a stop on the Croisette. Venturino climbed into the other seat of the roadster and motioned for her to take the next right.

"*Ciao*, baby. You made fantastic time."

"I'm not too late?"

"Don't worry about it," Venturino said. "Our young friend is waiting in a café across from the port with his ticket in his pocket. As soon as I get the passport to him, he'll be on his way. The tender won't go until he's on it."

Erika pulled up for a traffic light. "I don't like it. No matter what story you cooked up, it still calls attention to him. And that's the last thing we want."

"No story," Venturino said. "He arrives a little late, and finds the tender hasn't left. His good luck."

A grin spread across Venturino's handsome, predatory features. "You see, when you called from Frankfurt, it gave me an idea. I checked around and discovered, as I expected, that the tender's engineer and I had a mutual friend. The tender, like your airplane, developed engine trouble."

5

Paul Faure, the French student who was going to Columbia University in New York to do a year of graduate work in some obscure aspect of geology, stood at poolside on Lido Deck with two coltish California blondes who had been spending their junior year abroad at the University of

Grenoble. They were twin sisters, and both had crushes on Faure.

He was darkly handsome, and so suave. And that gorgeous bod, the California sisters said, like a Greek god. They loved to watch him in the first-class pool, tirelessly swimming laps. Each sister was determined to get Faure into bed with her before the voyage ended. Neither told the other.

"Yes, I have a single cabin," Faure was saying in answer to a question. "I hate sharing a room with a stranger, don't you?"

His accent was divine, just like a younger Charles Boyer. Each California sister hoped she would soon be promoted from stranger to bedmate.

He had climbed from the pool only a minute ago and was still breathing deeply, his sleekly muscled chest rising and falling. Droplets of water beaded his darkly tanned skin. He got a towel from his deck chair and began to rub himself briskly.

"Cold?" asked one of the sisters.

Faure looked straight at her. "Wet," he said.

The California sisters laughed uneasily. They never knew when Faure was making fun of them. It never occurred to them that he couldn't because he had no sense of humor.

Sulayman Husayni put on a terry-lined beach jacket, part of the wardrobe Giovanni had brought him in Cannes. He waited for the California sisters to speak. His English was more than adequate, but he had no small talk. He never did, except with Maryam. He hadn't realized how much he would miss her. The California sisters were good camouflage, though, and he suffered their inanities.

". . . a siesta every afternoon," one of them was saying. "The Spaniards are right." Her voice became a meaningless babble.

Sulayman saw the Americans, Beck and Chaffee, approaching the apron of the pool. They wore shirts over their swim trunks; Chaffee had leather sandals on his feet, Beck espadrilles. Beck was beginning to tan, Chaffee to peel.

"It does, doesn't it?" one of the California sisters asked.

Faure looked at her. He had huge brown eyes. And oh, that dreamy mustache. He was handsomer than any Latin lover in Hollywood.

"Mean strong and stalwart in French," the California sister repeated. "Your family name."

"No, that's *fort*," said Paul Faure. "It sounds almost the same, but our name is spelled *F—a—u—r—e.*"

"You should change the spelling, then," said the other sister. "It would suit you so perfectly."

They were nineteen, tall, blonde, leggy, brainless—and obviously ready to spread their legs for him. Sluts! thought Sulayman. But what could you expect from a country like America?

Sulayman had never made love with a woman. Once years ago their tutor, an unctuous fat man named Mohammed Ali Assad, had tried to seduce him. Sulayman was thirteen then, shy and unformed. Assad might have had his way if Maryam had not walked in. Sulayman would always remember what happened then. It was as if Assad had attempted to defile Maryam herself—she flew at him, shrieking and kicking, raking his face with her sharp fingernails. When Sulayman joined in, Assad fled.

Their mother's cousin the grand mufti of Jerusalem somehow got word of what happened. The twins never saw Mohammed Ali Assad again. Later they learned the fat tutor had been castrated.

One of the California sisters had flopped facedown on an air mattress at poolside. She had undone the straps of her bikini top and her sister was anointing her back with

Coppertone. The prone sister raised her head and rested it on her folded arms so that Sulayman could see the pale side of her breast.

It was so obvious, so intentional.

He thought of Maryam emerging from the sea on the beach at Damyatta Mouth north of Cairo, as graceful as a fawn, and as fresh and un-self-conscious.

The prone sister smiled at him, a lazy smile, and raised her head further to look at her wristwatch. He could see her nipple. Her forehead was shiny with sweat. She let her head fall. She looked sun-drugged.

The sun did not bother Sulayman at all.

Beck and Chaffee were seated at a small round table on the far side of the pool. A steward placed drinks on the table, a tall amber one for Chaffee, a bright yellow one for Beck that turned cloudy yellow-white when the waiter added water. The Americans were talking. Sulayman wished he could hear what they were saying. He wished too that they had settled into a discernable routine beyond that imposed by the shipboard schedule itself. But there was plenty of time, almost five days before they reached New York.

The second California sister was stretched out on a second air mattress, the brown Coppertone bottle at her side, the straps of her bikini top unfastened.

"Paul, would you be a sweetheart and oil me?"

He poured the warm suntan lotion into his palm and spread it lightly across her back. It reminded him of massaging Maryam's shoulders the night before he left Paris. He began to knead the California sister's shoulders the same way. He added more lotion and stroked her. She made a soft sensual sound of arousal.

Sulayman wished he could hear what the Americans were saying.

Chaffee grimaced. "You actually like that licorice stuff?"

Southard had just taken a long swallow of *pastis*. "Maybe it's an acquired taste. I drink it when I'm in France. I usually drink native."

Chaffee shook his head in mild disbelief. "You're the only guy I know who looks on drinking as work."

Southard laughed.

The deck rolled slightly, the water in the pool sloshing from side to side.

"Want to try a session tonight?" Southard asked.

"I was wondering when you'd get around to it, professor." Chaffee was watching the muscular, darkly tanned young man put sun lotion on the bare back of one of the sisters from California. "Look at her, will you? Five ten in her bare feet and built to scale. California—they're making a new breed of female out there."

Southard turned to look. He thought Chaffee was wrong. The girl on the air mattress was not a new breed at all. She reminded him, in fact, of a younger Erika Graf.

The tanned young man with the mustache did not remind him of anyone.

6

SOUTHARD: Third interview with Christopher Chaffee. On board the *Andrea Doria*, at sea, Monday, 23 July, 9:50 P.M. I'll start with the usual, Kip—have you any objections to answering my questions?

CHAFFEE: No.

SOUTHARD: Okay then. How long after she moved in with you did Major Graf suggest that she might be able to help you?

CHAFFEE: Let's see. I already told you about that business in Paris, how I was feeling sorry for myself and talking a lot?

SOUTHARD: Right.

CHAFFEE: Well, one night we both got a little bit drunk. You want the truth, we were stewed to the gills. That's when she told me who she really was.

SOUTHARD: Just like that? "I'm Major Graf of the MfS"?

CHAFFEE: (laughs)

SOUTHARD: Then how?

CHAFFEE: It's tough to remember, exactly. She said she knew how lousy I felt because she'd been through that kind of experience herself.

SOUTHARD: What kind of experience?

CHAFFEE: You know. An absentminded mistake, one crummy little mistake in a line of work where . . . what was the word she used? Something you associate with religion . . . yeah! Anathema. She said an absentminded mistake was anathema in our line of work.

SOUTHARD: And then she just introduced herself? Try to remember the exact words, could you, Kip?

CHAFFEE: No introduced, no. But we started in talking about it. Our work, our kind of work. One thing led to another. Pretty soon she was Erika, not Margit.

SOUTHARD: Erika Graf? Her whole name?

CHAFFEE: That came later, I'm not sure when. She was already helping me by then.

SOUTHARD: Meaning, giving you intelligence pieces?

CHAFFEE: Yeah, that's right. It must have been when she started giving me transcripts of meetings between her boss Wollweber and General Shalin of the GRU—you know about those.

SOUTHARD: What was discussed at those meetings?

CHAFFEE: I can't read Russian.

SOUTHARD: Were any of the documents in any other language?

CHAFFEE: (pause) No.

SOUTHARD: Not in German?

CHAFFEE: No.

SOUTHARD: How many pieces did you get from her in all?

CHAFFEE: Of ass? Or intelligence (nervous laugh) Jesus, I don't know, I wasn't counting. But Washington's got them, right? (nervous laugh)

SOUTHARD: You tell me.

CHAFFEE: (shouts) Well I just did, didn't I?

SOUTHARD: Take it easy, Kip. Now I want you to think this one over before you answer.

CHAFFEE: Sure.

SOUTHARD: It's important. Take your time.

CHAFFEE: I said sure.

SOUTHARD: At what point in your relationship did you begin to suspect you were being used as a conduit for disinformation?

CHAFFEE: Well, I figured she was up to *some*thing right from the start. I mean, why give me that Khrushchev speech? She wasn't that sorry for me. She had to be softening me up.

SOUTHARD: Did you tell her you suspected what she was doing?

CHAFFEE: Hell, no. I just went on playing the stud, and brother she liked it. So what's the big deal?

SOUTHARD: (pause) If it was obvious to you, don't you think she'd know it?

CHAFFEE: Huh? Know what?

SOUTHARD: That you'd figure she was using you.

CHAFFEE: Well, yeah. I guess maybe. (clears throat)

SOUTHARD: (long pause) Kip, did you give her anything in exchange for the pieces she gave you?

CHAFFEE: Hey, wait a minute! Just a cotton-pickin' minute here!

SOUTHARD: People help each other. Friends do that. And you were lovers.

CHAFFEE: I swear to God (stops)

SOUTHARD: Whose idea was de Cheverny?

CHAFFEE: Hers. No, mine.

SOUTHARD: Which is it going to be, Kip?

CHAFFEE: It was my idea. She went for it right away. Listen, Ben, like, even if I'd've wanted to, what kind of pieces could I give her?

SOUTHARD: I'll play back the first tape if it will refresh your memory any. You had the chronology wrong then, and you had it wrong when we talked in Rappallo.

CHAFFEE: What are you trying to hand me? What are you talking about?

SOUTHARD: Paris. You lost a briefcase, okay. And it bothered you. You started drinking. Probably you missed a few contacts.

CHAFFEE: Yeah, I did.

SOUTHARD: The drinking got heavier. And then Erika Graf met you down on the Riviera.

CHAFFEE: Sure, so what's the—

SOUTHARD: (interrupting) When the dentist in Passy and his six assets were blown, it wasn't because of any beating you gave to a greedy agent, was it? And they weren't blown because you did a lot of talking in a lot of bars, either.

CHAFFEE: I don't follow. What's the question, professor?

SOUTHARD: I mean blowing them was what you gave Major Graf in exchange for what she gave you. Isn't that the way it happened?

CHAFFEE: (long pause) Yeah, all right. Yes.

SOUTHARD: You're in more trouble than I thought, Kip. You see, it all comes down to intent. When someone's channeling disinformation, the big question is did he realize it too late? Or did he know all along?

CHAFFEE: I didn't say I knew. I suspected.

SOUTHARD: Right, suspected. You should have passed along those suspicions. But maybe they weren't strong. Were you 90 percent sure she was using you? Or just 50, or 20, or 10? If that were the only question, a good lawyer could demolish the prosecution on intent.

CHAFFEE: Lawyer? Prosecution? What is this anyway?

SOUTHARD: You're in a hell of a jam, Kip. Intent isn't at issue anymore. You blew our assets in Paris to the French counterintelligence service—and I don't have to tell you practically half their staff gets its orders from Moscow.

CHAFFEE: I'm only a resident, for Christ's sweet sake. A glorified cut-out. A go-between. I don't even know any top-secret material or like that.

SOUTHARD: But our Paris assets did. A pretty strong case could be made against you for treason, Kip.

CHAFFEE: They never do that, you know they don't! The publicity.

SOUTHARD: I mean an internal trial. The Agency as judge, jury, executioner. You didn't think they'd let you walk away from it, did you?

CHAFFEE: (long pause) Ben. Hey listen, Ben. Isn't there anything I can do? Anything, whatever you say, to square things. We're old friends, Ben, right? Ben, listen, I (sobs).

7

By the time the *Andrea Doria* was within 150 miles of the Nantucket Lightship on Wednesday afternoon, July 25, she was sailing through light, patchy fog.

Senior Captain Piero Calamai was resigned to it. Name a perilous condition at sea, and you could expect to find it in the North Atlantic. Storms, fog, ice, gales, hurricanes—Piero Calamai had seen them all. To sail past the Nantucket Shoals in July without encountering fog would have been unusual.

Expecting the fog to thicken as the liner steamed west, Captain Calamai came into the wheelhouse from the port bridge wing and ordered the standard precautionary measures.

One of the two radar sets was tuned to a range of twenty miles, and one of the two watch officers was stationed at the screen to begin his vigil over the sweeping wand of light.

By electronic control from the bridge the twelve watertight doors in the bulkhead deck, A Deck, were shut, sealing the ship's watertight compartments and making her theoretically unsinkable.

The engine room was instructed to reduce speed from 23 to 21.8 knots, a token compliance with Rule 16 of the International Regulations for Preventing Accidents at Sea, which stipulated a moderate speed in bad weather.

The compressed air foghorn began to boom its warning every minute and forty seconds.

Senior Captain Calamai, harking back to preradar days, even ordered the lookout down from the crow's nest to a post at the very prow of the vessel.

He would have reduced speed significantly if it had seemed necessary. But the so-called Rules of the Road had been handed down from the nineteenth century, before radar changed the concept of visibility. Besides, a storm had delayed the ship and there was still time to be made up. A ship's captain prided himself on punctual arrival whatever the weather.

The fog grew denser. By the end of the afternoon Captain Calamai knew he would spend the entire night on the bridge, and from his cabin he got the blue beret he wore at such times. It was warmer than his uniform cap and his hair was thinning. He had a light supper sent to the bridge—a cup of soup, cold beef, a piece of fruit.

Every hundred seconds the foghorn boomed mournfully.

The *Andrea Doria*'s thousand-odd passengers looked forward to arrival in New York with mixed emotions. Most of them didn't want the voyage to end. But by afternoon the festive mid-ocean feeling had slipped away.

They had paid the ship's photographer for the enlarged color prints they would throw into a drawer at home. They had folded their bouffant gowns in yards of tissue paper and readied their luggage for the crew to take away before dinner. They had checked the result of the last ship's pool.

Now they prowled the *Doria* restlessly, feeling awkward and somehow unmasked in their street clothes.

They held endless consultations on how much, and whom, to tip. They conferred only slightly less about the proper handling of customs inspectors. They exchanged addresses and telephone numbers they would never use, in a rite of disengagement from shipboard friendships.

They went out on deck, hoping to see the first New England fishing boats, but they saw only fog.

So they congregated in noisy groups in the bars and lounges and card rooms. Most of them laughed a lot. The laughter rang false.

The last day at sea is always a letdown.

The first day at sea for the almost four hundred passengers of the Swedish-American Line motor vessel *Stockholm* was filled with confusion and excitement.

Staterooms and public rooms were explored, baggage was lost and found, fellow passengers appraised with convivial caution, the Jones Beach pylon and Long Island's receding shore viewed through binoculars.

The gleaming white-hulled *Stockholm*, with the sleek, racy lines of a yacht, was the smallest passenger liner in North Atlantic service, less than half the size of the *Andrea Doria*. Her lines were deceptive. She had a top speed of only eighteen knots, but her sharp reinforced-steel prow was designed to cut through northern waters in the wake of an icebreaker.

In midafternoon she was steaming due east from New York in calm seas under a clear sky, and would passs one mile south of the Nantucket Lightship in about seven hours before turning northwest toward Scandinavia.

The *Andrea Doria*, steaming due west through fog, would pass one mile south of the lightship at about 10:20 P.M.

8

SOUTHARD: Fifth interview with Christopher Chaffee. On board the *Andrea Doria*, at sea, Wednesday, 25 July, 10:25 P.M. I'll start the same way, Kip. Have you any objections to answering my questions?

CHAFFEE: No.

SOUTHARD: All right. Now, you've already told me that you didn't remember—or didn't keep count of—how many intelligence pieces Major Graf gave you. Is that right?

CHAFFEE: What's the difference? Washington can count.

SOUTHARD: You also told me all the pieces—transcripts of high-level MfS and GRU meetings, weren't they?—were in Russian.

CHAFFEE: MfS and GRU transcripts, that's right.

SOUTHARD: In Russian.

CHAFFEE: We already established that.

SOUTHARD: You mean you already told me that.

CHAFFEE: Why should I lie about a thing like what language it's in?

SOUTHARD: You know you're in trouble, Kip, don't you?

CHAFFEE: (nervous laugh) Quit rubbing it in, okay?

SOUTHARD: Why are you?

CHAFFEE: (pause) I gave her the names of some people in Paris.

SOUTHARD: "Her" being Major Graf?

CHAFFEE: (shouts) Well who do you think I mean?

SOUTHARD: Whose names did you give her?

CHAFFEE: I already told you. The other night. You got it on tape.

SOUTHARD: You gave her the name of a principal in Paris and several of his agents.

CHAFFEE: Yeah.

SOUTHARD: How many?

CHAFFEE: Six.

SOUTHARD: Plus the dentist. That's seven of our people you blew, Kip.

CHAFFEE: (shouts) All right. All right!

SOUTHARD: (fast now) Can you read Russian?

CHAFFEE: No.

SOUTHARD: Any Slavic language?

CHAFFEE: No.

SOUTHARD: French?

CHAFFEE: I live in France, for Chrisake.

SOUTHARD: German?

CHAFFEE: (long pause) Yeah, I can read a little German.

SOUTHARD: Did you read the transcripts Major Graf gave you?

CHAFFEE: I told you I can't read Russian.

SOUTHARD: No, I mean the German ones.

CHAFFEE: Not those either.

SOUTHARD: (softly) What did you do with them, Kip?

CHAFFEE: Oh shit.

SOUTHARD: (angry) I didn't need to tell you what kind of trouble you were in. You already knew. So unless you were even dumber than I think, you'd have taken out some insurance.

CHAFFEE: (thirty-second pause) I don't want to play all my cards yet.

SOUTHARD: How well do you read German?

CHAFFEE: Fluently. Yeah, I'd say fluently.

SOUTHARD: How many of the transcripts Major Graf gave you were in that language.

CHAFFEE: It's too soon. I'm telling you it's too soon. It isn't time for bargaining yet.

SOUTHARD: It's way past time.

CHAFFEE: No, it's too soon.

SOUTHARD: (softly) Kip. Your trial's already begun.

CHAFFEE: Jesus!

SOUTHARD: There's no question about your guilt. There never was. The only question is how much you're willing to cooperate. You know what the options are at an internal trial?

CHAFFEE: How the hell would I know anything like that? All I am, I'm a high-level messenger boy.

SOUTHARD: From retirement with pension all the way to termination with prejudice. (pause) Kip, believe me, you need an advocate—and I'm the only one you're going to get.

CHAFFEE: (very long pause) There were three of them.

SOUTHARD: Three of the transcripts Major Graf gave you were in German?

CHAFFEE: Yeah.

SOUTHARD: And you read them?

CHAFFEE: All right. Yeah. I read them.

SOUTHARD: Where are they?

CHAFFEE: I (pause) I put them in a bank vault in Nice.

SOUTHARD: Kip.

CHAFFEE: Okay. Okay. I mailed them to myself.

SOUTHARD: Where?

CHAFFEE: The States.

SOUTHARD: Where in the States?

CHAFFEE: I mailed them to myself, care of general delivery at (stops)

SOUTHARD: What post office?

CHAFFEE: (pause) I thought you were my friend.

SOUTHARD: I want to help you.

CHAFFEE: If I tell you now, I got nothing left to bargain with. I got to keep something for later. For Prestridge. He's the tough one, he's a fanatic. I think I—

SOUTHARD: (interrupts) I'll talk to Adam Prestridge when the time comes.

CHAFFEE: —ought to wait until—

SOUTHARD: (interrupts) If you lose me you won't have anybody.

CHAFFEE: (pause) I don't know. I don't know what to do. Whatever I do is gonna be wrong.

SOUTHARD: You said you mailed the three German transcripts to yourself care of general delivery. All to the same place?

CHAFFEE: All in one package, right.

SOUTHARD: Kip, I want you to tell me where you sent the package. What city.

CHAFFEE: Goddamn it, give me a break! I need time. You're all over me. I don't know what to do anymore. I'm up the creek no matter what. I've got to get out of here. (footsteps) I can't stand it any longer. (slam of door)

Southard smoked a cigarette thoughtfully. Chaffee had run out of last night's session too, run out crying the identical words: I can't stand it any longer. Southard had given him twenty minutes, then gone and found him outside on Boat Deck. He came back meek as a lamb, and he answered a key question. Southard expected it would be the same tonight. He'd let Chaffee mull it over for a while, then go up and join him on Boat Deck.

9

Sulayman had begun to think he'd never have a chance even at Chaffee, let alone Beck.

Either they stayed together like lovers, sometimes spending hours together in Beck's cabin, or they were in crowded places like the Belvedere Lounge or the Grand Bar, the theater, poolside, the dining room.

Then last night the red-haired one, Chaffee, had taken a brisk walk on Boat Deck alone. It was dumb luck that Chaffee had picked Boat Deck, Sulayman's favorite place aboard ship. It was usually private there. The wind blew hard. Chaffee might have been an indoor type, might have preferred the glassed-in Promenade Deck instead.

It would have been a simple matter to slip a knife between Chaffee's ribs on the deserted Boat Deck last night and pitch the body over the chest-high rail but Sulayman hadn't done it. He just passed Chaffee once on the starboard side of Boat Deck and returned to his own cabin.

To dispose of Chaffee first, he had thought then, would put Beck on his guard. Beck was the primary target, Chaffee a dividend if he could get it.

But now it was the final night. If he didn't make a move tonight, he'd get neither of them.

Their cabins were the worst kind of killing ground. The Upper Deck corridors were rarely deserted for even a few minutes at a time. Some passengers stayed up all night, drinking, dancing in the Belvedere Lounge, playing bridge in the card room. There were the night stewards too, a steward station for every few cabins, ready to answer someone's ring. There were even the boys who went along the corridors at night picking up the shoes left outside cabin doors and taking them to be shined.

Sulyaman would have to make a decision if Chaffee came out on Boat Deck again tonight. Go after Beck in his cabin—or settle for Chaffee? Beck was clearly tempting, and just as clearly dangerous.

Sulayman pondered his choice.

The fog wasn't what you'd call a pea-souper, but it was heavy.

Kip Chaffee had got his raincoat and was wearing it now as he paced fore and aft along the starboard Boat Deck. The deck planking was slippery. He could see moisture on the keels of the lifeboats hung from their davits. There was wind, generated by the ship's headway, but the night was warm.

Chaffee went to the rail. He peered down through the darkness. Despite the fog he could see the bow wave creaming white.

He had to make himself think.

Now or later? Southard, who was his friend, or a court of inquiry run by that creepy fanatic Prestridge?

The foghorn moaned periodically, a low note with all the sadness in the world.

Chaffee glanced up, his view partially blocked by the bridge wing. He could see a dim light in the chart room.

He went the length of the starboard Boat Deck and back once more. Then he walked it again and turned and started back and saw someone coming toward him, not pacing as Chaffee was, but just strolling. Chaffee recognized him as they drew close. That French student, what was his name? Faure, Paul Faure.

Chaffee wished he could make up his mind. He ought to be able to make a simple decision like now or later. But so much depended on it. His whole fucking future.

He raised his hand in casual salute to Paul Faure. The French student raised a hand in return, and it took Chaffee a second to realize the hand wasn't empty. The hand had a knife in it, for Christ's sake, and Faure just sort of swung it easily at Chaffee from the side. As easy as the motion seemed, Chaffee did not have the time to block it. Maybe, a small voice whispered inside his head, he really didn't want to block it. Maybe it was easier this way, with Paul Faure taking the decision out of his hands. But he was trying to block it. He just couldn't. He wondered why he didn't feel any pain. He wondered if that Kraut cunt Erika had sent Paul Faure. Then he started to feel the pain and it wasn't much really but Faure was half shoving, half lifting him, and he thought he was resisting but Faure leaned him against the rail and began to fold him over it like a suit of clothes.

Sulayman had trouble wrestling the wounded man against the railing. He was all floppy arms and legs, like a rag doll. When Sulayman got his arms over the top rail, he sagged, his weight flopping back. When Sulayman tried to lift him bodily, he grabbed the middle rail and held on. When Sulayman pried his fingers loose it was only to have him slide to the deck. Sulayman had to start all over again, lifting him, fighting the tangle of long arms and legs. Sulayman was sweating.

Chaffee's right hand was gripping the rail again.

Sulayman heard the ship's foghorn, then running footsteps.

The fog bank enveloping the *Andrea Doria* extended 180 miles with the Nantucket lightship 19 or 20 miles from its western edge. The *Doria* had been sailing for eight hours now through fog and, having passsed the lightship at 10:43, was nearing the edge of the bank. Here the fog was thickest.

The *Stockholm*, a few miles west and closing fast, maintained full speed. What looked like haze on the horizon in the clear moonlight night was the edge of the fog bank.

Each ship had the other on its radarscope now, each had plotted the other's course. In the *Stockholm* wheelhouse it was expected that the approaching vessel would pass somewhat less than a mile off the port beam, given the present bearings.

When the radarscope indicated a distance of six miles, the *Stockholm*'s watch officer went out onto the port wing to see the lights of the approaching ship.

He was mystified when he saw nothing.

Soon, distant and eerie, he could hear a foghorn.

In the wheelhouse of the *Andrea Doria* it was calculated that the approaching ship would pass a mile or so to starboard and, on that heading, was probably a fishing trawler making for Nantucket Island. It was decided to let the smaller vessel pass between the *Doria* and the shoal waters off Nantucket. The larger *Doria* would keep to the left.

This might have been a violation of the Rules of the Road, which specified that ships on or close to a collision course must both turn right in order to pass port-to-port. But the words *close to* are open to interpretation, and in the wheelhouse of the *Doria* it was thought there was ample room for a starboard-to-starboard passing.

To the *Andrea Doria*'s left, after all, was the safety of the open sea.

11

Sulayman had no way of knowing who was running toward him along the slippery deck. It might be Beck, come to join his friend. It might be anyone who had come outside for a breath of air and had seen him grappling with Chaffee, trying to lift him over the railing. Sulayman had to make up his mind in a second.

He let Chaffee slump to the deck and ran.

Chaffee was on his knees now, gripping the middle bar of the railing. Southard raced past him in pursuit of the other man.

Tendrils of fog coiled along Boat Deck, reached out, caught the receding figure, released it. Southard couldn't close the distance. The man ran with reckless disregard for the slippery footing and, if anything, increased his lead as he sprinted aft. Fog swept past Southard. Again his quarry was lost to view.

At the rear of Boat Deck steep metal staircases climbed up to Lido Deck and down to Promenade Deck. Southard heard the pound of shoes on stairs, but in the fog the sound seemed all around him and he could not tell if the feet went up or down. Then there was silence. It would be pure guesswork — and if he guessed wrong, the man might return to finish Chaffee. He stood for several seconds listening. Still he heard nothing.

He returned along the deserted deck to Chaffee.

Perhaps, thought the *Stockholm*'s watch officer, something was wrong with the approaching ship's lights. Or possibly it was a warship, running dark through the night on secret maneuvers. The possibility of fog never occurred to him. The night was clear, anyone could see that.

When the pip was inside the two-mile ring on the five-mile radarscope, the lookout on the bridge wing finally saw the approaching ship's running lights.

The two ships were then closing at a combined speed of forty knots. Less than three minutes separated them.

Still, everything seemed in order to the *Stockholm*'s watch officer. The forward light of the approaching ship appeared slightly to the left of the higher aft light. This meant a routine port-to-port passing. To make sure, the watch officer called for two full turns of the wheel to starboard, and the helmsman complied.

The watch officer next received a call from the crow's nest confirming a ship's running lights twenty degrees to port. When he hung up his telephone the lookout in the crow's nest then saw the impossible—the other vessel's lights were crossing, forward light swinging to the right under aft light. The other ship was going to cross the *Stockholm*'s bow!

Walking out onto the port bridge wing, the watch officer saw the great black hull, studded with porthole lights, looming directly ahead. Horrified, he ran back inside to the engine-room telegraph. But by then it was too late.

On the bridge wing of the *Andrea Doria*, Captain Calamai watched with disbelief as the masthead lights of the other ship moved further apart, indicating a turn.

The red sidelight told him the turn was to starboard.

The unknown vessel was heading straight for the *Andrea Doria*.

13

Sulayman slipped into the cabin and leaned against the door, both hands flat against it. He was breathing hard. His pursuer had not followed him down the two ladders to Upper Deck. He still did not know whether it was Beck or not, and whether he had recognized him. There was nothing he could do about that now.

"I thought you were never coming back."

Sulayman whirled.

One of the California sisters sat in his bed, long blonde hair hanging free, blanket held coyly to her chin.

"How did you get in here?"

"Aren't you just a teensy bit glad to see me?"

"I asked how you got in here."

"The night steward. The nice night steward let me in," said the California sister.

"Get out!" Sulayman shouted.

Instead, she lowered the blanket to reveal that she was naked, at least from the waist up. And she laughed.

That seemed to trigger a series of events that Sulayman did not comprehend.

The floor shook underfoot.

He was picked up and slammed back against the cabin door.

There was an ear-splitting sound of metal grating against metal.

Something white and gleaming seemed to replace the cabin for an instant, showing sparks.

He was on the floor. He got up groggily. He smelled scorched paint and the sharp odor of ozone.

The girl was gone.

The bed was gone.

The far wall of the cabin and the hull beyond were gone.

Sulayman looked out at the dark night.

Southard did not identify the source of the faint light which dimly showed the ruins of Chaffee's cabin until he felt the cool night air.

A jagged-edged hole had replaced the outer wall of the cabin and through it Southard saw the moon. He saw it but could not understand what it meant. In that first moment after he regained consciousness all he could understand was that they had finally steamed out of the fog.

He remembered helping Chaffee down to the cabin, remembered how Chaffee was shaking, could not stop shaking, and how his lips were blue. He remembered leaving the door ajar and pressing the call button beside it, and easing Chaffee onto the bed, then unbuttoning the raincoat to find out where the blood was coming from. The wound was between the sixth and seventh ribs on the left side. Blood seeped out steadily. He remembered removing the pillowcase and folding it into a makeshift compress, remembered feeling how cold Chaffee's skin was. Shock was setting in. He would have to get the doctor himself if the steward did not come soon. He would phone just as soon as he got Chaffee covered with the extra blanket and elevated his feet somehow. The bulky kapok life jacket would do. Southard remembered opening the life-jacket compartment above the closet, and then he felt a jarring, wrenching thud and the closet seemed to detach itself from the wall and topple forward, which made no sense at all because the closet was built in, and the edge of the door to the life-jacket compartment struck Southard's head.

He had no way of telling how long he blacked out. Now he saw the moonlight in the cabin, what was left of the cabin.

The far wall was gone, ripped off jaggedly at floor and ceiling, sheered off smoothly as if by design at one side, where the head of the bed had been. The bed dangled half in, half out of the gaping hole. The side wall with the closet was buckled inward, the opposite wall outward.

Southard heard cries and shouts outside, and feet running. An explosion, he thought, maybe one of the ship's boilers had exploded.

Still on his knees, he could feel the ship rolling to starboard. The moonlit sea outside seemed to rise to meet it. The ship did not return to even keel. It wasn't rolling; it was listing. The bed tilted and slid and fell out of the cabin.

Southard tried to stand. His head came into contact with something. Part of the ceiling had come down. Dust still settled through the moonlight. Southard ducked under a metal beam canted diagonally across the cabin and was able to get to his feet in a crouching position, his head bumping the ceiling as he took an exploratory step.

He heard a groan. Chaffee called, "Ben? Ben, what happened?"

Ahead the ceiling was lower and he had to crawl under debris to reach Chaffee. He felt a sharp pain when he tried to put weight on his left arm; something was wrong with the shoulder. Chaffee lay near the jagged hole where the exterior wall had been. Another metal beam was down, this one running from the bathroom wall to the edge of the hole. Chaffee was on his back, both legs pinned by the beam.

Southard got his weight under the beam, as close to the middle as he could, and strained upward. Something shifted and grated in his left shoulder. The beam would not budge.

He crawled closer to Chaffee. The floor was stickily wet and he could smell the coppery smell of blood.

"Ben?" Chaffee sounded bewildered, a child waking from an unpleasant dream.

"I'm right here, Kip."

"Ben? I . . . listen, professor. Your way. We'll do it your way. You were right. I'll tell you where . . . where I sent the, Erika's transcripts, okay? Then everything will be just fine." His voice seemed to gain confidence. "They'll pension me off, *n'est-ce pas?* They'll have to. Then I'll be able to go back to France and get a little place somewhere and . . ." Chaffee laughed, a soft sighing sound. "Here's the funny part. I want to paint. Really paint, never mind how I got my start. I was just painting whatever would sell, but now . . . I think the talent's there, I think there are some good paintings in me, only . . . Ben?"

"Yeah, Kip?"

"I think maybe Erika took that away from me too. Why would she do that, Ben? Why would she send him to kill me now when . . ."

"Who? Who did she send?" Southard said urgently.

"That French kid, you know the one, hung around with those blondes? Faure, Paul Faure. I don't see why . . . everything was going to be all right, as soon as I . . ." Chaffee's voice was fainter now but calm. "The only think is, I don't think I'll make it, Ben, I think I'm going. Funny, I'm not scared . . . it doesn't matter now, any of it. I said I'd give it the old college try, and I did." Chaffee gave another soft laugh. "That's how come when I had to think of a place to send them. . . ."

Southard thought he laughed a third time. Then he realized the sound in Chaffee's throat was the last one he would ever make.

Chapter Eighteen

1

Southard sat in the back seat of the car surrounded by newsprint—the *Times,* the *News,* the *Mirror*. Banner headlines celebrated the disaster of the year.

Every story cited the same few statistics. The *Andrea Doria* went down at 10:09 A.M. Thursday, July 26, in 225 feet of water at 40°30′N 69°53°W. Casualties were 25 dead, 17 missing.

From there they passed to conjecture, also repetitive.

If the *Stockholm*'s watch officer was unable to see the other ship's lights, how could he not realize there was fog ahead?

Why did the *Andrea Doria*'s captain decide to pass starboard-to-starboard?

Why had the *Doria* listed so severely, over 15°, minutes after the collision? Why had the watertight compartments overflowed, one into another, at the bulkhead deck? How could a theoretically unsinkable ship go down in less than twelve hours?

Why were the davits constructed so they could operate only up to an angle of seven degrees, making all the portside lifeboats useless?

There were authoritative answers for every question, instant experts at every newsdesk. And of course the ghost of the *Titantic* was conjured up.

Much was made of the rescue operation.

The *Stockholm*, still seaworthy despite her demolished prow, took on board 545 survivors, the United Fruit Company freighter *Cape Ann* 129, the U.S. Navy transport *Pvt. William H. Thomas* 158.

The great liner *Ile de France*, outward bound from New York, turned back at the SOS and reached the scene of the disaster at 1:45 A.M., all lights blazing. Positioning herself within 400 yards of the *Doria*'s starboard side in the bright moonlight, the majestic French vessel shielded the sinking liner from the motion of the waves. Then she sent eleven lifeboats to take aboard, in all, 576 passengers and 177 crew.

The *Ile de France* was the last of the rescue ships to sail for New York, as the damaged *Stockholm*, with a Coast Guard cutter trailing, was understandably the first.

Southard impatiently folded his copy of the *New York Times* to the page which listed the survivors and stared at it. It did not change.

Paul Faure, French citizen, had been among the survivors taken to New York by the *Stockholm*. And Curtis Beck, U.S. citizen, had reached New York hours later aboard the *Ile de France*.

Now Southard, his broken collarbone securely trussed, a dozen stitches closing the gash in his left upper arm, was being driven down the New Jersey Turnpike in a car sent from D.C. by the Agency. As they passed the Bordentown exit, the driver tilted his rearview mirror and glanced back at him.

"You doing all right, Mr. Southard? I've got a thermos of coffee if you—"

"No thanks."

"A chocolate bar?"

"No."

"For God's sake, a shipwreck—I mean, this is 1956."

Southard mumbled a reply. The shot of morphine had worn off. The shoulder was beginning to hurt more.

The driver said, "What I heard, the crew abandoned ship before most of the passengers even had a chance to get into a lifeboat. Well jeez, what can you expect from a bunch of wops?"

"You always hear stuff like that. The crew was okay."

The driver said: "According to what I. . . ."

The driver said: "Well, I heard. . . ."

The driver said: "Here's what I. . . ."

The driver said: "The way I see it, the owners won't lose a penny. They'll hire themselves some smart Jew lawyers and—"

They were approaching a rest area. "Pull in there, would you?" Southard said.

The driver pulled off.

"Now get out," Southard said. "Get out, give me the keys, call Washington and ask them to send a car for you."

"But I'm supposed to . . . my ass'll be in a sling if . . ."

"There's this alternative. You could drive the rest of the way to D.C. without making any slurs against wops, spics, polacks, niggers, kikes or CIA officers. You think you can do that?"

The driver stared straight ahead. His neck reddened.

They drove out of the rest area and again did a steady seventy-five on the turnpike.

Southard decided he had been arbitrary and unfair. Everyone wanted to talk about the shipwreck, it was big news. The odd possessiveness he felt as eyewitness, as near victim, was foolish and childish. The *New York Times* knew far more about the collision than he did.

"Think the Dodgers can take the pennant this year?" he asked.

The driver smiled in the rearview mirror. "Nosiree," he said, eager to resume talking to the survivor. "Philly, that's my club. With a classy guy like Robin Roberts on the mound, how you gonna stop them? The Dodgers? Not a prayer. Too many Negroes. Mind you, I always say more power to them if they can make it in the big leagues. But you take a spade, there's somebody's gonna fold in the clutch, if you see what I mean. Look at that fat old catcher Campanella, he never did. . . .."

Southard sighed. He opened the newspaper again and propped it in front of his face.

2

Sulayman reached Washington by train at about the same time Southard did by car. He assumed, correctly, that that was where Curtis Beck would go.

The Mukhabarat station chief was expecting him. They met in a Chinese restaurant near Dupont Circle for an early dinner. The station chief was a bald fat man who reeked of cologne.

"I know of you, of course," he said, nervously clearing his throat. "But I have no instructions concerning you."

Sulayman stared at him. "No, you wouldn't. That is why I had to see you in person."

"What is it you want?" the fat man asked uneasily.

"First, U.S. identification papers."

"For deep cover? On such short notice, you understand—"

"All I want is adequate identification to buy firearms."

The fat man smiled and relaxed. "'Here, that is no problem. Here a driver's license will suffice."

"I need money."

"Within reason that too will be no problem."

"And I need to know the identity of the CIA operative who has been calling himself Curtis Beck in Europe."

"Beck," said the fat man. "No, I don't know the name."

"It's important," Sulayman told him.

346

"Mr. Husayni, please believe I would do anything within my power to help you. But—"

"Then find out who he is."

"To do that, I would have to collect a debt which I hoped—"

"Collect it."

The fat man looked at Sulayman's eyes and saw there what Sulayman's reputation had told him to expect. He saw death.

He lowered his gaze and said, "I will do it."

3

In his office near the Watergate barge and bandshell the next Monday morning, Allen Dulles stood up behind his desk and said, "Benton! Come in, boy, come in. You're looking better than I'd expected. A lot better."

The director was looking chipper himself. His step was firm as he came around the desk to shake Southard's hand.

"Sit down, Benton, tell me what it was really like. Did you know the *New York Times* had a veteran correspondent aboard? Their Madrid man, coming home on leave. They kept waiting for him to find a way to file his on-the-scene report." Dulles shook his head. "Poor bastard was crushed to death in his berth."

Southard hadn't sat down yet. He tossed a bulky manila envelope on Allen Dulles's desk. It had République Française airmail stamps on it, and a blue *par avion* sticker. It was addressed in a looping, almost childish handwriting in green ink to Christopher Chaffee, General Delivery, Chapel Hill, North Carolina. Chaffee had had a couple of years of college at UNC.

Dulles looked from the envelope to Southard.

"Chaffee's insurance. We've inherited three German transcripts of MfS meetings—probably doctored."

"Not necessarily," Dulles said. He picked up the phone and dialed four digits. "Sometimes they really want us to have something, but need to pretend they don't. That business about biological warfare last year, for example." Dulles lifted a hand and spoke into the phone. "Could you come in, please?"

Southard tapped the envelope. "This is part of a whole disinformation campaign, Allen. With just enough truth, or more than enough, to make it convincing."

"I'm not saying it isn't. But we *have* had more time with the Russian transcripts since you left. I'm just suggesting—" Dulles reached over to the phone console, where a light was flashing, and flipped a switch. "Send Mr. von Stolz right in."

Von Stolz was a bull-necked man wearing a brush cut. After the fall of Admiral Canaris's Abwehr in 1943 he had spent two years in *Amt* IV of the Reich Central Security Office before joining the Gehlen Group after the war and the CIA in 1954. He greeted Dulles and Southard, each by surname, each with a single stiff nod of his head.

Dulles handed him the envelope. "For immediate evaluation, please," he said. "These came from the same source as the Russian ones you've been working on."

Von Stolz waited five seconds to make sure there were no further instructions, then nodded stiffly to each man again and left.

"An unregenerate, irredeemable Prussian," said Dulles. "But he also happens to know more about what's going on inside Eastern Europe than anyone this side of Reinhard Gehlen. Sit down, will you? You're making me nervous."

Southard drew a chair up to the desk.

"Now," said Dulles, "about this Paul Faure. Did your inquiry to the immigration people turn up anything?"

"Plenty." Southard shook his head. "In the last three days he flew out of Idlewild for Europe seven times, and out of Logan twice. Also he crossed the St. Lawrence into

Ontario or Quebec two dozen times by bridge or ferry. Never under the name of Paul Faure, of course."

Dulles tamped tobacco into a billiard pipe. "Of course. So we don't even know for certain that he's left the country."

"He must have. For all he knew, Chaffee might have lived, at least long enough to identify him. Or I might have recognized him. When he didn't see either of us among the survivors the *Stockholm* picked up, he wouldn't wait around to see if we got off any other ship. He'd cut and run."

"Would he? Maybe he'd want to finish the job."

"If he did hang around, it wouldn't have taken him long to find out Chaffee was dead."

Dulles scowled through a haze of blue smoke. "It wasn't Chaffee I had in mind."

"Me?" Southard stared at him. "Not a chance. When you get to my level, let alone yours, you're supposed to be immune. Fieldmen may be fair game, but no top people, isn't that the rule? Or else the rival agency that ordered the hit starts to lose top people of its own."

"That's the theory," Dulles agreed. "Actually we don't practice retaliation much. We don't have to. The threat alone makes a useful deterrent."

"And Erika Graf understands it as well as anybody. Besides, even if she was crazy enough to send Paul Faure after both of us, it's too late now. The only reason for killing us would be to stop us telling what we knew. Okay, he got Chaffee. But I'm here in Washington, I've dictated a full report. So I can't be a target anymore, if I ever was."

Dulles had to admit the force of Southard's logic. Still, when he was alone, he sat smoking pensively. He would feel better if he knew for certain that Paul Faure had left the country.

Finally he shrugged. There was no point in having

349

resources if you didn't use them.

He called security and ordered around-the-clock babysitters for Benton Southard.

4

Sulayman found what he was looking for in a pawnshop on Pennsylvania Avenue, not a mile from the White House. It was a Springfield 03 rifle, the model developed from a Mauser design before the First World War and still used by U.S. Army snipers in World War II. It was not fitted with a sniper-scope, but Sulayman found a 5X telescopic sight and had it mounted at a gunshop on F Street. He also bought three boxes of .30-06 ammunition, merely by showing a District of Columbia driving license.

He took a room in a boarding house on Wisconsin Avenue in Georgetown, a block and a half from Southard's apartment in a converted Federalist era house on Q Street, and began to familiarize himself with his quarry's habits. He soon learned that Southard had a bodyguard of whom he was, or seeemd to be, unaware. Southard spent ten and twelve hours a day at his office in a two-story cinderblock building in Foggy Bottom. He dined out, with a variety of women, usually at Naylor's on the Municipal Fish Wharf. Naylor's was where Sulayman decided to hit him.

One week to the day after the *Andrea Doria* sank, Sulayman rented a car and drove into the Virginia countryside to get the Springfield zeroed in. By that weekend, the first in August, he was ready to move against Southard.

Southard, however, went out of town. When he got back, Sulayman had a whole new routine to learn. Southard wasn't alone.

350

"He drinks tea and he had a bald place on top of his head and he tells funny stories that make me laugh." Suzie Southard looked up at her father sideways from the middle of the front seat of the Chrysler. "I hate him," she said.

They were driving north toward Washington on U.S. 17.

Suzie was wearing a blue and white piqué sunsuit. Her blonde hair had been cut short for the summer, shorter than Southard liked it. There was a Samsonite suitcase on the back seat.

"He sounds very nice. Why don't you like him?"

"Because he wants to be my daddy. And I don't want anybody to be my daddy except you."

Southard's former wife had been married that morning in the Wren Chapel of the College of William and Mary to a professor of economics named Durant.

"Well, I'm not going to stop being your daddy. But I can see why he'd want a daughter like you. Anybody would."

"I hate him!" Suzie began to cry.

Southard pulled to the side of the road. Suzie hugged herself to him and snuffled against his shoulder.

"Hey, doll, just because he's married to your mother now, that doesn't mean—"

"Yes it does! I heard mother say so. He's going to de—deplace you in my life."

"He can't unless you want him to, doll. There's nothing to worry about. Now tell me, did he ask you to call him daddy?"

"N—no. I call him Eddie, just like mother does."

"See? He won't take my place, he'll just have a place of his own. What's wrong with having another person to love you?"

"I hate him," Suzie repeated, but the conviction was gone.

"No you don't. You just said he makes you laugh. I'll bet you like him already."

Southard was able to see Janet's viewpoint. Durant, a widower in his late forties, had seemed an affable enough sort, if professorial. He was stable. He would be home every night. When he traveled during the summer break in the college year, he would take his family with him to the expected tourist places.

What could Southard offer his daughter but stolen weekends, long absences, the unwholesome excitement of uncertainty?

"Are we going to your house, daddy?"

"That's right, doll. I've got the whole week off, so we can see all the sights in Washington. That sound like fun?"

"Wow! Can I cook for you, daddy?"

"Well, breakfast anyway." Southard reached over and ruffled Suzie's short blonde hair.

When Janet had phoned, asking if he could take Suzie for the coming week, his first reaction was unmixed pleasure. But that same afternoon he had spotted someone following him and, though he soon identified his shadow as an Agency security man, it made him reconsider seriously the threat of the man called Paul Faure.

He could see how Graf would send someone after Chaffee. But Southard himself was another mattter. He had gone over that with Allen Dulles. He was too highly placed in the Agency; any attempt on his life would trigger retaliation. More important, there was no longer any reason to kill him. The Agency now knew everything he knew.

Still, Allen Dulles's concern was touching.

Omar Hamza, the Mukhabarat station chief, hung up the telephone and mopped his round, sweating face with a cologne-scented handkerchief.

New York had called—his opposite number at the

consulate there—with an urgent message for Sulayman Husayni.

Cairo had called on the scrambler phone with the same message for Sulayman Husayni.

Finally his GRU control had phoned from somewhere. The GRU connection was new and Omar Hamza had reason to think the man, whom he knew only as Able, was the GRU chief resident for North America. Hamza had been told to cultivate the connection for all it was worth. Perhaps Able did not realize this. Or perhaps the GRU had money to burn. Whatever, the GRU was paying Omar Hamza a princely sum to do what the Mukhabarat had ordered him to do for nothing.

Able had the same urgent message for Sulayman Husayni.

Husayni was to abandon the operation and leave the country at once.

Omar Hamza had no idea what the operation was. But it was a simple message, as concise as it was imperative.

And as impossible to deliver.

Hamza had not the slightest idea where to find Sulayman Husayni.

6

Suzie was skipping ahead past the tigers and leopards to the monkey house. Southard caught up with her in front of the chimpanzee cage. Two chimps, one seated on a hanging rubber tire, one on the ground, were jabbering at the crowd of tourists Suzie had joined, lecturing them, perhaps scolding them.

"They're funny," Suzie said. "They make me laugh."

Southard grinned when he realized she had used the same words to describe the chimps and her stepfather.

"What's funny, daddy?"

"You already said. The chimpanzees." Maybe funny was just her newest favorite word.

It was the third day of Suzie's visit and Southard was feeling better about his status as her father. He loved Suzie and she loved him. The problems created by his career would sort themselves out.

Suzie had proven herself a tireless tourist, asking the same eager question each morning as she made breakfast, and a mess, in the kitchen of the Q Street apartment. "Where are we going today, daddy?"

So far they had gone for a barge ride on the Chesapeake and Ohio Canal, and seen the Kenilworth Aquatic Gardens, the Aquarium, the Wax Museum at Fifth and K, Fort Stevens, and now the National Zoological Center in Rock Creek Park. Today, after the zoo, they would have a picnic in the park and then see the dinosaurs at the Smithsonian.

Getting Suzie out of the zoo, though, took some doing. She wanted to watch the bears, she said, especially the big white polar bear, even if he did just sort of sit around.

"It's too hot for him."

"It's not hot, daddy, not for summer."

"No, but he's a polar bear. It's always cold at the poles."

"Does he come from the North Pole or the South Pole?"

"I, uh, the North Pole."

"Right on it? How can they tell when they're there?"

"Well, they live a long way north. Places like Greenland."

"And Iceland, I'll bet."

"No, Iceland isn't really very cold."

"That's silly, daddy. *Ice*land—it *has* to be."

After the bears, she fed the goats and sheep little pellets of animal food.

"I wonder what they taste like."

"No idea, doll."

A moment later: "Daddy, I need a drink of water. They

354

taste like . . . like . . ." Suzie made a face, for once at a loss for words.

She was an avid thrower of peanuts to the elephants, but she regarded the peanuts themselves with a jaundiced eye.

"Do they taste like just plain peanuts?"

"Sure."

"Are you *positive*, daddy?"

"Yup."

She shelled one and sampled it doutbfully. "You're right, they're people peanuts."

Southard couldn't get her to leave the Great Flight Cage. She caught on to the idea of a habitat right away. "It's so big it's almost like they're not in a cage at all. But I'll bet they still want to fly away sometimes."

"I guess so."

"They ought to let them."

"Then you wouldn't be able to see them."

"We-ell," Suzie pondered the dilemma.

Outside the zebra enclosure Southard saw Kimball. "Hey, Scotty," he said.

The security man looked startled, then smiled ruefully. "The idea is, Mr. Southard, I'm supposed to be invisible. Mr. D thought you wouldn't like it if we were obvious about it."

"No problem, Scotty."

"I thought I was lucky, getting the day shift. But that kid of yours is walking my feet off."

Southard introduced Kimball to Suzie. He was boyish and tousle-haired and it was obvious she took to him at once.

"Listen, Scotty, we're having a picnic near that field that's set up for show jumping."

"This side of Military Road?"

"That's it. Plenty of food, so why don't you join us?"

"I made the sandwiches, Mr. Kimball," Suzie said. "Well, some of them," she added after a look from her father.

"Then I'm sure they're good," Kimball said.

"They're delicious," said Suzie. "I hope."

They drove the short distance in two cars and spread the picnic out on a slight rise that looked down over the equitation field. A woman in riding habit was jumping a gray stallion. There was corned beef and salami and beer and milk and the peanut butter sandwiches Suzie had made.

"They're my specialty but you have to make them thick."

"So I see," said Kimball, talking with difficulty.

"I knew you'd like them."

Sulayman watched them spread a blanket about twenty yards from where they parked at the Military Road end of the Equitation field. He could tell they would be there a while. He kept driving, turning left on Military Road and left again on Connecticut Avenue, where he parked near Tilden Street. He took the long, bulky package from the car and walked back through the woods that began at the western edge of the field. He could see them through the trees now, a hundred yards away. A simple shot with the Springfield. But he didn't like it that the bodyguard was right there with Southard and the child. They were on high ground at the edge of the woods and if the bodyguard rolled to his own right from where he now sat he would be out of Sulayman's line of fire, protected by the side of the slope. If he was quick he might make it. The Springfield was bolt-action, not semiautomatic.

Sulayman would wait until they returned to their cars. The men would separate then. He would hit Southard and disappear back through the woods while the bodyguard was still climbing out of his car wondering where the shot had come from.

Suzie got into the Chrysler before Southard. She sat

behind the wheel, grasped it with both hands, stared intently through the spokes and made a sound like an engine revving.

Southard was standing with Kimball between their cars. "On to the Smithsonian."

"That kid of yours is a doll but she's gonna wear off my feet clear up to the ankle." Kimball got into his Chevy.

"Move over, Juan Fangio," Southard told Suzie.

"In a minute. I'm not there yet." She made a final revving noise and slid over. Southard climbed in.

"Are dinosaurs really bigger than elephants?"

"You'll see for yourself at the museum."

Southard put the key in the ignition.

"Let me do it, daddy?"

Suzie rose up on her knees beside him.

Sulayman squeezed off the first shot just as the child's head appeared in the 5X sight, so close it looked like he could have reached out and touched her. The blonde head exploded, and Sulayman thought the bullet went right through and hit Southard too.

The child unnerved him. He hadn't meant to shoot the child. He got off a second shot, quicker than he intended, the sight-picture unsteady. He thought it was low. Not much, but some. Southard slumped out of sight.

The security man was quick. He was already on the ground between the cars, but still uncertain exactly where the shots had come from.

Sulayman saw the woman galloping the gray stallion back toward the north end of the field, taking a hedge beautifully. He debated firing off a round to keep the bodyguard pinned down but decided it would only tell him which direction the fire had come from. He dropped the Springfield, peeled off his cotton gloves, and jogged through the woods the few hundred yards back to his own car.

He wished Maryam were there.

Part Four

Chapter Nineteen

1

The searchlight swept back from the east, catching the last of three men scrambling frantically for the safety of the gully fifty yards to the near side of the chain link fence. Instantly a whistle shrilled. Tracer bullets from a machine gun stitched a low trajectory through the darkness and through the beam of light. Then the gun was still. Dust settled. The light moved on past the gully, completing its half-circle sweep. In ninety seconds the light would be back but by then the three men would have crawled north in single file along the shallow gully to the fence, ready to move as soon as the light went by in the other direction. Ninety seconds again, this time to scale the seven-foot chain link fence with its V-shaped pair of overhangs holding coiled barbed wire.

Their exit from the far end of the gully, or their sprint to the base of the fence, triggered two floodlights suspended from the metal-pipe frame of the fence. The fatigue-clad figures could be seen clearly as they rushed the chain link with a pair of two-by-twos and a heavy blanket. From the time they reached the base of the fence until the last one dropped from the top to land on the other side, eight and three-tenths seconds had passed on Adam Prestridge's stopwatch.

"An acceptable time," he said, "would be a full second longer, so these boys cut—what? 12 percent—off that. They

361

are good. They don't come any better. And don't think they were slow getting to the defilade. That ninety-second sweep is timed so they can't make it, and you saw how close they came."

The translator repeated in Polish what Prestridge was saying. The Polish actor, whose name was Wadislaw Wazyk, whispered something to the Hungarian doctor, whose name was Noah Landler.

"If they wanted to go through the fence instead of over it," Prestridge continued, "they'd use a six-foot pry bar, and some of these Hungarian teams get through in under half a minute. Not even our own Rangers can top that."

The two East Europeans stood for a while smoking cigarettes on the platform of the observation tower with Prestridge and the translator. All wore U.S. Army fatigues without insignia. They had spent an hour and fifteen minutes here on the barrier penetration range, mostly on the ground, mounting to the observation platform only when live rounds were fired.

Their staff car now returned to the base of the tower. They descended the ladder and were driven slowly away.

"Next is the corrugated steel roll-up vehicle door," Prestridge said, the translator a few words behind. "Sixteen-gauge steel. You could blast your way in with a shaped charge—say, five kilos—in about seven-tenths of a second. But allow these men a tenth of a second more and they can go through with a six-inch pry bar and a two-by-four. And no noise. They're being trained to get over or through or under any barrier at all, as you've seen."

"I am impressed, sir," said the Polish actor in careful English. "They are skillful."

"They're terrific, that's what they are," Prestridge said, and the translator smiled and repeated that in Polish. "In actual fact, gentlemen, our own best security people would have one hell of a time stopping them."

The car went slowly along an unpaved track. Here in the

Taunus Mountains thirty miles northeast of Wiesbaden, West Germany, the night wind in early October was chilly.

"Very well trained indeed," said the Polish actor in his deep voice. The voice, of course, was important. The Hungarian doctor's lacked the timbre of the actor's, but he was a man who believed passionately, and his heart and soul were in his voice.

The staff car climbed onto the crumbling slab of an ancient asphalt road. Prestridge leaned back, and removed the wire-rimmed government issue glasses he was wearing instead of his customary pince-nez. "We have five thousand Soviet bloc refugees here in this one camp, and the best guerrilla warfare people in the U.S. Army training them. Poles and Hungarians, East Germans. Even a few Ukranians. And we've got transportation—pilots on standby around the clock at airfields right here and in Japan and England, and once the field near Thessalonica is ready, it'll be just a milk run from there up into the southern bloc countries. And these are only the vanguard to lead the forces of counterrevolution, gentlemen. To roll back the Iron Curtain."

In the headlight beams Noah Landler saw what looked like a small warehouse. Then he could see it was only a false front, the concrete wall, the corrugated garage door, the wooden supports behind.

He had a fleeting sense of unreality that seemed to war with the total conviction in Adam Prestridge's voice.

The staff car stoppped, and as they climbed out Prestridge looked at his watch. A single streetlamp to the left, twenty feet out from the corrugated metal door, cast pale shadows. The three men waited for the new team to attack the new barrier.

Landler did not know where they were, only that it was somewhere in West Germany. They had been blindfolded on the drive to the camp from the plane that had flown them from Munich-Riem Airport. It did not matter. The important thing was not where, but what.

Seeing, as Adam Prestridge said, was believing. It had not sounded so trite when translated.

Noah Landler was seeing.

He could still hardly believe that he was here, in the West, a free man. It was less than a month since he had sent the message through the pharmacist in Sopron and driven with his wife and daughter to the border, less than a month since Istvan Varady himself had come with the skiff and taken them across the lake and then to Munich. There had been too many signs—the traffic police stopping him twice and subjecting him to a rough search, the medical college questioning him about the use of proscribed drugs, his wife losing her position with the Budapest library, the hooligans attacking him one night, knocking him down and taking his wallet. Istvan said the fact that they forced him out of the country instead of imprisoning him meant they were afraid of people like him. Istvan said there were too many ready to follow people like him now, in or out of prison. Noah Landler did not know what was so important about himself. It did not occur to him that he spoke with a passionate idealism which might be contagious. A man is used to the sound of his own voice.

Landler and the Polish actor Wadislaw Wazyk were employed by Radio Free Europe.

Landler's broadcasts to Hungary would carry even more conviction now. Seeing was believing. The Americans really *were* planning for the time when. . . .

He watched the new team of trainees silently approach the corrugated metal door.

2

Just to the east of the Chinese Tower that stood almost in

the exact center of the Englischer Garten was a group of drab cinderblock buildings that had been hastily erected shortly after the inception of the CIA. These housed Radio Free Europe.

The transmitters that broadcast to Soviet block countries from West Germany and Portugal were a powerful fifty thousand watts, and the controversial organization was a big one. Here in Munich alone it had some eleven hundred employees, many of them Eastern European refugees. Corporations like General Motors, Ford and Standard Oil were known to fund Radio Free Europe, but no one at Munich headquarters seemed willing to say who actually ran it.

More than half of RFE's programming was music and entertainment geared to the tastes of the targeted countries. About half the remaining airtime was devoted to hard news. The rest was commentary—the commercial, the paid political announcement. Much of it got through, despite almost two thousand Russian jamming transmitters located in bloc countries. RFE switched frequencies often and usually operated at night when jamming transmitters were least effective.

The paid political announcement, generally speaking, went: Communism cannot meet the basic needs of the people in Eastern Europe, so Soviet power will gradually erode until, ultimately, the satellite countries are free.

The question was, who made the announcement?

One good guess was the CIA. Though Adam Prestridge would have denied this, he rarely visited Europe without a stopover in Munich and a call at the Englischer Garten. The day after his tour of the secret base in the Taunus Mountains with the new Polish and Hungarian commentators was no exception. Back in impeccably tailored civilian clothes and his customary pince-nez, Prestridge stayed long enough to give a final pep talk to Wazyk and Landler. It wasn't necessary. As Wazyk said, the base was impressive.

One function of Radio Free Europe that caused controversy was the interviewing, and often recruitment, of Iron Curtain refugees.

The innocuously named New Assets Office was located on the second floor of Building Three in the RFE compound. It was here that Noah Landler had been processed on arrival in early September. And it was here, in the Hungarian section, that Istvan Varady worked as a translator.

Istvan, his once handsome face marred now by the welted scar tissue above his eye and slashing across his cheek and by the broken nose that had healed crooked, lived alone in a small room in the student quarter of Schwabing, within walking distance of the English Garden. Although he did his job well, he was surly and uncommunicative, careless in his dress and often unshaven.

He was, that is, until the arrival at RFE of the new assistant to the broadcast director just downstairs on the first floor of Building Three. Becky Kahn was an American, probably of Jewish extraction, and Istvan was entranced by her dark beauty—the weightless bounce of her auburn-highlighted hair as she walked, the sparkling dark brown eyes, the small aquiline nose, the lithe figure usually clad in a straight skirt and a cardigan sweater buttoned down the back. Becky was, by Istvan's estimate, in her early twenties, only two or three years older than himself.

For Istvan she epitomized, in her open face innocent of any makeup but lipstick, in her youthful but alluring clothing, in her lack of pretension, that freshness which makes American women so appealing to jaded European eyes.

He had lived like a monk since leaving Austria in July. It was hard not to think of Friedl, but he knew he had done the right thing. Friedl had wanted to be loyal but he could not burden her with his scarred ugliness. He had broken with her and come to Munich for her own good.

Half an hour after Adam Prestridge's brief inspection of New Assets, Istvan crossed the cafeteria to where Becky Kahn sat.

"May I?" he asked, a tray in his hands.

She looked up, frowning and then smiling. "Yes, of course. Please do." She had a rich, beautiful voice. "You're in New Assets, aren't you? Istvan something."

"Varady." He sat beside her, not across the table.

"I'm Becky Kahn."

"I know."

He slanted his chin so that the worst of his scars were averted. He could do nothing about the gaping spaces where three teeth were missing, except not smile much. German dentists cost the moon.

She picked up a wedge of her bacon and tomato sandwich. "If I seemed sort of standoffish for a couple of seconds there, I'm sorry. You surprised me, coming over. Did you know everybody calls you the mystery man?"

Istvan's face closed. Head bowed over the sectioned tray, he began to eat his roast pork, peas and mashed potatoes.

"Did I say something wrong?" she asked.

"They want to know where I got the scars," he said bitterly. "That's the mystery."

"The what, scars? Oh, I see." He could almost believe she hadn't noticed them before, did not find them repellent now. "No, it's just that you keep to yourself so much."

"I've only been in Munich a couple of months. I don't have many friends yet, that's all." He turned his face full to her, watching her eyes warily. She did not react to his disfigurement in any way he could see.

"That must be interesting, working in New Assets."

Istvan's shoulders went up. "It's a job. I was a new asset myself back in the summer. What does 'assistant to the broadcast director' mean?"

"I'm a gofor."

"Please? Isn't that some kind of small animal?"

She laughed good-naturedly—at herself, not at Istvan. "Gofor. Spelled g—o f—o—r. I mostly run errands."

"You should do broadcasting yourself. You have a perfect voice for it."

She smiled, and changed the subject, "I saw you walking to work this morning. Do you live near here?"

"Schwabing."

"Me too. Where's your place?"

"Ungerer Strasse, near where it branches off Leopold."

"I'm on Herzog. We're practically neighbors."

Becky Kahn was still eating her bacon and tomato sandwich when Istvan finished his chocolate layer cake.

"Excuse me," he said, "but aren't you Jewish?"

"Sure. Why?"

He pointed at the sandwich.

"Oh, you mean the bacon. I happen to like bacon."

"I'm sorry," Istvan said quickly. "I didn't mean to offend."

"You didn't. Not very many American Jews keep kosher. The dietary laws are left over from three thousand years ago in a different climate. Moslems don't eat pork either, you know. But it's silly not to eat it now."

"Especially in Germany. Half the fun is the sausages and beer. Do you like beer?"

"How could anyone not like German beer? It's almost possible to forgive the Germans everything—for their beer."

It was a witty remark, but Istvan was almost sure the girl had difficulty saying the words.

"Well, could I take you some night to the Hofbräuhaus?"

"Oh, I'd like that," said Becky Kahn.

Istvan got through the afternoon without thinking once of his disfigurement.

Deborah's left hand ached where Hauptsturmführer Kerrl had shut the door on it in Auschwitz.

The hand had begun hurting the moment she stepped off the Lufthansa DC-4 at Munich-Riem Airport in mid-September, it ached dully all day long at the English Garden, and the pain increased when she was alone in the furnished two-room flat on Herzogstrasse.

The left hand told her she was back among Germans.

If there weren't so many Americans on the staff of Radio Free Europe, she doubted she'd have been able to go through with this assignment.

Not that young Istvan was a German. She gathered he was part Austrian, which was the same as German, maybe worse. But he was part Hungarian too. And anyway she had liked Istvan instinctively. There was something that made her want to reach out to him, like a stray puppy. He must have been gorgeous, he must have broken hearts right and left in Budapest and Vienna, before whatever it was had happened to his face. Not that the scars were as bad as he thought. It was his attitude, his certainty that he looked hideous, the way he sat with his face averted—he was somebody who cried out for sympathy. No, not sympathy; it was too much like pity. Affection.

Deborah changed into black slacks, ballet slippers and a turqoise blouse. The college-coed wardrobe had been Klaus's idea. Istvan Varady, after all, was only a kid, nineteen or twenty—a kid, and lately a voracious reader about all things American. Maybe Klaus had been right, because shy Istvan had finally got around to talking to her. She had no idea why Klaus wanted her to befriend Istvan. The why would come later, if at all. They had never given the why in Paris. Still, this wasn't Paris. Their training was over, the groups separated. She wondered if she would ever see the twins again. It was odd, but they had been through so much together that, despite everything, she sometimes found herself perversely missing them.

Deborah went down the two flights of stairs.

No, this wasn't Paris. The streets of Schwabing, like the Latin Quarter, were crowded with students at this hour. Virtually all of them German.

She had to walk among them, had to get used to it.

The Germans were blond, brunette, tall, short, thin, fat, like any other people. But any other people hadn't murdered her father in Berlin and gassed her mother at Auschwitz.

She sat at a sidewalk café two blocks from her apartment and ordered black coffee. The waiter was very polite.

Her hand throbbed with pain.

4

"This is Becky," Istvan said a few nights later in the Festival Hall one floor up in the cavernous Hofbräuhaus. Noah Landler had just joined them. Istvan had to shout to be heard. They were seated at a long table, jammed together with strangers. Hundreds of beer-drinking, laughing, singing Germans filled the hall. Buxom waitresses carrying trays heavy with foaming liter steins rushed from the banks of kegs to fan out among the tables.

Landler bowed over her hand. He had warm eyes and a bushy mustache. He sounded different now, the passionate ring she had heard so often in the studio gone from his voice.

"Becky. Yes indeed," he said in German. He had a nice, fatherly smile. He was about forty, she thought. "I seem to recall Istvan mentioning someone named Becky once or twice."

They talked for half an hour. Landler couldn't stay long, he had to get home for dinner. The conversation was inconsequential but Landler couldn't have been more charming, the quintessential cultured European.

After he left, Deborah asked, "If he's a doctor, how come he doesn't practice medicine here?"

"He has more important things to do." Istvan drained his stein. "He liked you. I could tell."

"I liked him too. A lot."

"He's married," Istvan said quickly, "very happily married."

"So?"

Istvan was visibly blushing. "Nothing," he said. The waitress came. He asked for the check, averting his head in that odd way that made Deborah's heart go out to him.

The Mossad contact was a middle-aged man who called himself Hans-Peter. Deborah met him in the small square between the Frauenkirche and the police station. He was stocky and bullet-headed with a thick neck, and he spoke the dialect of Bavaria.

At their first meeting this appearance had upset her, and he had sensed it. "Look, I can't help it if I look like a leftover from Hitler's Brownshirts. Just so you know, I was a newspaperman and they didn't like what I wrote and I spent a good chunk of the war in Dachau. So can we maybe conduct our business without you looking at me as if you wished I'd drop dead?"

She liked Hans-Peter after that.

Now she told him, "Landler's the target, I think."

"Couldn't you have gotten to know Landler routinely through your own work?"

"Yes, but not so well. Istvan Varady's his closest friend—probably his only real friend—here in Munich. So he's bound to trust anyone Istvan trusts."

"You said target."

Deborah shrugged. She could almost be businesslike about it. "They gave me a lot of training, you know. But it

371

all boils down to this. I'm an expert at abducting people. Or at killing them."

"This is a nice place," Istvan said.

They were in Deborah's flat on Herzogstrasse. She was wearing an apron over her skirt, and a bandanna from which a strand of hair had escaped. She had promised him a home-cooked meal.

"American," she said. "Or as close to it as I can come with Münchner ingredients."

The meal was Daddy Sam's favorite—Southern fried chicken and corn bread and cole slaw, followed by deep-dish apple pie à la mode.

"Explain it to me," Istvan asked afterwards. "What's supposed to be so terrible about American cooking?"

"You liked it?" Deborah smiled. Careful, she told herself, you're starting to sound like a Jewish mother. She had even insisted that Istvan have second helpings, and the first had been gargantuan.

They sat side by side on the overstuffed sofa and talked for about an hour. The conversation turned to Dr. Landler. Istvan said, "So far he's adjusting all right to being an exile. I wasn't sure he would."

"What about you?"

"Me? In a way I've been an exile all my life."

Istvan began to tell her about his father. At first he described their relations dispassionately. But as he tried to recount to her the last harrowing scene when he got out of prison, his voice became more and more strained. He stopped halfway through the story, abruptly. "It's too . . . I just can't. . . ."

Deborah turned to him and kissed his cheek, the lightest touch of her lips. He gave a choked cry and wrapped his arms around her and held her hard against him. He put his mouth on hers, forcing her lips apart, thrusting his tongue between them.

She pulled away from him and stood quickly.

He saw the distaste on her face.

His own face went blank, no expression at all. He traced the scars slowly with his fingertips. "Because I'm ugly," he said, his voice flat. "That's why. That's why you can't stand to have me touch you."

"No, Istvan! That's not it. You don't understand . . ."

But by then he was no longer there.

He was back the next night with a dozen long-stemmed red roses. He handed them to her with an embarrassed smile. "Forgive me for last night?" he said.

"There's nothing to forgive."

She made coffee. It was obvious he wanted to talk, had to talk. And just as obvious that his audience had to be her.

To explain the final confrontation with his father before he left Budapest, he had to go back to the night he was taken by the secret police, back to Noah Landler's involvement with Miklos Manyoki, back to the American who had come to find him at Neusiedler Lake.

". . . so I met this Beck at his hotel and — what is it?"

"The American you've been talking about, is that Curtis Beck?" That was the name Southard had used in Paris when he drove her up from Nice to Paris. And she knew he had been in Hungary after his friend died there. It must be him.

"He didn't give a first name, as far as I remember," Istvan said.

"Was he tall and good-looking, with sandy hair cut short and light blue eyes that sometimes change to gray when he smiles?"

"You must have looked into his eyes more than I did," Istvan said dryly, "but it sounds like the same guy."

What would Becky Kahn say now?

"I used to know him in the job I had before this. I haven't seen him since April, though. Last I knew, he was back in Washington. Actually, his real name is Southard. Curtis Beck is just a name he uses when he's over here on—"

"Wait a minute, did you say Southard? Benjamin Southard or something like that?"

At first Deborah was glad when Istvan interrupted. She'd already said too much—even if Southard's real name was safe with someone like Istvan—but she had to talk about him.

"It's Benton. Benton Southard."

"Oh, God," Istvan said. "That's the name, I'm sure of it."

Deborah just looked at him.

Istvan was studying the floor. He looked like someone who had bad news to break and wasn't sure how to go about it.

"It wasn't too long after I got here," he said in a subdued voice. "The reason I remember, a few people at the English Garden were pretty upset because they'd known him too."

Deborah registered his choice of a past tense. She waited for him to go on.

"You know that American newspaper out of Paris that you always see around the compound—the *Herald Tribune?*"

Deborah nodded mutely.

"It made the front page, the article about him. Benton Southard, said to be a high-ranking officer of the CIA in Washington . . ." Istvan got the rest of it out in a rush. "He was shot. Him and his daughter both. They didn't expect him to live."

Chapter Twenty

1

The conversation at GRU headquarters on Znamensky Street in Moscow a few hours before dawn the next morning also concerned Southard.

General Shalin, chief of the GRU, was an insomniac who often got by on two or three hours of sleep out of twenty-four.

Colonel Kossior, his operations chief, required a full eight hours—nine if he could get them.

Shalin's driver delivered Kossior to Znamensky Street at 2:45 A.M. Kossior had dressed hastily and he looked more rumpled than usual. Even his unshaven face seemed rumpled. He blinked in the bright light of General Shalin's large corner office at the rear of the GRU quadrangle. On one wall was a heroic portrait of Lenin exhorting the multitudes. Facing it were portraits of the porcine Khrushchev and the goateed Marshal Bulganin. There was no portrait of Stalin; that had been removed on the twenty-fifth of February. General Shalin kept up with the times.

Colonel Kossior stood for ten minutes while his superior removed documents from a stack on the left of his desk, flipped through their pages, signed them, and transferred them to a stack on the right.

Finally he screwed the cap onto his fountain pen and pointed it at Kossior. "Sit down, Dmitri Platonovich."

Kossior did so gratefully. With his wife he had stayed up

past midnight planning their Crimea vacation. And then after less than two hours of sleep had come the summons from Shalin. Whatever its reason, he knew it spelled trouble. Shalin did not use the knock-on-the-door-in-the-middle-of-the-night, certainly not with his own people, unless it did. Then Shalin's ability to go long hours without sleep served him well.

"You know of course why you are here," Shalin said. That was another of his techniques.

"Comrade general, I have to say I do not know."

Shalin rose. His gray suit was as well pressed as Kossior's was rumpled. He went to the window and breathed deeply of the night air. He stretched his arms and flexed the muscles of his back. Then he sat down again, looking like a man who has just had an hour's nap or a refreshing swim.

"You *don't* know?" he said.

Kossior wanted to say he was exhausted, he couldn't think on two hours of sleep, he would rather come back in the morning. He said nothing.

"You are here because a Palestinian amateur was ordered to assassinate the CIA's counterespionage chief for Europe. You are here because I was not informed of this at the time. You are here," Shalin said, "because when our good friend General I. A. Serov of the KGB found out, he told the Central Committee, who tonight came within two votes of ousting me from my command."

Kossior sighed. He hadn't known about the vote in the Central Committee.

It would be worse than he thought.

"But naturally," said Shalin, "once it got as far as the Central Committee, you would, my dear Dmitri Platonovich, say nothing until you saw which way the wind was blowing. I commend you. You show signs of being a survivor."

"Comrade general, I swear I knew of no proposal to replace you."

Shalin shrugged that aside. "As my operations chief, you *did* know of the shooting in Washington?"

Kossior nodded bleakly.

"Why was it attempted?"

"It was felt Southard was learning too much about the Manyoki affair."

"Learning about things like Manyoki was his job," Shalin said impatiently. "You've been a professional long enough to know that killing high-ranking enemy officers is counterproductive. Capture and interrogation, yes, if the potential for gain is exceptional. Assassination never. Because the opposition must, at whatever cost, retaliate to prevent recurrence. And no espionage service can function when its chief priority becomes the protection of its senior officers." Shalin paused. "You realize, Dmitri Platonovich, you would be an appropriate target for retaliation. Or, since Southard's child was killed, one of your own three daughters."

Kossior came totally, horribly, awake. That was something he had not thought of. Danger to himself he had learned to accept. But Irina, Tatiana, Feodora?

"It might have happened," Shalin said harshly. "It won't now. Washington has been signaled unofficially that we regret the shooting, which resulted from an error in judgment by a foreign agent in our temporary employ."

That was in fact the case, as Erika Graf had reported it to him, and Kossior began to hope this middle-of-the-night interview might not be a complete disaster. "The original plan was to kill Southard on shipboard," he said. "That was sound. The assassin exceeded his orders in attempting to do so in Washington."

"The error in judgment which concerns me was not the Arab's. Were you running him yourself?"

"No, comrade."

"Who was?"

"Major Graf."

Shalin thought about that for a moment. "Graf," he said. "Graf and you, Berlin, 1953 . . . wasn't Southard involved in the Golovin affair?"

"He had some slight connection with it, yes."

"And you tell me it was Manyoki about whom Southard knew too much?"

Kossior could not answer that question; only Erika Graf could. The idea of removing Southard had been hers. But Kossior was a man who believed in taking responsibility for his subordinates' actions. Besides, he liked Erika.

"I had no reason to fear Southard as a consequence of events in Berlin three years ago or for any other reason."

"The decision to kill him was yours?"

"Not directly."

"Was it Major Graf's decision?"

"Yes, comrade."

"And she has your complete confidence?"

"She does."

"I wonder," said General Shalin. "We know the Southard child is dead because her funeral in Virginia was covered by the local press. But we don't know about Southard himself. He has simply dropped from sight. If he lived—or even if he could talk before he died—could he have told his people the assassin came from us?"

Kossior thought that over. "Probably," he said, and explained about Kip Chaffee. "He'd know it was Major Graf, and he could assume she was getting direction from Moscow."

"In that case, Washington might have signaled the KGB—unofficially, of course—demanding an explanation. The KGB would know they didn't do it, and therefore we did." Shalin shoved his fingers through his graying hair. "But what if Southard couldn't talk?"

"You mean Washington would not have known that we were responsible?"

"And neither would the KGB. Unless." Shalin said

slowly, "someone working for you, someone who knew about the assassination plan, was actually working for the KGB."

Shalin got up abruptly.

"Is this what we can expect of your highly touted Special Groups? Not just failure but betrayal?"

Kossior wished it were not the middle of the night, with his head throbbing painfully and his eyes threatening to shut. Still, he had to be decisive now or lose everything.

"You have no grounds to call them failures," he said boldly, "let alone traitors."

"What is their current status?"

"The officer directly supervising them has split the groups up. This indicates not poor performance but rather the satisfactory completion of their training. Most members," said Kossior, gaining confidence as he spoke of the project he was responsible for, "Most members have returned to their homelands to form the nucleus of terrorist organizations. For example, the Palestinian Husayni, who shot Southard, is now in the Middle East and has already stepped up fedayeen strikes into Israel from both Egypt and Jordan."

"And those who have not been sent home?" Shalin asked.

"Are being used as planned and as needed to protect the disinformation project concerning Soviet response in the event—"

"I know the purpose of the project," Shalin said impatiently. "These, then, are the best people to emerge from your Special Groups?"

"Highly trained," said Kossior, nodding earnestly, "highly motivated, and of proven ability."

"They had better be all that and more. Because if they fail in any way, especially after the fiasco in Washington, Serov and his Chekists will have us exactly where they want us."

General I. A. Serov of the KGB, having business in East Berlin, had arranged for Andrei Golovin to join him there.

They met in Karl Marx Allee (formerly Stalinallee) and walked past the huge apartment blocks whose construction workers had started the riots in 1953 that had led, indirectly, to the elder Golovin's death. The buildings were less than three years old but already dilapidated—gingerbread masonry crumbling here, a jagged crack in a concrete wall there, a general air of shabbiness. It came as a surprise to Andrei Golovin as it did to anyone returning for the first time from an extended stay in the West.

"Yes, I can see your problem," General Serov said. He was a small and wiry man with receding reddish hair. His thick-soled shoes gave him a springy step as he matched the strides of the taller Golovin.

"If I do one thing," Golovin said, a frown on his handsome face, "the KGB suffers. If I do the other, Russia does. Suppose they get away with killing the Hungarian. Then Shalin and the GRU point to their Special Groups as proof of their preeminence in Westwork."

"And if you stop them," General Serov said, "Landler remains alive to continue his broadcasts to Hungary. That, you say, is bad for Russia. Landler is a charismatic speaker, and the obvious man to take up the torch of Manyoki. Landler alive could mean, at worst, a revolution in Hungary."

"That's the dilemma, comrade general."

They approached an apartment building that had been cordoned off. Men with sledgehammers were demolishing a row of balconies. A small crowd jeered. Two Vopos in green uniforms, each with a shoulder-slung submachine gun, stood impassively nearby.

Serov said, "Don't let them kill him. Stop them."

"But in that case—"

"In that case, Andrei Leonidovich, two things will happen. The failure of the attempt, particularly a flamboyant failure, will discredit the GRU Special Groups and shift Westword back into the KGB's province."

"But Hungary?" Golovin asked.

General I. A. Serov rocked back and forth on his thick-soled shoes. "The more charismatic Landler is, the more persuasive, the better I'll like it. Because he'll drive the Hungarian malcontents out into the open. Right where we want them."

Serov's other business in East Berlin had been to put the finishing touches on a defection.

While he walked with Golovin on Karl Marx Allee, three miles to the west a man in civilian clothes carrying a Finnish passport was admitted through Checkpoint Charlie.

Once across the border, he revealed his identity as Lieutenant Vasily Novikov of the GRU, and asked for political asylum.

Novikov's credentials were good enough to satisfy the U.S. Army C.I.C. interrogator in West Berlin, and get him flown that night to Camp King. And the information he brought was valuable. Novikov said his job was liaison between the GRU's East German headquarters at Wünsdorf and the MfS on Westwork operations of mutual interest. The information was genuine; it was Novikov, in reality a KGB officer, who was not.

In the course of his debriefing at Camp King, he would mention that the source of certain papers was code-named Lazarus, a mole in the British intelligence service who had been run by Colonel Kossior since July.

General Serov thought they might fly Novikov from Camp King to Washington. Whether they did or not, he would accomplish his mission.

Then, after a suitable period, he would redefect.

"Just exactly who," Erika said, "is Jehan Khalid?"

"An Egyptian girl whose father is in a Tel Aviv prison serving a life sentence for spying," said the man Erika knew as Klaus Steinbrenner.

"What else can you tell me about her?"

"They were sitting at a café on the crowded Marienplatz. It was the day after Andrei Golovin's return from East Berlin. Two-car trams rolled by, traffic roared around the column of the Madonna, and tourists crowding the sidewalk readied their cameras for the daily performance of the New City Hall glockenspiel.

"Her group was the best I had in Paris," Klaus Steinbrenner said, "and it was mostly the Khalid girl's work. She seemed the obvious choice for this assignment. And in fact she's already become quite friendly with Landler."

"What's her cover?"

Erika watched Steinbrenner's face and knew he was debating not answering her question. But he said, "She's in broadcasting at Radio Free Europe, where Landler works. She carries an American passport with a Jewish name."

"Why Jewish?"

"It seemed a good idea. Landler is a Jew."

"What's the plan?"

Across the Marienplatz the glockenspiel opened for business. Figures of lords and ladies in silks and court wigs danced to a clockwork minuet, and on the next level knights on colorfully caparisoned horses jousted.

"When he's dead, you'll read about it in the papers," Klaus Steinbrenner said.

Erika lit a black-tobacco cigarette and blew an angry plume of smoke. "Steinbrenner, listen to me. I don't like a confused chain of command any more than you do. But we do have to work together."

"If you mean I ought to tell you every step of our planning, the answer is no. You happened to see me walking with Jehan Khalid—my mistake. So all right, I told you what I know about her. But for the rest, I'd say your need-to-know rates about zero."

The glockenspiel closed shop, the tourists began to disperse. Then from a pair of doors high on the façade of the New City Hall, the unexpected cuckoo emerged, trilled his note and went back in. The doors snapped shut. Not one tourist in fifty had his camera poised in time.

Steinbrenner smiled. He was blond and handsome, in his middle twenties. "The tourists never manage to catch it," he said. "It fooled me the first time too."

"Oh? A stranger in Munich, are you?" Erika blew another plume of pungent smoke.

"Yes. My first time here."

"This glockenspiel's famous for its little surprise all over Germany."

"Is that a fact?" Steinbrenner asked in an insolent voice.

"You're not German, are you?"

"What difference does it make what I am?"

"You're Russian."

"I'm a man from Mars if you like. But I still won't tell you what you don't need to know. Now if you'll excuse me—" He put a ten-mark note on the table, weighting it down with his glass, and began to rise.

She caught his wrist. "Not yet, Herr Steinbrenner."

Her grasp was surprisingly strong. He could either risk a scene or sit down again. He sat. "Well?"

Erika tried to think. Who was behind Steinbrenner's refusal to answer her questions? Not Kossior; they knew they had to trust each other. Then General Shalin himself? Possibly.

It was no wonder someone mistrusted her. She had blundered badly over Southard. That was symptomatic of the way she was letting her past, her personal life, dictate her present professional life. And now it was the Egyptian girl Jehan Khalid.

That, finally, was why she was here, antagonizing Klaus Steinbrenner, insisting stubbornly on information she had no need for. Because she had seen the girl again, here in Munich, and somehow now she seemed, in her walk, in her manner, more what that other one might have become had she survived.

Impossible, of course. But how ironic that, whoever she was, she had now assumed the role of an American Jewess.

"Well?" Steinbrenner said again. "What is it?"

"I—nothing, Herr Steinbrenner." She let her eyes fall and her voice was contrite. "I only wanted to say, you are right. I have no need to know. Can we put it down to feminine curiosity?"

"By all means, Frau Major. I know of you as a competent professional. Still, what woman is without curiosity?"

4

It was simple, first on the crowded paths of the English Garden, then through the busy streets of Schwabing at rush hour, to follow the Khalid girl to Herzogstrasse. There was a bierstube across the street from the building she went into, and Erika sat at a table just inside the window. In twenty minutes Jehan Khalid came out. She had changed into a white blouse and slacks and let her dark brown hair fall free.

Erika got up and went outside.

The Khalid girl seemed to change her personality within half a block. At first she moved purposefully with the lithe self-confident stride of the girl in Monaco. But soon she lost the graceful freedom; her stride shortened, her carriage became stiffer. She looked almost as if she expected to be physically assaulted. She had walked like that on her way home from the English Garden too. It was very strange.

Erika followed as Jehan walked the length of Ludwigstrasse toward the city center.

The strangest part was that Jehan Khalid was aware of the way she walked. Several times she paused, threw back her shoulders, and stepped out briskly. But she never managed to keep it up for long.

Erika followed her along the side of the Frauenkirche, the dull red brick wall half-hidden behind a scaffold of pipes and boards. When Jehan reached the small, crowded square between the church and the police station, Erika realized she was meeting someone.

It was not Klaus Steinbrenner. It was a stocky bullet-headed man who looked like a storm trooper out of uniform. Now, just as the Arab girl approached, he removed an unlit cigar from his mouth. That might have meant nothing or it might have signaled that he was free of surveillance. She in turn ran her finger quickly around the waist of her slacks as if to be sure the white blouse was tucked in, a natural gesture, easy to miss. The stocky man walked off and Jehan Khalid fell into step with him.

Erika followed them west along Neuhauserstrasse through the early evening crowds. When they parted at the Karlstor, Erika followed the bullet-headed man.

An hour later, from a public phone, she called a local number. Thanks to the welcome the Bonn government gave to refugees from the East, the MfS had a well-staffed operation in every West German city.

Erika gave her code, described the stocky man, and said: "He lives in, or at least went to, a building at Beethovenstrasse 154. There are ten apartments, nine with names on the mailboxes." She read the names from a small notebook. "I'm particularly interested in foreign connections, possibly American or Israeli."

When she phoned back the next day, she was told:

"Hans-Peter Kempke, bachelor, forty-eight. Former print and radio journalist. Interned in Dachau under the Hitler regime. Now produces television documentaries."

"And the foreign connections?"

"Depends what you mean by a connection. He knows just about everybody in Munich, including half the American community, but nothing we've turned up is more than superficial or social. On the Israeli side, there is something. Kempke spent eight weeks last year filming a documentary in Israel. Whether there's anything earlier we don't know."

It wasn't much to go on, but maybe it was enough.

Erika spent the rest of the day prowling aimlessly through the streets of Munich. She had never been indecisive before, and it bothered her. At dusk she found herself back in the Marienplatz, standing beside a public phone. She had to force herself to pick up the receiver. And then, after all, the circuits to Berlin were busy.

She ordered a beer at the café where she had met the man called Klaus Steinbrenner. She shut her eyes and pictured Jehan Khalid's face. On it she tried to superimpose the other one, the child from Auschwitz. The faces blurred and slid apart, as though insisting on their uniqueness.

Drop it, said one part of her; you don't really want to find out.

You must, said the other part, you must do it now.

She would finish her beer, she decided, and try the call again. If the circuits were still busy, that would be it.

The call went through immediately.

When the MfS bureau in West Berlin heard her code name, better known than any but that of Minister Wollweber himself, she was switched at once to the appropriate department.

"I want to check on a girl called Jehan Khalid," she said. "J—e—h—a—n   K—h—a—l—i—d. Egyptian. Freienwalder Strasse has her photograph on file. Obtain copies from Quast on my authority, and use them to

386

confirm her identity. The only relative I know of is the father, currently in jail in Tel Aviv for spying against Israel. Perhaps you can locate other family in Egypt." Erika listened for a minute. "Good enough. When you have an answer, signal my office, Normannenstrasse. And remember, *absolutely* as soon as possible."

5

Three times during the year Radio Free Europe stepped up its broadcasts to every country behind the Iron Curtain except Albania—tiny Albania had so few radios that RFE ignored it altogether.

The first step-up came in the spring when reports began to filter through of the secret meeting at the 20th Party Congress.

The second was early in June after the U.S. State Department released its accurate, though incomplete, version of the Khrushchev speech.

The third was when Noah Landler became the Voice of Free Hungary.

That Landler's was the most effective voice ever used by Radio Free Europe soon became obvious. When Noah Landler spoke, all Hungary listened. Within hours, his words were repeated in coffee houses and taverns across the Magyar nation. It was said he spoke with the voice of the martyred Manyoki. The dream was simple—free elections, an end to Russian occupation and exploitation of Hungary. The warning was more difficult—no single satellite country dare act alone. The Red Army had plans, plans Miklos Manyoki had seen in Moscow, to deal with revolt. But the plans depended on shifting forces from one bloc country to another as needed. There could be no plans to deal with a general uprising of the Warsaw Pact nations. And there were men, even now, in Poland and East Germany and

Hungary, working together, planning together. The key was patience. Wait, coordinate, rise. . . .

Russia's first response was to step up jamming activity.

The second response was to crack down on satellite citizens caught listening to Radio Free Europe broadcasts.

The third was a campaign of harrassment against RFE itself. The MfS Westwork bureau in Munich drew this assignment.

They began relatively modestly. RFE employees from behind the Iron Curtian were warned their relatives at home would suffer reprisals. Employees were wakened in the middle of the night by threatening phone calls. A few had their homes ransacked.

But the Voice of Free Hungary became more effective, and the campaign of harrassment intensified.

Members of the MfS Westwork bureau in Munich infiltrated Radio Free Europe and worked in the English Garden compound itself.

It soon became a frequent occurrence for tetrahedron nails to be scattered at night in the parking lot. Flat tires were only a nuisance, but cumulative nuisances impaired efficiency.

One day the saltcellars in the cafeteria were laced with atropine. Several RFE staffers were hospitalized with symptoms ranging from double vision and nausea to breathing difficulties and irregular heartbeat before the tainted salt was discovered. No one died, but the warning was clear; atropine had hospitalized several people; strychnine would have sent them to the morgue.

By late September, security at the English Garden compound was tighter, and in-house harassment ceased.

Swiftly the rest dwindled to where it had begun — threats against RFE employees or against their families behind the Iron Curtain. And even this campaign lost its effectiveness. Reprisals behind the Curtain simply did not occur. Tension had been building all summer there, and the authorities were afraid to light a new fuse. At home in Munich, too, the threats on RFE staffers were shrugged off as a stale joke.

Except in the case of Noah Landler. Those threats RFE took seriously.

The bodyguards assigned to the Landler family worked around the clock, and they worked in pairs.

6

More and more, Istvan Varady's nerves were laid bare by events in Hungary.

Back in Budapest, with a censored press, or in Vienna, with its own concerns, he would have known only a fraction of the Hungarian news he had to confront here every day. And here he could not just crumple it in an angry fist and fling it into a wastepaper basket. Most of the time it was his duty to translate it. Since Landler had arranged his transfer to the Hungarian news desk, he was earning more, but he would gladly have gone back to his old job. Just so he could sleep nights.

"I mean, Becky, you take the AVO prison at Recsk," he said on Monday evening at Deborah's apartment on Herzogstrasse. "Now they're sending people there whose only crime is they talked out against the Russians." His face looked gaunt, as if he didn't eat properly, as if he'd forgotten how to sleep.

Deborah had a pot of *Saftgoulasch* simmering on the stove, its aroma of paprika and onions filling the apartment. It was cold, the central heating not yet turned on despite the change in weather. Dusk was settling on the street outside. Deborah drew the curtain that closed off the kitchenette and went to switch on the lamp by the sofa where Istvan sat in near darkness.

"Don't," he said quickly. "I like the twilight."

Deborah went to the window. Pedestrians walked

389

hunched against the wind, fallen leaves swirling at their ankles. She would humor Istvan for a while about the light. But he was so wrong—the scars merely kept him from being the most beautiful boy she could imagine.

Istvan shifted his weight on the sofa. "They have real specialists in torture at Recsk prison. They really learn their trade there," he said. "It's a disciplinary assignment for AVO men. I know because my father was sent there when I was a kid. They teach them there, at Recsk, how to hurt a man, how to do internal damage without marking him. I wasn't so lucky. They put me in jail at Fo Street."

"Istvan. Stop that."

"Stop what?"

"Feeling sorry for yourself. You *are* lucky. You were able to get out."

"Through my father. . . . A father like mine, you call that lucky? The AVO are inhuman," said Istvan, his voice rising. "Every time I hear of a new atrocity I think maybe my father's responsible."

"And if he is? You're not to blame."

"I can never go back to Hungary, because of my father."

"Listen, Istvan, visiting the guilt of the fathers upon the sons went out a long time ago, in civilized places. You aren't responsible for what your father does. You simply have to stop torturing yourself."

"How can I help the way I feel, inside? Why do you think I had to run away from Friedl?"

"What I think," Deborah said, sitting at the end of the sofa, the plump middle cushion separating them, "what I think obviously won't count for much because at the age of nineteen—"

"I'm almost twenty."

"At the age of twenty you think you know more about human nature than I'll know if I live to a hundred."

Softly in the gathering darkness Istvan said, "Because I was impotent."

390

"What?"

"That's why I ran away from Friedl. Because I couldn't do it. Because I was impotent with her."

"Oh."

Deborah didn't know what to say.

"She's still seventeen," Istvan said. "Her whole life ahead of her. Look at me—would you want to spend the rest of your life looking at a face like that?"

"Istvan, I never even think of those scars on your face until you mention them."

He made a sound which was a fair imitation of laughter. "That's what Friedl wanted me to believe. But don't you see, she knew me before it happened."

"Then she'd know there's a lot more to you than just your looks," Deborah said gently. "Tell me about her. What's she like?"

"She's beautiful. She has these really big blue eyes and long blonde hair and golden skin, and when she smiles . . ." Istvan stopped.

"Yes?"

"Funny, I never noticed," he said. "It's like when *you* smile, the same . . . the way you put your whole heart in it."

In the darkness, Deborah did smile, ironically. She could hardly tell Istvan she had always been warm and open with children. "You were telling me about Friedl," she said.

"Well . . . we used to laugh together all the time. People used to look at us on the street."

"Because you laughed so much?"

"Because we were a beautiful couple. Me! I was part of it! Now they look at me with pity. They sidle away from me on the street. They take their children indoors so they won't have to see my face."

"Don't be silly, Istvan."

"I know what I look like. That's why . . . it was my first weekend back in Vienna. My brother was out of town, so we

391

had his place to ourselves. We . . . remember, she's only seventeen, so don't think it's strange," Istvan said defensively, "when I tell you we never slept together before. Oh, we came close, but . . ."

"That's normal," Deborah said. "She was seventeen and you'd never slept together. Nothing strange about it."

"When we got to my brother's place I could tell she thought I was ugly. Look at me — this twisted face."

"How can I, when you won't let me put any lights on?" Deborah said, exasperated. "Did she *say* she thought you were ugly?"

"No, that's just it. She kept telling me I wasn't."

"Oh, Istvan, you're hopeless!"

"That's funny."

"Is it?"

"I mean, that's just what Friedl said."

"She sounds like a very bright young lady."

"You talk as if you're old enough to be her mother or something. What are you? Twenty-two, -three?"

"I'm twenty-four."

"Ancient. Decrepit. Remind me to help you up the stairs next time."

Deborah went to the curtain and pushed it aside. A small light burned in the kitchenette. She stirred the goulash, took off her apron and came back, leaving the curtain open. She could see Istvan, his face in shadow. The faint light made the welted scars on his forehead and cheek look like greasepaint imitations. He moved to the far end of the sofa, further from the light, averting his face in that sad, defensive way he had. She wanted to touch him. She wanted to touch his scars to prove to him they were nothing. But she didn't dare. She sat on the sofa, close to the middle, facing toward him.

"That smells great in there," Istvan said.

"It's only goulash."

"Never say 'only goulash' to a Hungarian." She could just

make out the gleam of teeth as Istvan smiled. "That's what Friedl was going to cook for me at my brother's place. She never even got around to peeling an onion. The minute we were alone together we both wanted . . . at least I thought we both—" The gleam was gone. "Do you mind my telling you this?"

"I'd like you to."

She was so unsure of herself in so many ways, and yet Istvan was more insecure still. How could she refuse him?

He did not speak for a minute. Finally he said, "I can't."

"You can."

She reached out in the near darkness and found his hand. It stiffened at her touch and she thought he would retract it. But he held on.

She felt something stir in her, a maternal feeling. . . .

"It was going to be all right. I thought it would be fine. It was going to be beautiful," Istvan said. His voice was low, that special soft tone more difficult to hear than a whisper. She leaned toward him. Their arms touched.

"She—I guess she could tell how upset I was about my father and all. So she sort of started things. When she asked me to undress her I was pretty awkward but she stood there while I took off her clothes. She had this look on her face like—like she would do it for me but she really couldn't bear to look at me."

Deborah said nothing.

No, you're wrong, she thought; the girl was seventeen, she was shy, it had nothing to do with what happened to your face.

"She was beautiful, standing there," Istvan said in that voice softer than a whisper. "Then she said, 'Now let me do it to you,' and she undressed me, slowly, very slowly . . . looking everywhere but at my face. . . ."

No, Deborah thought, she just wanted to look at the rest of you, it's perfectly normal.

". . . and I started touching her as if my fingers could see

393

". . . Well, you're an older woman, you know how it is . . ."

No, I don't, Deborah thought, I don't know at all.

". . . but I could feel how she was stiff, almost rigid . . ."

Of course she was, Deborah thought; it was her first time, and she was afraid she would be clumsy, afraid she would spoil it for you . . . Just as I spoiled it for Ben. She had tried not to think of it, the death of this man she had trusted so easily, as easily as she had trusted Daddy Sam—and with as much reason, she felt. Sam Brodsky had made her life more than a matter of mere survival; he had saved her from a complete oblivion of the heart. Ben Southard had done the same and she had finally been able to share some of her pain, and to hope to share herself.

". . . then she took my face in her hands. This face! She kept touching it, as if she couldn't help it. She started to cry. And after that I . . . I was no good for anything."

Istvan suddenly lunged to his feet. He went to the window and leaned on the sill, breathing heavily. Deborah stood too. For a long time she tried to find the right words to make him understand. But she already knew words wouldn't help.

She put her hand on his shoulder and turned him slowly. He looked so forlorn. There was no resistance in him. When he saw that she was staring at his face, he shut his eyes but then he opened them and did not turn away. Tears glistened on his cheeks. He needed her, he needed her.

"Undress me," she said, in that voice softer than a whisper, the voice he had used, and he undressed her. His hands were sure. She did not help him at all. "You're beautiful," he said in that shared voice. It was cold in the room. That was why she felt the tips of her breasts puckering so. "Now I'll do it to you," she said, and she unbuttoned and removed his shirt, knelt to take off his shoes, unbelted and removed his trousers, slipped off his shorts and stood facing him, her hands reaching out for his face, the dear scarred face of this child who needed her.

"You're beautiful," they both said, and he did not seem to mind that she was looking at his face, at the scars there. He took her hand in his. He led her to the sofa. Or did she lead him? He had a hard firm beautiful body. He was on her, his eyes shut, a smile of joy on his face. It transfixed her. He transfixed her. She was helping, moving with him, it had to be right for him. Now, she thought, now do you understand how beautiful you really are? And she knew, she could sense with every nerve in her body, the intensity of pleasure he must be feeling because, at last, she was feeling it herself.

Chapter Twenty-one

1

There was the one called Houdini who in the early days of the Agency had walked all the way around the Black Sea—Turkey, Russian Georgia, the Ukraine, the Moldavian SSR, Romania, Bulgaria, back to Turkey—speaking no local languages but smiling his head off and shooting pictures with a Kodak Brownie, just to prove you could get away with it. Houdini was too old for fieldwork now and he resented the way the eastern establishment types were easing the aging OSS people out. What did they have Houdini doing now, in 1956? Teaching Agency trainees at the Farm the finer points of breaking and entering—saber saws, oxyacetylene torches, bulk explosives w/tamper, hand hydraulic bolt cutters—all pointless because in practice you called in support specialists and didn't even get your hands dirty. Houdini was luckier than some. He had fresh air and exercise and as an instructor he got a certain amount of respect. Still, he wound up regularly twice a year at the R&R Center near Big Stone Gap in the Virginia mountains. Part of his therapy was watching film clips of exotic places he would never see again. Houdini was a devout movie goer and he had only four years until retirement.

There was Billy the Kid, who had helped give Mossadegh his walking papers in Iran in 1953 and put young Riza Shah Pahlevi back on the Peacock throne. Billy the Kid told anyone who would listen that we were backing the wrong horse in that part of the world. It became an *idée fixe* with him and more than once a year he did his talking at Big Stone Gap. There were plenty of talkers at the R&R Center, their essentially captive audience listening with glazed eyes until they could recite a chapter from their own memories. They were encouraged to talk, at Big Stone Gap. Talk was therapy. When working, Billy the Kid held down a desk at Temporary C Building on Pennsylvania Avenue, and over the desk flowed an endless river of paper, unclassified material, requisitions, Congressional Inquiries that could have been answered by mimeograph, and Billy the Kid had to lower his face toward his first drink in the morning, the one before he got out of bed. Often it was only half a drink when his face got there. Billy the Kid would be pensioned off early, by 1960.

Bumblebee was there, all two hundred fifty pounds of him and that deep, commanding voice, Bumblebee, who got the name in England thirteen years ago when OSS sent him to a Moon Squadron flying out of Kent. The Moon Squadron's Lysanders were so small they looked like model airplanes, and the Special Operations blokes at the field took one look at him and said he was aerodynamically unsound, like a bumblebee. So they strapped a parachute on Bumblebee's back and gave him a single practice jump before flying him over to France in a four-engine Lancaster, from which he jumped, possibly the heaviest man ever to do so. It was said that he made a small crater when he landed. He got the job done in the mountains of central France (what the job was, not even Bumblebee ever said, for he wasn't one of the talkers) and he stomped south to the Pyrenees and over them and across Spain to Portugal, where he got a seat on the Sunderland flying boat to London like a commuter catching the 5:15. From the night they gave him the green light in the Lancaster until the afternoon three months later when he walked into the Officers' Club on Grosvenor Square, he somehow managed to put on fifteen pounds. Last winter they had Bumblebee on the phone all day long with state, arranging embassy cover slots for assistant case officers on their first overseas assignments. But five, six weeks ago over drinks at the Mayflower bar Bumblebee had, with one swat of his huge and dimpled right fist, broken the jaw of a State Department man in three places, no one could determine why, and Bumblebee was now lying low, indefinitely, at the Agency R&R Center near Big Stone Gap, where the psychologists had pronounced him homicidal.

2

There was the one they called Par Two, and unless you knew his history you thought the name was golf-derived. Houdini and Billy the Kid and the other talkers soon gave up trying to talk to Par Two. Par Two kept his small room immaculate—it was in one of the cabins on the western edge of the Big Stone Gap center—and he spent most of his time in the sun on the tiny porch reading every newspaper he could get his hands on. They thought that Par Two was looking for something but he wasn't. At least not anything specific. Par Two lived in his newspapers so he would not have to live inside himself. There were high stacks of papers, arranged by date, beginning with the twenty-sixth of July, the day the *Andrea Doria* went down, the day Egypt's strongman Colonel Nasser nationalized the Suez Canal company. A few of the papers from early August had neat holes cut in them. It was thought at Big Stone Gap that Par Two had clipped articles for safekeeping. But Par Two had thrown those articles away. They were not part of the world which he could inhabit yet. In the neat stacks of newspapers Par Two read and reread, maintaining his link with reality, performing his own cure.

In the newspapers, Adlai E. Stevenson was nominated in

398

Chicago to face Ike for the second time. The drama was in the choice of his running mate. On the third ballot Estes Kefauver of Tennessee just beat out the junior senator from Massachusetts, John F. Kennedy. When Ike and Nixon were renominated the next week in San Francisco, the dump-Nixon campaign never got off the ground. In the neat columns of printer's ink, Anthony Eden said Her Majesty's Government would as a last resort use force to insure unrestricted passage through the Suez Canal—except for Israeli ships, of course. In the world of Par Two's newspapers, fedayeen terrorists swooped into Israel from Egypt and Jordan, killing farm workers at outlying kibbutzim, machine-gunning buses, setting off pipe bombs in crowded marketplaces. Much of the international press, heeding the politics of petroleum, decried the reprisal attacks by Israel as excessive. Par Two's stacks of newsprint informed him Khrushchev and Bulganin had ordered an end to the liberalizing trend in Warsaw and Budapest, or else; de-Stalinization was coming back to haunt the Russian leaders. Sources close to Secretary of State John Foster Dulles said the United States "would not tolerate" Soviet armed intervention in Poland or Hungary.

One day in October, Par Two stopped living in the world of his newspapers. Somehow he knew it was time, and he stopped like a heroin addict going cold turkey. For the first time in the rec hall he would talk to Houdini and Billy the Kid and Bumblebee, who knew him from the OSS days.

"Why don't you get out?" each said in his own way. "You're young enough to start over, make a new career, a new life."

But that was not what Par Two had in mind.

He went to the director of the center and said, "When are you going to let me out of here?"

Four days they tested him—word association, ink blots, pictures you wrote a story about—and they said his personality was well integrated. They had already, in Big

Stone Gap's adjacent medical facility, declared him physically fit weeks ago. The wounds left by the .30-06 round that had passed through his neck had healed cleanly. The bullet that had lodged in his back had required a lengthy operation to remove, but it too had left no permanent damage.

The personnel man at Big Stone Gap said he could not reinstate or reassign Par Two because Par Two's job classification was higher than personnel handled. Allen, said the personnel man, would give him something commensurate with his experience. At Big Stone Gap everybody referred to the DCI as Allen.

A job commensurate with his experience was not what Par Two had in mind either, unless it would help him accomplish what he had to do.

He had been an ideal patient in the medical facility, which for some reason was not called a hospital, and at R&R he gave the answers to the psychological tests that were expected of a healthy, nonhostile personality. You could fool the tests up to a point, if you knew what the testers were looking for, and he had long ago learned how from his ex-wife, since it was her line of work.

He wondered how — or whether — his friend who had died in Hungary had fooled the psychologists. But then he told himself that would not have been necessary. His friend had gone back into the field just to prove he could do it. His friend had not gone back into the field to kill people.

The nickname they gave him at Big Stone Gap, he decided as he was flown out in an Agency Beechcraft, would have pleased his friend. But the name bothered Par Two. Sometimes he thought his friend had not been entirely honest with him, and sometimes he even thought his friend had only saved his life out of a feeling of guilt.

He took a taxi from National Airport to his apartment in Georgetown, gathered the almost ten weeks of mail into a pile without reading any of it, and used his thumbnail on the seal of an unopened fifth of Jack Daniel's. It was then four in the afternoon. At six-fifteen, when he had drained the bottle, he went into the bathroom to wash his face. He saw the faint scars on his neck. Even the one on the left, where the bullet had exited, was nothing much. He had that odd sense of dissociation, seeing his reflection, that you sometimes get when you are drunk. He did not gesture or speak to the image in the mirror. He simply saw a face and had to shut his eyes. He opened them again to make sure it was his own face. But by then he could not see well enough to tell because he was, finally, crying.

Everyone had always said Suzie looked just like him.

Chapter Twenty-two

1

The walls of the DCI's study on the third floor of the big house on Highlands Place were covered with photographs of Allen Dulles in the company of Ike, of Churchill, of the Free French General Charles de Gaulle. There was a photograph of FDR giving a younger Dulles an envelope in the presence of a beaming Wild Bill Donovan. Dulles was seen shaking hands with Tito and with Chiang Kai-shek. He was smiling beside Nasser and smiling beside Ben-Gurion. There was a tight two-shot with Edward Teller and one with André Malraux. He was squared off with Nehru, neither of them looking happy, but the Indian prime minister had autographed the photo under the words, "To Allen Dulles—we understand each other." He was seen with the king of the Belgians and the princess of Monaco.

He sat at table with Konrad Adenauer and a man whose face was turned away so you could see only the curve of his cheek, and that man was said to be Reinhard Gehlen. He was photographed with Dick White, the new head of Britain's Secret Intelligence Service, when he was still with MI5.

He appeared in photographs, all signed with affectionate comments, beside Marlene Dietrich and Paulette Goddard and, incredibly, Greta Garbo. There were more women, all beautiful.

Allen Dulles's small study at Highlands Place, unlike the

bigger library downstairs, was the mirror of the man. He had, Southard thought, probably the only safe network in the world of espionage—a network of friends in high places who had been cultivated and who could be relied upon.

Dulles puffed his ever-present pipe. "Never been up here before, have you?"

"No, that's right," Southard said.

For several minutes Dulles moved about the room, displaying souvenirs, recounting anecdotes. He made no reference to what had happened in August; he had said everything that was called for at the time. Except for avoiding too-hearty jokes, his delicacy consisted in acting absolutely normal.

Finally he sat behind his desk, and said, "We've been thinking, Benton, that maybe you ought not to go back to the CE desk, at least not for the time being."

"No objection," Southard said. "I more or less expected that."

"In fact, we've been thinking it might do you good to take a few weeks off, before we decide on a slot for you."

Southard said he had no objection to that, either.

Allen Dulles laughed his Santa Claus laugh. "We're neither of us fooling the other, are we? I assume it was Janet who showed you how to cook the test results?"

"A long time ago," Southard said.

"Well, she did a good job. So did you, up to the limit of what can be done. The only problem is, when you give contrived answers, the testers can tell they're being deceived."

"Sure. But according to Janet, that still leaves the question, what's he hiding? And there's no way they can answer that one."

Allen Dulles's affable smile blurred in a cloud of blue smoke. "You're not homosexual, you're not a problem drinker or a compulsive gambler, you're not in debt and, except maybe by Joe McCarthy's standards, you're a loyal

American—what *are* you hiding, Benton?"

"Nobody hides anything from you, Allen. You know what I have to do. Or you wouldn't have offered me convalescent leave."

Dulles drew on his pipe. It made a bubbling sound. He took it from his mouth and looked at it in mild reproach.

"I could withdraw the offer."

"I could resign," Southard said. "I've got some money in Switzerland. Not much, but enough. I could do it on my own."

Dulles did not dispute that. Instead he made more smoke. Finally he said, "We aren't quite after the same thing, you know."

"I didn't say we were."

Allen Dulles frowned. "Everything we hear from the Middle East points to war. Everything we hear from the Soviet bloc points to revolution. Yet we're told the British can't mount an invasion of Egypt, the Russians won't intervene in the satellites, and the people who are trying to sell this to us are the ones you . . . are interested in. And, let us say . . ." Dulles was speaking with obvious reluctance now ". . . the climate of opinion here in Washington . . . at this time . . . is all too receptive."

Dulles took out his handkerchief and patted his brow. "Frankly, Benton, I'd be more inclined to help you if you'd agree to do some of this my way."

"I've got an open mind," Southard said.

"Their code name for it is Lazarus," Dulles began, and for the next half-hour he talked and Southard listened.

2

First he saw Werner von Stolz, the former Gehlen operative. When the two men shook hands, von Stolz dipped his head in the suggestion of a bow. Southard

404

almost expected a Prussian heel click.

He had come about the transcripts Kip Chaffee had mailed to himself in Chapel Hill North Carolina. What von Stolz had to say surprised him.

"They are transcripts of meetings between General Shalin of the GRU and the East German minister for state security, Wollweber. All three are in every respect genuine."

"Isn't that strange?"

"I evaluate the material," said von Stolz with Prussian precision. "I don't evaluate the evaluation. The material is absolutely authentic. A man's speech patterns, vocabulary, word order, idioms—these form a composite almost as distinctive as a fingerprint. Shalin and Wollweber speaking, beyond a doubt. Of course, they could have been saying only what they wanted us to believe," von Stolz went on, apparently forgetting the limits on his own evaluation, "but why go to that trouble? The most effective weapon in a campaign of disinformation is the truth. Take this part where—you've read the transcripts?"

"Just last night," Southard said.

"Here, then, where they're discussing the effect of Manyoki's ideas in the satellites. Shalin guarantees that if there should be intenal trouble in East Germany, the MfS will have a free hand. Why should he do that?"

Southard thought a moment. "Why not? East Germany is the most stable of the satallites. Since the riots in 1953, hordes of East Germans, literally millions, have simply walked across the border to the West. They've hardly got any dissidents left. So of course Shalin can afford to say he won't interfere."

"Indeed," said von Stolz. "But why make a point of letting *us* know?"

"Again, why not? It's what we want to hear. And it's the truth. But maybe we'll read more into it than we should. Maybe we'll decide that what goes for East Germany goes for the rest of the Warsaw Pact countries. So we wind up doing the Kremlin's work—disinforming ourselves."

"Exactly, Mr. Southard," von Stolz said, dipping his head again in the suggestion of a bow. "From your reasoning, one would never know you were American."

Southard's next visit was to his own office, where Bob Eagleton sat behind the desk. Eagleton, a Bostonian who had worked under Southard for six months, seemed embarrassed. "They're letting me play acting chief," he said, "but you'll be back before I get to put my feet up."

Southard had come for his own experts' evaluation of the transcripts Kip Chaffee had sent to Washington.

"We think they're phony," Bob Eagleton told him. He picked up a document which purported to be a missing section of Khrushchev's secret speech. "I don't mean the style. Khrushchev wasn't speaking extemporaneously and when you're dealing with a team of speech writers the style's a pastiche anyway. It's the content. For example, this reference to. . . ."

Southard only half listened. He doubted Eagleton would tell him anything he had not already grasped. But he curbed his impatience; he had accepted Allen Dulles's *quid pro quo*.

" . . . contention that if a Warsaw Pact country revolts and we move in in force before the Kremlin does, they won't lift a finger. I don't buy it."

"They can't expect us to buy it. But they can hope we'll borrow it."

"I'm not sure I follow, Ben."

"The point isn't to get us to believe it. The point is to get us to broadcast it back behind the Iron Curtain."

"Jesus, who'd do a thing like that?"

Southard wondered what this wholesome, indignant, middle-aging boy was doing here. He would never last as CE chief. He wasn't devious enough.

"You ever been to Munich, Bob? Ever visit Radio Free Europe?"

"Sure I did."

"What do you think it's there for, Bob?" Southard asked gently.

"But, but any Soviet bloc dissidents who thought there was a chance we'd send in troops would come out in the open and fight. They'd be committing suicide. We couldn't broadcast anything like that."

"Maybe you're right," Southard said. He knew Eagleton was wrong. "But a broadcast can be explained away—even disclaimed. An armed invasion can't. If we encourage the dissidents to come out of the woodwork, the Russians attack them. We come out of it looking, at worst, naive. The Russians look like the bubonic plague.

"The only thing is, the Russians don't care. Their god is history, and they wind up with what really matters to them—tame satellites for another generation."

Eagleton's eyes looked bleak. "I thought they were just trying to put some disinformation over on us."

"You don't think disinformation's an end in itself, do you? It's a way to manipulate us. And in this case they're even willing to give us a propaganda victory."

"Some victory," Eagleton said.

Southard shrugged.

Southard went next to the former brewery in Foggy Bottom to see the Agency's chief of counterintelligence. Bart Hague was an ex-FBI agent who had had a bellyful of J. Edgar Hoover.

"Hey, Ben, good to see you back, buddy. What's the story over at CE anyway? Does Bob Eagleton really have your job?"

"Allen said you could give me a rundown on the GRU defector Novikov."

If Bart Hague was offended by Southard's curtness, he

did not show it. "Novikov, huh? So that's the reason you're slumming here at CI." Hague pressed a button on the phone and lifted the receiver. "Sal, let me have the Novikov file, please." He told Southard, "Except for one item, as you'll see, Novikov came over with the sort of routine stuff that's valuable only because it confirms what we already have. Novikov's just a lieutenant. He served out of Wünsdorf liaising between the GRU and the Normannenstrasse."

"Why'd he come over?"

"He says it's idealogical. But he's been in grade five years and he may have realized he was going nowhere. He was unhappily married. Also there was a German girl in there somewhere, but he says they split up. The girl took him for a lot of dough. He was in debt."

"Couldn't he think of any other reasons?"

Hague laughed. "We thought he laid it on with a trowel too."

A middle-aged woman came in with a file folder. After she left, Hague said, "Now, if he's a phony defector it could mean—"

"Practically anything," Southard interrupted. "What was the one item that wasn't routine?"

"The business about Lazarus. Novikov says that's the code name for a mole in British intelligence who was activated in July by the GRU operations chief, Colonel Kossior. Since then he's been filing information on the state of British military preparedness. Novikov brought photocopies." Hague removed them from the folder.

Southard quickly scanned the pages.

• British Army of the Rhine seriously underequipped; had to borrow equipment from friendlies to participate in joint maneuvers.
• Motor transport, antitank guns, automatic weapons all obsolete or of poor quality.

- Sixteenth Parachute Brigade, deployed in Cyprus against EOKA guerrillas, without jump training for twelve months.
- RAF troop carriers limited to five squadrons of Valeta and Hastings transports; troop delivery capacity only one parachute battalion.
- Only two LSTs in commission in Royal Navy, both Malta-based; barely sufficient to transport one infantry battalion and a few tanks.
- Cyprus, at 250 miles nearest British base to projected battlefield, lacks both deep-water harbors and adequate airfield.
- Malta the alternative, 1000 miles distant, six days by slow convoy.
- Libya closer, where Tenth Armoured Division deployed, but refuses H.M.'s government permission to use Libyan territory as staging point for invasion.

There was more, but Southard had seen enough.

"If we can believe Kossior's mole Lazarus," Hague said, "the British would barely hold their own against Leichtenstein in a fair fight. So when they threaten to use force against Nasser in Suez, they're obviously bluffing."

"Do we know who this Lazarus is?"

"We think so. We've been going over Novikov's copies of the reports Lazarus sent to Kossior, and they match, point by point, reports the Agency in London got from another source."

"What assets did we use to get them?"

"That's the strange part—no assets. These are extracts from preparedness estimates made by the Ministry of Defence and presented to us by Britain's intelligence liaison to London station, a man named Kendal Tarrant, as a personal gift."

"Do the estimates check out?"

"Too soon to tell," Hague said. "I shot them over to my

contacts at Defense Intelligence, but they said maybe yes, maybe no."

"So," Southard said, "we assume Novikov is sent over to inform us that a mole called Lazarus in British intelligence was activated to report to Russia on Britain's ability to attack Suez. And when we check Lazarus's material against what Kendall Tarrant gave London station, we find they agree straight down the line. What does that mean to you?"

"Either the information is accurate, and Russia wants us to know it is, or the information is false but they want us to accept it as accurate."

"Or it's false and they want us to believe *they* accept it. Or even the other way around."

Hague raised his hands before his face in an exaggerated protective gesture. "Hey, I'm just a simple country by. You CE types go ahead and sort it out."

There was still another possibility, but Southard did not mention it.

The whole elaborate charade of Novikov's defection could have been arranged merely to expose Kendall Tarrant as the mole Lazarus. Except that Southard could see no reason why the GRU would want to do that.

3

Southard checked the departure board and hurried through the crowded concourse of Union Station. On the phone Mrs. Perlmutter had told him David was just off for New York. He liked to take the Congressional Limited when he went north, but he had been held up at the office, as usual, and would wind up on the late afternoon local.

It was leaving from Track 11. Southard got there and went out on the platform just before they shut the accordion gate. Redcaps were descending from the train, pocketing tips; a conductor shouted. "All 'board!" Southard swung up the nearest steps. There was one dining car and a string of coaches. Southard began to work his way forward, scanning every passenger who was big enough, looking for the ginger-colored hair. But he didn't recognize Perlmutter that way. He saw him in the third coach lifting a suitcase onto the overhead rack, blocking the aisle, broad torso resplendent in a Harry Truman shirt. It might be autumn in Washington, but David Perlmutter still dressed for the beach at Waikiki.

Southard waited until Perlmutter sat, then swung into the seat beside him. The train began to move. Perlmutter glanced at him once, then a second time.

"Benton Southard, for crying out loud. How the hell're you doing? Didn't I read somewhere you got shot?" Perlmutter's florid face turned redder. "Oh God, I forgot. It wasn't just you . . . awfully sorry . . . please accept my sincere. . . ." His voice trailed off into incoherent snatches of conventional condolences.

"Thanks, I'm okay now. I'm learning how to deal with it."

That was true enough, Southard thought. He just didn't mean it in the usual sense.

The train moved slowly north through the freight-marshaling yards.

"That's some station," Perlmutter marveled. "Where else would you find anything like it? I mean, the concourse is longer than the Capitol and it's just one room." Perlmutter was sounding like Perlmutter again. "The main waiting room, you know what it was modeled after?"

Southard shook his head.

Perlmutter looked surprised. "The Baths of Diocletian in Rome. Boy, the things people don't know about their own country."

The conductor came through. Perlmutter showed his round-trip ticket for New York. Southard bought one for Baltimore.

411

"What's in Baltimore?" Perlmutter wanted to know. "I thought they rolled up the sidewalks at night there."

"I needed to talk to you. It was either ride to Baltimore or wait until you got back. You hear anything more from Kaplan?"

"Say, don't tell me you're still interested in that girl in Paris," Perlmutter said. "What's her name again?"

"Raven."

"Sure, that's it. Raven. Look, I don't know anything. I never did. I was just passing along Kaplan's messages. There was one more, not long after—that is, about the middle of August, but it wasn't any different from the others. Then they stopped. I'd like to help, but no can do. Kaplan doesn't owe me any more favors. You want to know the truth, we don't even like each other."

"Is he still there?"

"In Paris? As far as I know."

For the rest of the short haul to Baltimore, they talked little. Perlmutter looked out the window at the passing American scene, equally entranced with fields of cows, freight yards, and track-side slums. Southard thought about his flight to Paris the next day.

He had not really expected Perlmutter to know anything, but Kaplan might not be the same dead end. It would cost him nothing to find out, a few hours at most. Then he would fly to the Riviera to track down Giovanni Venturino.

As the train was pulling into Baltimore, Perlmutter rose to shake hands with Southard. They had already said good-bye when Perlmutter called him back.

"Hey, you know where the train crosses the Delaware line into Pennsylvania there's this little town called Chester, and right by the tracks there's a big sign that says, 'What Chester makes, makes Chester.' You wouldn't happen to know, would you? Just what the hell *do* they make in Chester?"

Southard stared at him, "Sorry."

As he turned to leave again Perlmutter said, "One of these days I'll have to get off there and find out."

Southard spent a frustrating twenty-four hours in Paris. He saw the station chief, Harry Sullivan, right away, and the first thing he found out was that Kaplan was on home leave. Sullivan said he'd try his other Mossad contacts. But the next morning he reported drawing another blank.

"Raven is no longer run out of Paris station," he said. "They sent the file on her to Tel Aviv last month."

"Is that where she's gone?"

"Maybe Kaplan would know. If anybody else here did, they weren't saying. Probably they didn't know, because they've been cooperating with us all across the board this summer, and they would have told me. Is there anything else we can do for you? Or somewhere I can reach you in case—?"

"No," Southard said. "I'll be on the move."

As he boarded the plane at Orly for the flight to the coast, he asked himself whether he had ever seriously hoped Deborah could help him. Her only encounter with Erika Graf, as far as he knew, was in Monaco when Graf had helped Venturino finger the Tolosano woman.

Maybe, he admitted to himself, he had just wanted to find Deborah, just wanted to see her again. And that was a complication he could not afford now.

Chapter Twenty-three

1

Deborah met Klaus Steinbrenner at the bandshell near the Maximillian Bridge. A crowd had gathered to hear the third Sunday morning concert in October. The day was crisp and bright, but a fresh breeze blew along the Isar and stirred the fallen leaves that turned the riverbanks russet and gold. The band was playing a medley of waltz tunes from *Der Rosenkavalier*.

"When do they get back from the mountains?" Steinbrenner asked.

"Tonight on the 10:15 train from Innsbruck. I already—"

"You told me they drove up there."

"It was a rented car with a driver. Dr. Landler didn't want to come back by car at night."

"Tomorrow?"

"At the studio from eight in the morning. He broadcasts several hours a day now, some of it live. But you know that too."

"What were the security arrangements for their trip to the mountains?"

She knew by now how Steinbrenner's mind worked. First the repetitive questions, the routine questions, then the important ones.

"Their own driver and another car. Four men in that. I

414

assume all but the drivers will return on the train with the Landlers."

"You *assume?*"

"How could I ask a question like that?"

Steinbrenner said, "Let me have his complete schedule for the week as soon as you can."

"I told you, he often changes—"

"He has a date book, doesn't he? An agenda?"

"Yes."

"Surely you can get access to it."

It was the first time Steinbrenner had demanded a day-by-day accounting of Dr. Landler's activities. It worried her.

"Yes, all right."

Steinbrenner didn't say good-bye. He never did. He just turned and left Deborah standing there listening to the band burst into Johann Strauss's "Radetsky March."

Hans-Peter timed it so they turned into Rindermarkt at the same moment. Today Deborah was particularly glad to see him. He was the only person in Munich she could talk to.

"You know," the stocky Bavarian said, "you still walk like you think someone's after you. Which *does* make you easy to follow."

"Being in Germany makes me nervous. I can't help it."

"Come on, then, I'll buy you a drink. There's a nice little place behind the Peterskirche. Not German. Italian."

Over the Chianti he said, "You met Steinbrenner again?"

"Yes. I don't like it. I don't like telling him all the things he wants to know about Dr. Landler."

Hans-Peter tried to reassure her. "He's safe, believe me. His family too. The security precautions are very thorough."

"Yes, but—"

"You're just nervous. You said so yourself."

"It's the same as spying on him. It *is* spying on him. I don't want to do it anymore."

Hans-Peter patted her hand. "Be sensible. It isn't spying on him if it's for his own good."

"Telling Klaus Steinbrenner isn't—"

"It is, if you're the one who tells him. Because then you tell me."

"I want to stop."

"Then they'll use someone else, and we won't know what they're up to."

"I want to stop," Deborah said. "I want to go home."

She looked surprised, as if someone else had spoken those words.

Hans-Peter studied her face.

"I'll tell them," he said.

2

On the telegraph wires strung alongside the two-lane asphalt road south of Beersheba white eaglets perched. A jeep passed, and behind the jeep an ancient bus, battered but serviceable. The hot wind blew hard. In the jeep, the four Israeli soldiers drew kerchiefs over their lower faces. The eaglets flew off. The telegraph wires sang. Then the wind died down. Sand had drifted across the road. The telegraph poles marched north and south, unchanged. White eaglets settled on the wires again.

The road passed between barren walls, and carved in deep clefts in the rock here and there could be seen the sign of the cross, almost twenty centuries old. The walls dropped away, the road crossed another sand barren, the walls rose again; the road climbed and fell and went through a valley where giant rocks stood sentinel, guarding nothing. Ahead loomed a water tower. The bus followed its jeep into a transit camp for immigrants. Passengers got out and stretched. The hot asphalt was sticky. The bus driver talked to the corporal who drove the convoying jeep. They watched another jeep go by, a driver and three soldiers with Uzi submachine guns, heading south in a swirl of dust. The passengers took their newspapers and their lunches of pita stuffed with felafel or grilled lamb, and walked toward the palm trees and the little man-made lake. It was green there, green with water piped down from the north. In the old days the British had said nothing could grow in the desert south of Beersheba. But here and there it was becoming a garden. The water pipes, underground, sometimes aboveground, followed the road south. The residents of the transit camp were Yemeni immigrants who would be settled in the new places of the Negev. They watched children from the bus playing in the shallow water of the lake. The bus carried thirty-five passengers that day. It ran south from Jerusalem through Beersheba to Eilat on the Gulf of Aqaba, a daily service. The passengers boarded, the soldiers climbed back into their jeep, the little convoy headed south toward the new orchards and tilled farmland of Sde Boker eleven miles away. South of Sde Boker the road plunged into the wilderness of the lower Negev, passing close to the Jordanian frontier. The Mountains of Moab loomed in Arab territory, high and stark against the deep blue desert sky.

Cousin Yasir could see them coming, the small dot that was the jeep and the larger dot that was the bus. The bus scratched dust from the road and the dust spread, a pale yellow cloud against the sky. Cousin Yasir squatted over the detonator box, his hands already on the plunger. His checkered headcloth was grimy, and beard stubble covered his receding Husayni chin, a homeliness of feature his twin cousins Sulayman and Maryam had almost been spared. Yasir's dark Husayni eyes were narrowed against the sun's glare, the armpits of his khaki shirt were black with sweat. He watched the road. He could make out the tiny figures of the Israeli soldiers in the jeep now. He could hear the engine of the bus laboring as it climbed the long hill out of the arid valley of Arava ninety miles south of Beersheba. Here the road came closest to the frontier and the Mountains of Moab at cousin Yasir's back.

One jeep carrying soldiers had already gone by, twenty minutes ago. Cousin Yasir had wanted to push the plunger then. It was almost more than he could bear, to let four uniformed, armed Zionists pass unharmed. "Wait," Sulayman had told him. Now cousin Yasir knew why.

In addition to himself and Sulayman, there were Maryam and four young fedayeen. Cousin Yasir carried a 9-mm Czech automatic holstered at his side. The others had Kalashnikovs.

The jeep was close now. He could see the faces of the driver and the other man in front. Their uniform blouses were short-sleeved. They wore kerchiefs around their necks.

Maryam was unslinging her Kalashnikov. Cousin Yasir did not expect her to use it, nor Sulayman his. The objective, from a training standpoint, was to blood the four young fedayeen.

The jeep came up the long hill, drawing further ahead of the bus. The man next to the driver raised his hand, and the jeep stopped one hundred yards short of death. With the raising of that hand Allah had granted the soldiers another moment or two of life. But they were dead. Oh yes, they were dead!

The bus struggled up the hill, groaning in low gear. Cousin Yasir remained crouched with the others in the wadi that came down from the higher hills in Jordan and joined the road for thirty yards before leaving it on the far side. There the asphalt had crumbled and hard, cracked earth showed through. Cousin Yasir had camouflaged the explosives beautifully where the wadi and the road were one.

He felt no fear. When he was working with explosives he was competent and powerful and nothing could hurt him.

The jeep began to move, level now, the bus close behind. Cousin Yasir could see faces in the open windows of the bus. He saw an old man with a straggling beard, and a woman in a head-scarf. He saw two children. One of them might have been laughing. He saw two men of military age. Later he would tell himself the bus had been carrying troops.

"Now," Sulayman said, but Yasir was already shoving down on the plunger.

There was a flash and a roar, and the jeep flew up clear of the ground and tumbled off the road on its side, wheels spinning. Four mannequins in soldier uniforms floated out of it, unraveling, a detached arm or leg seen briefly before the cloud of sand and dust swallowed it. The bus stopped forty yards back. People were screaming, tumbling out the doors. Some climbed from the windows. The four young fedayeen ran out of the wadi, shouting, raising their Kalashnikovs. They fired short bursts on full automatic and the people scrambling from the bus fell down, first a few, then more and more. Two of the fedayeen chased some of them down the road to where the wadi went out between low sandstone walls on the other side. The walls were too steep to climb. Two children tried and fell back. The Kalashnikovs fired, in short bursts as the fedayeen had been taught. One boy clung to the wall like an insect. A Kalashnikov hammered and he dropped.

When the dust settled, cousin Yasir saw what was left of the soldiers who had been in the jeep. He had done that. He felt strong and righteous.

There was still screaming. It came from the bus. A few passengers had remained inside. One of the young fedayeen entered from the front and one from the rear. Soon the Kalashnikovs fired their short bursts. The screaming stopped.

Sulayman walked to the jeep. One axle was broken, the chassis crumpled. He walked back to the bus. He looked at it for a moment, then fired a single round into each of the tires and watched the bus settle onto its wheel rims. The Zionists would have to send another vehicle to cart away their dead.

In the wadi the young fedayeen had gathered. Maryam was talking softly to them, patting a shoulder, touching a hand. At her brother's signal they all moved east through the wadi at a quick trot toward the sanctuary of Jordan. The young fedayeen ran with easy confidence. They knew they had done well; next time they would go out alone, and before long they would be training others. Cousin Yasir came behind in his awkward waddling run, dropping back as the bus had done on the long hill. He was gasping for breath with every step but he was happy. Without his explosives they could have accomplished nothing.

Sanctuary in Jordan was a new thing—the West Bank and all the way south to the Gulf of Aqaba. In the small Zionist state none of the roads were safe now.

The cities would be next.

Alongside the road, white eaglets settled again onto the telegraph wires.

3

One hundred sixty miles to the north Akhmed Khalid looked through the small barred window high in his cell

420

and watched the gulls wheeling over the shore beside Ahuzat Bayit Prison. He did not find the gulls very interesting, but they were all he had seen of the outside world for almost a year and he equated their flight with freedom.

In 1920 Ahuzat Bayit was just a small settlement. Then organized Arab violence broke out against the Jewish residents of Jaffa. Many moved to the settlement at Ahuzat Bayit, and large numbers of immigrants joined them. In fifteen years the little village became Israel's largest city, Tel Aviv. Jaffa was now the suburb, and Ahuzat Bayit was only the name of a bleak stone prison complex on the far side of the Yarqon River.

The maximum security facility housed convicted Arab terrorists and spies. Though the prison authorities maintained a scrupulous correctness in dealing with them, there were the expected accusations of mistreatment in the Arab press. Beginning in 1955, periodic visits by the Egyptian Red Crescent were permitted. Major Sam Brodsky signed the letter from the Shin Beth urging the penal authorities to permit such visits. Brodsky had long advocated them. Not only would the Red Crescent representatives bring reading matter and packages and letters from home; unless they were hopelessly prejudiced, they would confirm the humane treatment of the prisoners.

The visits of the Red Crescent held no interest for Akhmed Khalid. A professional spy, he had served the Mukhabarat well for many years. He had been compromised and captured, tried and convicted, imprisoned. He accepted his lot as the will of Allah. He had not been mistreated, so he had no complaints to voice. Nor did he ever receive packages.

Yet on this third Sunday in October the Red Crescent representative, in the company of a prison guard, paid a call on Akhmen Khalid.

His name, he said, was Abu Majid. He was a jowly, overweight man and the climb to the second tier of the prison had left him wheezing and panting. He sat on the edge of the hard bunk, Akhmed Khalid facing him on the small stool. The guard stood just inside the cell door.

"I've brought you a letter," Abu Majid said. "From your cousin in Cairo."

Akhmed Khalid had no cousins he knew of, in Cairo or anywhere. He was instantly alert. He said smoothly, "That *is* a surprise."

Khalid slipped the letter from the envelope, already opened by the prison censor. He had better keep talking, he decided, until he understood what was wanted of him.

"He must be writing out of family duty. In any case, he can't be asking for money this time."

That drew a laugh from Abu Majid and a faint smile from the bored guard. Khalid now knew that the guard understood Arabic.

Akhmed Khalid unfolded the stiff sheet of paper. A photograph was enclosed. Khalid glanced at it quickly and turned his attention back to the letter. He looked first at the signature. His nonexistent cousin was named Mokhtar. Then he started to read it aloud, hoping to get some sign from Abu Majid.

"Be assured that we think of you proudly . . . to your family and to all Egypt you are a hero . . . prayers go to Allah daily for the time when the prison gates open to return you to your native land . . .

"Meanwhile, all is well with . . . um, yes . . . betrothal of Alya to medical student, good family . . . her sister still teaching . . .

"And then just last week . . . delightful surprise visit of your Jehan to her cousins . . . so long since they'd seen her . . . how the three of them have changed in ten years, grown from awkward schoolgirls into beautiful young women . . . felt sure you would want to see the photograph of them together . . ."

Akhmed Khalid hadn't heard from his daughter Jehan since February. He wasn't disturbed by her long silence. They had never been close, Khalid had seen to that. Emotional involvement would have made his work more difficult. She had probably gone to her fiancé in Beirut. She was making a new life for herself, which was what he wanted.

Khalid looked now at the photograph, studying it carefully. Three girls, heads together, faced the camera.

He went back to the letter. Sure enough, his new found relative had told him what he needed to know. ". . . with Alya to her left and Amina to her right . . . in all modesty we can rejoice in Allah's gift of such daughters . . ."

So the one in the middle was supposed to be Jehan.

What were they trying to tell him? That this unknown girl was using the name of his daughter and that, if challenged, he was not to repudiate her? Was that it? But here in prison there seemed little chance that—

And then he knew.

They weren't telling, they were asking. They did not know what Jehan looked like any more than his fictitious cousin did. Only Akhmed Khalid did, and somehow he had to tell Abu Majid, tell him under the nose of the guard leaning against the steel door.

Akhmed Khalid sighed heavily. "I thank you, Abu Majid," he said formally. "I am sure that you, like Mokhtar, wished only to do me a service. You cannot have known how the sight of this photograph would afflict me."

The Red Crescent man leaned forward on the edge of the bunk to see the photograph. "This one is your daughter? A lovely girl. You must not bemoan the separation, but be glad that she is free."

423

"Glad? How can I be glad when I see what this year has done to her? Always before I could look into my Jehan's eyes and see the smiling eyes of her dear dead mother. But now? Now her eyes are bleak and sad, and there are hollows in her cheeks. Even her proud, jutting nose seems diminished."

"Perhaps it is only a poor photograph," Abu Majid suggested. "A bad likeness."

But Akhmed Khalid shook his head. "If you had told me this was someone else's child," he said with another heavy sigh, "I would have believed you."

Then Abu Majid did a clever thing. He looked not at Akhmed Khalid but at the guard, and his shoulders lifted in the barest suggestion of a shrug, as if to tell the Israeli he was used to this, some prisoners were never satisfied.

Khalid folded the letter and returned it to the envelope along with the photograph. Abu Majid offered cigarettes, two packages. They, like the letter, had been opened. Khalid and the Red Crescent man smoked and conversed aimlessly for five_ minutes. Khalid's family was not mentioned again.

"Have you any complaints?" Abu Majid asked.

"I'm in prison. I'll be in prison the rest of my life. Is that a complaint?"

The guard suppressed a smile, and a few moments later escorted the Red Crescent representative down the corridor.

Akhmed Khalid waited ten minutes and then carefully burned the letter and the photograph over the clay pot he used as an ashtray. With his thumb he pulverized the ashes. Then he flushed them down the toilet.

All the rest of the day Akhmed Khalid was pleased with himself. He did not know why they had asked him about his daughter, but he had answered them. Once more he had been useful.

Abu Majid was driven to Jerusalem in an Israeli Defense Forces staff car. He would cross on foot at the Mandelbaum Gate, take a bus to 'Amman and the evening flight to Cairo. As they drove through Jerusalem, he broke out in a cold sweat. Pain gripped his chest with a constricting pressure. He spent five minutes trying to convince himself it was indigestion, but by the time his escort dropped him at the Israeli side of the gate he knew better. He had had a heart attack two years before. Weak, sweating, the pain worse, his legs rubbery, he somehow made it to the checkpoint. The message was important. He had to cross into Jordan.

When the Jewish soldiers had finished with his papers he looked so obviously sick they suggested sending for an Israeli doctor.

"Nothing . . . something I ate . . . don't trouble . . ."

He lurched past the control point and collapsed in Jordanian territory.

Chapter Twenty-four

1

Southard saw Le Matou's mistress three days after the little Frenchman's funeral.

His nickname meant tomcat in French; his real name had been Rasquier, Michel Rasquier. Rasquier was the name his mistress used too, though there was a legal Madame Rasquier in the north somewhere, Lille, she thought. She spoke about it frankly. It had not bothered her while Le Matou was alive and it did not bother her now.

The unmarried Madame Rasquier ran a small hotel in the town of St.-Laurent-du-Var on the main highway just west of Nice. Madame Rasquier was plump and pretty, perhaps thirty-five. She wore black, but Southard did not think she had been crying recently. They sat at a small table in the hotel restaurant drinking coffee.

"Every day for ten years, this happened in my imagination. I'm surprised he lived as long as he did, working for *le Milieu*. Not that he considered it work. He was like a small boy playing cowboys and Indians. He had no regrets, monsieur.

"He spoke of you highly. You're surprised? He told me everything, he sought my advice, he believed in my intuition." Madame Rasquier's face was wistful. "He bought this hotel for me. He came here whenever he could.

Now all that is finished. You know that he died a hero?" the unmarried Madame Rasquier demanded fiercely, as if daring Southard to refute her. "A veritable hero. All the newspapers said so."

Southard had seen a follow-up story in *Nice-Matin*. Le Matou had spent several weeks as bodyguard-chauffeur to the Communist Deputy Thierry de Cheverny. Their car had been overtaken and forced off the road on the Middle Corniche between Monaco and Nice. Le Matou had killed one of the attackers. He and de Cheverny had both been shot dead, Le Matou's bullet-riddled body sprawled over the politician's as if he had tried to shield him.

"It was an odd sort of job for him, wasn't it?"

"You didn't know him that well, monsieur. Michel detested Communists."

"Then why--"

"Thierry de Cheverny was the exception. How Michel admired him! A rich man with a spirit of noblesse oblige, a socialist dreamer who could have changed the party totally, could have taken it out of the hands of that gutter thug Thorez. That was why they killed him."

Or, Southard thought, because they erroneously believed he was leaking information to Kip Chaffee. He asked, "Does the name Margit von Weber mean anything to you?"

"Of course. You came to Nice in April looking for her. It is as I said, he always told me everything, he believed in my intuition."

Southard tried the name Zia Lucia. Madame Rasquier knew her as a former brothel keeper who ran a small private rest home in Rapallo on the Italian Riviera. "For *le Milieu*, you understand."

"What about Giovanni Venturino?"

Madame Rasquier's face, so expressive until then, looked like wood. In a flat voice she said, "Venturino killed them. Venturino sent the men who gunned them down. The police will do nothing. Venturino was Union Corse. After that, according to de Cheverny, he worked for Thorez. Now he is a figure in the international set. He has society's protection three different ways. Michel always lived outside society, like a gypsy. He was always on his own."

Like a gypsy, Southard thought, or like a spy.

"The Venturinos of the world always win. Always." For the first time there were tears in Madame Rasquier's eyes.

2

Venturino crossed the gallery between the American Room and the Cercle Privé shortly after two the next morning, possessively holding the arm of an Italian starlet who looked like and sometimes stood in for Sophia Loren. The girl wore a white strapless gown that set off her dark beauty, Venturino a custom-tailored midnight blue *smoking*. His cruel, handsome face was smug with fresh conquest. Both he and the Italian starlet had good color and their dark eyes glowed. They might just have come from bed.

Porfirio Rubirosa had just risen from a seat on the croupier's left at the roulette table. Venturino punched his arm. The name Sophia Loren was whispered in the crowd standing two deep at the bar.

"Carlotta fools them every time, don't you, baby," the Dominican playboy said. He lowered his head to kiss the Italian starlet's bare shoulder.

"She's even more beautiful," Venturino said.

"And she has more imagination the one place it really counts," Rubirosa said.

Venturino looked at Carlotta and then at Rubirosa.

"Tell him," Rubirosa said to Carlotta, "about Rome last week."

"I never remember last week," Carlotta said. "I never

even remember last night."

She looked like what Venturino believed to be every man's impossible dream, the virginal Earth Mother. With a few words she and Rubirosa had spoiled that for him.

"Tell me about Rome, *cara,*" he said. His hand closed on her upper arm. Her face was suddenly pale.

"Giovanni," Rubirosa said, "it doesn't matter. It was only a joke."

But Venturino thrust the girl away from him. "Get out of here, you cheap tramp."

She went to Rubirosa, and left with him. There was an awkward silence around the table until the croupier said, *"Messieurs, mesdames, faites vos jeux."*

Venturino laughed as if the brief scene had been a joke. He got chips from the croupier instead of going to the cashier's window and he played for about an hour, winning a few hundred thousand francs by placing chips conservatively on red and black, odd and even, not enjoying it. Since the de Cheverny business was over, he had felt let down for days.

He shoveled all his chips at the croupier in a grand gesture. *"Pour le personnel,"* he said, and over the croupier's profuse thanks heard Ari's voice.

"You think I don't pay my rakemen enough?" the Greek shipowner asked.

"It's for luck."

"Here?"

"In life."

"Like spilling wine to the gods," said Ari Onassis.

"Yeah, sure," said Venturino. He punched the Greek's upper arm lightly and headed for the bar.

The barman placed a glass of Patrimonio in front of him, but Venturino pushed it aside and asked for a double whisky. Then he went out to the terrace and walked around to the sea side. Under a low moon the lights of the harbor were bright. Venturino had always liked this view, especially at night. Tonight he didn't. He spat and went back around the side of the casino and told the doorman to get his car.

Soon the Bentley came purring to a stop. You could have built a house of cards on its hood, the kind of idle it had. Venturino began to feel better. He tipped the doorman extravagantly too. Money made things easy, it uncomplicated life. He had that much in common with Onassis: both of them appreciated that crucial fact. He drove west out of Monte Carlo along the coast road.

After a few minutes he heard a sound behind him. In the rearview mirror a man appeared suddenly in the back seat.

"If this is a holdup you are making one bad mistake," Venturino said.

The man waved his hand in the darkness, and what might have been a gun. "Turn off on the Cap d'Ail road."

"The kind of mistake that can get you killed," Venturino said, but he made the turn for Cap d'Ail.

The man did not speak again for a while. They drove on a narrow curving road past dark houses toward the sea. There was an overlook, a small restaurant shut for the night, and a single car in the parking lot.

The man leaned forward. Venturino could see the gun now. "Pull in there."

Venturino stopped the Bentley alongside the other car. He turned the engine off and pocketed the key. The surf sighed faintly on the shingle beach below the restaurant.

"Get out of the car."

Venturino could feel the man frisk him quickly but expertly, underarms, sides, belt, inside of legs. He wasn't armed.

They walked down the path in the moonlight, Venturino a few steps in front, to the shingle beach. Their shoes made a crunching sound on the stones and their footing was uncertain.

"This is far enough," the man said. "Turn around."

Venturino started to turn and something exploded against his face. He fell down, twisting, his upper body splashing in shallow water.

"Get up."

Venturino could feel the left side of his face puffing, over the eye, cheek, jaw, everything.

"What do you want from me?"

The man hit him again with the gun and Venturino tumbled facedown into the water. He got up slowly. Blood ran from his nose. The first blow had been too sudden. He hadn't felt fear then. He began to feel it now.

The man spoke. "I'm going to ask you questions. One question, one answer. No answer, I hit you. An answer I don't like, I hit you. Understood?"

Venturino stood there. The man swung and Venturino fell down. He gasped.

"I asked if you understood."

"I understand," said Venturino. He snuffled blood into his nose, almost gagging on it.

"What do you know about Margit von Weber?"

"She's a rich Kraut broad, a café society type that—"

Venturino didn't see the blow coming but he was sprawled on the edge of the shingle again. He saw the man's legs. He thought the man was going to kick him.

"Wait!"

"Get up."

Venturino was on his feet swaying. His ears rang. He saw the man blurringly as two men. Then they coalesced.

"Maybe it was my fault," the man said. "Maybe I asked the wrong question."

The way he said that frightened Venturino more than anything else had.

"I have standing orders from party headquarters in Paris to give her any help she needs. Is that what you want to know?" Venturino asked in a rush of words.

"What kind of help did you give her last April?"

"Last April?"

Venturino went down again. He came slowly to hands and knees. Something was dripping steadily on the shingle. It was coming from his mouth.

"She brought in three kids to do a job. I got them a place to stay and—"

"Get up."

The man had to help him.

Venturino explored with his tongue. He had lost a tooth.

"And you fingered the Tolosano woman for them, right?"

"Jesus," Venturino gasped. "Yeah."

"Did you ever see them again?"

"One of them."

"Which one?"

"There were two girls and a boy. It was the boy."

"When did you see him?"

"Middle of July."

"What for?"

"Another job for Margit von Weber."

"What kind of job?"

"I put him on a ship in Cannes—the one that sank, the *Andrea Doria*."

"Who told you Beck and Chaffee would be aboard?"

"Jesus!" Another gasp from Venturino. "It was a whorehouse madam in Rapallo called Zia Lucia."

"Where's Margit von Weber now?"

"She left. I don't know where she is! Honest! I haven't seen her since July."

The man was silent for a few moments, as if lost in thought.

Then he pointed the gun at Venturino in a way he hadn't done before.

"No," Venturino said.

The gun was pointing at his chest.

"No, Holy Mother of God, no!"

Venturino saw the muzzle flash and heard the first round fired and might have heard the second except for the pain, the enormity of pain and the impossibility of breathing, and he thought it wasn't supposed to hurt at all, not when you got shot, it was supposed to hurt later, but he hurt, he was pain and only pain, and there would be no later.

Southard changed cars in Nice and crossed the Italian border before dawn.

For a while he considered driving to Rapallo through the early morning and going to Zia Lucia's hillside villa. But he rejected the idea. Zia Lucia was on the edge of things only.

He stayed on the *autostrada* as far as Verona, where he took the road north through Bolzano to the Brenner Pass. He would cross Austria and be in Munich that night.

He had figured all along that sooner or later he would need Reinhard Gehlen's help.

3

Adam Prestridge stopped over in Munich on his way to Adana, Turkey. Adana had been raising questions.

The reconnaissance photographs taken on superfast Kodak film by the U-2's cameras were astonishingly clear, even when shot from an altitude of ninety miles. The U-2 had filmed, the middle of last week, what looked like a French invasion fleet assembling at Toulon — cruisers and destroyers at the Darse Neuve near the naval arsenal, half a dozen LSTs in the more protected anchorage of the Darse de Castigneau.

That alone wouldn't be too difficult to explain. The U-2 could photograph ships but not sailing orders. France, after all, was fighting a war in Algeria.

But Valetta, the British deep-water harbor on the island of Malta, would be more difficult to explain away. The

Royal Navy was there in force—cruisers, destroyers, and six LSTs instead of the two reported by Novikov and Lazarus as operational. Granted, the reading of the U-2 high-altitude films was a new skill, and one of the specialists at Adana was inclined to believe it was a dummy fleet like the one assembled in 1944 in East Anglia to persuade the Nazis D-Day would hit the Pas de Calais—a plywood and rubber armada that had worked. But Prestridge did not think the Valetta fleet was a dummy.

Not that Prestridge cared if the British and French invaded Suez; his only worry was that they might do it too soon. He had reason to believe they would not; they could expect Washington's protestations of outrage to be more muted once the American presidential election was over. The election was still two weeks away, and two weeks might be long enough.

Because it was all happening, finally, as it was meant to happen. The situation in Hungary was daily becoming more critical, the people listening to Noah Landler and clamoring for Prime Minister Imre Nagy to pull down the hammer and sickle and raise the Kossuth flag in Budapest. Unless our allies diverted world outrage by aggression in Suez, Hungary would become the first tear in the Iron Curtain. It wouldn't merely be rolled back; it would be ripped apart.

Prestridge, comfortable in a gray herringbone tweed now that cool weather had set in, took a taxi to the English Garden. He adjusted the pince-nez that he liked to think made him look like FDR and strode into the office of the broadcast director, who already had the tapes ready. He played excerpts of the week's broadcasts, while Prestridge read them in English translation.

"This Landler's very good," he said.

"He's the best we have."

"But why the cautionary note?" Adam Prestridge asked. "He's practically telling them *not* to resist the Russians."

"Not unless the Poles or the East Germans do it at the same time, no. That's the only way Landler thinks it has a chance of working," the broadcast director explained.

"I wish you'd get him to stop harping on a simultaneous uprising," Prestridge said. "It isn't likely. And it spoils the effectiveness of what he has to say."

The broadcast director said that no one could edit Noah Landler. "He'd quit if we tried."

Prestridge did not answer at first. In balance, Landler was valuable. He drew big audiences, that was the main thing. "All right then. You know your man. Keep up the good work."

That afternoon Prestridge's Super Constellation was airborne for Turkey.

4

Iser Harel's office was on the top floor of a three-story building near the Defense Ministry in Ha Qirya, the government quarter of Tel Aviv. It was an office of shirt-sleeves and open collars, of first names and no protocol. The office was very much the man.

The man hadn't slept for days and his staff was equally exhausted.

First there had been the grueling flight in the French DC-4 to the military airport of Villacoublay outside Paris, seventeen hours in the four-engined plane, two refueling stops. Then there had been the even more grueling conference with the French prime minister and the British foreign secretary in the Paris suburb of Sèvres. The whole affair had had a theatrical air of secrecy about it—the seventy-year-old Ben-Gurion stuffing his wild lion's mane of white hair under a broad-brimmed hat for the two-mile drive to the château, Chief of Staff Dayan substituting dark glasses for his eyepatch, Shimon Peres's less-known face undisguised, Harel himself the nondescript little man who wasn't there.

The long flight in the DC-4 had exhausted Ben-Gurion, and the old man had deferred to Moshe Dayan and Peres all during the conference. Not that it affected the outcome, but it had pained Iser Harel to see the prime minister so obviously an old man.

At Sèvres war became a certainty.

That Israel had to fight was obvious. The fedayeen were back in strength, better equipped, better trained, better led, a deadly commando force capable of striking anywhere at any time. And every week the Egyptian army received more tons of Russian equipment. Israel could fight now — or be overwhelmed later.

That France and Britain had to fight now was debatable. But Nasser could cut off their oil supplies without warning, threatening their existence as industrial powers. The threat would have to be dealt with sooner or later, and the timing for war seemed opportune now.

In America, attention would be absorbed by the election campaign until after November 6.

In Eastern Europe, three days before the conference at Sèvres, Russian troops were fired on by units of the Polish army. The Russians had merely been crossing from East Germany in a routine transfer of forces, but for the first time a Warsaw Pact country had challenged the Soviet Union's right to garrison troops on its soil. Warsaw remained tensely quiet, but the news brought the population out in the streets of Budapest, singing patriotic songs, carrying the red-white-green Kossuth flag, marching to Parliament Square. Faced with the ominous quiet in Warsaw and the outburst in Budapest, Russia was in no position to intervene in the Middle East.

Dayan would launch his forces at the end of the month. War was now barely a week away.

Iser Harel wished that the chief of staff was at the

Defense Ministry now, drawing up final battle plans. He wasn't. He had been in Harel's office half an hour, and now he was saying, "You know I have the greatest respect for the Mossad, but as good as your people have even been, they've got to be even better now. With the army fighting in the Sinai, the whole country will be vulnerable to fedayeen attack."

Moshe Dayan leaned forward, his arms outspread, both hands on the desk. "Find out what they're planning, Iser. Otherwise there'll be a bloodbath."

After the chief of staff left, Iser Harel had a cup of dark strong coffee. It made his stomach sour; it always did. He went through his file of Arabic-speaking operatives and his file of Egyptian assets. He knew he was stalling. The latter were unreliable, the former lacked access.

Harel sent for a man named Hirschland, who ran the Mossad's West German desk.

"Raven's in Munich, isn't she?" Iser Harel said.

Hirschland seemed surprised by the question. "That's right. In fact, I've got her file out right now. I was just writing a memo to—"

"Get in touch with her control. I want her reassigned."

"But—but that's the point. I've just heard from her control," Hirschland said. "She wants to come home. He says she's burned out."

Iser Harel shut his eyes. He heard the steady roar of traffic on Petah Tikva Road. Seven months; the girl had been magnificent. But whatever he had told Sam Brodsky, in the final analysis she was an amateur. Seven months in the enemy camp, it was amazing. No wonder she was burned out.

Iser Harel opened his eyes slowly. Hirschland looked at him, waiting.

Iser Harel told him what he wanted.

She had access. She was the only one who did.

Times like this, Iser Harel hated his job.

Chapter Twenty-five

1

Deborah and Istvan were walking along Leopoldstrasse in Schwabing. It was dusk, and all along the sidewalk rows of candles were being lit. On a blanket, wood carvings were displayed. Next came an oil painting of an alp, candlelight turning its glaciers golden. There were dirndl-clad dolls and tiny porcelain statuettes. Watercolors of big-eyed children stared between rows of candles at ornate beer steins.

"It's an interesting tradition," Istvan said with a show of enthusiasm.

"Colorful."

"I mean the candles."

"That's what I meant too."

They walked slowly, looking at the sidewalk displays. Once their hands touched. They both pulled away quickly.

"It's really old," Istvan said.

"What is?"

"The tradition—lighting the sidewalk with candles."

"How old?"

"I don't know exactly," Istvan said.

They stopped on the corner of Herzogstrasse.

"I could make us some coffee."

"No! I mean . . . listen," Istvan said, "I wanted to tell you . . ."

A gaunt poet sat cross-legged on a cushion on the

sidewalk, reciting verses in Italian.

"That's nice poetry," Istvan said with a fresh burst of enthusiasm.

"I didn't know you understood Italian."

"Actually I don't. But it sounds . . . uh, poetic."

"What was it you wanted to tell me?"

Except for a few accidental encounters at the English Garden, Istvan had been avoiding her all week.

"You were wonderful," he blurted.

She looked at him. "You were pretty wonderful too."

"But that isn't what I wanted to say."

"Oh?"

"Not that you *weren't* wonderful. I mean, you still are. I mean, listen, Becky."

She listened, Istvan was silent. He crossed the street. She followed him. Istvan turned and faced her. "You're looking at me," he said. "And it doesn't bother me anymore. You did that for me. I just have some marks on my face."

"That's all they ever were."

"That isn't what I meant to say," Istvan told her.

"Either?"

"Either."

"Then what?"

He looked down at the sidewalk.

"You're the greatest person I ever met in my life," he said.

She sighed and felt a salvaging tenderness toward him. But she wondered how she could disabuse him of what, after all, was only puppy love.

"I phoned Vienna," he said.

"Vienna?"

"Vienna." Still looking down at the sidewalk. "I called Friedl. I, uh, I asked her to come to Munich."

For a moment she stared at him in astonishment. Then she threw her arms around his neck and, right there in the middle of the crowded Leopoldstrasse, she kissed him full on the mouth.

"Istvan, that's wonderful! When did you call her? What did she say? Is she coming right away?"

He was so swept up in her sudden exuberance that he found he had his arms around her waist. "You're not mad or anything?"

"Don't be silly. I can't tell you how glad I am. Of *course* I want you and Friedl to be happy. Oh, Istvan, I love you!"

That didn't quite make sense, but he seemed to understand what she meant. Soon they were walking along the candlelit sidewalk hand in hand, while Istvan told her everything Friedl had said—or most of it. She could get away at the end of the month, she couldn't wait to be with him, they were bursting with plans . . .

Finally Deborah managed to get a word in.

"Istvan," she said, "you've got to promise me one thing. As soon as she gets here, you'll let me meet this paragon of a Friedl of yours."

2

Deborah met Hans-Peter in Lenbachplatz the next day at noon.

Only an ornate façade or two and the undamaged baroque splendor of Trinity Church remained of what had been the most opulent square in Munich. An architectural gem from the days of the Kingdom of Bavaria, it now held broken remnants of walls and gaping weed-grown lots. Here and there a construction site had been fenced, here and there the ruins of a palace stood propped by great beams, awaiting restoration. But Lenbachplatz, more than a decade after the air raids that had virtually leveled Munich, was not essential to the life of the city.

Lenbachplatz was crowded. "It's a compulsion," Hans-Peter said. "Something in the German character makes them come here. Guilt, maybe. Or self-pity."

Deborah gave him an icy look.

"Hey, I can't help it I was born German."

"I'm sorry. It's just that . . . it still upsets me, telling Steinbrenner every move Dr. Landler's going to make."

Hans-Peter didn't meet her eyes. He said, "You won't have to anymore."

"You mean it? Am I going home?"

Hans-Peter looked uncomfortable. "Well, not right away. First they're sending you somewhere else. In fact, they want Steinbrenner to know you're going there. They want you to get his approval."

"What are you talking about?"

They crossed to Pacellistrasse and began walking back toward the center of town.

"They want you to get permission to return to Egypt, as K. I assume that's your black identity. You're to rejoin the twins, whoever they are. Does all this make sense to you?"

"Yes," Deborah said slowly, "I'm afraid it does."

"Miss," said Hans-Peter, "how long have they been running you black?"

"I'm sorry, Hans-Peter, I don't know what you mean."

"You're right," he said. "It's none of my business."

"No, really. I don't know what 'running me black' means."

"When's the last time you were home . . . your own name . . . your own life?"

"March. It was in March."

Hans-Peter sighed. "You'll tell Steinbrenner?"

She nodded.

Ahead loomed the onion-doomed towers of the Frauenkirche.

"Then this is it, I guess. Good luck," Hans-Peter said stiffly. He cleared his throat. "You're a very brave girl, you know."

"Not really. I'm just doing what I . . . You're a nice guy,

441

Hans-Peter." She didn't feel it necessary to add, for a German.

And then it really hit her.

Egypt.

The Mossad had ordered her to return to Egypt.

Twenty minutes later Golovin was standing with Erika Graf not far from where Deborah and Hans-Peter Kempke had parted. Golovin's back was to the pipe-and-board scaffolding on the side of the Frauenkirche. Erika's right hand gripped an upright as if she were blocking his escape. In a way she was; Golovin was in a bind and he knew it.

"If Landler has protection around the clock," he was saying, "what can I do?"

"Use the girl."

"I do. I have from the beginning. She tells me every move he makes."

"I mean *use* the girl. He trusts her. So do his babysitters. The girl can kill him."

Golovin believed that she could. He had always known that, if his aim was the death of Noah Landler, the girl was his best weapon.

Now Erika Graf had reached the same conclusion and he could stall her no longer.

What to do?

The GRU wanted Landler asssassinated. The KGB wanted the assassination to fail. But if he didn't keep the GRU's confidence he couldn't carry out the KGB's orders.

It was even possible that Graf could have him recalled.

"I'll use the girl," he told her.

As they separated, Erika felt as uncertain as he did. She had not heard from Berlin yet, had no idea what the identity check on Jehan Khalid would reveal. Forcing the girl's hand might give Erika her answer.

Jehan Khalid would kill Noah Landler without a qualm.

But if she was that other one?

Erika lit a black-tobacco cigarette and watched Klaus Steinbrenner disappear around the corner of the church.

What would that other one do?

3

In a hospital room in Jordanian-occupied East Jerusalem, Abu Majid lay staring up at the ceiling. A tube taped to his cheek disappeared into his nostril, and through this Abu Majid was breathing oxygen. He heard a muezzin chanting from the balcony of a nearby minaret. Abu Majid was no religious man. He would not ordinarily have prostrated himself to say his evening devotions, but now he wished he could. It would mean he could climb out of bed, leave the oxygen cylinders and the smell of carbolic behind, and resume his life. Well, what was left of his life. This second heart attack almost killed him, the Jordanian doctor said. A near thing, Abu Majid, a very near thing.

For three days he had been asking—begging—to see a man from the Egyptian Embassy in Amman. Either the doctor and the nurses had ignored his request or for some reason unknown to Abu Majid the man had been unable to come.

The younger of the two nurses came in, the one who looked so seductive in his white uniform, the one with the soft fair skin and full red lips that so attracted Abu Majid. "You're looking better," the boy said.

"I'm feeling better."

"After your nap this afternoon, I'll sponge-bathe you," the boy said, and Abu Majid looked forward with pleasure to the touch of the skilled young hands.

The boy shut the valve on the oxygen cylinder and removed the tube from Abu Majid's nose, startling him.

"You don't need these anymore, doctor says. You're

getting well, in *sh*a'Allah."

"In *sh*a'Allah," said Abu Majid automatically.

The boy smiled slyly. "We have a surprise for you."

Abu Majid watched the red lips expectantly.

"Do you feel strong enough for a visitor?"

"From Amman?"

But it had to be. No one else knew Abu Majid was here.

"Five minutes only," the boy said, "and then you'll have a good rest before your bath."

It wouldn't take him five minutes. It would take just a few seconds for Abu Majid to complete his mission.

All he had to do was tell the Mukhabarat man from Amman that the photograph was not of Jehan Khalid.

4

Reinhard Gehlen was using an office in a small factory in the Munich suburb of Pullach. The factory manufactured components for the electronics industry and the sign on the door said Herr Doktor Schneider was vice-president for research and development.

Southard went in. He thought the impossible was about to happen, thought he would see Gehlen's face. But he was mistaken. Shafts of brilliant sunlight entered the room through the venetian blind covering the large window behind the desk. Reinhard Gehlen sat in front of the window, puffing on a cigarette, its smoke rising through the shafts of sunlight. Gehlen's face was a dark featureless oval between Southard and the window. Southard could not even estimate his height because he had no idea how high off the floor the seat of Gehlen's chair was.

"Sit down, Mr. Southard, and tell me how I can help you." The German's arm moved slightly; he might have been looking at his wristwatch.

"I want to find Erika Graf," Southard said.

"Yes, I thought that was what brought you to see me again," Gehlen said, his voice troubled. "I had hoped I was wrong."

"Do you know where she is now?"

"It wouldn't take me long to find out."

"How soon should I get back to you then?"

It was several seconds before Gehlen spoke. "I'm afraid you misunderstand, Mr. Southard. I'm not going to be able to help you this time."

Southard heard a click and pale flame flickered in the shafts of sunlight. Reinhard Gehlen blew cigarette smoke that rose into the bars of light and shadow.

"Two nights ago," he said, "a reformed hoodlum named Giovanni Venturino was shot to death on a beach near Monte Carlo. Venturino was known to work for Major Graf whenever she was on the Riviera."

Gehlen's chair creaked as he shifted his weight. "What you did in France is not my concern. But you must not pursue your vendetta on West German soil, Mr. Southard. You would be making the same mistake that Erika Graf's people almost made in Washington."

"Did you say *almost?*" Southard half rose from his chair.

"Please, Mr. Southard." Gehlen lifted a hand. "You have my sympathies, believe me. I merely meant that they did not succeed in killing *you.* But what they attempted in Washington, I will not permit you to do here in my country. West Germany is the eye of the storm. If you killed Major Graf, they would have to strike back. Nor would it stop there. Sooner or later the Gehlen Group would be caught in the cross fire. I cannot let that happen.

"Of course," Reinhard Gehlen said, "Major Graf does not spend all her time in the Federal Republic, and what you do elsewhere is your affair. But I would strongly advise against this particular course of action anywhere."

The unseen face, the dry delivery, the pompous words, the advice that fell little short of command, all brought

Southard to his feet coldly furious.

"It doesn't matter who we work for, we're all professionals together, is that it? So she can order all the mayhem she wants and get away with it, because in our world when you reach a certain level professionals don't go around killing each other. Somebody should have told her that in August. Somebody should have told her that three years ago in Berlin."

"Berlin was a different situation altogether. There was a power struggle on the other side. You and Gideon Parr were caught in the middle."

"Yes? And where did you fit in? One of your men was driving the car that took Leonid Golovin for his last ride. Who did you owe that kind of favor?"

"You disappoint me, Mr. Southard. If Erika Graf ever had the sort of hold over me that you're implying, she would not be alive today."

"I didn't mean Erika Graf," Southard said. "The one who had the hold over you was Gideon Parr. He knew all about your wartime background. He told me he did. And he *isn't* alive today."

Gehlen said nothing. For an instant he seemed to Southard no more substantial than the smoke coiling through the bars of sunlight and shadow. Then the instant passed and Southard said: "It was you who got word to Erika Graf to be at the Hungarian border that night last March when Parr died, wasn't it? Because you knew they'd been lovers. Because you knew she would never let them take him alive and force him to betray himself. But most of all because if they did, in the process of wringing him dry they'd have learned what he knew about you."

Reinhard Gehlen said softly. "That's why I've been helping you, Mr. Southard. Because in a way you are Gideon Parr's heir."

"He kept your secret, didn't he? Why would he do that?"

"But surely you can answer that question yourself.

446

Because we were useful to each other. Isn't that always the reason?"

For the first time Southard heard fervor in Reinhard Gehlen's voice. He knew then that, finally, that had to be the criterion in the world they all inhabited.

Because we were useful to each other. Isn't that always the reason?

He wondered if it had been Gideon Parr's only criterion in life, his substitute for friendship, his understanding of morality, his reason for loving.

"Mr. Southard, I must remind you—"

But Southard had already pushed the door shut behind him and in the room with Reinhard Gehlen he left the ghost of Gideon Parr.

Chapter Twenty-six

1

Southard drove to Dachauerstrasse and parked in the lot behind the four-story building that housed the U.S. Army finance office for the Munich area. He spoke to the MP at the front desk. Soon he was on the third floor outside a door marked SPECIAL DETACHMENT. It was the Munich cover for the CIA.

Southard caught Charlie Townsend just as he was closing up the office. He and Townsend had served together in the OSS. Townsend was competent but had little ambition; now he was just putting in his days until retirement. Southard told him what he wanted.

"Major Graf?" he said doubtfully. "Yeah, I guess we can put out some feelers. But it's going to take time. We're understaffed as it is," Townsend complained.

"I didn't mean just here. Berlin, Frankfurt, Stuttgart — I want all of Germany covered."

Townsend brightened. "That I can do. I'll get it right on the telex. The reason we're shorthanded here, they took six of my people and turned them into babysitters for some high muckamuck over at Radio Free Europe. What the hell, maybe they know what they're doing. It looks like Hungary's ready to explode, don't it? And from what I hear, this Landler's broadcasts are dynamite."

"Landler? Dr. Noah Landler?"

"Yeah, that's the name. Dynamite. Say, if you're not

doing anything for dinner, how's about we grab a bite together?"

Southard begged off and a few minutes later was driving through heavy evening traffic toward the Englischer Garten.

2

Through the soundproof glass wall of the control room Deborah could see Noah Landler seated, a microphone, a glass and a pitcher of water on the small table in front of him, a copy of his speech in his hands. Dr. Landler was dressed carefully in suit, starched white shirt, conservative tie; his dark hair was brushed, his mustache trimmed, his strong, homely face freshly shaven — all as if he expected his audience in distant Hungary not just to hear but to see him. Deborah could see his lips moving as he rehearsed for the final time what he had written.

There were four seats in the small control room, Deborah and the engineer in the first row of two, Adam Prestridge, who had returned from Turkey, and the broadcast director in the semiupholstered chairs behind them. The engineer removed his earphones when a man came to the door at the rear of the control room, and Deborah could faintly hear a violin playing. The man said something to the engineer and left.

"Switching frequencies again," the engineer told the broadcast director. "Ivan's got his jamming transmitter working overtime."

"How bad is it?" Prestridge asked.

"No big deal. We lose part of our audience for a minute or two. They pick us up again. And we'll be taping the speech for rebroadcast later anyway."

The engineer fitted the earphones over his head. The clock on the studio wall, visible both from the control room

449

and to Landler, jumped half a minute. It was now 6:59 in Munich and in Budapest. One minute to go.

Noah Landler looked up from his speech to the soundproof glass wall of the control room. Almost imperceptibly he shook his head.

Deborah knew what was preying on his mind.

Yesterday in Budapest the blood had started to flow. Breaking under the pressure of their daily confrontation, Russian soldiers had turned their machine guns without warning on the crowds milling in Parliament Square. More then two hundred died in the senseless slaughter.

All night Hungarians streamed past the nearby United States Legation, crying in bewilderment, "Why don't you help us?"

They had, after all, been listening to Noah Landler's broadcasts.

In the control room Adam Prestridge drummed his fingertips on the wooden arm of his chair. He looked at the clock.

The engineer twisted knobs on the console in front of him and pointed dramatically at Landler just as the clock on the wall nervously bit off the final half-minute.

Landler sat there. He hunched his shoulders in what Deborah knew to be a characteristic gesture and planted his elbows on the table on either side of the low mike.

"This one's a beauty," the broadcast director said. "Really strong stuff. It practically makes me want to hitch a ride to Budapest myself."

Prestridge's fingers continued the drumming sound. "What's he waiting for?"

The engineer waved both arms, trying to attract Landler's attention. He pointed at the clock.

Noah Landler sat hunched silently over the microphone.

Then he got up and walked out of the studio.

"Put on one of his old tapes," the director said. "Hurry up, Max."

"Which one?"

"Any one you can lay your hands on. Meanwhile keep the music going."

Adam Prestridge left the control room without a word.

Ten minutes later he sat facing Landler across a table in the small lounge outside the studio. Though they had been arguing the whole time, neither man had raised his voice. Landler knew they were too far apart, and their disagreement was irrelevant now anyway.

Still he said, "It's all a question of propaganda, isn't it? In Bohemia during the war the Nazis had a showplace concentration camp called Theresienstadt. Red Cross officials were permitted to visit it. Theresienstadt was the only camp they ever saw. They were told, come, see for yourselves, what's all this rubbish about the extermination of the Jews? The camp was sanitary and not overcrowded, the inmates were worked hard but not worked to death, they had medical care. There were even pots of geraniums in the barracks windows. And you? For you there is the training camp in the mountains here in West Germany—a few thousand political dissidents from the Soviet bloc practicing parachute jumping, night fighting, unarmed combat, barrier penetration—pots of geraniums in the barracks windows, Mr. Prestridge."

"If you think there is even the remotest similiarity between a showplace concentration camp and—"

"A showplace training camp? I was taken there because I was ready to believe, just as the hopeful gentlemen of the Red Cross were ready to believe in Theresienstadt. I was fool enough to let you use me. It's a matter of human nature, after all. A man believes what he wants to believe."

Prestridge leaned forward across the table, his eyes earnest behind the glitter of his pince-nez. "You're wrong, you know. The camp exists. It's real. Its purpose is real. There are other camps. There are planes, big C-54

451

transports, waiting right now at airfields here in West Germany. There's a U.S. Army regimental combat team on standby ready to board those planes. Airborne troops, doctor. Paratroops. They'll drop on Budapest within hours after they get the signal to move."

A change had gradually come over Prestridge's face while he spoke. The faint suggestion of a smile, superior but not arrogant, touched his lips; he had removed the pince-nez and in his eyes was a tranquility of belief as strong as the deepest religious faith.

Noah Landler thought of all that had remained unsaid: that possibly even Miklos Manyoki had been wrong, because no rioting in the streets of Budapest could throw off the Soviet shackles, no revolution in the Soviet bloc could succeed, no dream of freedom could be permitted to spread—for the gray faceless bureaucrats in the Kremlin knew that once it reached the non-Russian population of the Soviet Union itself, that union was doomed. No, whatever happened in Hungary, Russia would keep her empire and the West would win a propaganda victory over the corpses of Hungary's Freedom Fighters.

But he said none of it. His words would not reach Adam Prestridge. The man had not intentionally deceived him. He was a fanatic, a true believer, his faith unshakable by mere words, his ability to delude others less important than his need to delude himself.

Dr. Landler had no wish to see the effect on Adam Prestridge when the events of the next few days, as they must, destroyed his faith.

He had no wish to see Budapest, either, but he knew he had to go there.

3

It was half an hour later. Landler sat drinking cofee with

Istvan and Deborah at a formica-topped table in the RFE cafeteria.

Istvan had taken one look at the doctor's face and asked, "How soon are we leaving?"

The question seemed to surprise Landler. "I'm a doctor, they'll need me. But why should you—no, forgive me, Istvan. Of course you have to go. We'll take the train to Vienna tonight."

Deborah wanted to object. It was senseless to return to Hungary knowing what awaited them there. But she was going to Egypt, wasn't she? If anything, that could be even more dangerous. But they wanted her to go, in Tel Aviv. How could she refuse? Time enough to return to Israel when her work was finished. She almost managed a smile. Egypt was a lot closer to home than Germany, anyway.

Klaus Steinbrenner had surprised her by his ready assent, even if he had sounded peevish. "If you think they need you in Egypt, go. I won't try to stop you. That's what you were trained for, after all." He said nothing else, not even good-bye. Just turned and walked off, as he always did.

"No," Dr. Landler was telling Istvan now, "it would be unfair to blame the Americans. They have their fanatics, naturally—show me a country that doesn't and I will pray at the gates for them to let me in. Faith in the goodness of man may be naive but . . . what's the matter, Istvan?"

Deborah saw it too, the speculative frown on Istvan's face as if he were trying to remember something. Then suddenly he was smiling and he pushed back his chair and walked quickly past the side of the table where Deborah and Dr. Landler sat, both his arms outstretched, and he said: "Good God, everybody thought you were dead, Herr Beck."

And Deborah turned and saw him.

Chapter Twenty-seven

1

From the water, fragrant with the scent of bath oil, rose Erika Graf's leg. She regarded it, the faintest suggestion of amused narcissism on her face. Erika had been endowed with a superb body, as firm now as in her early thirties as the body of a girl ten years younger. She examined the arched instep, the long smooth curve of the calf, the thigh almost too muscular, like a dancer's. She let the leg slide back into the water and cupped a breast, feeling warmth, weight, firmness, texture of skin. Men went wild over this body. By now she accepted that as normal. What sometimes still surprised her was her strength. It seemed almost unfair. She was as strong as most men. Not a few of the junior officers who submitted to a half-hour of unarmed combat practice with her in the basement gym at the Normannenstrasse came away with their egos bruised.

Erika, her blonde hair coiled on top of her head, slid down until her chin rested on the surface of the water. With a languid foot she turned on the hot tap. Steam rose and she could feel the sweat running down her face.

The long hot bath, the awareness of her body, the self-absorption, all usually took Erika's mind off things. But not tonight.

It had been almost eleven when she ran the bath, perhaps half an hour ago, and still the questions kept coming back at her. Would Steinbrenner have told the girl by now? Would the girl have had time to do it yet? Was Landler already dead?

All one question, really—was the girl Jehan Khalid or wasn't she?

The telephone in the bedroom rang. She rose, her skin flushed with the heat of the bath, water cascading from her body. She could feel a pulse pounding in her throat as she went swiftly, dripping wet, into the bedroom. Steinbrenner. It had to be Steinbrenner calling to tell her that it was done. Calling to tell her, without knowing he was telling her, that the girl was Jehan Khalid.

She grabbed the receiver. "Hello?"

"Fräulein Erna Bauer? Berlin calling."

For a moment she was disoriented; she had been so certain it would be Steinbrenner.

"Yes, Erna Bauer speaking."

She heard the operator say, "I have your party, sir, go ahead."

"Erna? You remember your uncle Alfons, don't you?"

Erika completed the recognition code. "Uncle Alfons! It's been a million years! What are you doing in Berlin?"

"I've opened a print shop," said the man called uncle Alfons. "Unfortunately, I'm not getting the business I'd hoped."

That meant the girl in the photograph supplied by Richard Quast wasn't Jehan Khalid.

There followed a short conversation about a personal life meaningless to both of them, and then it was over.

The girl was an imposter.

Erika sat unmoving for several seconds with her hand on the telephone. Then she got up and walked to the open window. Streetlamps penetrated the heavy fog only a few feet. A car came cautiously by. Erika left the window and saw a lit cigarette on the edge of the telephone table. She did not remember lighting it. She ran a hand slowly over the curve of her hip. It was like touching someone else. She went to the window again. She could smell the fog, moist and earthy like the Oświecim marshes in Poland those rare nights when the wind blew from the south and you could not smell the chimneys of Auschwitz.

2

Steam billowed from the locomotive, the great pistons began their first labored movements, the wheels turned and Deborah saw Istvan waving from the window of the wagon-lit compartment he shared with Dr. Landler on the night express to Vienna. The wheels clattered on the tracks, the train moved faster and faster, the open rear door of the last car disappeared into the fog at the end of the platform. A uniformed figure carrying a lantern walked slowly back.

Deborah squeezed Southard's arm against her side.

"Take me somewhere," she said, "where there's music and candlelight and—no, take me walking along the river. Is that all right?"

They stood on Ludwig's Bridge listening to the Isar rush below them. Fog lay heavy on the water.

Everything about him was at once strange and familiar. She hadn't remembered how tall he was. The top of her head just reached his mouth. There were droplets of mist in his dark blond hair. The hair was fairer than she remembered. His eyes were cold now in the spill of light from the lamps over the bridge roadway, hard and full of a hurt she hadn't been aware of before. They would change when he looked at her, and the line of his mouth would soften too. But then without warning she would see a small cold contraction of the flesh around his eyes, and he was gone from her again.

"I'd better get you home," he said. "It's late."

She hadn't intended telling him until later, but she had to bring him back from wherever he had gone. "I'm flying to Rome tomorrow," she said.

He misunderstood. "Are they bringing you in? It's about time."

"From Rome I'm catching a plane for Cairo."

"Cairo? What's wrong with them? How much do they think you can take?"

"I'm the only one they've got who can do it. It's not as awful as it sounds. The fedayeen think I'm one of them. Why," Deborah said lightly, "it will be a reunion, won't it—me and the Husayni twins." She laughed, or tried to. She wanted to be bright and brave about it so she could bring him back from wherever it was he went.

Tomorrow she would be in Egypt, so tonight belonged to her. She wanted the night to stretch out and stretch out, their night, she wanted it filled with laughter and gaiety, she wanted music, she wanted a bottle of the best wine in the world, the wine they had drunk in France, she wanted. . . .

"I'm scared," she said. "I'm so scared."

He held her. He tilted her face up. He kissed her hair and her cheek and her mouth. Their mouths held together. She felt his touch all through her. The joy, the new joy of her discovered body was there, but it was more than that. It was him. It overwhelmed her, the feeling of not knowing him and of having known him forever. Laughter, other people's laughter, gaiety, music, wine—there was no time for any of that. Tomorrow night she would be in Egypt.

"Take me somewhere."

Erika, in belted trench coat and mannish hat, was walking. The wind rose, the fog lifted in tatters, the wind dropped, the fog crept back. Erika would turn up one street, down another, go straight along a third. She walked beneath the Victory Arch on Ludwigstrasse. Now I know, she kept thinking. Well, I wanted to know. Isn't that what I wanted? Erika walked faster. Soon she was in Schwabing. She paused on a street corner. You don't want to go there, she told herself. But she did want to, she couldn't help it. Five minutes later she reached Herzogstrasse. She looked up through the fog at the apartment windows. They were dark. The girl was asleep. Erika wanted to go in there, to rush up the stairs, to wake the girl and tell her get out of Munich, hurry, go back where you came from. . . .

Erika walked to Leopoldstrasse and found a public telephone.

Andrei Golovin had always believed in his own good luck, and it was working for him now.

Graf had phoned. The conversation was brief.

"Has she done it yet?"

"No . . . not yet," Golovin said warily.

He had not even spoken to the girl about killing Landler. She had come to him giving him the excuse he needed. She was going home; her place was in Egypt now, she said. Overexcited, naturally—and therefore unable to employ effectively the skills in which she had been so well trained. He said none of this to Graf on the phone. It wasn't necessary because Graf asked: "Call her off—can you do that?"

Graf gave no reason, no explanation.

After a moment Golovin said, "Yes, I can do that."

It was chilly in the room and now Golovin slipped a sweater over his pajamas.

Why had Graf changed her mind?

Could the GRU have decided Landler was worth more to Russia alive than dead? No, not likely. Once they began a project, the GRU seldom backed off. They did not share the KGB's flexibility.

Besides, Golovin thought, even his own orders from General Serov to prevent the assassination were suspect. How much was Serov influenced by the situation in Hungary, how much by the struggle of his KGB against Shalin's GRU?

Maybe Graf's motives were not what they seemed either. She hadn't said a thing about Landler; she'd only told him to call off the girl.

Then possibly the girl was the key.

But with Jehan Khalid leaving for Egypt tomorrow, Golovin doubted he would ever know.

Erika returned to her room at the Hotel König. She lit a cigarette, inhaling deeply. She opened a bottle of Schinkenhäger and took a long swallow. She kicked off her low-heeled shoes but did not undress. The window was open. She could still smell the fog. A late car passed slowly, its headlights swinging across the ceiling. She shut her eyes but the image remained. She knew there would be no sleep tonight. She saw stabbing through the mist the searchlights at the end of the rail line in Auschwitz, the Jews blinded by them, tumbling from the packed cattle cars to the ground, the Ukrainian guards whipping them into line, the guard dogs straining against their leashes. It was on a night like that, a night in February 1943, when the last transport of Berlin Jews had been shipped east, that the girl who was not Jehan Khalid had reached Auschwitz.

Erika herself had already been there two months. The work was easy, as long as something inside you had gone dead.

While Southard got the room key from the night porter at the Hotel Drei Löwen, Deborah stood looking at the two huge photographs and the equally large architect's sketch filling one long wall of the lobby.

The first photograph showed the hotel entrance as it had looked before the war—busy, prosperous, with several men in derbies emerging, and a mustachioed doorman in an elaborate uniform holding a huge umbrella over a couple in evening dress as he opened the door of a high, square, ancient taxi. There was a date: May 1930.

The second photograph showed a pile of rubble with part of the porte cochere canted on its side, the letters *ÖWEN* visible. The camera had caught half a dozen passersby, thin faces frozen in despair as they trudged by, heads down, leaning forward as if walking into a strong wind. There was a date: May 1945.

The architect's sketch showed what the façade of the Drei Löwen would look like when restoration had been completed. There was no date.

"You know, I would have expected this second picture to bother me," Deborah said when Southard joined her. "Because they deserved whatever they got, and who needs their self-pity? But tonight I'm not so sure. You know what I think, right now tonight? That some of them were just people and they didn't deserve it. Because they were victims of the Nazis too."

5

Erika sat at a table in one of those late-night clubs that were called private because you had to show your membership card, usually a fifty-mark note. In an urn on the table was an almost empty bottle of Sekt, Erika's second, and a telephone. Every so often the phone buzzed and a number denoting one of the other small tables in the cellar room lit up. Erika would answer, and fend off the advances of whatever man, a few tables away, had called. It had happened a dozen times; twice women had called. Erika watched them pairing off at the other tables, watched some couples leaving together. The entertainment, in addition to that provided by the customers themselves, was an amateurish soft-porn film alternating with the listless performances of two strippers.

It was four-thirty. Erika signaled the waiter and ordered another bottle of Sekt. She would stay until the club closed, perhaps half an hour from now. She knew she had drunk too much. The room was too bright, the room swayed; her face felt slack, her eyelids were heavy. She saw the girl. She kept seeing the girl. It had been worse in the hotel room, but even here.

One day the girl had appeared, a plaster cast on her hand, outside the special barracks where privileged women inmates slept one to a bunk and had almost enough to eat. The girl, she could tell, was trying not to cry. The plaster cast surprised Erika. A broken bone usually meant the death barracks at Birkenau; Auschwitz was hardly a rest camp. Erika had to assume that someone, Hauptsturmführer Kerrl himself perhaps, did not want the girl to die. Or did not want the girl to die yet. But Kerrl would forget.

Though Erika had heard her play in the camp orchestra, this was the first time she had seen the girl so close. Erika had just put her motorcycle on its kickstand and the girl passed near enough to touch. She was small and dark and she walked nervously, her movements graceless, the camp walk, a neuter walk of exhaustion and fear. All that was normal. It was her face that stunned Erika. She mounted her motorcycle and kicked down hard with her black boot on the starter. For a moment she had lost the capacity to think. She almost drove off. Then she remembered she had come here to requisition half a dozen women for temporary duty in the greenhouse that supplied the I.G. Farben offices with flowers throughout the year. She climbed off the BMW and went into the office near the special barracks. She saw to it that the girl was included in the work detail for the greenhouse.

Now the telephone on Erika's table buzzed. The third bottle of Sekt was half empty. She matched the number that had lighted up with a table. Average height. Well dressed. Rimless glasses, bloodless lips. Accountant. Married. Late-night argument with wife, wife with another man, wife out of town. The bloodless lips smiled thinly at her. She did not pick up the phone. She paid her bill, far too much for three bottles of Sekt. She had to get out of there. Up the stairs. The street. She walked fast, her strides long. She was going nowhere as fast as she could.

6

Southard stood at the window of the hotel room. It was not yet dawn. Wisps of fog blew along the street. He did not want to wake the sleeping girl. He did not want to think about her or about how he felt. But he could not help smiling, remembering.

She had come to him with an odd, touching, finally exciting ingenuousness. Everything seemed new to her. Kiss me, she had said. She was up on one elbow in bed. Kiss me everywhere. I want to see what you do, is that all right? Everything excited her. When he kissed her throat she cried out. When he kissed her breasts she laughed, a sound both joyous and lewd. The touch of his lips on her thigh made her whole body tremble. After a while she said, now I want to try. And she explored him. She explored him with hands, with lips. She breathed the scent

462

of him. She was in a place she had never been before. She made little sounds of delight. She spoke his name often. Her breath soon came in gasps. Her eyes were almost closed, her lips were parted. They looked bruised. I never knew, she said. My God, I never dreamed.

She lay looking up at him, her hair spread dark on the pillow, her arms reaching up. Now, she said. Now. For a moment she was passive under him. Then she cried out again with delight and again she said, I never knew! Her hands caressed his back. Her movements were languid at first. He was kissing her. Then he saw her eyes. They were wide open and tears were running down her cheeks but she was smiling. He said, you're beautiful. He said her name. Deborah, he said. Debbie. Her eyes had squeezed shut. Her fingernails dug at his back. Her mouth was open. She thrust upwards. She made an exultant sound, long held, rising, falling. Then they lay in each other's arms. He could feel her heart pounding against his ribs and the hot little puffs of her breath on his throat. He stroked her hair. He kissed her eyes. I never knew, she said against his lips. I never—is it always like that? She was crying. I'm so happy, she said. But tell me it isn't always like that. I couldn't stand it if it was. He said, Debbie. He said, darling. She was kissing his cheek. She said, tell me, how long does—no, never mind. He asked, what? She said, well, I was just wondering how long it took until—oh! and that laugh at once joyful and lewd, it doesn't take any time at all, does it?

Later she said, Benton? Do you like Benton or Ben? I like Deborah, he said. And she said, you were so mean and hard that time in France when you were questioning me . . . how did I know you were nice, going to be nice? She also said, this is a lovely room. Isn't this a lovely room. He said, I love you, without realizing he was going to say it. He said, listen to me. You don't have to go there. I don't want you to go. She said, yes, I have to, and he knew he had no right to stop her. She kissed him and he said, I love you, and first there had been the not knowing he would say it, and then the knowing, and now it was something he had to say. She smiled, eyes shut, lips shut. She slept.

At the window he watched the dawn seep slowly through the fog and he knew that until tonight he had not cared that he might die. She had changed that. She was part of him. But what he still had to do was something she would never know about.

He heard her. Her steps were light. He felt her hand on his shoulder.

"Hello," she said.

"Hello."

He turned, and she came into his arms. He held her.

"I love Benton Southard," she said. "Isn't that a lovely thing to say, first thing in the morning?" She moved back against his arms and smiled up at him. "I love looking at you. I can't understand why every girl who sees you doesn't fall in love with you. Maybe they do. I'm starving. Is it too early for breakfast?"

"It's too early here. But there's the airport," he said. "What time's your plane, doll."

It was something he had not called her before and it made him smile, a sad smile, and then he felt his face grow hard.

"My plane? Not for hours and hours. What is it, Ben? You look . . . far away somewhere."

He said, "It has nothing to do with you," and he saw the hurt on her face. He wanted to take the hurt away.

"Last spring when I got back to Washington," he told her, "I asked a Mossad man named Perlmutter to get me reports on you."

"You did?"

"I wanted to find out if you were all right. I had to know." But still that wasn't enough. He had to say it,

464

wanted to see her face when he said it. "The reason I had to know," he said, "was because I couldn't stop thinking about you. Because I was already in love with you."

A few minutes later he went around the corner for his car. A wind had blown the fog away but the sky was leaden. It looked like rain. He drove her to Herzogstrasse so she could get her things.

7

When Erika left the telephone club she had no intention of going to Herzogstrasse. But she hadn't intended going there before, either. It was past six-thirty. She had no idea how long she'd been walking. A strong wind had dispersed the fog to reveal dark sullen clouds coming low and fast from the west. It grew colder. She felt the first few raindrops on Leopoldstrasse near the phone booth she had used for her call to Steinbrenner. The rain came down harder. The wind lashed it along the sidewalk. A man with an umbrella hurried by, walking a blond Alsatian puppy like the one her little sister had named Shatterhand after the Karl May character. The wind blew and the skirts of Erika's trench coat flapped. Shatterhand had lived to be five and died in an air raid. It wasn't much of an air raid that November of 1942, but it hit their block in Hamburg. Men were digging in the ruins when she returned. She got a spade somewhere and helped. They found her mother that night. They found the dog that had been named Shatterhand the next morning. They found her sister at noon. Her father never learned about the air raid because a few minutes before they found her sister's body the telegram came saying that he had fallen for Greater Germany.

She was working that November out of the Winterhilfe office on the Alster Canal. It was just a door-to-door canvasing job, but that too was doing something for Greater Germany. She was nineteen.

It was as if there was another death in the family—something inside her turned hard and cold and uncaring. She paid no attention to her appearance, she drank, she woke mornings in strange beds with SS men and soldiers on leave whose names she did not remember. Her mother's brother came for her. He was dark and slender like that side of the family. Before the war there had been jokes: they almost looked Jewish. There had been no jokes now for a long time. Her mother had been small and dark, her sister the same. Erika resembled her father, big-boned, blond. Her sister had always needed caring for. Polio had crippled her when she was an infant. She had a quick, nervous walk which, with her brace, almost hid the limp. Erika looked after her. In the beginning it was like playing mother, there was that much difference in their ages. Now she was dead. They all were dead.

Her uncle wore the uniform of an SS Sturmbahnführer. He took her with him to the General Government in Poland. They were not close, it was only a family obligation. He did not work at the extermination camp called Birkenau. He commanded the garrison that kept order among the slave laborers at the I.G. Farben synthetic rubber factory, only one part of the vast complex of Auschwitz.

Erika's uncle found her work. Soon she was in charge of the labor details assigned to groundskeeping. It was necessary, her uncle said; the Polish landscape was so ugly.

The girl, the violinist with the broken hand, reminded Erika of her sister.

She liked working in the greenhouse and Erika had her assigned there permanently. Soon the cast was removed from her hand. That the injury hadn't sent her to the gas chambers was Erika's doing, because SS men were always looking for those who were injured or too weak to work. Erika said the girl was the best worker in the greenhouse. That was the first time she saved the girl's life.

Now in the rain in Munich she ducked into the recessed doorway of the bierstube across Herzogstrasse from the girl's apartment. The rain was coming down in sheets. The sky was even darker than before. A car came slowly along Herzogstrasse and stopped in front of the doorway. A man got out. He turned and faced Erika for an instant, not twenty feet away. He was Benton Southard. He ran around the front of the car and opened the door on the other side. The girl got out and stepped forward into his arms and said something and he laughed and they ran together, arms around each other's waists, splashing across the street. Soon lights came on in the girl's apartment. Erika did not move. The name kept going through her head.

Benton Southard in Berlin in 1953.

Benton Southard in Budapest in March.

Benton Southard in Italy with Kip Chaffee in July.

Now Benton Southard here. In Munich. With the girl.

Twenty minutes later they came out. Southard was carrying two suitcases. He let the girl into the car, then opened the back door and put the bags on the seat. Then he went around to the driver's side. Erika could see them through the rain-misted window. The girl moved closer to him as he slid into the car. She tilted her head for a kiss. They held each other for a long moment. Then the engine coughed and caught raggedly and smoke came from the exhaust pipe.

The car drove away. Erika walked slowly back through the rain toward the Hotel König.

Golovin met Erika Graf at the Petershof that afternoon. Her face looked drawn. She began to speak as soon as he sat down. "Jehan Khalid's an imposter," she said. "She's being run by the CIA."

His first reaction was disbelief. "That can't be. Her credentials are impeccable."

"I had her picture sent to Cairo. They don't know who the girl is, but they know she isn't Jehan Khalid."

He was getting over the disbelief, beginning to think. But he needed time to adjust. "You said the CIA."

"She left Schwabing early this morning with a CIA officer named Benton Southard."

He was careful not to respond to the name. Klaus Steinbrenner would know nothing of Southard, nothing of the death in Berlin in 1953 of General Leonid Golovin.

Instead he said the first thing she would expect him to say. "Is that why you called off the operation last night?"

She was playing right into his hands. There was no way, now, that he could be faulted for failing to have the girl kill Noah Landler. But it was better than that. The Golovin luck again, he could sense it. It was always there when he needed it most.

"Obviously," she said. "But that's not important now. Don't you see what this means? The Special Groups are finished—at least all the ones that trained in Paris. There's no way we'll ever know which of them have been compromised."

He made the best job he could of nodding glumly. "What will you do?"

"I'm taking the first plane to Berlin. I'm going to recommend that all operations be suspended, all contacts with the Special Groups cut."

They would follow her recommendation. They had no

choice. He suspected he himself would shortly be summoned to Special Groups Control, Wünsdorf. Where he would stress how adeptly Jehan Khalid had penetrated the other groups. They would have to accept failure, try to cut their losses. And even if they made him the scapegoat it wouldn't matter. There might be some small unpleasantness. He would weather it.

Their failure had been his real mission. General Serov would protect him.

"Where was she going?" Graf asked. "Do you know?"

"She said she was going home to Egypt, right after the Landler thing was over," Golovin told her. "When that was called off, she probably went anyway. Unless the CIA had other plans for her."

But those were precisely the plans they *would* have, he told himself. The Middle East was ready to erupt. Probably the CIA had instructed her to get permission to return to Egypt.

"The CIA or the Mossad," Graf said. "If you'd been doing your job, you'd have known she was reporting periodically to a Mossad contract agent right here in Munich. What do you think made me suspicious of her? Why do you think I ordered an identity check?"

The more she told him, the better it sounded. The CIA would only be after information. The Mossad's aim would be to destroy the fedayeen.

Graf was looking at him scornfully. "Can I trust you to do *something* right. You *do* know how to get word to the Egyptians?"

Once again she was playing into his hand, this time with her scorn.

"Yes, Frau Major," he said, getting to his feet. "I'll let them know."

He would. In two or three days.

Time enough, with luck, for Jehan Khalid to undermine the fedayeen—and thereby the GRU, which had orchestrated the death of his father.

And if he were ever called to account for the delay, what difference would it make? He worked for the KGB, not the GRU. General Serov would pin a medal on him.

Chapter Twenty-eight

1

They did not take a boat south from Illmitz because they were told Russian troops patroled the lakeshore there. They walked east instead all night on a track through the marshes. They were still in Austria when the new day dawned bright and cold. Two Austrian border police were riding bicycles on the unpaved road between the bridge over the Einser Canal and the village of Andau.

"Where do you think you're going?"

Istvan said nothing. Landler was too exhausted to talk. He just pointed east.

"Are you crazy? The traffic's the other way, friend."

"We're going in," Istvan said.

Both border policemen had dismounted from their bikes.

"Have you any idea what it's like over there?"

Istvan shrugged impatiently. "We're going."

"There are watchtowers along the canal. Machine guns. Wait for tonight and it will be easier to get through."

Dr. Landler shook his head. His face was haggard. Mud caked his trousers and windbreaker. "No," he said.

"Then if you're going," the other border policeman said, "don't use the bridge. See those birch trees? Keep north past them, through the reeds. There's a drainage ditch that empties into the canal. You can wade across. What are you?"

They looked at the policeman blankly.

"Are you journalists or what? Journalists are going in."

Istvan didn't bother answering.

"I'm a doctor," Noah Landler said.

"Then you ought to have more sense. Haven't you heard what it's like over there?"

"That's why we're going," Noah Landler said.

Istvan tugged at his arm impatiently. The border police climbed on their bikes and pedaled slowly toward Andau. One of them turned to look back, but by then Istvan and Dr. Landler had left the road and were striking out cross the marsh toward the birch trees.

That afternoon in the town of Magyaróvár ten miles inside Hungary they walked silently up the main path through the cemetery. The path was bordered by plane trees, their leafless, skeletal branches clawing at the sky. Hundreds of people were walking slowly up the path toward the cemetery chapel. When Istvan and Noah Landler reached it they stood for a long time. Istvan remembered the silence most of all and the smell. The bodies were in rows on the floor. There were not enough coffins in Magyaróvár. The blood had not been washed away and no effort had been made to cover the wounds cosmetically. Istvan saw gaping chests and pulped faces and heads split open. There were flowers everywhere, their scent mingling with the smell of blood.

"The AVO did this," someone told them, and then four or five people began to talk. There had been too many deaths, too unexpectedly, for a normal display of grief. They looked like people who had been watching a horror movie and then found themselves inside it, unable to get out.

"They only wanted to take down the red flag at the AVO barracks and put up the tricolor of Hungary. There were trenches in front of the barracks. The AVO waited there with machine guns."

"And grenades," another voice said. "They threw grenades."

"One moment the officer was talking with the crowd, and the next he jumped into the trench and gave the order to fire."

There were eighty-two bodies in the chapel. They had lain there since yesterday. The AVO officers were still in the cellar of the barracks. Their men had fled after beating back the first mob. Now most of the people of Magyaróvár stood outside the low stone whitewashed AVO building. When Istvan got there it was almost sunset. Dr. Landler was at the schoolhouse, where the wounded had been taken.

Istvan hadn't been outside the barracks ten minutes when one of the AVO officers made a run for it. He was caught a few hundred yards away on Lenin Street. Some men brought a rope and fastened it to the branch of a plane tree. Before they could hang the AVO officer an old man with bristling silver mustaches rushed up and pulled the officer's pistol from his holster and shot him behind the ear. People grabbed the old man. "He is my son," he cried, and stood there and watched while they hoisted the body of his dead son on the rope and hanged him anyway, and all the while he kept nodding and looking at the pistol and the neat hole drilled behind his son's ear.

The crowd broke into the cellar then and dragged the other two officers out. These begged for mercy. They were punched and kicked and beaten with sticks. They were clubbed with bottles and when the bottles broke they were slashed with shards of glass. They were stomped on. Soon they were rags that had been AVO uniforms, stuffed with bloody flesh. The crowd silently dispersed. Istvan saw the old man with the silver mustaches linger near the hanging dead man. He thought of his father without hatred. For one instant he was afraid for his

473

father. The instant passed.

Istvan wanted to go to Budapest. Everyone said if the AVO were to be crushed, they must be crushed in Budapest; if the Russians were to be beaten, they must be beaten in Budapest. He went to the schoolhouse where Noah Landler was. Landler was just coming out. His face was drained of color. There were hollows under his eyes. He had removed his windbreaker. His shirt was covered with blood.

"I'm not needed here any longer. They have doctors."

"I'm going to Budapest," Istvan said.

Landler nodded at him and took a step and his legs gave out. Istvan caught him.

At dusk workers from the bauxite mines outside Magyaróvár commandeered six trucks. When he heard they were going to Budapest, Istvan persuaded them to take him and Noah Landler with them.

2

Southard was drinking his second cup of coffee in a working-class café in the Kreuzberg district of Berlin. His snap-brim hat and tan topcoat made him look out of place among the men in coveralls crowding the café. It didn't matter; the operation was supposed to attract attention. But it offended Southard's professionalism.

He remembered his last conversation with Allen Dulles. It was why he was here now.

"Their code name for it is Lazarus," Dulles had begun. "He's a Russian mole, the man British intelligence assigned as their liaison with us."

Dulles sighed. "Dear God, first they gave us Kim Philby as liaison in Washington. We *told* them. We could do everything but prove it in a court of law. But he was part of the Old Boy net. They thanked us for our concern,

concern they called it, and got him a top job with a newspaper and he's probably still working for them. Now they've given us Lazarus—a man named Kendall Tarrant—in just about the same job, only he does it in London. All summer he's been busily disinforming us on Britain's ability to invade Suez. And once this fellow Novikov defected, we learned Lazarus was a mole and was giving the same reports to the GRU. It was his easiest way to tell the Kremlin exactly how he'd been disinforming us."

Allen Dulles lit his pipe. "Well, that's the background. Now, there's this new fellow Dick White running British intelligence. They brought him over from M15, which is about like giving J. Edgar Hoover my job. But fortunately White's a good cop, and he's not establishment. He'll shake them up. He won't let them get away with any more Philbys. He'd choke them with their Old School Tie first.

"I said we weren't after quite the same thing, you and I, but I'm willing to give you a free hand provided you do something for me."

Dulles told him what he wanted.

Now Southard glanced at his watch. It was a few minutes past noon. Through the window of the café in Kreuzberg he saw a Volkswagen van pull to the curb. *Wannsee Landscape Gardening* was lettered on its side in German. Southard paid his bill and approached the van. After an identification code was used, the driver pointed to the side door. Southard got in, expecting to see the British chief of station, but the man who smiled at him and shook his hand said: "Hello, Mr. Southard, pleasure to meet you. I'm Dick White."

"What I don't understand," the head of the Secret Intelligence Service was saying ten minutes later as they drove west toward Wannsee, "is what they hoped to accomplish by the Novikov defection."

"It was their best chance to convince us Tarrant's reports were accurate. When he was passing them to us as coming from your Defence Ministry, we'd naturally suspect you wanted us to think you couldn't invade Suez—it is on, by the way?"

"Operation Musketeer. It's on for the beginning of the month as long as the Israelis move first."

"They don't have any choice but to move," Southard said.

"No, of course they don't. If they want our support they'll do it how and when we say. They're fighting for their lives."

"Anyway, Tarrant kept telling us you were nowhere near ready. If we knew the same information was being passed to Moscow by one of *their* people, we'd be more inclined to believe it than if—"

"Than if it were coming from us. Lovely," said Dick White. "Then tell me, why didn't you believe it?"

"A couple of reasons. Our U-2s took some pictures of Toulon and Malta. Besides, there were a few people in your Defence Ministry who were willing to answer some crucial questions."

Dick White expelled a long breath. "After Philby and Tarrant, I'm surprised you'd trust any of us."

"I can trust you, Mr. White. I was told I could by a man *I* trust."

"Yes, well, I . . . the maddening thing is, we're damned sure there were other moles recruited at Cambridge at the same time as Philby and Tarrant. But we're convinced Tarrant doesn't know who they are any more than we do."

"So we've found out as much as we can from him and sending him to Russia will be no loss. What we intend now is that the Russians, with a little help from us, will suspect this isn't just a case of the Old Boy net allowing one of

476

their own to escape prosecution by defecting. It's in our best interests to make them think we've doubled Tarrant to find out who the other moles are. He'd be the ideal one to do it. He already works for the GRU, and if he were a routine defector, they'd keep him on. As it is, we're effectively invalidating any information he offers them. Is he in Berlin yet?"

"The filthy sod flew in the day before yesterday. Eager to begin a new life. He's been told there's to be a swap, and he'll be released as soon as our man in the East Sector is. Not a shred of truth to it, of course," Dick White chuckled softly. "I can just see him explaining it to his GRU interrogators."

"What about the safe house? Did that go all right?"

"Perfectly. One of our people allowed himself to be followed there. As you'll see, it's the ideal location. A villa in a new development near Wannsee. Construction everywhere. They could hide a camera a hundred different places and those Exakta telephoto lenses they use are bloody good."

"Then we can figure they'll be photographing anyone coming or going?

Dick White said, "*We* wouldn't pass up an opportunity like that, old boy, would we?"

3

The photographs were taken from an electrician's truck parked outside a villa under construction diagonally across the street from the blown safe house. The film was taken twice daily to the East Sector and developed at the Normannenstrasse.

On Friday the twenty-sixth, a Volkswagen van belonging to a firm of landscape gardeners had delivered a man who was identified, after consultation with GRU-Wünsdorf, as

Kendall Tarrant, code-name Lazarus, a GRU mole in the Secret Intelligence Service.

Since it was the KGB, not the GRU, who had sent the defector Novikov to blow Tarrant's cover, the GRU had no way of knowing that Tarrant had been forced to defect.

On Sunday the twenty-eighth, the same Volkswagen van delivered two men to the SIS safe house. The photographer ran into bad luck that day. As he was about to shoot, a moving van came slowly past. Neither man was visible in the first exposure. In the second and third, the man on the left could be seen clearly. But the man on the right appeared only in partial profile in the third frame.

The man on the left, when the second two exposures were matched against MfS files, was identified as Dick White, new head of British intelligence. No one at first could identify his companion.

The presence of Dick White in the Wannsee safe house meant it was something really big. Though it was Sunday night, MfS chief Ernst Wollweber hurried to the Normannenstrasse. By eleven, operators were busily summoning all Westwork specialists then in East Berlin.

Erika Graf, who lived in suburban Pankow, was among the last to arrive. She had just returned from Munich the day before.

Erika had no trouble identifying the man on the right in the third exposure as Benton Southard.

Southard left the safe house at sunset with Kendall Tarrant in a two-door DKW. Southard, now hatless and wearing a shabby raincoat, was driving.

As far as Tarrant knew, Southard was a German who spoke little English. Tarrant's German was only fair. The tall, distinguished-looking Englishman had been brooding ever since his arrival two days before from London. But now that the hour of his defection had arrived, his spirits rose. They would find work for him in Moscow, important work. He was sure his control, so obviously an Anglophile, would be helpful. He even dared to hope that his wife Carol might one day be persuaded to join him. Awfully decent of the chaps to arrange a swap for him, but then, when you got right down to it, despite their ideological differences he was still one of them.

His German driver was uncommunicative. They drove east on Kurfürstendamm past the floodlit ruin of the Memorial Church, followed the Landwehr Canal for a while, then turned north on Wilhelmstrasse. The German parked. The streetlights had come on. The German got out of the car; so did Tarrant. One suitcase, minimal personal belongings. The only way to start a new life.

They were then just four blocks from Checkpoint Charlie, the sole entry point into East Berlin for foreigners. The driver pointed. Tarrant knew where he was. He saw the great bulk of the Brandenburg Gate looming against the sky. He was on his own now.

The driver did an unexpected thing then. He suddenly offered his hand to Tarrant. In automatic response, Tarrant shook it.

That photograph, taken on high-speed film, reached the Normannenstrasse late the same night.

4

Erika awoke from the dream in a cold sweat. She got out of bed and poured herself a glass of Kümmel. It had been a dream only in that she had been asleep.

The girl had come down with the flu. Even in the warmth of the greenhouse Erika could see her trembling. One morning when she made her rounds the girl wasn't there. Erika checked the barracks. Then she climbed astride the big BMW bike and raced past the administration buildings between the slave labor camp and the death camp. Ahead were the tall chimneys of the crematoria. The ovens never stopped working; a pall of sweetish, nauseating smoke hung over the camp. Erika sped past the well-tended lawns and the flowerbeds that covered the underground extermination room. Three SS men were standing near a small truck, smoking. It was their job to drop through the vents the blue crystals that would evaporate on exposure to air, releasing the Zyklon-B gas.

Erika could hear the music of the camp band. They were playing a medley from *The Tales of Hoffmann*. The doomed shuffled in a long column, five and six abreast, toward the huge metal doors open now to receive them. The sign over the doors said BATHS. Erika braked the BMW and rode slowly along the ranks of the doomed. They had just arrived in the cattle cars, Jews from Macedonia and Thrace. They believed they had been brought to Poland for resettlement, believed they were going now to shower and be deloused. But a few dozen slave laborers had been moved the night before to the holding barracks in Birkenau. They knew. Ukrainian guards with horsewhips kept them separate from the others. As she stopped the motorcycle Erika heard the crack of a whip. A prisoner's face was laid open from ear to chin. Others kept him from falling.

Then Erika saw the girl. Head bowed, she trudged forward with the others. Her hair was clipped short and stuck out in tufts from her scalp. She must have hurt her leg; she was limping. Erika pushed past the Ukrainian guards. One of them laid a hand heavily on her shoulder and tried to pull her away from the column of prisoners. They had stopped shuffling forward and stood watching. The other guards grinned when Erika shoved their comrade aside. His face flushed and he shouted, taking the coiled whip from his belt. Erika struggled with him for possession of it and won. The other guards were jeering openly at him now. Erika flung the whip disdainfully at his feet. She took the girl's arm and they went together to the BMW. The girl climbed on behind Erika without being told and clung to her as they raced away. Erika got her into the hospital and after a few days she returned to the barracks and resumed working in the greenhouse.

It would happen twice more. The first time the women in the barracks assumed the girl had been sent directly to the hospital. The second time, on her return, there were mutterings. Who was she, to be brought back from the dead? The third time they began calling her the ghost. They shunned her. They assumed the tall blonde who came on the motorcycle was using her sexually.

By the end of that year the fact that the girl had a protector was accepted and she was not taken to Birkenau again. She was painfully thin but she could still put in a day's work. Sometimes in the greenhouse Erika brought her a piece of hard sausage or a cold chicken leg, anything she could give the girl quickly. They never spoke. The girl feared her as much as the other women did. They called her the Valkyrie. They said she chose who would live and who would die. Once her hand touched the girl's when she slipped food to her, and the girl turned and ran. After that she left the food where she knew the girl would find it.

The months passed, the war retreated west from Russia to Poland, artillery flashed red at night on the eastern horizon, bodies were burned at a frantic rate in the ovens. By then security was lax, more and more guards were deserting. The camp underground grew bold. They shorted the stockade wires and, a few at a time, those prisoners who could walked off. No one tried to stop them that late in the war. Where could they go?

One day the girl was gone. Erika never learned whether

she had died or fled west with the others, away from the advancing Russians, away from the *stormoviks* and artillery. Erika left the camp a few days later and when the war ended she was in Leipzig.

Now in her apartment in Pankow she sat near the window drinking Kümmel and chain-smoking. The first meeting with Colonel Kossior had not gone too badly. She was the one who had unmasked the imposter, after all. Kossior was furious, but not with her. He had spoken by phone with Moscow and met with her a second time, with her and the man she knew as Klaus Steinbrenner.

Steinbrenner, the colonel said. It was Steinbrenner's fault. Steinbrenner knew the girl, he had talked to the girl, he had trained the girl, he had worked with the girl. Surely Steinbrenner should have suspected. But Steinbrenner had not.

That second meeting was not at GRU-Wünsdorf but at the Normannenstrasse, and Kossior seemed impatient. He had something else on his mind. Twice his phone rang, twice he spoke to Wünsdorf. The second time his benign, homely, bureaucratic face turned pale, and he dismissed her and Steinbrenner.

Erika's phone was ringing as she let herself into her garden apartment in the rear of the big old villa in Pankow. Minister Wollweber's office was calling. She went right back to the Normannenstrasse. Wollweber himself was in the room when she studied the Exakta prints and identified Southard shaking hands with a man near Checkpoint Charlie. When she returned to Pankow it was after one. The dream woke her two hours later.

Southard was in Berlin.

But the girl was in Egypt, and probably dead already. What could Southard do now?

The shock of seeing the girl with Southard had made her tell Steinbrenner. Otherwise, would she have denounced the girl at all? She would never know.

Southard was in Berlin.

The girl was dead by now.

But if somehow the girl was still alive?

Southard was here in Berlin.

She took the first *S-Bahn* in the morning into the American sector. She walked until the streets came to life with the new day. The post office in Potsdamerstrasse opened at eight-thirty. She gave the number to the long distance operator. It was fifteen minutes before she was directed to a booth.

"Herr Doktor Schneider's office."

"Is he in, please?"

"Herr Doktor Schneider is in conference."

He was invariably in conference. He detested the telephone. She knew that.

"He'll speak to me," she said. "Tell him it is Major Graf."

Ninety seconds passed, and then Reinhard Gehlen's voice came over the phone. "Is this some kind of joke?"

But Erika's voice and a reference to the Parr operation in March were enough to convince him of her identity.

I want to get a message to Benton Southard, she thought she would say. But what she said was, "I have to see Benton Southard." She knew then it was something she had to do herself. "I know he was in Berlin yesterday, and that's where I'm calling from."

"Did you know he's been looking for you?" Gehlen said uneasily. "He asked me to help him find you."

"Then that makes it easier, doesn't it?"

"Hardly. He holds you accountable for the death of his child. He intends to kill you."

Erika accepted that; if Gehlen said so, it was true. "Let me worry about that. Can you get a message to him? Can you set up a meeting?"

"I can get a message to anyone in West Germany," Reinhard Gehlen said matter-of-factly. "But why should I?"

"Because then I'll owe you a big one. Bigger even than what I did for you in March."

Gehlen did not speak for several seconds. Then he said, "Make it somewhere public."

"Yes, all right. The Victory Column in the Tiergarten then. Let's say every hour on the quarter hour, beginning at 6:15."

"And the same tomorrow evening?" Gehlen said.

"Tomorrow? Even tonight could be too late."

"I am not a magician."

"Yes, then tomorrow night too."

"You are a fool to do this."

"Just arrange it," she said.

Later that morning when she got back to the Normannenstrasse, Minister Wollweber sent for her.

He smiled thinly. "Sometimes, Major Graf, I think you lead a charmed life. You had an interview scheduled this morning with Colonel Kossior, I believe?"

"Yes."

"It would have gone badly. Moscow has terminated the Special Groups. He would have had to make scapegoats of you and this Steinbrenner fellow to save his own skin. But the situation's changed. Colonel Kossior was ordered back to Moscow unexpectedly this morning. Does the name Tarrant mean anything to you?"

"No."

"A British defector. He's being interrogated now. Colonel Kossior was running him, you see, and it appears that Tarrant was doubled. Kossior will have some answering to do in Moscow. He'll be far too busy to worry about you."

The mist rolling in from the Danube smelled of gunpowder and raw gasoline. Istvan had seen streetcar wires and power lines down all over the west bank of Budapest. Two overturned streetcars blocked the entrance to the Margaret Bridge. Behind them the tracks had been ripped up to make a crude tank trap. There were burned-out cars, and always the bodies of the dead. Not many Russian tanks had crossed the river yet, but they would come. Istvan had heard that they had broken through the barrier on the Chain Bridge to the south. But he had heard many things. He had heard that the Americans would come, or the United Nations.

Across the Margaret Bridge now two huge T54s came to a clanking stop and lowered their 75s. Istvan shouted to the men at the barrier to get out. There were dozens of Molotov cocktails in the overturned streetcars. A few men listened; most did not. The 75s began to thud, smoke puffing from their long snouts, the tanks rocking back. The first two shells fell short. Stones flew up from the roadway of the bridge. The second salvo screamed overhead and part of the wall of a riverfront building was blown away. By then Istvan was running. The 75s thudded again at the far end of the bridge and there was a direct hit on one of the overturned streetcars. It cracked open and spilled out benches and bodies and an enormous blossom of flame.

Istvan ran up the steep cobbled street. He thought that things would go better for them up here, especially in the rabbit's warren around Castle Hill. During the war the retreating Germans had made their final stand there; the artillery battle had ripped five hundred years off the city. From the rubble Castle Hill was being rebuilt not as it was before the war but as it had been in medieval times. Architects and masons, carpenters and glaziers, were finishing the job accidentally begun by Russian artillery during the Second World War.

There were tank traps now along the narrow cobbled streets of the new old town and the flow of water from burst mains had flooded excavation pits. In a courtyard behind an arched doorway men were making Molotov cocktails. Istvan recognized some of the bauxite miners from Magyaróvár. They hadn't been able to cross the river yet either. The real fighting, it was said, was on the other side. They were pouring gas and oil into wine bottles, beer bottles, milk bottles. They tore up curtains and clothing to be stuffed into the necks of the bottles as wicks. Istvan sat down and began to fill bottles. He did not remember when last he had been off his feet. He had not slept in the two days since they had entered Hungary. He heard explosions from the direction of the waterfront. By dusk the sky above the river was red. It looked like sunset—in the east.

A man came running into the courtyard. He was laughing and shouting and pounding people's backs. "The Americans are coming! I heard it on the radio. Hold out, they said, hold out."

A cynical voice asked, "Did they say *when* they were coming?"

It was Istvan. He felt the same way Noah Landler did now about Radio Free Europe.

"No, but why else would they tell us to hold out? They're coming, I tell you."

Istvan kept filling bottles, kept tearing cloth for wicks.

The tanks did not come up the hill that night.

A few minutes after dawn there was suddenly a shrieking in the air, and MiG-17s flew low over Castle Hill. They were soon gone, leaving the terrible roar of their afterburners behind. Then they returned, flying into the sun this time. They were so low that a few men with automatic rifles ran outside but the MiGs had already come and gone. Istvan left the courtyard. It did not seem possible that so much damage could have been done in so short a time. The cannons of the MiGs had pulverized the new old city on the slopes of Castle Hill. Istvan saw crumbled walls, collapsed roofs. Shattered glass covered the cobbled street. Istvan walked higher up the hill, then along the zigzag walls of the ramparts, still climbing but making his way south. Soon he reached King Sigismund's Gate Tower. The roof of the restored tower had fallen in. Dust was still settling as Istvan mounted the stairs of the tower, picking his way over broken roof tiles and beams. At the top he looked down across the zigzag ramparts and the new old town to the river. Even from here he could hear the faint rumble. T54s were crossing south of Margaret Island on the Chain Bridge and the Elizabeth and Petofi bridges. They came like toy tanks, scale models, but they came relentlessly. The overturned streetcars and burned-out cars looked like toys too. These toys were smashed. The tanks crossed the river and started up the hill. Istvan saw bursts of orange as Molotov cocktails were thrown.

He descended from the tower and hurried to Sword Street. The aid station had been set up in the steep-roofed Gothic building at Number Seven. Istvan entered the narrow street at the top and started down. Suddenly walls were crumbling around him and stones were flying. The Russian tanks had elevated their guns and were now lobbing shells blindly into the new old city. Yellow dust filled the air. The ground lurched under his feet. He fell and got up and fell again. The bombardment receded down the hill toward the waterfront as the guns were lowered. Slowly the dust cleared. Istvan went to the aid station. The front wall was smashed and men were carrying the wounded out on stretchers. They were all wounded in there except for the three doctors and the few women helping them. Someone shouted that Istvan should keep away, the roof might collapse at any moment. He went in. They were bringing the last of the wounded from the rubble. The dead they left where they were. He found Noah Landler seated at a small table near a window. The window glass had been blown out. Landler seemed to be resting, his arms folded on the table, head down. Istvan called to him and when he did not answer went over and shook him gently. Noah Landler slid sideways and then Istvan saw the blood. The blood was everywhere, on his shirt, on the table, in a puddle on his lap, on the floor. The gash across his throat was no longer bleeding but that was because all the blood that could had run out of him.

Chapter Twenty-nine

1

Southard spent Monday with Dick White hammering out the details of a report on the Tarrant defection that would satisfy the Home Office in London and Allen Dulles in Washington. It took far longer than it should have. The British station chief insisted on filing a minority report to protest the blowing of his brand-new safe house. Southard did not get back to the Hotel am Zoo until after a late dinner.

The hotel concierge handed him a gray envelope along with his room key.

Southard tossed the envelope on the desk when he entered his room. His back was stiff, his eyes felt gritty. He kept hearing the British station chief's petulant Oxbridge drawl as he lectured Dick White on the subject of Berlin real estate. He stripped and showered, then toweled himself dry and returned to the bedroom. He saw the envelope on the desk. No one except Dick White and the station chief knew he was here, and he had just come from them. He lit a cigarette and opened the envelope.

The handwritten note was dated today, the twenty-ninth, and instructed him to be at the Victory Column in the Tiergarten any hour on the quarter hour from 6:15 through 11:15. The gray stationery, the misspelling of the word *Vorteil* and the proxy signature Schneider authenticated the message as coming from Reinhard Gehlen.

Southard shaved and dressed. It was 10:30 by the time he finished. He debated arming himself. He put on his topcoat and shoved a short-barreled Sauer 6.35-mm automatic into the pocket.

It wasn't far to the Victory Column. He decided he could walk and still get there well before 11:15. He cut through the parking lot of the Zoo station. On the elevated tracks a train clattered by. He walked north beside the park and crossed the Landwehr Canal on a footbridge. Soon he was walking on the broad Strasse des 17 Juni—June 17 Street—which ran east through the Tiergarten. At the midpoint, in the center of the Grosser Stern, soared the column commemorating the last war Germany had won, in 1870.

June 17 Street commemorated something else. That was the date the construction workers had rioted in East Berlin in 1953.

2

Erika reached the south side of the Grosser Stern on foot at 11:12. Traffic roared around the circle. The gilded figure of Victory, over two hundred feet above the street on its red granite column, was floodlit. Erika waited for a break in the traffic and crossed. It was too late, she knew. It had to be too late by now. It seemed a lifetime ago that she had betrayed the girl to Klaus Steinbrenner in Munich.

As she neared the pedestal of the Victory Column on its island in the middle of the busy traffic circle, Erika saw Southard.

He watched her coming, the proud carriage, the lithe stride, the long blonde hair, the woman Gideon Parr had loved, the woman who had caused the death of Gideon Parr, the woman who had caused the death of Suzanne

Southard.

Why had Gehlen sent her here?"

He felt the weight of the Sauer in his pocket. No one else stood on the broad safety island in the middle of the Grosser Stern.

She was wearing a belted trench coat. In the cold night air he could see her breath as she approached. Headlights whirled around the Victory Column, flashing on red granite and bronze.

"Southard," she said.

"Erika."

She seemed to flicker like an image in a prewar newsreel as the headlights swept by. A gust of wind almost took his hat. He raised his hand and she swayed back away from him. Then she spoke. Her voice was harsh.

"The girl Jehan Khalid is in Egypt, with the fedayeen. They have been told she is an imposter. Can you get word to her?"

He had not known what to expect. Anything but this. Something tightened and twisted deep inside him.

He did not react in any way that she could see. She was going to tell him it might already be, probably was, too late. But she didn't. Knowing that would not help him.

He said, "How long have they known?"

"There's war. Fighting started in the Sinai this morning," Erika said, not answering his question. "The message might not have got through. You may still have time to warn her."

"Why are you doing this?"

She couldn't answer his question in any way that would make sense to him. My sister, she thought. I do not want my little sister to die a second time.

"I just have to. You wouldn't understand."

Headlights swung around the traffic circle, light and darkness flashing across his face.

"You're going to kill me, aren't you?" she said.

All he had to do was pull the trigger. The shot would not be heard over the roar of traffic. The single tongue of flame would be lost in the glare of headlights.

But she had come here to tell him this.

"Not that it will do any good," she said in that same harsh, unrelenting voice, "but I want you to know—I tried to call the assassin off in Washington. He'd broken contact."

Her voice changed. It was soft then and uncertain. "I'm sorry the child was killed, Southard. Now do what you have to."

She stood, waiting. Her eyes were shut.

He moved past her and plunged through a break in traffic and was gone.

Chapter Thirty

1

The report from Egypt was the last to reach the Mossad in Tel Aviv before the outbreak of war. It had come the usual way, from the embassy of a Western European country that also maintained a legation in Cairo.

A copy was sent by the Mossad to Shin Beth, and that copy went to Major Sam Brodsky, who now, at three o'clock in the morning in his office at the Defense Ministry in Ha Qirya, was trying to study it dispassionately. That was impossible. The report had come from the agent Raven, and Sam could not think of Raven as a Mossad code name, but only as Deborah Brodsky.

His office at that hour was possibly the quietest place in the Defense Ministry. Footsteps pounded along corridors, voices shouted, telephones rang. Even now General Dayan's paratroopers, who had dropped from sixteen DC-3s, were securing their position deep in the Sinai at the Mitla Pass, the gateway to the Suez Canal, and armored columns were racing across the desert to link up with them.

Sam Brodsky knew the war was necessary. What he did not like was the moral slant the Anglo-French planners had imposed on it. Israel would attack first across the Sinai, advancing on the canal. Egypt would of course resist. Britain and France would call for a cease-fire, which Egypt would not accept, not with Israeli troops camped on the canal. The Anglo-French would issue an ultimatum. Israel would accede, Egypt ignore it, and Anglo-French forces would move in to occupy the Canal Zone, ostensibly to keep the warring armies apart. All of this would, *de facto,* return control of the canal to England and France. The call for a cease-fire, the ultimatum, the invasion—it was all so transparent.

The moral implications troubled Sam Brodsky because the Anglo-French scheme all but buried the real and pressing need for Israel's preemptive strike against Egypt.

If anything proved that, once and for all, it was the report he was reading now.

Deborah had sent it two days ago. As of then, she had known only that the fedayeen were planning coordinated attacks throughout Israel. She still did not know exactly where or how soon.

The telephone at Sam's elbow rang.

"Major Brodsky."

"Sam, this is Marv Saunders over at the American Embassy."

"How are you, Marv?" The CIA station in Israel was small but first-rate, and Saunders, a political attaché, was station chief. He and Sam had done business together before. "What are you doing up in the middle of the night? *You're* not fighting a war."

"We just got a cipher from Berlin with a message for you. It's short, I can read it or have it sent over by—"

"Read it, would you?" Sam said, trying not to show his impatience. He had enough on his mind without having to worry about cryptic messages received by the Americans in the middle of the night from Berlin.

"It says, 'Inform Shin Beth Major Sam Brodsky that Mossad agent Raven blown to fedayeen recently stop Raven believed in Egypt now stop am flying Israel soonest end Sigma Seven.' That's all of it, Sam. Shall I repeat? Sam? Hello?"

"No, I heard it," Sam Brodsky said in a dull voice.

"I'd better explain the code. Sigma Seven's a big one—CE Europe. You know him?" Marv Saunders asked.

"Do I know who?" Sam wished Saunders would get off the phone. He wanted to think.

"The CE chief for Europe, Benton Southard. Because we had a TWX from Berlin station confirming he's on his way."

"What for?"

"Search me. But he's booked commercial flights as far as Turkey."

"We're closed to commercial traffic."

"I know. Southard planned to get an air force plane down from Turkey. The point is, the plane will radio prior to entering Israel airspace so—"

"Got you," Sam Brodsky said. "We won't shoot your boy down."

"Well, that's it then."

"Yeah. Thanks."

Sam got coffee from the pot on the hot plate. He read the Raven report again. It ended on an almost exultant note. "The next time will be by telephone. I'm coming in with the fedayeen."

Sam groaned, a sound of total despair.

War or no war, there were ways they could infiltrate—from divided Jerusalem, from Jordan, even from the sea.

And there were ways they could send messages in.

Was Deborah in Israel now?

That was the final terrible irony. Seven months living among the enemy, first in Egypt, then in Europe. And she would come home to die.

Andrei Golovin sat in the darkness waiting.

He had familiarized himself with the room: its dimensions, its furniture. Sofa. Low coffee table. Two wing chairs, with small table between. Sideboard. Dining table and four chairs. Lamp on small table. Light switch at the doors leading to the garden, French doors that opened inward, the only entrance to the apartment. Weapons available in the sideboard, flatware and a set of steak knives. Weapons available in the kitchen. But he would not let her reach the kitchen.

He got up and made his way around the room again. He could probably handle the darkness as well as she. Better, if you counted the element of surprise. But even if she hit the light switch to the left of the French doors, it wouldn't bother him.

He had run strips of cellophane tape across a pane of glass, tapped it with a rock, removed the single sheet of shattered glass held together by the tape, and reached in to unlock the door. That was almost two hours ago. The bedroom had been empty. That had surprised him. He had thought he would find her at home; it was already late. He liked the location of the apartment—in an ell off the back of the villa, as private as a separate house.

He had not decided to kill her until this evening.

It had almost seemed at first that Kossior would accept full responsibility, something unheard of both in the military and in the bureaucracy. But in the course of their meeting at the Normannenstrasse, Golovin could see that the colonel was already recognizing that blame—and guilt—always move downward in an authoritarian hierarchy.

That suited Golovin. Kossior's career was destroyed, no matter what, but he would try to shift as much blame as possible to his subordinates. Golovin would be protected by General Serov, and that left Graf. Her career was finished too.

But then suddenly Kossior was recalled to Moscow. There were rumors at GRU-Wünsdorf that he was involved with a defector still being run by the enemy. If so, Kossior would be tried, perhaps even shot.

And there would be no one left who needed Erika Graf as a scapegoat.

Golovin had accomplished his mission for the KGB. The Special Groups had been discredited, the project abandoned on orders from General Shalin. The GRU, in fact, could not dissociate itself from the fiasco fast enough.

But what Golovin had set out to accomplish for himself was still incomplete.

He would complete it tonight. Klaus Steinbrenner would, and then Klaus Steinbrenner would cease to exist.

Golovin waited in the darkness.

Erika came along the path past the big linden tree at the side of the garden.

She had taken the *S-Bahn* into the East Sector only as far as the Alexanderplatz station. She wanted to walk herself into a state of exhaustion. It hadn't worked. She felt drained emotionally but physically keyed up.

She unlocked the French doors, then shut and locked them from the inside. Only then was she aware of something, she wasn't sure what. She felt the surge of adrenalin through her body as she turned to face the darkness of the room. She was just reaching for the light switch when something grabbed her throat. She managed to hit the switch and the overhead light came on. She saw Steinbrenner. She brought her left hand up hard, surprising him, breaking his grip. With her right hand she chopped behind Steinbrenner's ear. His knees buckled and he staggered back from her and for one instant she stood immobile, not comprehending. Then he came at her again and she lunged for the sideboard. She was reaching for a knife when Steinbrenner got his arm around her hips from behind. The drawer came out and she fell back against him and they both went down with the contents of the drawer spilling all around them.

Golovin was astonished by her strength. Her blow to the side of his head had almost put him out. His ear still rang and it was hard to focus his eyes. Now she forced him over and down on his back. She was groping on the floor for a knife. He caught her wrist. The knife point touched his cheek, held there. She could not drive it into him and at first he could not force it away. But his head was clearing, and soon he began to move the straining hand that held the knife, move it and turn it, bending the wrist back. The knife clattered on the floor. Golovin put his returning strength into one convulsive movement that rolled them over twice. Even then it wasn't settled. Her elbow caught him across the bridge of the nose. She tried to gouge his eyes but he twisted his head away. He clubbed the side of her jaw with his fist. His breath came in ragged gasps but he was straddling her and his hands found her throat.

The light pulsed red. Steinbrenner's face seemed to expand and contract. Through the redness tiny circles drifted. She thought Steinbrenner was speaking. He was trying to tell her something. His voice came and went, and at first the words had no meaning. But then she understood. Golovin, he said. General Golovin. My father, he said. By then she no longer felt the pressure on her throat, but it was there. It pushed her down into herself where she saw the girl, the girl and Southard, and then Southard at the Grosser Stern, traffic flashing by,

Southard, who had not killed her because ever since that night in West Berlin three years ago her death had been waiting for her here.

Chapter Thirty-one

1

All day Russian tanks had been rumbling east out of Budapest. There were motorcycles too, and trucks to carry the wounded. Self-propelled 100-mm artillery rolled by, huge guns pointed backwards on the horizontal in case the retreating columns met resistance. But there was none. The Russians were leaving. That was all that mattered.

Cobblestones were torn up on Stalin Street and broken glass crunched underfoot. Istvan waited for the exultation. It did not come. He had crossed the river to Pest and there had been no tanks to stop him. He was too tired to exult and there was too much death on Stalin Street. No building was undamaged. Bodies lay in doorways and on street corners where they had fallen. Istvan saw a Russian soldier sprawled on the curb, his skull a cracked, empty shell. Black crepe flags hung from every building. No window that he could see was intact. People came from side streets. Walking north on Stalin Street they became a crowd. They flowed like a stream around a burned-out tank. Its treads had been forced off somehow. A dead crewman hung half out of the turret. Suddenly there was shouting. A tank, limping on damaged treads, clanked into Stalin Street, its turret scorched by gunpowder, its red star dulled with grime and dust. The crowd parted for it, jeering. There was something grotesque about the tank now that its gun was silent. It looked like a terrified elephant lumbering to overtake the fleeing herd.

Istvan heard talk in the crowd. The Russian occupation of Hungary was over. There would be free elections. Hungary would withdraw from the Warsaw Pact. Istvan was too exhausted to know what to believe.

Telephone lines dangled from their poles. Some high-tension wires were down. Sporadic gunfire could occasionally be heard far to the east, but it was like an echo or a memory only. Istvan passed a café. A truck carrying flour sacks had been hit by tank fire. The café terrace was white; it looked snow covered. Every chair was white and smashed. A few corpses lay there, dusted thickly with flour. Now trucks with red crosses freshly painted on their sides came slowly by. They were open in back and Istvan looked in at the wounded. Then came the other trucks, the ones with the words DEAD BODIES painted on their sides. Twenty trucks, thirty. The wind had died down and it was almost dusk. The smell of death hung in the air. Seeing the dead-body trucks had changed the crowd. There was an ugliness now. Istvan could feel it in himself. He saw the dead bodies and once again he saw Noah Landler, dead, seated at a table in a house on Sword Street on Castle Hill across the river. It was personal. That was the only way you could grasp it. They all had their personal dead. They began to walk faster. Many carried Russian semiautomatic rifles. Istvan carried one himself. They were moving with a purpose now, past the overturned streetcars, the piles of rubble, the broken walls, the dead that had not yet been picked up. It began to rain. Soon it was a drenching downpour. Istvan expected the crowd to disperse but it did not. The rain washed the air clear of dust and gasoline fumes and the smell of death. The crowd became silent except for the drumming of shoes on cobblestones. Istvan saw ahead where they were going. The grimy brick and plaster façade, pocked by shellfire now, filling an entire block — 60 Stalin Street, the AVO prison on the east side of the river.

Something told Istvan not to stay with the crowd, something told him to leave, to go somewhere else, anywhere else. It was the way he had felt when his father had driven him in the big black *amerikai* along this same street. Here, here was where Istvan had jumped from the car — rubble now, and even in the pouring rain the smell of death lingered. Istvan kept walking. The crowd had slowed and was spreading out to join others already surrounding 60 Stalin Street. A blackened T54 was overturned outside the main entrance, the rain washing grime and dust off its side so that its red star gleamed. Boys climbed on the tank, young boys, ten or twelve years old.

Suddenly there was an animal sound from the crowd, all their voices one brute voice. Istvan at first had no idea what it meant. Then he saw the white flag dangling from the balcony. It hung limp and rain-sodden. Istvan felt the rain streaming down his face. The crowd raised its single brute voice again. It parted for a group running heavily with a telephone pole that battered against the great metal-studded wooden doors barring the courtyard of Sixty Stalin Street. The telephone pole was carried back and then brought forward again, the men holding it on either side running hard, their faces contorted. The pole struck the doors and they shook. A third and a fourth time it struck the doors. Wood splintered. The pole was run forward again but just then the huge bolt on the inside of the double doors was released and the men carrying the pole went running with it, out of control, through the open doors and into the courtyard.

Again Istvan had the urge to leave. Instead he followed those who streamed through the wide entrance into the courtyard. Three black *amerikai* were parked facing the far wall and their headlights had been turned on against the gloom of the dusk and the heavy rain by the time Istvan went inside. A group of AVO officers in khaki with blue metal markings had been herded against the wall. They cowered in the brightness of the headlights in the rain. Rifles were raised but no one shot at the AVO. A strange thing had happened to the crowd. On entering the courtyard it became silent. No single word was spoken. When Istvan reached the cars there was still no physical contact between the crowd and the AVO. A small space separated them and it was as if no one wished to cross it. Then a hand reached out to pluck a blue badge from a khaki shoulder. A second hand ripped an epaulet. There was only the sound of tearing cloth and the rain. Then a rifle butt was thrust forward, a face smashed. AVO hands were raised in front of AVO faces. The one who had been hurt was dragged by the crowd across the narrowing space between them and the AVO. Istvan heard a muffled scream. The AVO with the smashed face was pulled down, then up and quickly sideways and back and forth. His cap was gone. He wore only tattered strips of khaki where his uniform blouse had been. He was dragged down again. The part of the crowd near him seemed to march in place in double time. They were stomping the AVO. Then the entire crowd surged forward with no sound but the shuffle of shoes on cobblestones. Istvan remembered the Fo Street cellars. He moved with the crowd. A second AVO was cut from the tight knot of khaki and blue in front of the headlights, and a third. Then, just before the crowd took all the rest, Istvan saw his father. He remembered the old man and his AVO son in Magyafovár, the pistol shot behind the ear. He could see his father but his father could not see Istvan because the light was behind him. Istvan could see in his father's eyes the blind terror, the slaughterhouse terror, and then he saw his father go down. The crowd moved. They might have been peasants trampling grapes at harvest. Istvan felt nothing. He went outside.

2

It was raining in Frankfurt too when Adam Prestridge's taxi stopped in front of Building D of the I.G. Farbenindustrie complex on the former Rothschild estate.

The U.S. Army had taken over the Farbenindustrie buildings, undamaged during the war although the nearby Rothschild mansion had been demolished. The second floor of Building D housed the CIA's European nerve center under the cover name Department of the Army Detachment. Prestridge walked past reception, nodding at the two MPs and the girl at the desk. His raincoat was folded neatly over one arm and he wore a three-button gray flannel suit. He passed through the teletype room, where six machines were clattering, to the telephone exchange. A separate room in the rear housed the scrambler phone closest to Munich, which was why Prestridge had flown here. He got through to the director of Central Intelligence in twenty minutes.

The discussion lasted less than half that time and it destroyed Adam Prestridge.

"Hello, Allen! It's good to hear your voice. I'd have been in touch sooner but—"

"I wish to hell you had," Allen Dulles interrupted. "Just what are you trying to do over there at Radio Free Europe anyway?"

"We've been telling them to hang on," Prestridge said excitedly, "telling them we're coming. What's holding the Pentagon up? They should have dropped supplies on Budapest days ago—machine guns, bazookas, antitank guns. And that regimental combat team in Wiesbaden ought to be airborne by now."

"Adam, no one in Washington ever seriously considered dropping hardware on Budapest. As for sending in troops, there's not the remotest possibility we could do that."

"What do you mean there's not?" Adam Prestridge shouted. "We'll never have a better chance to liberate Eastern Europe."

"Adam," Allen Dulles said, "exactly what is it about a third world war that appeals to you so much?"

"Who's talking about a world war? It's a calculated risk, sure. But if we move fast enough, the Soviets will have to back off."

"You've been out of touch, I'm afraid," Dulles told him. "How can we do anything about the Russians when our own allies are on the brink of invading Egypt?"

"Then the emigrés," Prestridge said. "My emigré army. At least let me send *them* in." His voice sounded unfamiliar to him, not his own voice at all, almost a whine. "A CIA operation, nothing to do with the military except for air transport."

"Adam, we both know those emigrés of yours never figured in any plans short of total war."

"But they're good. They're better than our own Rangers. Five thousand trained saboteurs, waiting for the chance to—"

"I'll grant you've done a fine job with them. But there's no point in discussing this any further. I want you to stop all RFE broadcasts to Hungary for the time being. They can only make matters worse."

"Stop all broadcasts . . ." Adam Prestridge echoed the words in disbelief. He removed his pince-nez and rubbed his eyes. He took off his jacket and loosened his tie. His hands were shaking.

"Believe me, Adam, I know how you feel." Allen Dulles's voice was gentle now, almost sad. "Don't you think

I wish there were something I could do? But I'm the DCI, not the president—and the president hopes to be reelected one week from today. What we *can* do is keep the world informed. So I want you to make sure you get good tapes."

"I thought you told me to stop the broadcasts," Adam Prestridge said.

"I mean tape what's coming out of Hungary, the broadcasts the Freedom Fighters are making. The ones they *will* make when the Russians come back in. The world must hear what it's like."

Prestridge did not remember hanging up. He was in the teletype room and then outside. The two MPs did not at first recognize the sweaty, coatless, somewhat disheveled man as Adam Prestridge.

As he left, the receptionist shook her head. Poor man, she thought, he must be coming down with something.

3

The precipitation that was rain in Budapest and Frankfurt fell as snow in Moscow. It lay ten centimeters deep in Red Square and inside the Kremlin walls. General I.A. Serov's black Zim cut fresh tracks to the mustard-colored building in the exact center of the fortress complex. The KGB chief arrived a few minutes after General Shalin of the GRU and in his eagerness to win everything that night he made a mistake. As he entered the small conference room, he heard General Shalin tell Khrushchev, who sat at the far end of the long, narrow table: "The Third World always judges the West more harshly than it does us. This is particularly true as long as our problems are confined to Europe."

I.A. Serov spoke immediately, not pausing to weigh his words. "Are you suggesting, general, that the bombing of a few airfields in the Nile Delta will be seen in the same light as the destruction of Budapest and the death of thousands of Hungarians?"

"Are *you* suggesting, general," Shalin shot right back at the KGB chief, "that we are not morally justified in putting down counterrevolution with whatever force is necessary?"

Khrushchev smiled and said nothing. His policy was well known to Serov—let them argue, let them go for each other's throats. Then neither would become strong enough to threaten the ultimate authority, as Serov's predecessor Lavrenti Beria had tried three years ago.

Serov, sensing his mistake, retreated from his position in good dialectical order. The verbal jousting continued for almost an hour, the trick being to oppose Shalin's views and arrive at a new stage in the argument which rendered them impractical, inoperative or, best of all, foolish. Shalin gave as good as he got. Both men were trained dialecticians. Finally Khrushchev got to his feet.

"The conversation has been enlightening," he said. "I thank you both."

The two generals quickly rose.

"You will stay, Serov."

I.A. Serov, his face impassive, watched the gray-haired, scholarly looking Shalin leave the small conference room.

Khrushchev resumed his place at the head of the table. He did not sit. Neither did Serov.

"He is finished, of course," Khrushchev said, "He will be out as soon as a suitable replacement can be found."

"A pity," said Serov dryly. "I rather liked the man. He was always so well meaning." In Khrushchev's vocabulary, he knew, *well meaning* was not complimentary. Intentions were irrelevant. Only results counted.

Khrushchev laughed. I.A. Serov smiled.

Then Khrushchev crashed a fist down hard on the table.

"You wanted his head. You have it. But you went too far."

"Comrade, you yourself gave me the tapes of your conference with him and his operations chief. So I assumed—"

"I said you went too far. To destroy your rival, you destroyed the credibility of the GRU itself."

"Not really," Serov said smoothly. "The idea of destabilizing the West by the use of trained guerrilla forces drawn from Western and Third World countries is sound. It failed only due to a typical GRU security lapse. But history is patient. The project can be tried again. May I suggest that the KGB—"

Again the fist crashed on the table.

"And who is Lieutenant Novikov?"

"We defected him in order to—"

"Tell me, General Serov. Suppose you saw a vicious, mutually destructive rivalry between two intelligence services in the West, what would you do?"

"Try to make it worse. Naturally."

"That is the opening you have given the enemy."

"With respect, I fail to see how," Serov protested.

"You used Novikov's apparent defection to damage the GRU by betraying their man Tarrant. This made it necessary for Tarrant to defect. It also made it possible for the CIA to double him. And there is evidence that's precisely what has happened."

"As long as we know," Serov said, "what's the harm?"

"I'll tell you the harm you've caused," Khrushchev said. His voice had grown softer. He would not pound the table again, Serov knew from experience. He had reached the more dangerous stage, the soft voice, the faint smile, the criticism that was worse than accusation.

"Tarrant will be debriefed, interrogated—twenty years with their intelligence service, can you imagine what we might have learned from him?"

508

Serov was about to speak, but Khrushchev silenced him with a gesture. "We will learn nothing. Worse than nothing. Because his purpose is to disinform us, isn't it? We won't know when he's telling the truth, when he's lying, when he only wants us to think he's lying."

"But there are collateral sources of information that can be used to confirm—"

"On the contrary," Khrushchev said. "Any source seeming to confirm Tarrant will be automatically suspect. *That,* comrade general, is the state to which you have reduced us. People who have been trusted for years by our intelligence services will be treated warily. In the absence of reliable information, the services will atrophy. It is true, comrade general, that caution is essential to your profession, but you have encouraged it to become paranoia. The results are apparent now on Znamensky Street. And before long you will see them at the Lubyanka."

Khrushchev stared down the length of the table. He waited ten seconds before speaking again. Then he said, "*If* you are there to see them, comrade."

Chapter Thirty-two

1

In Tel Aviv the afternoon was unseasonably hot for early November and the passengers complained when the No. 41 bus that ran south along Hakovshim Street to the old port of Jaffa was stopped for a check of identity papers. It was an ancient diesel bus, a relic; it vibrated alarmingly even while idling.

The man checking papers, a veteran of the 1948 war named Dov, had a wooden leg and was classified 3-C, a classification so safe, he would tell people, it was almost like the old Bob Hope joke—"3-C? That means in case of emergency you're evacuated before women and children."

3-C or not, the one-legged veteran of the 1948 war was once more serving in his faded khaki defense forces uniform.

This war was going well in the Sinai, but Dov couldn't keep up with the war of words—the French and British ultimatum, the protests from the United States, where Dov had relatives, the threats from the Soviet Union, where Dov also had relatives, the resolutions before the United Nations saying in diplomatic double-talk that Israel had no right to fight for survival even if there were fifty Arabs for every Israeli, all vowing to push the Israelis into the sea—it was far too much for Dov to follow.

He moved along the aisle of the bus checking papers. Thirty-five passengers, so it might take ten or fifteen minutes. Half the passengers were Arabs from the look of them. Not that Dov had anything against Israel's own Arabs—some of his best friends were Arabs; if you lived in Jaffa that was almost inevitable—but there was a war on and you couldn't take chances. A whistle hung from Dov's neck on a lanyard, and a billy club from his belt. He always forgot to put the billy club on the side with his wooden leg. It was less uncomfortable there.

"Papers, please."

Dov went slowly along the aisle. The floor rattled underfoot and there must have been a leak in the exhaust system because the bus reeked of diesel fumes.

This dark, handsome couple here, Dov guessed—Arabs or else Yemenites. They wore white slacks and shirts somewhat less than fresh, they had big dark eyes, and the girl had a thick, lustrous mane of jet black hair. Dov didn't care if she was a Yemenite, an Arab, a Maronite Christian, or what—she was a real looker. The two were brother and sister, no doubt about it, there was a definite resemblance. The young man was almost too pretty, even with the thick dark mustache.

"Papers."

They were, according to their papers, Arabs who lived in the north at Acre.

Across the littered aisle was another looker. Maybe not exotic like the girl from Acre, but pretty. Local, Dov decided. Nice Jewish girl. She wore a beige cotton blouse and skirt, somewhat less than fresh like the whites across the aisle, but with this unseasonable heat, and the humidity, what could you expect?

"Papers."

So much for the nice Jewish girl. Her papers were Israeli like those across the aisle, but she too was an Arab, and she lived in Jaffa, same as Dov. Her ID photo was not flattering. Were they ever?

He returned the booklet to her and as their hands

momentarily touched he felt a scrap of paper pressed into the palm of his hand. He looked then at her eyes. Dov was a bulky man and none of the other passengers could see her face the way he was standing over her. Her eyes pleaded. Dov pocketed the scrap of paper and continued along the littered aisle.

2

Less than three miles to the northeast, in his office in the Defense Ministry, Major Sam Brodksy was saying: "It's a funny thing. I'm usually lousy when it comes to faces, but I remember you. Last June in Washington. You were just coming out of Allen Dulles's house in Cleveland Park, and I was going in."

"Sure. You and Iser Harel."

It was late afternoon, 5:40, Thursday, the first day of November.

Sam poured two cups of coffee from the pot on the hot plate. "Now what's this all about, Mr. Southard?"

"Have you heard from her? Is she okay?"

"I wish to Christ I knew. The last we heard from her, she was in Egypt. She thought she'd be coming in with the fedayeen. Since then, nothing. Now, where does the CIA fit in?"

"She was involved in a GRU operation in Munich that—"

"You saw her in Munich? How was she?"

"I put her on the plane last Friday. Even though she was on her way back into Egypt, she wouldn't let me make a big deal of it—but you know Debbie?"

Sam studied Southard's face carefully. "That sounds kind of personal. You friends or what?"

"Let's hold that for later, all right? I got the warning from an MfS officer that Debbie's cover was blown and we

512

telexed Saunders to pass the warning to you."

"An MfS officer? Why would he do that?"

"Not he, she. And I don't know why she did it."

"Then maybe it isn't true," Sam said with a faint note of hope in his voice.

"Not a chance," Southard told him. "You said she'd be coming in with the fedayeen. Could she be here already? What are you doing to find her?"

"What are we doing?" Sam asked, offended. "Tel Aviv alone has three-quarters of a million people. How can we hope to find her? She's got to come to us. And she hasn't." Sam looked at Southard's coffee mug, which was almost full. He refilled his own. "That's what breaks your heart. There's nothing you *can* do. Just wait and hope. Every time the phone rings I think it's going to be her. If I don't go home at night I think maybe she's there waiting. I telephone my own place." Sam shook his head. "You got any kids, Mr. Southard?"

Southard stared out the window. "No," he said.

"Well, if you did you'd know what I mean. And it's more so with Debbie and me, because she's adopted. You see, she was a survivor of Auschwitz and—"

"I know. She told me."

"—I brought her and a bunch of Jewish DPs here to Israel."

"I know that, Debbie told me all about it."

Sam gave him a perplexed look. "She did?"

"In France last April."

"You know each other since April?"

"That's when we met, yes. Why?"

"I was just wondering. What I still don't get," Sam said, "is why you flew here."

"I almost didn't make it. The air force said they couldn't fly me into the war zone unless it was official business. So I found a Turkish crop duster to fly me in. That's why it took so long."

"Then if it's not official business, what is it?"

Sam finished his second cup of coffee. He poured a third.

"I had to be here," Southard said.

"Why?"

"Because of Debbie."

Sam drank the third cup of coffee. "Mr. Southard," he said, "are you married?" He added quickly, "I was just wondering."

"I was. I'm divorced."

"Oh, I'm a bachelor. Never found the right woman, I guess. And Debbie always sort of . . . well, you know . . . she was keeping house for us ever since I adopted her so I—"

The phone rang. "Yes?" Sam said irritably. As he listened, his face changed. "Send him right in." He spoke quickly to Southard. "Guy's doing a security check on a bus. Girl hands him a note for me."

The man wore khaki, and had a slight limp. He looked nervous.

"Where was she going?" Sam asked.

"No. 41 bus, major. Carmel Market to Jaffa."

"When?"

"Forty, forty-five minutes ago."

"Where's the note?"

Dov took out the scrap of paper. Sam smoothed it on the desk. "It's hard to read," he told Southard. "I'm not even sure it's her handwriting."

"Hold on a minute. We still don't know it was Debbie who gave him the note."

Sam got a photograph from his wallet. Dov looked at it and said, "That's her all right."

"She's alive. Thank God, she's alive," Sam said.

Southard asked Dov, "Was she alone?"

"How can you tell, on a bus? I don't remember her talking to anyone."

514

"A brother and sister," Southard siad. "A little older than the girl who gave you the note. Dark brown eyes. Hair jet black. The girl's is probably long. The boy may be wearing a mustache. Both about medium height. Complexion lighter than most Arabs."

"They sat right across the aisle from her. Arabs from up north in Acre."

"Could you be sure they were going all the way to Jaffa?" Southard asked him. "Does the bus make any stops on the way?"

"There's a stretch of bombed-out road there on the way in. You know the place I mean? That's where I lost the leg in '48. Arab sharpshooters were using the minaret of the old Hassan Beq mosque. They had a clear field of fire all the way to Hayarkon Road. I was in the platoon that flushed them out. Anyway, no stops until Jaffa."

After Deb left, Sam and Southard turned to the note that Deborah had penciled in tiny script on the scrap of paper. It said:

Crossed from Jordan Tuesday night with twenty fedayeen trained in explosives. Split into groups headed Jerusalem, Haifa, Herzliya, Tel Aviv, Jaffa, Beersheba, Rehovot to mount simultaneous bombing attacks. Trying to learn exact locations, time. Am with Husaynis at Aleytsion Hotel, Jaffa.

Sam picked up the telephone.

3

They got off the bus at the Jaffa waterfront, Deborah and Maryam each carrying a shopping basket. Andromeda's Rock rose out of the turquoise sea just beyond the harbor entrance. There were a few small boats but the port of Haifa and Tel Aviv's own new port had left the harbor at Jaffa a commercial backwater. Except for a few warehouses still in use, it was given over now to restaurants and cafés.

Deborah was elated. Daddy Sam had surely read her message by now. The man on the bus was a member of the defense forces; when he saw the note was for Major Brodsky of the Shin Beth, he was certain to deliver it.

They had been in Israel almost two full days, Deborah with her old Jehan Khalid papers, the twins with documents supplied by the Mukhabarat.

They had flown to Jordan and crossed the border at night in the desolate country near the Mountains of Moab. A man in a truck had picked them up and delivered them to Beersheba, where the three-man teams separated. After that it was public transportation, security checks everywhere, and for Deborah the fear always that someone—an old schoolmate, a friend, a co-worker from Kol Israel—might recognize her.

The twins had been with her always. She'd never been able to get away by herself for more than a few minutes, and never far. She couldn't chance using the telephone; there was no one Jehan Khalid would plausibly be calling. She had written the note last night in the bathroom of the hotel here in Jaffa.

The Aleytsion Hotel stood on the opposite side of the large central markets from the covered streets of the bazaar. As usual, no privacy for Deborah. Not that they were suspicious of her; it was natural for Maryam and Deborah to share a room. The twins knew people at the Aleytsion, fedayeen sympathizers; the manager of the dingy, foul-smelling hotel surely was one. Deborah had heard Sulayman talking to him.

Now the three of them were sitting on the jetty. The sun was low on the horizon. Deborah sat with her back to it, looking toward the warren of streets that was the Old Town. It seemed more Arab than Israeli—the men wearing headcloths and robes, the laden donkeys, the sidewalk peddlers, the mounds of dates and open melons swarming with flies.

The twins were facing the Andromeda Rock offshore, Maryam with her legs drawn up and her arms around her knees.

"I was thinking," she said. "If all goes well, we'll be back in Jordan tomorrow night, and in Cairo the day after."

Deborah herself could get on a No. 41 bus and be home in an hour. The temptation had been almost irresistible earlier that afternoon when they had gone into Tel Aviv to shop. Every bustling street, every balconied apartment block, the raw newness, the feeling that the city was growing right before her eyes—Deborah was home and she was homesick. In Europe she had never been so far away.

But then they got off the bus at the Carmel Market, and Deborah had no more time to think of herself. The shopping expedition might tell her part of what she needed to learn. Sulayman went off alone, leaving Deborah to accompany Maryam.

Their first purchases seemed innocuous enough—three small flashlights shaped like fountain pens, a spool of insulated copper wire, a couple of rolls of electrician's tape, a pair of scissors. But the quantities and the manner of purchase of the remaining items revealed to Deborah the pattern she was looking for. They went to four hardware shops to buy a total of twenty-four 1.5-volt batteries. And in the jewelers' quarter they spent an hour and a half going from shop to shop until they had a dozen cheap pocket watches.

Everything they needed to make twelve timing devices for explosives.

Now it all was packed in two shopping baskets at Deborah's feet on the jetty. And from what Maryam had just said, the bombs would be put together tonight.

Sulayman tossed a pebble into the water. "It looks like we'll have to get along without cousin Yasir."

"He may still make it," Maryam said. "Cousin Yasir was never on time for anything in his life."

"If I know cousin Yasir," Sulayman told her, "he's probably made up his mind to stay sick in bed in Cairo until we get back."

"Don't worry. We'll do fine without him, now that Jehan's with us again." Maryam turned to Deborah, reached out and squeezed her hand. "I still can't get over it, Jehan dear, the way you walked in on Monday just exactly when we needed you most. Honestly, it was—"

Sulayman stood abruptly. "Let's get something to eat. It's going to be a long night."

As they left the jetty, Deborah's mind was racing. A long night? But that hardly made sense. You don't kill people by blowing up a train station or a public building or a marketplace in the middle of the night. Then what had Sulayman meant?

By 8:30 they had finished dinner and were walking along Aleytsion Street. It bisected the old quarter and ran past the central markets, deserted now, and the flea market, still full of noise and confusion, toward the narrow covered streets of the bazaar.

They weren't going back to the hotel. The hotel lay in the opposite direction.

They passed through a wide gateway. Deborah knew the bazaar. She'd often come here to shop, as often just to look. There were woodcarvers and coppersmiths, rug merchants, basket weavers, potters, glassblowers. There were sellers of ivory and jade and semiprecious stones. There were dealers in used furniture and "antiques" which you could watch being created before your eyes.

It was nearly closing time but the din in the covered streets was terrific, shoppers still crowding the stalls and haggling with fierce joy. It was all so congested, all such a jumble that it was hard for Deborah to tell if the shops spilled into the covered streets or the streets spilled into the open-fronted shops.

There were no doors anywhere. None were needed. When the last merchants left and the bazaar was shut for the night, roll-down iron shutters would seal off all five entrances.

From the street of so-called antiques they turned left past the ivory and jade shops. Chessmen were being taken in for the night, displays of jade jewelry returned to their cases. They entered the street of the rug merchants. The shops were larger here, the oriental carpets piled knee-deep on the floor. They passed the basket weavers and Deborah began to think they we going to leave the bazaar because ahead were only the tobacconist and the exit that led to Taib Tabitha Street. But another turn took them along the street of the potters. Deborah saw jugs and bowls, vases, candlesticks, lamps, and finally a narrow shop where ceramic figurines were displayed. They went in. There were no customers. The ivory chessmen were duplicated here in clay. There were lifelike statuettes of water-carriers and donkeys, of camels, of old men smoking nargilehs, of all the artisans in the bazaar plying their trades—basket weavers, glassblowers, potters, the lot.

A bead curtain parted in the rear of the shop and a man beckoned. The back room was small. Deborah saw a table, four chairs, and shelves cluttered with unglazed clay figures.

"Peace be with you," the man said. He was tall and thin with a purple birthmark on his left cheek.

"And with you, Yusuf," Sulayman said quickly. "Has Yasir come?"

"No, but if he does they'll let him in."

Sulayman was immediately wary. "Who will?"

"Rashid has the keys."

"Open those iron shutters in the middle of the night, and you'll wake the dead."

"No, there's another way in. A small door on Kabir Street. The sweepers use it. But they won't be coming tonight."

Sulayman shrugged. "It hardly matters. Cousin Yasir probably won't be either."

Deborah heard a noise on the other side of the curtain. Yusuf went out to deal with a customer. Soon he was back.

"They came Tuesday," he said. "There they are on the top shelf, the twelve apostles."

Deborah looked at the shelf and saw only a row of unglazed clay figures like the others.

Outside a whistle shrilled. The police were coming through to shut the bazaar for the night.

"How bad will it be?" Yusuf asked.

"Don't come in the morning," Sulayman told him.

"God be with you," Yusuf said, and was gone.

Deborah heard the shrill of the police whistle, more distant now. Footsteps shuffled past outside, voices faded. There was silence.

Then suddenly a loud scraping sliding sound was followed by a clanging crash. The first of the bazaar's iron shutters had been pulled down and secured for the night. The second, third and fourth banged down. Then there was another silence.

A small lamp burned on the table in the little room behind the curtain. Outside, the covered streets of the bazaar were now almost night dark.

The final iron shutter crashed down.

Maryam and Deborah put their shopping baskets on the table and began unpacking them. Out came the scissors, wrapped in a sheet of newspaper. Out came the penlights, the rolls of tape, and the spool of insulated copper wire. Flashlight batteries were unwrapped, two dozen in groups of six. And last the watches, twelve cheap pocket watches that Deborah laid in a row.

Sulayman nodded approvingly and placed beside the row of watches a plastic bag containing tiny screws, the sort used in the hinges of eyeglasses. Then he took from his pocket a small soft leather case. He opened it to reveal a set of miniature jeweler's tools.

He went to the shelf where the figures Yusuf had called the apostles stood. They were about eighteen inches tall. Bearded and robed, they did have a biblical look, with eyes turned heavenward and arms crossed in a pious attitude. He took one of them down and put it on the table.

"Not a bad setup, is it?" he said. "Nobody would think of looking for us in here because there's no way we can get out until morning. Who'd willingly lock himself in?" Sulayman smiled. "So that gives us the whole night, undisturbed. Of course, without Yasir we're going to need it."

He picked up the biblical figure and tossed it to Maryam, who held it a moment and smiled before giving it to Deborah. It wasn't as heavy as it should have been, not if it was solid clay. And it had the sticky feel of plasticine.

Two explosives, TNT and hexogen, Deborah remembered from her training, mixed into a rubber compound base. You could cut it into strips or sculpt it. Cousin Yasir, at El Mansûra, had often amused himself by carving likenesses of Ben-Gurion or Golda Meir. You could attach it to any surface—say, the underside of a table or the chassis of a car. You could detonate it with fuses or blasting caps.

Yasir was a superb *plastiqueur* and without him the

521

work would go slowly. But that was no problem. As Sulayman said, they had the entire night.

"The beautiful part of it is," he was saying now, "that when they open up in the morning we just mingle with the crowds and walk out."

Deborah now knew where, at least here in Jaffa. And after they converted the pocket watches into timers she would know when. It had to be early in the morning, the first crowds of the day. The sooner it was, the less likelihood that any of the plastique bombs would be found.

But even if her message had been delivered to Major Brodsky at the Defense Ministry, what good would it do? It told him she was at the hotel on Aleytsion Street.

And she was locked in here for the night with the Husayni twins.

Chapter Thirty-three

1

Iser Harel did not reach Sam's office until shortly before midnight. He had been in the Sinai at the site of an overrun fedayeen base.

"Brand new weapons," he was saying, "cases of them. Kalashnikovs and Model 40s still—"

"Iser," Sam interrupted, "we've heard from Debbie. She's here. She's in Jaffa." He showed Harel the note. "This came this afternoon."

"What have you done so far?"

"We've got two men watching the hotel, but no sign of her or the Husaynis."

Harel looked at Southard. "Is there some Washington connection I don't know of? What's the CIA's interest?"

"We have none," Southard said. "I'm here on my own."

Iser Harel gave him an appraising look. "Well, if Major Brodsky is satisfied, so am I."

The phone rang. Sam picked it up eagerly. But it was only one of his men calling from Aleytsion Street to report no change at the hotel.

Of the two girls Deborah was the more dextrous, so she constucted the timing devices while Maryam worked on the apostle figures.

From the base of each figure Maryam removed a plug of the claylike plastique. Inside was a hollow space, a balsa-wood cylinder with the black button of an electric blasting cap visible at the upper end, and a pair of insulated wires leading from it. Maryam fished out the wires and left one dangling loose. The other she taped to the positive terminal of a battery, which she shoved into the cylindrical cavity. Then she clipped a length of wire from the spool and taped it to the bottom of a second battery, which she shoved in after the first. Making sure the pair of wires protruding from the base were safely separated, Maryam replaced the plug.

Deborah sat across the table from her in the back room of Yusuf's shop. She had already removed the crystals from the pocket watches. Next, using the tiny magnetized screwdriver and tweezers in the tool kit, she removed the minute hand from each watch. That left the most difficult part. First she scratched a dot on each crystal about two-thirds of the way from the center to the rim. Then she began to turn the tiny drill from the tool kit in the first crystal. That one went all right, and the second. The third cracked, and Deborah held it up to the light, squeezing the rim gently between thumb and forefinger. It would be all right, she decided.

All right? What was she thinking of? The work had become an end in itself, its purpose obscured by its tedious nature. Making time bombs to blow up the bazaar in the morning, *all right?*

But what could she do?

When she finished drilling the last hole, Deborah went to work with the tiny screws and the wire. She removed enough insulation to run a double loop of wire around each screw, just under the head, and let a few inches trail. Later, this wire would be spliced to the one leading to the batteries.

With the magnetized screwdriver Deborah inserted a wired screw in the hole she had drilled in each watch crystal. Then she asked Maryam, "What time? Did he tell you what time?"

"No, but here he comes."

Deborah heard Sulayman's returning footsteps too. He had been outside, selecting locations for the plastique time bombs. He came back whistling. He was enjoying himself.

"I've found a dozen perfect spots already, and I've only been over half the bazaar," he said. "How are you two coming?"

He picked up one of the plastique apostles and looked at its base. "And the timers?"

"All I have to do is put the crystals back in," Deborah said.

He studied her work. "Nice," he admitted, "very nice. Set them for 9:15. I want all twelve to explode within minutes of each other. It will be crowded at 9:15." He went out again, whistling.

Deborah began to replace the crystals, orienting them with the screws just past the nine on each watch face. Again she had that odd, terrible feeling of being proud of the expert work she was doing, as if the replacement of watch crystals had nothing whatever to do with the manufacture of time bombs, nothing to do with terror, nothing to do with death. She put in the fifth crystal, then the sixth. She flexed the fingers of her left hand. The shaft of each tiny screw was long enough to contact the hour hand of the watch but not the watch face. When everything was wired together, this contact would detonate the blasting cap to explode the plastique.

Maryam was looking at Deborah. "It gives you a funny feeling, doesn't it? I mean, you're using a tiny screwdriver and drill and I've got a roll of tape and some batteries, and it doesn't seem like much, what we're doing, but in the morning right here in the bazaar maybe a hundred, maybe two hundred people will die. They're in bed now. They're sleeping. Or say a woman gets up in the middle of the night to feed her baby. They don't know this is the last night of their lives. Maybe they're dreaming. Or making love. Or maybe in Tel Aviv right now someone's writing a letter, and in the morning he'll take it to the post office on Allenby Road—"

Deborah kept her eyes on the watch in her hands but her mind was now all on Maryam's words.

"—and that's the last thing he'll *ever* do."

"Stop it," Deborah said. "What's the sense in talking about it like that?"

"You sound as if you don't like it," Maryam said, surprised.

"Do you?" Deborah challenged. She thought: Allenby Road post office. That's one. Keep her talking. Keep her talking.

"It's something that has to be done. Liking it has nothing to do with it."

"No, that's not what I mean," Deborah said. "The bazaar here, the post office in Tel Aviv—we'll be killing some of our own people. That's what's bothering me."

"It can't be helped. At least we'll keep it to a minimum. Why do you think we set the operation for a Friday?"

"Of course, I see now. For the Jews, it's the day before the Sabbath, the busiest day of the week. But for us it *is* the Sabbath. There won't be so many of our people in the places where the bombs are."

"There shouldn't be any at all in Jerusalem." Maryam laughed; it was not a pleasant sound. "How many Arabs do you find at World Zionist Headquarters?"

"Is *that* the place we're going to hit in Jerusalem?" Deborah said. "Perfect. Oh, that's beautiful."

"You mean you don't know what the targets are? No, of course you don't. You only joined us right before we left Cairo. I'll tell you," Maryam went on softly, her eyes glittering in the lamplight so that for an instant Deborah thought she could see through them into Maryam's soul. "No two targets alike. No pattern. No way for them to predict where we're going to strike. Here the bazaar. The post office in Tel Aviv. The Zionist headquarters in Jerusalem and the Weizmann Institute of Science in Rehovot. The lobby of the Sharon Hotel in Herzliya. And in Haifa? The big bus terminal on the waterfront near the Dagon Silo." Maryam's voice had fallen to a whisper. "If you want to know the truth, I *do* like it. Will a man here in Jaffa suddenly decide to come to the bazaar in the morning? Will a woman in Haifa take the train instead of the bus? One to die, the other to live? It's like being a capricious god, isn't it? Because we don't know who's going to die but we're going to kill them."

Maryam stared at her hands for a long moment. "Beersheba's the exception. We *do* know who's going to die there. Our own people, in a way, yes—but they fought for the Israelis in 1948, fought against us. So it's retribution, isn't it? Wouldn't you give a lot to be with the group in Beersheba that's blowing up the Bedouin Clinic?"

Deborah was resetting the eleventh crystal, but her fingers were trembling so much she had to stop. They were making bombs—here, in Haifa, in Jerusalem, all over the country. In the morning those bombs would kill people. She even knew exactly where.

And there was nothing she could do to stop them.

3

Cousin Yasir got the last bus from Beersheba. His papers identified him as a Lebanese businessman. He was wearing a suit but no tie and had shaved the beard stubble off his face. He looked at his reflection in the window of the bus—the protuberant eyes, the flat wide nose and fleshy lips, the receding chin—not exactly beautiful. But at this moment, traveling through the night from Beersheba to Tel Aviv on a half-empty bus, he felt powerful. Knowledge, as the grand mufti had always said, was power.

He wondered if they had already gone ahead without him. If they weren't at the hotel he would find Rashid. Rashid would know and Rashid could let him into the bazaar. But maybe he should find Rashid first in any event. A hotel was too public a place now. Yasir was frightened.

It was fright that had kept Yasir at home in Cairo on Tuesday. Half an hour to destroy a jeep and a bus near the Jordanian border was one thing. Hiding in Israel for Allah knew how many days was another.

But the knowledge he possessed now had overcome his fright, had made him come into the enemy country. He had lived with the knowledge a day in Egypt, a day in Jordan, unable to use it. But in thirty minutes the bus would be in Tel Aviv. Then a taxi from the station to Jaffa, find Rashid, find his cousins. . . .

Yasir had been entrusted with the the information by a captain in the Mukhabarat, and he would deliver it.

The bus sped through the moonlit night. Yasir felt important. He felt strong.

4

They parked a block from the Aleytsion Hotel under the iron-roofed open shed of the central markets.

Southard and the Shin Beth man named Porush waited in the unmarked Chevy. Porush wore a filthy white shirt and gray trousers. He had a long nose, heavy beard shadow and small dark eyes punched deep into his face. Major Sam had chosen well: Porush looked like an Arab and if Southard saw him behind the desk of a seedy hotel in the middle of the night he would not have looked twice. Southard watched Sam and the second Shin Beth man disappear into the hotel. They were inside five minutes and came out with a man who might have been Porush's brother.

"They're not there," Sam told Southard. "Haven't been in since this morning. Rooms 7 and 9. This fellow will answer some questions and then get put on ice." Sam opened the car door and gave the night porter a little shove. He told Porush, "It's not exactly the Ritz, but here's your chance to play hotelkeeper."

"I don't even *stay* in hotels much," Porush said.

"There's only twelve rooms, no room service, no ice, no room phones, and every room is taken. You think you can manage?"

Porush smiled. "I'll try."

"The night porter's name is Mustafa and he took sick."
Southard and Porush went to the hotel. The car drove away.

5

Sulayman brought a pack of American cigarettes back from the tobacconist. He put his feet on the table and began to smoke, seemingly in no hurry about anything.

Maryam gave him a look. "It's almost two o'clock," she said.

"What are you worried about? There's plenty of time." Sulayman picked up one of the watches and examined it. "Not bad." He started to hum. He examined a second; soon he had looked at all the rest.

He began drawing a rough floor plan of the covered streets of the bazaar, marking with an X each location where he wanted a bomb placed. He kept humming.

Maryam watched him impatiently.

"Look, I said there was no hurry," he told her. "These watches are Hong Kong's best, if that. They won't be wildly accurate. The later we set them running, the less time they'll gain or lose. If they all go off at once, or almost at once, the panic will be even greater. It won't be just the bombs that kill. People will trample each other to death."

He said it so matter-of-factly.

Deborah knew that each of the twelve figures contained enough hexogen and TNT to demolish a good-sized room.

Cousin Yasir got off the bus at the main station on Mezion Street in Tel Aviv at 2:20 A.M. The bus had been delayed at two security checkpoints on the Beersheba-Tel Aviv highway. Each time Yasir had pretended to be asleep so that his nervousness would seem only the disorientation of a foreigner awakened suddenly in the middle of the night on a bus traveling through a country at war. His papers were good. There had been no problems.

But the security checks took time. When the bus pulled in over an hour and a half later, few taxis were waiting on Mezion Street.

Cousin Yasir couldn't get one all to himself. He refused the offer of a shared ride and began walking instead down Jaffa Road.

Shortly before two-thirty, Major Sam returned driving the Chevy. Two Shin Beth noncoms were with him. In the trunk of the car were four Uzi submachine guns.

Sam parked in the darkness under the corrugated roof of the central markets. One of the noncoms went to the hotel and a few minutes later came back along the dark street with Southard.

"Find anything?" Sam asked.

Southard shook his head. "A change of clothes, a couple of small suitcases—that's it. What about the night porter?"

"Fedayeen connections, no doubt on that score. We'll let him go in a day or two, keep a watch on him, maybe turn up something. But that's not going to help us now."

They looked at each other. Deborah was here with the

Husaynis, somewhere in Jaffa. It was an ancient, cluttered town, a maze of crooked streets, climbing to the hill still strewn with rubble from the 1948 war, a town of dilapidated tenements and dingy shops, of abandoned warehouses sharing the waterfront with shuttered restaurants—Deborah could be anywhere.

Chapter Thirty-four

1

Rashid was eighty-two and he needed very little sleep. He was night watchman at one of the few warehouses still in use on the decaying Jaffa waterfront. Rashid walked through the warehouse every hour or so, hearing the scurry of rats among the sacks of grain and dried beans. He spent most of the night outside. A high moon, not quite full, hung over the water. Rashid sat on the jetty and dreamed. He was young again, he was serving in the bodyguard of Haj Amin al-Husayni, the grand mufti of Jerusalem and the spiritual leader of the Arabs of Trans-Jordan and Palestine. He went everywhere with the mufti, the mufti depended on him. Even into his sixties Rashid was a strong and active man. Then suddenly it had ended. During the war the grand mufti had come out publicly in favor of Germany, the Nazis, Adolf Hitler. He had fled Jerusalem one step ahead of the British army and spent the war years in Berlin. He was back now, a has-been.

Still Rashid maintained his interest in the Husayni family. At first he had seen promise in the mufti's young twin cousins, but now they disappointed him. They were dedicated, but arrogant and contemptuous of the very people they aspired to lead. Rashid did not believe their leadership would survive long. But then, neither would he. Rashid was an old man.

He wondered if Yasir would come tonight. Cousin Yasir interested him more than the twins. Ingratiating to the point of servility, yes, but Rashid thought he would outgrow that. Cautious to the point of cowardice, but Rashid thought that might be to his advantage. Dead leaders become only martyrs. Besides, Rashid believed that if a man was not born brave, he learned to compensate. A kind of intellectual stealth was one way of doing that. Yasir had it. The trait was not thought ill of among the people; it was necessary for survival in a harsh world. Once out of the shadow of his cousins, Rashid believed, Yasir might find himself. He wheedled but he was persuasive. He complained but he was innovative. And with his homely face and unbeautiful form, Yasir looked every inch the fellah, the man of the land.

Rashid believed that one day Yasir, who as a child had taken the name of the great Arab hero Yasir al-Birah, might amount to something. Yasir Rahman Abdul Rauf Arafat al-Qudwa Al- Husayni would be a man to reckon with. Unlike the twins, he had been wise enough to drop the al-Husayni. The grand mufti was finished. Why remind people you were related to him?

Rashid was walking back to the warehouse when he saw Yasir approaching.

"May peace be with you," Rashid greeted him.

"And with you peace," replied Yasir.

Rashid expected him, in the flowery old style, to spend a few minutes speaking of anything but what had brought him. But in this Yasir disappointed the old man. He said, "Where are my cousins? At the hotel?"

"No, this is the night, in *sha*'Allah."

"In *sha*'Allah," said Yasir without much spirit. "So they are in the bazaar?"

Rashid said they were.

"*Yallah*," said Yasir. "Let's go."

2

Maryam came out of the jade and ivory shop silently, startling Deborah. Both of them were barefoot, their shoes in Yusuf's back room. Barefoot they were more surefooted in the near darkness.

They were distributing the bombs.

Each watch was wired now, stem to blasting cap and tiny screw to batteries, each wound up and set to the correct time, each wedged securely into the piously crossed arms of its apostle figure.

One of the time bombs had been fixed to the underside of a display case occupying one side wall of the jade and ivory shop. That was their fifth. One to go. Sulayman had taken the other six himself.

They were walking toward the Taib Tabitha Street gate, the main entrance to the bazaar. Just inside it, across from the tobacconist, was the bazaar directory, a large board on which each shop, each craftsman, was indicated by a stylized symbol.

The last of their time bombs would be placed here at the entrance, wedged behind the directory board.

Deborah was carrying the plastique apostle cradled in her arms, the apostle in turn cradling the watch that would detonate it in five and a half hours.

It would, that is, if it stayed the way it was set now.

The glow of a high moon filtered through the skylight in the sheet-metal roof above Deborah. She could see the luminous dial of her own wristwatch; it read 3:45. She could see the beard of the apostle and the crossed arms. She could see the stem of the watch protruding. But, wedged in as it was, she could not see the watch face itself.

She would have to do it by feel.

If only she could stop, stand for a moment, use her flashlight, even take the watch from the apostle's arms. But Maryam was walking at her side.

How far forward should she reset the watch? If she could see, could do it accurately, how many hours would she advance the timing device?

Ideally, almost a full five hours. The sooner the bomb went off, the sooner the police came, the sooner she could tell them the other locations so they could be evacuated and the bombs removed.

She tried to remember the feel in her fingertips as they were setting the watches an hour ago. But what good would that do? The watches were not identical. A full turn of the stem might advance the hand one hour, two hours, even more.

Too little, and the bomb would not explode soon enough to give the police the time they needed. Too much, and the bomb would explode now, in her arms, blowing her to pieces.

Try to set the watch forward three hours then? Make it 6:45 on the watch now. That would detonate the bomb at 6:15 real time, wouldn't it? *Wouldn't* it? Suddenly she couldn't think. In the darkness the numbers were whirling before her eyes, without meaning.

She pulled out the stem, her fingers damp with sweat. For an awful moment she thought the stem had turned. Then what? What time did the watch say now?

But no, she hadn't turned it yet—she didn't think she had.

For an instant longer she waited. Then she gave the watch stem almost two complete turns and pushed it in with her thumb.

The directory board wasn't flush with the wall. It hung from a pair of hooks just inside the corrugated iron shutter that closed the Taib Tabitha gate. Cool night air seeped in at the edges of the shutter.

Maryam lit her flashlight. "Here, let me do it."

"No, that's all right, I've got it."

Deborah wanted to position the bomb as close to the iron shutter as possible. She had no idea whether the explosion would destroy it, but at the least it ought to blow the shutter off it tracks. She felt behind the directory board, eased the bomb in.

It was done. It would work or it wouldn't. The phrase went through Deborah's mind—in sha'Allah. She couldn't help it. She had been with them too long.

They were walking back to Yusuf's shop.

Suddenly Maryam put a warning hand on her arm. Deborah could hear the voices too. They went closer and stopped again. They listened.

Even after all these months Deborah recognized cousin Yasir's wheedling voice.

"I'm telling you," he was saying, "they showed the photograph to the real Jehan Khalid's father in prison. Whoever she is, the girl's not Jehan Khalid."

Deborah stood frozen for an instant, her mind a complete blank.

Then she shoved Maryam forward and turned and ran back the way they had come.

The covered bazaar was shaped like a ladder with three rungs, with Yusuf's shop located in one of the uprights. Deborah turned into the first cross street. Barefoot, she ran silently. At first she could hear running footsteps behind her. Yasir, Sulayman, probably both. She ran past the three lamp shops, stopped, heard only her own breathing.

But that didn't have to mean anything. She knew Maryam was barefoot. Maybe the others were too now. In the faint glow from the skylight she could see nothing, no one, the whole length of the cross street. Stay where she was?

She backed into a shop, one of the lamp shops, she thought.

Her elbow touched something. By the time she realized what it was, by the time she reached out blindly in an attempt to keep the stack of copper pots from tilting and falling, it was too late.

The tower of pots overturned, clattering, rolling, clattering again.

She jumped. She hadn't known you really did that when you were scared out of your wits, but that was what she did. Then she ran. A single shot crashed and she saw the spurt of flame ahead of her.

She spun and ran the other way, turning on to the street of carpet merchants. She went into the deeper darkness of the first shop. She was drenched in sweat.

Think, she told herself. Think.

And then she had it. It was so simple, why hadn't she thought of it in the first place? All she had to do was find a telephone. There had to be phones in the bazaar. Find a shop that had one, call the police, and then just wait for them.

She lit her penlight. Its narrow beam picked vibrant strips of color out of the darkness as it moved across the rugs displayed on the walls. Then she saw what had to be the corner of a desk. She went to it, played the flashlight beam over it. No phone. She slipped out of the shop and into the one next door. She half felt, half saw her way to a large counter running along one wall. The narrow beam of light again. A wooden box of some kind, a pen in a base of onyx or marble, a leather-bound blotter, a ledger. No phone. But there had to be one somewhere. How could they do business without a telephone? Well, rug merchants maybe, nobody called to say I'll be over later this afternoon to pick up a flying carpet, hold one for me. She giggled at the thought. And realized she was close to hysteria.

Sulayman knew, from the floor plan supplied to him by Rashid, the location of all eight telephones in the bazaar. He went directly to each shop that had one, following the shortest route, found the phone, and yanked the wire from the wall. Once he ducked into one of the potters' shops, hardly more than a hole in the wall. He thought he heard footsteps. His hand went to the gun tucked in his belt.

Silence. Perhaps he hadn't heard footsteps after all. He went to the next shop that had a phone.

Deborah finally found it in a furniture shop. She stood for a few seconds, just looking at it—black, old-fashioned, tall stem with mouthpiece at the top, receiver on a hook at the side. Then she shut her flashlight and picked up the receiver. Five minutes? Ten? How long would it take the police to come?

She had done it.

She put the receiver to her ear. She heard nothing. She spoke softly into the mouthpiece. "Hello, hello?" She jiggled the hook where the receiver had rested. No sound. Jiggled the hook again. Did they shut the lines at night? But that didn't make sense, they never shut phone lines at night, did they? The penlight again. She found the wire that led from the phone to a box at the base of the wall. The wire came free in her hands. It had been ripped out.

She was shaking. She held the loose wire and thought of nothing. Think, she told herself. You've got to think. But there was nothing to think of. Either they would find her or they wouldn't. Either the bomb would go off in time or it wouldn't.

She burrowed deeper into the shop.

4

A few hundred yards away at the central markets, Sam Brodsky was sitting on the fender of the Chevy. It was twenty to five. Waiting this far from the hotel bothered him, but waiting any closer would be worse. Here under the roof of the market shed, even the car wasn't visible from the street.

And Porush was at the hotel. Take it easy, Sam told himself. If they come, you'll know it.

The windows of the car were rolled down. The two Shin Beth men sat in the front seat smoking.

Every now and then Southard would prowl the nearby streets. He moved well; in seconds he would be part of the darkness, and when he reappeared it was without warning and almost at Sam's side.

He did so now.

"Anything?"

"I'm not sure. It wasn't that close. It could have been a car backfiring."

"Where?"

Southard pointed down Aleytsion Street. "Someplace over there."

"If it was a car," Sam said, "it would have to be on the other side of the bazaar."

"What about the bazaar itself?"

"Nobody there," Sam said. "It's locked up tighter than a drum at night."

5

"Just shut up, will you?" Maryam said softly. "She's in here somewhere and she can't get out, not until they open the gates. Now let's go find her."

Yasir groaned but followed her past the glassblowers' stalls. The darkness was alive all around him. Yasir kept to the middle of the street, away from the deeper darkness of the shop entrances, but the street was so narrow he could almost span it if he stretched his arms wide.

There was only one telephone left. Sulayman went to the tobacconist's and yanked the wire from the box. Then he lit his flashlight and studied the directory board, trying to determine where the girl who called herself Jehan Khalid might be hiding.

Deborah was in the rear of the furniture shop, on the floor behind a divan that smelled of dust and age. It was dark in the shop but she could see dim gray light where it opened on the street. The luminous dial of her wristwatch told her it was 5:50.

Only half an hour to go if the bomb she had put behind the directory board exploded when it was meant to.

Even with three of them looking for her, they might not find her before then.

Maryam and Yasir had finished searching the first cross street, the one which housed the coppersmiths. They could either turn right toward jade and ivory or left toward the street of furniture shops. The latter seemed a more likely hiding place. Maryam wasn't certain if Sulayman had been there or not. But then, if he had, Jehan might have doubled back.

Deborah heard them coming. If she made a run for it they would shoot. If she stayed where she was there was always the chance, however small, that they might not find her. She saw them silhouetted in the shopfront—Maryam and the plump figure of cousin Yasir.

Maryam came in at once, probing ahead with the narrow beam of her flashlight. Yasir waited at the entrance.

Maryam reached the jumble of hassocks on the other side of the divan.

The light touched Deborah's face as she got up to run.

"Don't," said Maryam gently.

6

Now that it was over, Yasir wondered why he had been

542

afraid. Not that the fear had paralyzed him. It had only made him careful.

She was just a girl, a Jewess probably. He was walking at her side, his hand gripping her arm, as if pursuit, discovery, capture had all been his doing.

Maryam came behind them with the gun.

The skylights spaced along the roofed-over street were gray with predawn light. From the far end of the street near the Taib Tabitha gate Yasir saw Sulayman coming toward them.

"We've got her," Yasir called. Mild exultation only. He'd delivered the message. The message was the important thing. Anyone could have found the girl really. Nothing to it.

Yasir remembered, later, feeling the girl's arm tense under his touch when she saw Sulayman. He remembered that Maryam had come up on her other side, was walking even with them—and then there was a shattering brilliance, and Yasir was hurled from his feet.

7

Southard grabbed a submachine gun and was running while the explosion still echoed along the street. He held the Uzi at his side, steel stock folded along the barrel. He heard Sam and the two soldiers pounding behind him. A hundred yards ahead he could see smoke rising from the gateway to the bazaar. He thought he saw a figure duck through it and vanish around the corner.

Let me be in time, he kept thinking. Let her be alive. He realized he was praying.

Cousin Yasir knew only that something had gone

terribly wrong.

He could hear nothing. Blood ran from his ear. He remembered getting to his feet. The girl who was not Jehan Khalid sat watching him, staring straight at him, or else she was dead, her eyes staring like that. He touched the blood running from his ear. Concussion. Nothing, nothing. He went through the smoke and felt his way along a shattered wall. He thought he heard Maryam's voice. That didn't stop him. Nothing would stop him now. He had to get out. He reached the corrugated iron shutter. It had buckled outward but was still intact. He pushed it. The shutter gave. It hung askew in the gateway. Yasir slipped outside. He ran through the smoke. His ears rang and he saw double for a moment. Concussion. Nothing, nothing. He knew a doctor, right here in Jaffa, a Palestinian, who could take care of him. He knew someone who could hide him.

Yasir Arafat turned the corner and was gone.

8

Southard came in seconds later. The smoke was clearing. He saw the man he recognized as Paul Faure and knew was Sulayman Husayni getting to his feet. Except for the left sleeve, Sulayman's shirt had been ripped off. There was blood on his chest, blood streaming from his nose. There was an automatic in his hand and he said something twice, harshly, in Arabic. He was pointing the automatic at the ground where Deborah sat, legs stiffly out in front of her, gazing up at him, ready to die. Kneeling near Deborah was a woman. Her white clothing was scorched and she had no eyebrows. There was a second automatic, this one on the ground out of the woman's reach, out of Deborah's.

Southard heard the iron shutter bang behind him as Major Sam came in. Then Southard squeezed the trigger of the Uzi. It bucked against his side and Sulayman was flung against the wall, the stream of bullets seeming to pin him there upright a long moment before dropping him.

That was when the woman screamed her brother's name and ran into the line of fire.

Epilogue

1

Allen Dulles propped his left leg on a hassock and gazed into the fire. Three seasoned applewood logs glowed on the andirons. Outside, the first snow of the winter was falling on Washington. It was the day after Christmas—what the British, Allen Dulles thought, called Boxing Day. The British had little to celebrate as 1956 entered its final week.

The small upstairs study in the Highlands Place house was warm. Despite the twinges in his foot, Dulles felt a sense of well-being. He was surrounded by the photographs which summed up his career; Allen Dulles's network of friends in high places was globe-spanning. You placed your bets early and if you won enough of them you could one day call on the leaders of political parties, of armies, of nations, for what you needed. This Allen Dulles had done brilliantly.

He went to the desk and thumbed through the thick report he had read this morning. Benton Southard had spent over a month on a fact-finding mission to Tel Aviv, to London and Paris, to Munich and Vienna. The report was impressive. Southard did not share that urbane bonhomie which had always served Dulles so well. He was not a fanatic like Adam Prestridge. Nor was he a chameleon like Gideon Parr. Southard was a seeker after truth, one of those driven men who had to pursue the truth no matter where it led. It made him, in his very different way, as competent as Allen Dulles. No, Dulles told himself, more so. Southard was the perfect intelligence officer.

He had, the day he left for London six weeks ago, told Allen Dulles he would resign from the Agency on his return.

Dulles smiled as he flipped through the pages of the report.

There was no question that the Hungarian Revolution and the Middle East war, occurring simultaneously, affected each other.

The question was whether they had been simultaneous by accident or by design. Put another way: How effective was the GRU campaign of disinformation aimed at the United States?

On the balance sheet of winners and loser, Russia came out, at least in the short run, on top.

Red Army tanks were already streaming back into Hungary as Anglo-French paratroopers landed in the Suez Canal Zone. Within a week the revolt was crushed, with twenty-five thousand Hungarians dead. It took the UN another month to condemn the Russians, and the Soviet empire remained intact.

UN condemnation of Britain and France, by contrast, was instantaneous, with the United States leading the condemners. Britain and France withdrew from Suez. Their empires, already moribund, died in 1956.

America did not, as Eisenhower and John Foster Dulles hoped, gain ground with the Arabs. No Arab government believed Washington was ignorant of the plans to invade Suez. They believed Washington only said it was.

Egypt was a partial winner. When the canal was cleared of scuttled ships and reopened next year, Egypt would still control it.

Israel was also a partial winner. She had destroyed fedayeen bases and broken the back of the Egyptian army. She had bought time in her fight for survival. But there were still fifty hostile Arabs for every Israeli.

Dulles flipped to the end of the report.

On the balance sheet of history, Southard had written, Russia might ultimately lose more than she had won.

The messianic aspect of Communism, which had beguiled the Third World for so long, was now revealed as a fraud. If Russia could not win and keep converts by ideology, she would do so by force. The Kremlin, its ideology unmasked as opportunism, might find itself besieged by that ultimate weapon, truth.

Allen Dulles returned the report to his desk and stoked the fire. Embers sparked and flew up the hearth.

The report raised as many questions as it answered. But the truth always did. And besides, the report had served its real purpose admirably.

Allen Dulles lit his pipe. A surprisingly youthful smile played across his features.

Returning from Europe, Southard had not mentioned his resignation. He was once again a man with a vocation. He couldn't resign. There was still too much to learn.

The smile faded slowly from Dulles's face. He could even hope that, with luck, the world they all inhabited would not destroy Benton Southard as it had Gideon Parr.

2

Among the tens of thousands of Hungarian refugees who crossed into Austria on the bridge over the Einser Canal, the so-called Bridge at Andau, was Istvan Varady. Things went easier for him than for most—he already carried an Austrian passport.

He enrolled that winter at the University of Vienna, where he began his medical studies. He remembered saying once that Noah Landler had more important things to do than practice medicine. That he could have spoken those words seemed impossible to him now. He himself had to become a doctor, to take Noah Landler's place. He did not need to tell Friedl that. She knew.

3

On Capitol Hill they soon regarded Ad Prestridge as a plain talker who said what he meant and meant what he said. Good old Ad was a bit of a glad-hander and backslapper maybe, but they were used to that on The Hill. Ad was, after all, a lobbyist, touting the virtues of the CIA. Ad wore loud plaid jackets and heavy horn-rimmed glasses and he had begun to put on weight. He was soon known as a drinker, a four-

Martini-lunch man, but that was all right, in fact it was just fine, because an astute Congressman could sometimes get good old Ad to reveal a secret or two, nothing world-shaking but it impressed the folks back home.

Adam Prestridge spent more and more time drying out at the Agency R&R Center at Big Stone Gap, where he would garrulously tell anyone who would listen how we had blown our last chance to roll back the Iron Curtain.

Early retirement with full pension seemed likely.

4

In Moscow, the trial of Colonel Kossior was as swift as his punishment was lenient. Kossior was exiled for five years to the town of Osetrovo in Eastern Siberia.

His wife did not accompany him. The filthy settlement on the Lena River, a place of long winters and much drunkenness, she felt, was no place for their daughters Tatiana and Feodora.

General Shalin of the GRU was transferred to command of the provincial garrison at Alma Ata in the Kirgiz SSR.

General I.A Serov of the KGB was transferred to command of the GRU. The Central Committee felt he could bring his considerable administrative talents to bear on the GRU, where morale had fallen as the KGB star had risen. Serov could not regard the transfer as a step up in his career, but only as punishment.

Serov suffered one irony most acutely. He had hoped to revive the Special Groups but, before he left the KGB, he had ensured that the project would never again be left in the hands of the GRU.

Serov also, like Shalin before him, began to suffer from insomnia. He worried about Andrei Golovin. Golovin knew just how Serov had sabotaged the GRU that he now headed.

To ingratiate himself with A.N. Shelepin, his new boss, Golovin might talk. Shelepin was young, the youngest KGB chief ever, and he was ambitious. Serov did not know who in his own office was Shelepin's man. But there had to be someone. The KGB had watchdogs everywhere, Serov knew that.

Shelepin had his own problems. Previously KGB watchdogs, infiltrated into all parts of the Soviet bureaucracy, had been accepted with resignation. But when Serov was transferred, he took a list with him, and neutralized almost every KGB watchdog in the GRU. Inspired by his example, other departments made a determined effort to ferret out their own watchdogs. The KGB's efficiency was impaired. Before long it was whispered that Shelepin was too young for his job.

5

Southard fingered his pearl stickpin nervously and surveyed the guests that crowded the downstairs rooms of the big house on Highlands Place. A good share were from the State Department or the diplomatic corps and looked perfectly comfortable in morning clothes. Southard was not, but since it was his own wedding reception, he had not expected to feel comfortable.

At his side Deborah greeted people easily, getting all the names right. She had only been here six weeks, but already, this New Year's Day of 1957, she seemed to know half the embassy people in Washington. Now she brushed back her veil and bent her head to exchange a confidence with Mrs. Abba Eban. The wife of the Israeli ambassador had appointed herself Deborah's special protector.

Southard smiled, wondering what it was about Debbie that made people want to protect her when, as she proved daily, she didn't need it at all.

He had barely got her to Washington in November when Allen sent him back overseas. He urged her to come with him. But she said no, Washington would be her home now and she wanted to get to know it. By the time he got back, she had found the house they would live in on Massachusetts Avenue north of Embassy Row, signed the lease, and half furnished it. She had absorbed everything about American life instantly, including, Southard thought ruefully, the advantages of a charge account at Woodward & Lothrop.

Southard looked down at her, and the gamine smile, the brave tilt of her chin, stirred in him again that instinctive protective urge.

It was what he had felt the day he met her, and what he felt that awful morning in Jaffa when he found her in the bazaar with Sulayman's gun pointing at her. Only much later did he remember that he had ever deliberately intented to kill Sulayman Husayni. When it happened, he was no longer thinking of revenge, but only of Deborah.

Now she smiled up at him and whispered that it would just be another hour or so, and then they could go home. Deborah had vetoed the idea of a honeymoon. They had both, she said, traveled enough in 1956.

Allen Dulles was feeling expansive. He could not remember an occasion when he had been more pleased to act as host. He thought Deborah would make a fine wife for Southard. And, he knew, Southard would make a fine deputy director for intelligence, as soon as the Senate confirmed his appointment. His talents had been wasted in counterespionage. Because he was good, he had naturally been taken into the CE elite. But he belonged in pure intelligence—he was a man who had to know.

Dulles flagged a passing waiter and took a glass of champagne.

Toward the end of the reception, Lieutenant Colonel Sam Brodsky put on his coat and went outside. A few inches of snow lay on the ground and the wind was cold, rattling the winter-bare branches of the big elms and sycamores.

Sam thought back to the bazaar in Jaffa, the moment after he had come in behind Southard. Deborah was on her feet. Sam did not recall if he had helped her, or if Southard had. But for an instant she just stood back and looked at both of them and then she walked to Southard and he took her in his arms as she said, over and over, "You're here, you're here," and Sam felt, along with the joy at her deliverance, a sudden acute sense of loss. It did not leave him when, seconds later, she was hugging herself against his chest and laughing and crying at the same time.

Now, in Washington, Sam returned inside. At first, as he entered the crowded room, he felt disoriented, like a foreigner at a party where he doesn't speak the language. Then he glimpsed the bride across the room in conversation with two of those attractive young Radcliffe or Smith College types who always moved in Allen Dulles's Washington circle. That glimpse, across the long crowded living room, told Sam all he had to know.

Deborah looked more American than the two women she was talking to.

It was, after all, Sam told himself, only fair. He had left America to settle in Israel. Now his daughter was completing the exchange.

BESTSELLING ROMANCES BY JANELLE TAYLOR

SAVAGE ECSTASY (824, $3.50)
It was like lightning striking, the first time the Indian brave
Gray Eagle looked into the eyes of the beautiful young settler
Alisha. And from the moment he saw her, he knew that he
must possess her—and make her his slave!

DEFIANT ECSTASY (931, $3.50)
When Gray Eagle returned to Fort Pierre's gates with his
hundred warriors behind him, Alisha's heart skipped a beat;
would Gray Eagle destroy her—or make his destiny her own?

FORBIDDEN ECSTASY (1014, $3.50)
Gray Eagle had promised Alisha his heart forever—nothing
could keep him from her. But when Alisha woke to find her
red-skinned lover gone, she felt abandoned and alone. Lost
between two worlds, desperate and fearful of betrayal, Alisha
hungered for the return of her FORBIDDEN ECSTASY.

BRAZEN ECSTASY (1133, $3.50)
When Alisha is swept down a raging river and out of her savage
brave's life, Gray Eagle must rescue his love again. But Alisha
has no memory of him at all. And as she fights to recall a past
love, another white slave woman in their camp is fighting for
Gray Eagle!

*Available wherever paperbacks are sold, or order direct from the
Publisher. Send cover price plus 50¢ per copy for mailing and
handling to Zebra Books, 475 Park Avenue South, New York,
N.Y. 10016. DO NOT SEND CASH.*

THE BEST IN HISTORICAL ROMANCE
by Sylvie F. Sommerfield

KRISTEN'S PASSION (1169, $3.75)

From the moment Kristen met wildly handsome Captain Morgan Black, she knew this savage pirate had captured her soul—and that she had stolen his heart!

SAVAGE RAPTURE (1085, $3.50)

Beautiful Snow Blossom waited years for the return of Cade, the handsome halfbreed who had made her a prisoner of his passion. And when Cade finally rides back into the Cheyenne camp, she vows to make him a captive of her heart!

REBEL PRIDE (1084, $3.25)

The Jemmisons and the Forresters were happy to wed their children—and by doing so, unite their plantations. But Holly Jemmison's heart cries out for the roguish Adam Gilcrest. She dare not defy her family; does she dare defy her heart?

TAMARA'S ECSTASY (998, $3.50)

Tamara knew it was foolish to give her heart to a sailor. But she was a victim of her own desire. Lost in a sea of passion, she ached for his magic touch—and would do anything for it!

Available wherever paperbacks are sold, or order direct from the Publisher. Send cover price plus 50¢ per copy for mailing and handling to Zebra Books, 475 Park Avenue South, New York, N.Y. 10016. DO NOT SEND CASH.

MORE ENTRANCING ROMANCES
by Sylvie F. Sommerfield

DEANNA'S DESIRE   (906, $3.50)
Amidst the storm of the American Revolution, Matt and
Deanna meet—and fall in love. And bound by passion, they
risk everything to keep that love alive!

ERIN'S ECSTASY   (861, $2.50)
Englishman Gregg Cannon rescues Erin—and realizes he must
protect this beautiful child-woman. But when a dangerous
voyage calls Gregg away, their love must be put to the test. . . .

TAZIA'S TORMENT   (882, $2.95)
When tempestuous Fantasia de Montega danced, men were
hypnotized. And this was part of her secret revenge—until
cruel fate tricked her into loving the man she'd vowed to kill!

RAPTURE'S ANGEL   (750, $2.75)
When Angelique boarded the *Wayfarer*, she felt like a
frightened child. Then Devon—with his captivating touch—
reminded her that she was a woman, with a heart that longed to
be won!

*Available wherever paperbacks are sold, or order direct from the
Publisher. Send cover price plus 50¢ per copy for mailing and
handling to Zebra Books, 475 Park Avenue South, New York,
N.Y. 10016. DO NOT SEND CASH.*

THE BEST IN HISTORICAL ROMANCE

PASSION'S RAPTURE   (912, $3.50)
by Penelope Neri
Through a series of misfortunes, an English beauty becomes the
captive of the very man who ruined her life. By day she rages against
her imprisonment—but by night, she's in passion's thrall!

JASMINE PARADISE   (1170, $3.75)
by Penelope Neri
When Heath sets his eyes on the lovely Sarah, the beauty of the
tropics pales in comparison. And he's soon intoxicated with the
honeyed nectar of her full lips. Together, they explore the paradise . . . of love.

SILKEN RAPTURE   (1172, $3.50)
by Cassie Edwards
Young, sultry Glenda was innocent of love when she met handsome
Read deBaulieu. For two days they revelled in fiery desire only to
part—and then learn they were hopelessly bound in a web of SILKEN
RAPTURE.

FORBIDDEN EMBRACE   (1105, $3.50)
by Cassie Edwards
Serena was a Yankee nurse and Wesley was a Confederate soldier.
And Serena knew it was wrong—but Wesley was a master of
temptation. Tomorrow he would be gone and she would be left with
only memories of their FORBIDDEN EMBRACE.

PORTRAIT OF DESIRE   (1003, $3.50)
by Cassie Edwards
As Nicholas's brush stroked the lines of Jennifer's full, sensuous
mouth and the curves of her soft, feminine shape, he came to feel that
he was touching every part of her that he painted. Soon, lips sought
lips, heart sought heart, and they came together in a wild storm of
passion. . . .

*Available wherever paperbacks are sold, or order direct from the
Publisher. Send cover price plus 50¢ per copy for mailing and handling to
Zebra Books, 475 Park Avenue South, New York, N.Y. 10016. DO NOT
SEND CASH.*

THE EXCITING RICHMOND SERIES
by Elizabeth Fritch

RICHMOND #1: THE FLAME   (654, $2.75)

Amidst the rage and confusion of the Civil War, Melissa Armstrong fights a personal battle for an ominous goal: to maintain loyalty to her family—without losing the man she loves!

RICHMOND #2: THE FIRE   (679, $2.75)

Now, in Richmond, Melissa knows a passionate love for a Cavalry lieutenant who helps her forget the only home she's known. If only she could forget that their destinies lie on opposite sides of the flag!

RICHMOND #3: THE EMBERS   (716, $2.95)

If time could heal a nation stained with the death and blood of the Civil War, perhaps Melissa's heart would mend one day also. But she never really believes it—until she rediscovers love.

RICHMOND #4: THE SPARKS   (962, $3.50)

Two years had passed since the Civil War had ravaged the land, and Abby Weekly knew that Richmond was the place to begin again. But as the state of Virginia struggled for readmission into the Union, Abby found herself torn between two men: one who taught her the meaning of passion—and one who taught her the rapture of love!

RICHMOND #5: THE BLAZE   (1054, $3.50)

The War Between the States is over, but the war within the Armstrong family has just begun, as two handsome cousins vie for the love of Abby, a determined young woman who fights for honor—with a passion!

Available wherever paperbacks are sold, or order direct from the Publisher. Send cover price plus 50¢ per copy for mailing and handling to Zebra Books, 475 Park Avenue South, New York, N.Y. 10016. DO NOT SEND CASH.

WHITEWATER DYNASTY BY HELEN LEE POOLE

WHITEWATER DYNASTY: HUDSON! (607, $2.50)
Amidst America's vast wilderness of forests and waterways,
Indians and trappers, a beautiful New England girl and a handsome
French adventurer meet. And the romance that follows is just the
beginning, the foundation . . . of the great WHITEWATER
DYNASTY.

WHITEWATER DYNASTY: OHIO! (733, $2.75)
As Edward and Abby watched the beautiful Ohio River flow into
the Spanish lands hundreds of miles away they felt their destiny
flow with it. For Edward would be the first merchant of the river—
and Abby, part of the legendary empire yet to be created!

WHITEWATER DYNASTY #3: (979, $2.95)
THE CUMBERLAND!
From the horrors of Indian attacks to the passion of new-found
love—the second generation of the Forny family journey beyond
the Cumberland Gap to continue the creation of an empire and live
up to the American dream.

*Available wherever paperbacks are sold, or order direct from the
Publisher. Send cover price plus 50¢ per copy for mailing and
handling to Zebra Books, 475 Park Avenue South, New York, N.Y.
10016. DO NOT SEND CASH.*